REIGN OF BEASTS

BOOK THREE — THE CREATURE COURT

TANSY RAYNER ROBERTS

For Kaia,
My books are never finished until you have read them
Red pen at the ready
And complained about how mean I am.

CONTENTS

THE WORLD

AMMORIA

© Jilli Roberts 2009

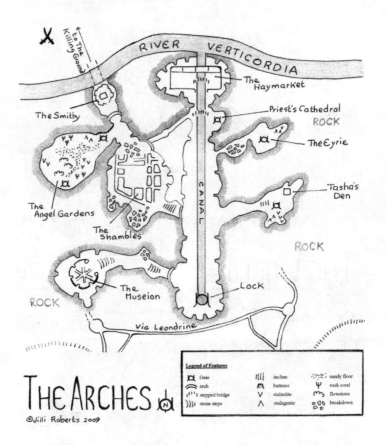

THE ARCHES

© Jilli Roberts 2009

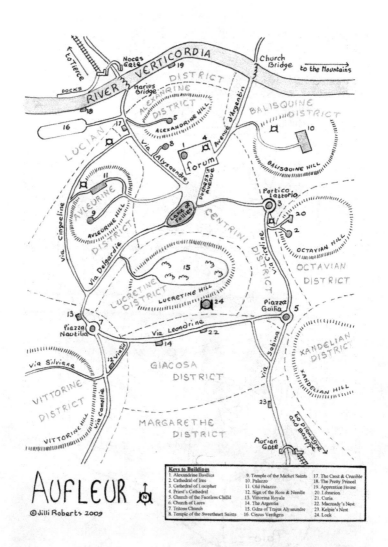

AUFLEUR

© Jilli Roberts 2009

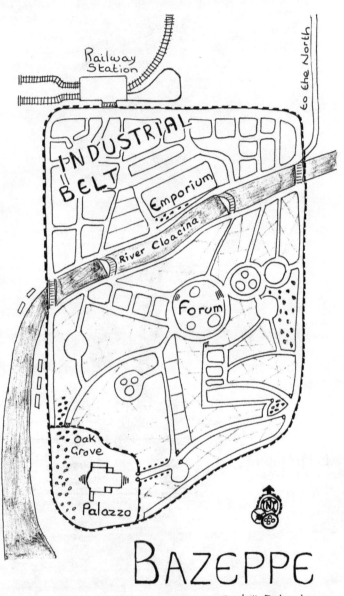

BAZEPPE

© Jilli Roberts

PART I
THE FIRST SATURNALIA

1

BOY

They called me Boy back then. The spruikers, the stagehands, the tumblers, the columbines, the songbirds, the masks. Even the other lambs of the crew, the ones who were younger than me. If I had a real name, it was long forgotten.

Madalena called me Baby. That wasn't my real name either, but it made me feel special. I would sit on her dressing table, swinging my legs, while she painted her face with cosmetick and told me stories of the old days, of the Pearls Beyond Price, of the songs they used to sing. I'd stay with her for hours: the only one who wanted to listen, the only one who didn't whisper behind her back about how she was pushing forty and maybe it was time for a new stellar to take her place. I didn't care about any of that cack.

Oyster wasn't much of a town. What do you expect from a place called Oyster? It was shellfish, shellfish and more shellfish. Folks came from all over to buy crab and mussels and, oh aye, oysters from our pier. Most families in Oyster had a boat, or crewed a boat, or were waiting for a place on a boat. The rest of them shucked the oysters or worked the market. The whole town smelled of salted shell.

Then there was the Mermaid. She was an old musette, peeling paint and shabby curtains, but she was ours, and she was famous, even more famous than the shellfish to the right kind of people. They came from all over to see the show in oyster season.

We were the lambs from the Mermaid. We didn't have to go to school, not even in summer when the musette was closed because the oysters were too scarce for us to pull decent audiences. Every young cove and demme in town wanted to be us. We didn't stink of fish. Just cosmetick grease.

Only the luckiest lambs in town got a chance to join the troupe. The stagemaster took on one or two every season, and half the time they wouldn't make it through — they'd rip a costume or drop a piece of scenery or prove to be no good at the tumbling and gurning between acts. The failures would be booted out swift as you like, back to the life of boats and markets and shellfish that was all Oyster had to offer them.

I was eight years old when I heard the name 'Aufleur' for the first time. It was the month of Fortuna, nearly winter, when the oysters are their meatiest. I'd been sent to fetch supper for the stagemaster and when I got back, Madalena was having one of her turns. I could hear the screams from the street.

As soon as I stepped backstage, I was seized by a mob of columbines, all spindly arms and fluffy tulle, surprisingly strong.

'Here he is!'

'It's the Boy!'

'Where have you been?' barked the stagemaster. 'Get up there, Boy, she listens to you. Talk some sense into the daft old haddock.'

I was pushed and shoved up the rickety steps to the stellar dressing room. It stank of gin and lime. Madalena had turned to her favourite activity in dark times — destroying one of her costumes. This was, I happened to know, her least favourite frock, with a murex fringe that made her look like a reading couch. She ripped it with savage glee, her false fingernails breaking off under the strain.

'Raddled, am I?' she screamed as I closed the door. 'Past my prime?'

'Did they say that?' I asked in a low voice.

'Might as well have! They want Adriane to play the Angel at Saturnalia. That's my role! The *stellar* role. They're raising her up to replace me!'

I'd heard rumours, of course. Whispers in the props room and the ticket booth. Madalena had too many years under her jewelled brassiere for anyone who knew how to count, and everyone knew that Adriane had been in and out of the stagemaster's loft above the box office at odd hours, emerging with her hair messed up and her knickers showing.

Aye, I knew what that meant, too. I was young, not stupid.

No one said to my face that Madalena's star was falling; they wouldn't, knowing she was the closest I had to a mam. I still heard the whispers. I wasn't going to be the one to break Madalena's heart, though, so I lied to her, bare-faced lie after lie, about how the Mermaid was nothing without her, no one would buy a ticket without her there, how she looked better than Adriane anyhow, and audiences liked a demme with meat on her bones.

Hard work for an eight-year-old, but I'd been born and bred to the stage. There are no better liars than mummers or masks. I'd been around the crew long enough to know the book by heart.

Madalena let me soothe her with my borrowed words, this time.

A few days later, when the stagemaster announced to the cast that Adriane would play the Angel, Madalena bit her lip so hard it almost bled. We all braced ourselves for a new bout of screaming, but she said nothing. She bowed her head and let the axe fall.

THERE WAS no bigger audience than the Saturnalia crowd. We always put on a special show from the Ides of Saturnalis through to early Venturis. The house came from as far away as Aufleur, the city to the north, and Bazeppe, far to the south. Some were brightly dressed Lords and Ladies, on pilgrimage to our town to eat oysters fresh with creamy mayonnaise. They were still licking their fingers and dropping the shells as they paraded into the Mermaid.

It was the same show every year: saints and angel, harlequinade, pantomime with saucy songs, cabaret of monsters. That last one was why the stagemaster was picky about his lambs, because it was us who performed it, done up in animal costumes and pretending to be fierce. It was a game, like everything else about Saturnalia: a festival of topsy-turvy. I sometimes think that was why Madalena gave in on the Angel role. She feared people might see her as another Saturnalia joke — the ageing dame pretending to be an ingenue.

It was the Kalends of Saturnalis and I was in the streets with Kip and Benny, pasting up the broadsheets for the show, when his Lordship came upon us. He was beautiful. No other word for it. I'll never forget how beautiful he was. His face was soft like a demme's, and he had long hair all hung about his shoulders. He wore a high top hat like the fancy toffs who paid three silver ducs to see the show from a private box, even though everyone knew the view from the dress circle was better. He had a long coat, and wore a chain at his throat. I couldn't figure if he was a theatrical or a genuine toff, and was so busy trying to work it out that I stared at him too long and Kip elbowed me in the side.

'Are you young seigneurs from the theatre?' he asked, and we preened, all three of us, to hear him saying 'theatre' about our lowly musette.

'Aye, sir,' said Benny, and Kip nodded along. I kept staring.

His Lordship smiled, and no matter how highborn he sounded, I knew in that moment he was an actor like us. Just another mask with something to sell.

'Is it a good show, your Saturnalia revue?' he asked next.

Kip and Benny fell over themselves to get out the usual patter: 'You won't see anything like this in your big city, squire; folks come from all over to see it; don't you know our columbines were trained by the Duchessa of Bazeppe herself; don't you know our cabaret of monsters act has been stolen by every musette north of here...'

He tired of the gabble eventually, and turned to me. His eyes were deep like coloured glass, all green and blue and maybe yellow if I looked hard enough. 'What do you say?' he asked.

'There ain't better,' I said, my voice coming out clearer than I'd expected.

The Lord smiled. 'Excellent to hear. You had best introduce me to your stagemaster, then. I wish to arrange a private show.'

~

THE DAY after the Kalends is ill luck for a performance, and
we still had more that a market-nine of rehearsals to go, but
his Lordship showed the stagemaster enough coin that he got
his show, straight away. The columbines and songbirds
complained, shrill gulls that they were. The masks weren't
any happier, but they knew better than to make a flap.
Adriane wasn't safe enough in her Angel costume to make a
fuss, and Madalena stayed quiet for once. No shrieking; she
watched the rest of them hop about.

The stagemaster quelled all complaint with one short
speech. 'This mad toff has forked over enough shine to see
the ceiling refurbished twice over. There'll be spare for a
meat dish a day and new costumes this winter, so shut the
fuck up about it.'

There was plenty of salt tossed around backstage to keep
what luck we had left all in the right places.

We started with the cabaret of monsters, us lambs peering
through our masks as we sang, trying to make sense of our
audience of one. His Lordship sat smack in the middle of the
dress circle and watched us hard, like a cormorant waiting to
snatch a fish out of the water. He sat through hours of our
best acts and never clapped once.

We did pretty well, I thought, though Adriane was so
nervous she tripped over her pearl-crusted hem and sang
half her notes too thin. Madalena did her best with her
smaller part as Mother Sospita, with only half a song and a
dozen lines to speak. At least the stagemaster had the grace
not to push the role of Ires the Crone on her.

At the end, when we were arrayed on stage waiting for
some sign of approval, his Lordship stood up and leaned
over the balcony. 'Do it again,' he said in a chilly voice. 'Only
this time, the one with the voice will play the Angel.' He
pointed directly at Madalena. Adriane looked as if she had
been slapped.

His Lordship turned and climbed the next set of stairs to the gods, the seats so high that we rarely sold them out. Those who liked a cheap ticket preferred the pit, where they had to stand but at least they could see whether the tumblers were coves or demmes. Our patron sat up there, chin in hand, as we went through the entire performance again, act by act, exhausted though we were. Madalena sang her heart out, the performance of her life, every gesture aimed skywards at her handsome benefactor.

~

DAYS LATER, we learned the true story of what his Lordship wanted of us. We were going to Aufleur. To this day I don't know how much his Lordship paid, but it was enough to make the stagemaster sweat and stutter like it was his first audition when he explained it to us.

The Lord had hired us, every mime and painted prop. For the first time in twenty-five years there would be no Saturnalia revue at the Mermaid in Oyster. Instead, we were to perform at a theatre in the city, a city so large most of us could barely imagine it.

We were taking the show to Aufleur.

Madalena was beside herself with excitement. She queened it over the masks and columbines, secure once more as the stellar of the company. Adriane made several visits to the stagemaster but he wouldn't budge. The Lord's coin pouch meant more to him than anything she kept in her cotton knickers.

I'd never been on a train before, nor had the other lambs. Me and Kip and Benny and Ruby-Red and Liv spent the whole journey staring out the windows, dizzy with the strangeness of being outside Oyster, loose in the world.

We piled off at the other end, staring at the sight before

us, the high dark buildings and domes, the finery of it all. Aufleur. The big city.

~

THE VITTORINA ROYALE had been a fine theatre once, there was no doubting that. But she had been abandoned for years when we first clapped eyes on her. I still remember the crest-fallen look on Madalena's face when she realised the grand city stage she had been imagining was just as old and rundown as the Mermaid. But then we walked inside, through the house, and Benny tugged my arm, pointing up at the ceiling. I swear I stopped breathing for a moment — I'd never seen anything so beautiful in my life. The ceiling was all mirrors and gilded saints, and when the lanterns were lit it gleamed above the stage like a sky full of stars.

'The Vittorina may be getting on in years, but she's a queen worthy of the best,' his Lordship said, and Madalena simpered at his words.

I suppose you've noticed I never named him. He told us he was 'Lord Saturn' — the same as the saint of revels. Seemed unlikely, but no one in theatre has the name they were born with.

'Where's your bean crown, then?' Ruby-Red asked him cheekily.

'Left it in my other coat,' he replied, pulling a face and making the young ones laugh. Such a quick tongue, that one.

~

WE MOVED INTO THE VITTORINA, making her our own, figuring out the ropes and tunnels and secret corners. We had from the Nones to the Ides to pull the show together, and we sweated to make it happen. He decided at the last minute that his private performance would be the dress rehearsal, the nox before the Saturnalia festival itself, which gave us an extra day, but it was still a scramble — and it meant performing on another *nefas* day which none of us liked at all.

Ill luck already dogged us. Props broke, costumes were lost, and it turned out that Aufleur had some daft law that restricted horses and wheeled vehicles during daylight hours, so we had to transport everything we owned across three districts in dodgy hand carts.

Matthias fell sick, a hoarse cough that racked his body and took his appetite. That left us without a merchant's son, and the stagemaster lined up the lambs, demanding that one of us take his place.

'Baby should do it,' said Madalena.

'The lad's too young,' the stagemaster said in disbelief.

She stretched and smiled. 'He has the voice of a princel, if you give him a chance.'

Madalena was happier here. She really thought this was her big break, her dream come true, singing to fine toffs in a city instead of in our own little musette back home. I missed the smell of salted crab and the sound of the sea.

The stagemaster reluctantly agreed that my pipes were up to the role of merchant's son, but I was too short to fit Matthias's costume so he made Kip do it instead. I tried not to care too much. There would be other roles. I minded more that Madalena was head over heels in love with the toff who called himself Lord Saturn, and she was going to get her heart broke clean through.

Her dressing room at the Vittorina Royale was no bigger than the one back home, though it had fancy giltwork around the mirror. I caught her gazing around sometimes like the room was a steak dinner. Something to be proud of, rather than something she'd been tossed by a cove who only wanted to impress some other lady.

Oh, aye. There was another lady. Of course there was.

2

INTRODUCING: THE MERMAID
REVUE AT THE VITTORINA ROYALE

*I*t was the nox before Saturnalia, and we were about to raise the curtain of the Vittorina Royale for the first time. The Lord told us we could open the doors to the general public from tomorrow, so Benny and I went out pasting posters like at home, except there were vigiles patrolling the streets here who'd give us a whack if they caught us pasting on public buildings.

We went as far as the Forum — a jaw-dropping place full of every kind of temple and building imaginable. Our posters were merry and bright and called us the Mermaid Revue, making us sound like some exotic troupe from the far south. But this show — the first show really though we all called it our second dress rehearsal to keep the bad luck at bay — was open to no one but his Lordship and his guests.

We peeped through the side of the curtain, watching them enter.

Lord Saturn wore that high hat of his, and a long coat that shone green and violet. He led his crew through to the dress circle — a gang of demmes and seigneurs dolled up to the nines. Liv and Ruby-Red giggled, laying bets on whether they were real aristos, another theatre troupe, or something a lot more scandalous. They always talked like that around me, assuming I was too little to know what they were on about.

I watched them, Lord Saturn's crowd. Finely dressed, but only some of them knew how to wear the clothes. They weren't aristos, that was for sure. They flocked around this golden demme with short curling hair and a frock more daring than anything a columbine would wear on stage. Her arms were bare, and you could see that she had taut muscles, like she knew how to haul scenery. That was no lady.

She was Saturn's, though. You could see it in the way she moved, the way she laid her hand on his, the look on his face as he presented her with... us.

We were a trinket to please his demme. The worst of it was, she wasn't even impressed. The whole time the saints-and-angel play went on, Saturn's lady looked bored, like she was waiting for the real show to start. Some of her retinue applauded at the closing song, but she shrugged one golden shoulder and they stopped.

Madalena sung her guts out. She almost convinced me (who knew her better than anyone) that she was a real angel made of sugar and steam. When that half-applause stopped, she looked like she was going to slit her wrists.

The harlequinade was next — columbines dancing and Larius swanning about as Harlequinus in the middle of it all. Madalena was supposed to change costume for the pantomime, but instead she shut herself in her dressing room and refused to come out.

The stagemaster shouted at her through the door, and finally sent me up to talk sense into her. She said not a word, no matter what I cajoled through the keyhole.

The harlequinade ended and we sent on the tumblers, though they only had so many turns to run through and it would become obvious soon enough that we had no pantomime to follow.

The stagemaster sucked in a breath finally and called for Adriane to find a frock so she could cover Madalena's songs. Adriane burst into tears, for Madalena had six separate numbers in the pantomime and she didn't know the words.

When all seemed lost, Lord Saturn himself strode backstage and demanded that Madalena open the door for him.

When she heard his voice, she let the door fall open a crack so he could push his way in. He took her face in his hands and kissed her, a grand finale kind of kiss that left her cosmetick smeared across his face. 'Sing for me,' he commanded. Madalena turned as if hypnotised, fumbling for her costume.

WE GOT through the rest of the show. Madalena performed the comic turns of the pantomime perfectly and vanished backstage again as the lambs trooped out for the cabaret of monsters.

Here's the funny thing: Saturn's golden lady, so bored through the whole proceedings, sat up and paid attention to us lambs in our animal costumes. I could feel her eyes on us — on me — as we went through our paces. When we took our bows, she stood and left without a word. A bunch of the young seigneurs followed her, chorus to her stellar.

Lord Saturn stayed. I don't know if I loved or hated him for that. He applauded in the empty musette. He showed up later at Madalena's door with an armful of flowers. Her cosmetick was streaked and she was tired as hell, but he told her she was beautiful, and meant it.

Madalena's smile, her real smile, not the one for the stage, was always something to see.

'Put these in water for me, will you, Baby?' she said, dumping the flowers on me as she strolled off with her new fancy man, arm in arm with him.

It was the last time I saw her alive.

～

THERE WAS an itch in my skin when I awoke. Nothing big, just a niggle, making me jig about impatiently as I went down to breakfast.

'What's up with you?' asked Ruby-red with her mouth full.

'Naught,' I muttered.

We were opening for real this nox. The stagemaster spent half the day convincing us that the golden bitch knew nothing about theatre and we shouldn't take her rudeness to mean three beans about how good our show was. We almost believed him.

There was enough to do that no one noticed until the afternoon that Madalena wasn't there. Not in her dressing room, not sleeping late, not anywhere in the Vittorina Royale. Gone.

The itch grew fiercer.

By the time we raised the curtain, Adriane was cinched into Madalena's angel costume and the stagemaster was red-faced and spitting.

We had a full house. It was the first day of Saturnalia, and nothing draws the crowds like a festival. Most of them were locals, and most of the centime seats went to other theatricals, out to see who had taken on the Vittorina Royale after so long without a performance in the old dame. It was the biggest audience we'd ever played for. Madalena wasn't there.

When it was over and we were sweating cosmetick, dizzy

with applause, already figuring out what parts we'd have to change for tomorrow, the stagemaster grabbed me by the collar. 'Tell Herself when she shows her face that she's fired,' he growled. 'We don't need her. We're going places.'

Madalena had never missed a performance before. Not once. I checked her dressing room. His Lordship's flowers were already starting to fade.

The itch spread to my feet. I went walking, trying to shake out the bad feeling, but all that did was remind me how big this city was, how none of us belonged here.

IT WASN'T me who found Madalena's body. That would tie the story up nicely, wouldn't it? If I sniffed out a trail of blood or used the devastating intellectual abilities of an eight year old to track her down. Instead, it was one of the columbines who found her in the alley behind the Vittorina Royale. Madalena was still wearing the bright scarlet and purple milkmaid's frock from the pantomime. Her body had been ripped apart, as if by animals. Blood everywhere.

They didn't let me see. Of course they didn't. They tried to keep it from me, because I was a lamb and the only one in the whole damn troupe who really loved her. But I heard stories, each of them bloodier.

Wild animals. How the frig do you get yourself torn up by wild animals in the middle of a city?

But you know the answer to that question, or you wouldn't be here.

THE AUDIENCES KEPT COMING. Even with Adriane's reedy pipes. Apparently our kind of revue had been out of favour for years in the big city and the crowds were hungry for it now. They lined up to buy half a shillein's worth of nostalgia — a nice way of saying we were old-fashioned but they liked us anyway.

No one spoke Madalena's name aloud. That's the way it is backstage. There's none like masks for superstition. Once you're gone, you're gone. They were as silent about her now as they had been about my mam all my life.

I snuck into the stellar's dressing room before they gave it to Adriane and stole the old poster Madalena had kept all these years of her and my mam, beaded up and laughing. *Come to the Mermaid and See the Pearls Beyond Price.*

I'd never asked her my mam's name, waiting for the right time to get her brandy-sozzled and softened up about it. Too late now.

~

AFTER THE EIGHT days of Saturnalia, the audiences trailed off. The stagemaster talked about heading home, eager to spend his Lordship's gold, to be the big man in Oyster when he hired on for the refurbishments of the Mermaid. We'd be famous: the lambs who went to the big city.

The day to return kept getting put off, though. There was talk of sticking around through Venturis. Some of the columbines sneaked off to audition in other musettes — there wouldn't be many of them coming back with us.

I wanted to go home so bad, but not without Madalena. The stagemaster had her cremated at some temple outside the city bounds and set in a stone without even her name on it, because that cost too much. No one had said a word about calling the vigiles — musette folk don't invite the law into our lives. Last thing we wanted was the city thinking we were trouble, maybe blaming us for other crimes.

I couldn't go home without knowing who had killed her and why.

I tried asking in the Forum if anyone knew of a Lord Saturn, but they laughed at me. Turned out there were no Lords in the city. A flower-seller took pity on me and said if he wasn't a Baronne or a Comte or even a Duc, then he was spinning a yarn.

'Some chancer with a bean crown making a fool of you,' she said sympathetically, and gave me a cake because she thought I was some scraggy street-orphan who had need of feeding. The cake was dry, but I still remember the taste of it.

As I headed back, I caught sight of a trio of seigneurs laughing and gaming in a corner of the Forum, by the Basilica. I knew them. They weren't dressed as fancy now, but they'd been in our audience on the eve of Saturnalia — the golden lady's chorus boys.

I followed them. When they split up near the main road, I followed the one with red hair because he'd be easier to track in a crowd. That, and he wore a bright green cravat tied badly, like he didn't know how. I'd spent enough time picking up pins for the wardrobe mistress that I could feel a bit superior. I could have done a better job of it.

Bad Cravat led me up and down the Lucretine before he turned and caught me, one hand grasping my collar like the stagemaster did. 'What are you, little rat?'

I should have been scared, right? He was bigger than me, though no older than Matthias, barely old enough to play leading man. But I wasn't scared, I was angry, and I fair spat the words at him: 'I want to see Lord Saturn. Take me to Saturn.'

His eyes flickered a bit, looking me over. I still had posters tucked into my belt — I'd been gathering them so we could re-use the backs for the new performances.

'You're one of those theatre pups,' he said quietly. 'Cabaret of monsters, aye? You were the ferax.'

It was uncanny that he knew me from that one performance, and me in a sweaty leather mask.

'Take me to Saturn,' I said again, brash and far too confident.

'Oh, you don't want that. Run back to your theatre.'

He released my collar and turned to leave, but I grabbed onto his belt. 'Did he set them animals on her? Were they his?'

Bad Cravat's face was all pale, sort of sick-looking, as he looked me over again. 'No,' he said finally. 'They were hers. Scurry home, ratling.'

With that, he prised my fingers from him and walked away. I tried to follow him again, but he turned into an alley and when I caught up he had vanished, like a stage trick.

3

SATURN AND TASHA

We stayed through Venturis and Lupercalia. Adriane had learnt from the best. Whenever the stagemaster made noise about heading back to Oyster, she'd scream like a fishwife and besiege him in his office until he gave in, over and over. One more show. Then another. Hardly anyone in the city had seen our old revues, so we had enough material to do something new every month.

The year turned.

My birthday came and went, and I didn't say a word about it to anyone. Madalena was the one who remembered it each year, with a new shirt if she was flush and a handful of sweets if she was down on her uppers.

Ruby-red turned twelve and made it into the columbine chorus. Matthias got sick again, and the stagemaster gave more of his roles to Kip. Benny left, because the boot factory paid more than the stagemaster ever would. Half the columbines ran off to other theatres, and half of those came back again, regretting it. There were always new demmes and coves lining up, hungry to see their star rise.

Saturnalis came around again and we'd been in the big city a year. The stagemaster didn't talk about us going home any more. We were stuck with each other.

We had a packed house on the Ides of Saturnalis. A new revue for once, though the play was still saints-and-angel — we'd started a fashion there. Half the musettes in the Lucian put on similar shows. Adriane was pregnant and still pretending she wasn't. The costumes were let out three times, and we knew better than to joke about it where she could hear. I had a solo of my own in the pantomime, playing a capering orphan with a secret past. The stagemaster said I had a gift for comedy.

Lord Saturn bought a ticket that first nox. He didn't bring any of his chorus. Just sat there in the front row of the dress circle as if nothing had ever happened. The stagemaster threw out a line in his introduction about our private bene-factor and Saturn bowed his head while all the fine demmes and seigneurs peered at him.

I knew Aufleur pretty well by then. Pasting posters for a year will do that for you. I'd got better at tracking people without being spotted, too. I practiced being quick and quiet, waiting for my chance. This time, I was going to find out his secrets.

I followed him home.

I'd never been up on the Balisquine before, the hill where the Old Duc lived. The vigiles would cripple any lamb they caught up there with a paste brush, and I knew about the lictors, too — axes, they carried. Didn't want to get on the wrong side of them. Saturn walked quick, like he had some-where to get to or something to hide. I could see the flick-ering lamps of the Duc's Palazzo, but he didn't go near it, which was a relief.

I scampered after him and crested the hill, looking across to a ruined old tower. There were white birds everywhere.

Owls, snowy white, all sizes. I'd never seen an owl properly before, just heard the occasional hoot or seen a silhouette over the city. They were beautiful in the half-moonlight. Bright as anything.

Saturn walked towards the tower, casting off his top hat, his long coat, his boots. Then he... changed. Flew apart into pieces and became all feathers and air, beak and claws. Hawks. I knew the shape of them from the bird-puppeteer who used to fill in between the tumbling spots back at Oyster. Saturn's hawks were larger, though. Sharper. He flew in a cloud around the owls, and then they all vanished into that ruined tower, down, down.

I walked slowly across the grass and reached out to grab the brim of his hat as if it might not be real. I waited, but he didn't return.

Hells, yes. I stole his clothes.

EVERY TIME I got a half-day off, I'd go up on the green around the Balisquine and lie in wait for his Lordship. Sometimes I saw the owls, sometimes the hawks, but never a real person. Not until sometime late in the month of Martial, with the cold of the city starting to ebb into spring.

'You again,' said the voice. It was Bad Cravat, who still hadn't learnt how to tie a piece of silk like a civilised person.

His suit was ill-fitting, and the wrong colour for his red hair. The wardrobe mistress would despair of him. He tried to speak like a seigneur, but his hands had seen rough work. He couldn't fool me.

'What do you want up here, ratling? Looking for another top hat to steal?'

'You know what I want,' I said boldly. 'I want Saturn. I want the... bastard' — I'd never said the word before; the stagemaster washed our mouths out if he caught us being coarse — 'who killed Madalena. Who let her be ripped apart by animals. I know enough to know that's not supposed to happen in *cities*!'

A look crossed his face. 'Was she dear to you, lad?'

'Don't you lad me, you're not that old,' I said. He wasn't nearly of age, I could tell that. 'She was the closest thing I had to a mam, and I want answers.'

'Get away from here,' he said, in a low voice. 'Don't come back.'

There was movement out the corner of my eye and I turned — just as a lion leaped out of the tower. Lioness, I should say. I'd never seen one apart from the mask Ruby-red used to wear in the cabaret of monsters. This was the real thing. She was long and muscled and golden, and she was looking directly at me. I swallowed hard.

She shimmered and shaped herself from lion to woman, all golden and glowing, eyes as yellow as her hair. Saturn's woman.

'Garnet,' she said to Bad Cravat, 'what have you brought?' She was practically licking her lips as she looked at me. 'Such a treat.'

'He's nothing,' Garnet said. 'A beggar child.' Who had taught him to lie? He was as bad at that as he was at choosing his clothes.

'Did you kill her?' I blurted. The lion lady raised her eyebrows, sort of prowling around me. 'Madalena. The Saturnalia before the one just gone.'

She laughed then, throwing her head back. 'You expect me to remember who I killed over a year ago?'

I was burning up all over. Madalena never harmed anyone and all she wanted was to be a stellar forever, for people to love her.

'The actress from the Vittorina Royale!' I yelled. 'The one who trusted Saturn to look after her! But he didn't, did he?'

'Tasha, he's too young,' warned Garnet, but she turned fluidly and slapped him, knocking him to his knees.

'I decide who is too young,' she said. Then she looked at me and smiled again, all teeth. I had thought she was beautiful, but she wasn't, not really. She only believed that she was.

'Come and find me this nox,' she said, and reached out to pull the silk cravat from around Garnet's neck. She rubbed it against her hair, her stomach, and passed it to me. It smelled of her, of perfume and lion and *bitch*. 'Find me,' she said again. 'And I will answer your questions. Even those you don't know you have.'

She shaped herself into a lion again and left us, her body gleaming in the sunlight as she trotted off down the hillside.

Garnet stood up, looking shaky. 'Go home,' he said. 'Not the theatre. Keep going to whatever ten-centime town you come from. This isn't for you. You don't want it.'

I breathed in the scent of the lioness, and tucked the silk cloth into my pocket. 'You don't know what I want,' I told him.

I LEFT the theatre that nox after the show ended. I could smell her in the alley out the back. *Tasha*. The scent of her was so strong and certain, I didn't have to inhale from the silk cloth in my pocket to be sure of it.

I followed her scent up the Via Delgardie and all the way to the Lucian district, which was still full of people at this time of nox — their musettes and theatres stayed open later than ours. I tracked her through a maze of side streets, and then she disappeared somewhere near the Circus Verdigris.

Only she didn't disappear, her scent went in and down between buildings, somewhere I couldn't follow.

'Good enough,' said a voice. A dark-eyed lad slipped down off a wall to face me. He was as tall as Garnet, broader in the shoulders, and he wore his fancy clothes better. Another came out of the darkness, a bright-skinned lad with curly blond hair, and then Garnet himself.

'Bring him down to her,' said Garnet.

The lads grabbed me and hauled me down into the darkness, into a space between buildings that I'd never seen for myself, down a path that shouldn't exist, deep into the undercity of Aufleur.

I didn't fight. This was what I wanted.

Tasha had a sort of den deep in the ruins beneath the real city. It was cozy, lit with oil lamps, and her scent was everywhere.

'Impressive,' she said, stretched lazily across a bed covered with cushions. 'See how the little rat burrows. One of us, boys. You can taste it on his skin.'

'What do you want with him?' demanded the dark lad, whom the others called Ash. 'He's a sprat. Is he going to hang around and pour drinks for us for the next few years?'

Tasha grinned. 'Not that. I have a better idea.' She reached out and took my chin in her hand. 'Do you want your revenge against Saturn, ratling? Do you want to know all his secrets?'

I forgot that I blamed her for Madalena's death, forgot that I had to be back at the theatre by sun-up or the stage-master would beat me, forgot that she was a *lion*. I leaned into her, trusting her. There was something about her that reminded me of what it was like to have a mam, of how it felt to be loved.

Tasha embraced me lightly, as Madalena did sometimes when she was feeling her years. 'Do you like me, little rat?'

'You smell of sunshine,' I muttered, half out of my senses. I had no idea what was happening, but everything about her drew me in, making me trust her.

Tasha laughed. 'Hear that, my cubs? The boy's a poet.'

And she tore me into pieces.

PART II
A SURFEIT OF KINGS

4

ONE DAY AFTER THE IDES OF BESTIALIS

DAYLIGHT

Sunlight shone into the broken theatre through holes in the walls and the sagging ceiling, catching motes of dust. The last of the bodies had been carried out by daybreak, but the place still smelled of death.

Isangell, the Duchessa d'Aufleur, had awoken to the news that there was a disaster in the Vittorine. The Proctor of that district was overwhelmed by distraught and protesting citizens. He sent to the Palazzo begging for more lictors to protect himself and his family.

The day after an Ides was traditionally nefas: ill luck. It was hard to argue with that tradition on a morning like this.

Isangell stepped into the ruined theatre, shivering at the sight of the damage. Broken glass was everywhere, thick slabs of it, some of the edges still black and crimson with dried blood.

'We will need to perform a cleansing ritual,' said the Matrona Irea in a solemn voice. By virtue of her senior position in the Priestesses of Ires, she was the only woman apart from Isangell herself who served as one of the City Fathers.

The Master of Saints, an elderly thin man with a hooked nose who had terrified Isangell when she was a child, snorted. 'Raze it to the ground,' he suggested. 'No amount of ritual can return fortune to this place.'

'A blood sacrifice could do it,' grunted Brother Typhisus of the Silver Brethren.

'Hasn't there been blood enough?' demanded Matrona Irea, and promptly launched into a lecture about the healing properties of honey cakes and blessed water while the other priests scoffed at her.

Isangell ignored the three of them, walking further into the theatre. She had dreamt of such places as a child, had begged her mother to let her attend a pantomime or a harle-quinade. She'd had a book full of columbines in pretty gowns like flower petals, and had imagined quite seriously running away to sing and dance with the theatricals. Her mama informed her in a haughty voice that musettes and columbine halls were not for respectable people. The closest Isangell came to such shows in her childhood were the circuses at the sacred games, with an occasional tumbler, songsmith or dancer thrown in between the many ritualised fights and battles.

When she was older, she disguised herself as a commoner and snuck into performances at the Argentia and some of the other musettes. It was a delicious secret, one she had shared with no one but her dressmaker.

This was awful. Broken statues and blocks of buttery golden stone had smashed one of the balconies, and now lay scattered across the stage.

Isangell pulled herself up onto the stage, feeling as if she did not belong there. She wasn't about to burst into song in front of the priests and her other retinue, but she was still going through the motions of some sort of performance.

The Proctor arrived, a blustering, bearded man surrounded by lictors.

'High and brightness!' he greeted her, breathing hard. 'Grateful as I am for your support, I require further assistance. The people talk of ousting me from office. Some measure of funding to restore and improve the safety of public buildings would go a long way to —'

Isangell turned away from him. 'Did you hear that?'

She hurried into the wings, ignoring his protests, stepping over broken pieces of scenery and a heap of scattered animal masks.

'Is someone still here?' she called.

A small noise cut through the silence, like a child's whimper.

'Hold on, I'm coming for you!' Isangell pushed further in, hearing a couple of lictors come after her, protesting.

She pulled back an expanse of canvas that covered a row of wooden nooks and looked inside. A grown woman sat hunched there, knees drawn up to her chin, eyes wide and frightened like a child's.

'I know you,' Isangell said as her eyes adjusted to the darkness. 'You were looking after my cousin. You're one of them.'

She did not dare say the words 'Creature Court' aloud with so many senior priests within earshot.

The demoiselle stared blankly out of her hiding place, not seeming to recognise her.

'Rhian,' Isangell said, hoping she remembered the right name. 'Demoiselle Rhian. Are you... can I help you?'

She gasped as the other woman's hand lashed out, squeezing her wrist painfully tight. 'You,' said Rhian, eyes wide and bloodshot, lips flecked with saliva. 'You have to tell them. The sky is coming. We will be the last city to fall, but we *will* fall.'

'Let me get you a dottore,' Isangell pleaded, trying to pull her wrist free.

'Not long now,' Rhian said, her whole body shuddering. 'Everything ends at Saturnalia.'

~

VELODY BURROWED out of her usual nest of blankets. The air was cool as she placed her bare feet on the floor. She still wore the ragged underskirts from the ridiculous antique museion dress she'd had on when she crossed over from that other place, the empty Tierce that hung in the sky. The dress itself lay over the corner of her bed, already fading. It wasn't bright emerald green any more, but a muted grey colour. The fabric crumbled like dried leaves. Velody took a deep breath, remembering the pain as Ashiol dragged her through the ceiling of that theatre, the screams of the wounded beneath them.

Velody went to her wardrobe, reaching in for where her work dresses always hung. She felt nothing but air. The wardrobe was empty. Further investigation revealed her clothes packed neatly in boxes at the bottom.

They didn't think I was coming back. Well, how could they?

Everyone had thought her dead. She wasn't sure they were wrong. She should be glad her clothes hadn't made it to a market stall already.

Months passed here while I was in a city that no longer exists, lungs not breathing, heart not beating, with a man everyone knew to be dead.

Garnet. Oh, saints. The cruellest Power and Majesty in the history of the Creature Court, and she had brought him back.

Velody dressed with shaking fingers on the buttons, and finally got up the courage to leave her room. Her step on the stairs was quiet and she noticed Macready and Delphine before they saw her. They were bundled together into a chair in the workroom, his hands in her hair, her legs across his, as they talked together in low voices. A couple, then. What else had she missed while she was away?

Velody slipped into the kitchen without disturbing them, expecting to see Rhian at the stove, making porridge or tea or something comforting. The kitchen was empty.

'Where were you?' said a voice behind her. Delphine stood in the doorway, her hand loosely held in Macready's. 'Tierce,' said Velody, telling the truth without thinking. 'What month is it?' It seemed ridiculous that she had to ask.

'Bestialis,' said Macready. 'The day after the Ides. Though most of the day is gone, so it is.' He looked Velody over as if she were the shade of her ancestors. 'What do you mean, you were in Tierce?'

Velody sat at the familiar old kitchen table facing them both, her hands flat against its comforting surface. It was such a difficult question, so complicated, and she was expected to answer without even a cup of tea inside her?

Tea was a distant memory. She had consumed nothing since she threw herself into the sky, except for that dried cake she had found among the ashes in the temple back in Tierce... and that brought back memories of Garnet's body hot inside hers, which was the last thing she needed.

Where was he now? She last saw Garnet and Ashiol fighting in the lake, years of stored-up anger spilling out as they pummelled each other. Then they were gone, both of them, and she had no idea what Garnet might do next. *Have I let a monster loose in the city?*

'Tierce is gone,' said Delphine. 'You told us that.'

It was true at the time. It felt like a million years since

Velody told Rhian and Delphine about the city of their birth, which they had all forgotten since it was swallowed by the sky in one of many battles, invisible to daylight folk.

Velody nodded. 'It's really gone now. For a while it was... in a place between here and the other side of the sky. But it crumbled underneath us, we managed to escape.'

Oh yes, she sounded insane. But Delphine had taken far more on trust this year.

'And by "we" you mean Garnet,' said Macready. There was a studied lack of accusation in his voice.

'Yes,' said Velody.

'As you say,' he said, and let go of Delphine's hand so he could busy himself with lighting the stove.

Velody could feel the distance he put between them. Many possible excuses ran through her head — *he's changed, he's different, you don't know* — but she couldn't say any of that to Macready. He and the other sentinels had suffered so greatly at Garnet's hands, when he was Power and Majesty. Besides, Garnet had left her swiftly enough, as soon as they got back to Aufleur. There was no reason to trust him.

Where is he?

'Where's Rhian?' she asked instead.

Macready and Delphine exchanged a glance.

'I've been looking for her all day, so I have,' said Macready. 'She didn't come home after the Vittorina Royale.'

Velody's throat tightened. 'She was there? When the ceiling came down?' What was Rhian doing in a theatre? Was she so much better that she could go out in public like that instead of hiding within the walls of their home? 'Mac, a lot of people were hurt —'

'You think I don't know that?' he snapped. 'She's not dead. The Proctor's men were all over the place today, carting bodies out of the theatre. She was not among them.'

'She'll come home,' Delphine said softly. 'She has nowhere else to go.'

'Lot of good that will do her if she...' Macready trailed off, looking uneasily at Velody. 'Tea?'

'What aren't you telling me?' she demanded. 'I'm not a child to be coddled.'

'No one's saying that, lass. But no one wants to pile it all onto you at once.'

'Rhian's the Seer,' Delphine said in a clipped voice. 'I'll have tea, please. Lots of it. With sugar.'

Velody stared at her. First Delphine was a sentinel, and now this. They spent so many months protecting Rhian from her own fears, and the very real threat of the Creature Court. Now she was one of them.

'It's my fault,' she said.

'Well, of course it is,' said Delphine.

~

ASHIOL WAS STILL SHAKING with fury as he returned to the Palazzo. Garnet was back. Velody betrayed him. Poet betrayed him. There was a conspiracy to put Garnet back in power. He was not going through that again.

Garnet could not be allowed to take power, not after the tyrant he became, last time he ruled the Creature Court. Ashiol could not stand by his former friend through the madness and vicious cruelties.

I was loyal last time. So loyal I knelt down and let him carve me into pieces without raising a fucking hand to him. I can't do it again. Can't be that again.

I will not serve.

The only way to avoid it was to become the Power and Majesty himself. If only Ashiol had got his act together after Velody's 'death' to demand the oaths. He didn't have the luxury now to wallow in grief and irresponsibility. He would drag the Creature Court to him, kicking and screaming if he had to.

He stood on the grass, staring at the bars on the outside of his windows, remembering how Macready had wrapped skysilver wire around them to ensure Ashiol remained imprisoned during his most recent madness. There was no danger of that now. Ashiol's thoughts were searingly clear for the first time in months.

He had allowed Macready to cage him, allowed himself to be *domesticated* by his own sentinels. Now he reached out, seizing the bars and letting the wire burn his palms as he wrenched it free. His animor gave him strength, but using it made the wire more painful.

When Ashiol was done, the bars lying twisted and broken at his feet, he climbed in the window and threw himself onto his bed. His hair was still damp from the unexpected plunge into the lake during his fight with Garnet and he rubbed it impatiently against the quilt until it felt dry.

He awoke later with Isangell's milksop of a factotum leaning over him. 'What do you want?' Ashiol growled.

'Her high and brightness requires your attendance,' said the little squit. If his nose turned up any more at the state Ashiol was in, it would have to be pinned to the ceiling. 'Would the Ducomte like to bathe first?' he added.

'No, the Ducomte would not like to frigging bathe,' said Ashiol. 'Bring me breakfast. Meat.'

'I could ring for it,' the factotum stuttered, reaching for the bell cord.

'No,' Ashiol snapped. 'You. Fetch. Now.' He leaped up and seized a random suit of clothing, tossed it on the bed. 'Why are you still here?'

∽

WHEN ASHIOL REACHED the Duchessa's rooms some time later, he was partially sated by a pile of bacon, sausages and steak, having sent the cringing factotum back to the kitchens twice to restock the platter. He felt almost human.

Isangell looked up as he entered. 'I'm glad you used the extra time to make yourself presentable,' she said dryly, her eyes sweeping over his bare feet and barely buttoned shirt.

'You summoned me, high and brightness?' Ashiol replied, not bothering to press the usual sarcasm out of his pleas-antries.

'Oh, stop it.' She was unusually sombre. 'I went to the Vittorina Royale today.'

'Did you enjoy the show?'

'Ashiol,' she said sharply, 'it was the site of a terrible disaster. As well you know.'

'I'm afraid I'm not up on the theatre gossip. Was the masked melodrama as dire as rumoured in the newspapers? The Orphan Princel isn't as good as he used to be, you know. I hear he's getting on a bit.'

'I know it was you,' Isangell said in a low hiss. 'Your people. I'm not a fool, Ashiol. Whatever happened to that theatre was not natural. The place is full of bricks and stone that shouldn't be there.'

Ashiol hadn't known that. 'What kind of stone?'

'Soft and gritty to the touch. Yellow.'

The sandstone of Tierce. Holy fuck. Had the sky thrown back more than Garnet and Velody?

'I don't know what you're talking about,' he said again. He had more to worry about than explaining a destroyed theatre to his daylight cousin.

'Oh, really?' she said. 'And I suppose you would be surprised to hear that half of the dead carted out of that theatre died not from blood loss or being crushed, but from the Silent Sleep? I find it very hard to believe the show was so dull.'

Ashiol tapped his foot on the floor. It was almost nox. He had to get to the Lords and Court before Garnet had a chance to bully them or Velody a chance to be nice to them. Of course it mattered if the Silent Sleep was taking a firmer hold on the city, but he didn't have time for it to matter.

'And then there's your Seer,' said Isangell out of nowhere.

Ashiol's foot stopped tapping. 'What do you know about her?'

'She's asleep in my bed. I found her tucked away in the wings of the theatre, ranting like a mad thing. Like you used to.'

'Charming.'

He jumped to his feet and pushed the bedroom door wide open. The bed was empty and rumpled. No sign of the Seer. (*Rhian*, he had to remind himself, not Heliora, who was gone to her grave.)

Isangell joined him in the doorway. 'She was here a moment ago.'

'Looks like you put bars on the wrong windows,' Ashiol said with some satisfaction. He turned away. 'I have to go.'

'Without doing anything? Without explaining anything?'

'Believe me, gosling, you don't want to know.'

'Don't call me that,' Isangell snapped. 'I'm not one of your animals. This game you play is getting serious, Ash. Real people are being affected by it.'

He gave her a fierce, empty smile. 'The game was always about real people. Now if you'll excuse me, I have to bring them to heel.'

5

ONE DAY AFTER THE IDES OF BESTIALIS

DAYLIGHT

*L*ady Livilla's rooms had no windows. Topaz and Bree shared one room and the rest of the lambs from the Vittorina Royale were crammed into another. Livilla had her own. Each room was connected to a balcony that overlooked a wide concrete courtyard with a canal running through it — and no sight of the sky, no hint whether it was daylight or nox. Topaz had learnt fast that you didn't ask Livilla questions, not if you wanted the smile to stay on her face. The lambs were good at keeping her sweet, cooing over her costume closet and delighting at the cakes and fruit she provided for them. They'd never eaten so well in all their lives.

Topaz still did not understand why she was here, or what this Creature Court expected of her and the others. All she knew was that Lady Livilla was kind, and protected them as the Orphan Princes had not.

They had a roof over their heads and meat in their bellies.

That was enough to secure the loyalty of a bunch of theatre brats.

The Orphan Princel was their first visitor. Topaz knew it was Himself when she heard his voice down below, singing the lead of the Bestialia chorus.

Livilla, busily dressing up the children, waved a hand. 'Send him away,' she said.

'Go on, then,' said Bree, determined to show Topaz which of them was higher in the ranks.

You may act the stellar, lovie, but you'll never rise out of the chorus, Topaz sniped silently, and went out onto the balcony.

'Ah,' said Himself, a sad smile crossing his face. 'That answers one of my questions. What are you doing here, Topaz?'

'The Lady gave us a home,' she said defiantly.

She owed Himself plenty, but he wasn't the one who looked after them when the theatre came down in pieces, when Bart died. He hadn't even glanced in the direction of the lambs. He did nothing to prepare them for this world of animal shapes and blood and threats.

'Send Lord Livilla out to speak to me,' he commanded.

Time was, not one of the lambs would have dared deny his word. He was the stellar and the stagemaster, and everyone knew they got what they wanted. *Not us, though. Not this time.*

'Did you know?' Topaz demanded, no longer caring that he'd been the one who had brought her to the stage, had cared for her so tender when she was hurt. 'Did you know I had a mess of crawling lizards inside me? Did you know this thing that all of us are?'

'Aye,' he said, and there was a world of hurt behind the small glass circles of his spectacles. 'I tried to give you a place to be safe —'

'We're safe here,' she snapped. 'No stones raining down to

smash us dead. Bart's gone, you know that? Do you even remember which one he was?'

'Send Livilla down,' Himself said again, nice as pie.

'She don't want to see you!' Topaz yelled. Why couldn't he get angry like a normal person?

A second man stepped out of the shadows and the look of him made her shudder. He was wrong, like Himself was wrong, like Topaz and the Lady and Bree and all of the lambs, now. His wrongness shone out of his bright white skin. He had red hair, and he wore a flash suit, all scarlet and velvet like he was the stagemaster here.

'She'll see me,' he said, in a voice that carried all the way up from the courtyard to her bones.

Topaz opened her mouth, but Lady Livilla came out, stood at the balcony with eyes as dark as a blackout.

'Hello, Garnet,' she said, all cool, though there was a tremble in her throat that Topaz was close enough to see. 'You made it back.'

'Aye,' said the scarlet seigneur. 'I might have expected a warmer welcome, my love.'

'I have more things to think about than whether you've decided to be alive or dead,' said the Lady.

'So I hear,' said Seigneur Garnet, sharing an amused look with Himself. 'Kidnapping children, Livilla? Really?'

'You've got the story wrong,' said Livilla, hands on hips. 'These courtesi were unclaimed. I rescued them from the theatre. They are mine to love and protect.'

Himself's cool expression cracked at that. 'Courtesi? All of them? *Livilla!*'

'Don't pretend to be shocked, Poet,' said Livilla. 'You knew exactly what those children were. You knew what that little song of theirs would do. As soon as Garnet came swanning back through the sky like he never left us, you abandoned those children without a thought.' She preened a little. 'They trust me.'

'They shouldn't,' declared Himself, looking shaken. 'Did you force out their powers? They're children!'

Livilla arched her eyebrows like a pantomime dame. 'Does this evoke traumatic memories for you, Boy? Are you going to cry?'

'You really are a stone cold bitch.'

'Right back at you, dearling,' said Livilla, dismissing him. Her attention was squarely on the other cove. 'These rooms are mine. Velody let me have them, and Ashiol too. You're not the Power and Majesty any longer, Garnet. And since you returned arm in arm with Velody, you are nothing to me.'

Garnet laughed at that. 'Accusing me of infidelity, Livilla? You, of all people?'

'I'm not accusing you of anything,' Livilla said frostily. 'I know what you are. You're going to have a war on your hands if you try to take power again. That means you can't afford to piss me off.'

'You're not choosing Ashiol over me,' Garnet said disbelievingly.

'I'm not choosing any of you. My courtesi were slaughtered by one of our own and no one was there to stop it from happening. No one gave a damn, because it happened to *me*. If anyone tries to take my lambs from me now, I will bring you all down.'

She turned dramatically and disappeared back into her rooms.

Garnet looked like he had been bludgeoned about the head.

'Topaz,' said Himself in his melodic voice, 'you can't trust her. What she did to you and your friends —'

'I don't know what she did to the lambs,' Topaz interrupted him. Livilla's antics made her bold. 'I know what *you* did. You used us. When I turned into lizards in an alleyway, she was there to look after me. Where were you?'

'Many things happened last nox,' he said, frustration dripping from him. 'Important things.'

'Aye, I figured it was something like that,' she said sharply. 'We don't need you. Push off.'

Without waiting to see if he did so, she went back inside to Livilla and the lambs.

Courtesi. It was an odd word. She supposed she would find out what it meant, eventually.

THE HORDE of black cats that was Ashiol poured into the abandoned cathedral at the edge of the Forum and swept down the staircase. He shaped himself into naked human form, startling a courtesa who was arranging tea and sandwiches on a tray. 'Oh!' she protested.

'My apologies, Damson,' he said briskly. 'He in?'

'He's not seeing anyone,' she said, and gestured discreetly without saying anything more.

Ashiol strode into the room she had indicated. Priest sat in a large, overstuffed armchair, smoking a cigar while his other remaining courtesa, Fionella, laid waistcoats and soft shirts into a large trunk that sat on the four-poster bed.

Ashiol eyed the scene. 'Going somewhere?'

'My boy,' said Priest, his voice rather less booming than usual, 'your timing is impeccable as ever.'

Priest nodded to Fionella, who drew an embroidered dressing gown from the trunk she was packing and held it out for Ashiol to shrug into. He did so, even going to the trouble of belting it for the sake of his host's pretence of modesty. 'How are things with you, Priest?'

'Ah, Ashiol. Don't pretend you care.'

'I've been preoccupied,' Ashiol said vaguely.

The Pigeon Lord was not looking his best. He had lost weight around the face and it made him look flabby and older than his years. Ashiol was Priest's courteso once, in the few months between Tasha's death and his own ascension to Lord. They'd got along well enough.

'Why is your courtesa packing a trunk?' Ashiol asked.

Priest sighed and inhaled from his cigar with no evidence of enjoyment. 'I think it's time for me to be on my way. Pastures new and all that. I didn't mean to stay in Aufleur so long, but events overtook me. You know how it is.'

Ashiol stared at him. 'You can't leave.'

'Can't I? You made a fair enough job of it, even if you gave up after five years. I think you'll find I have more staying power when it comes to exile.'

'But why?' Ashiol blurted, only to be met by an expression weighted with disapproval.

'You ask me that?' Priest said softly. 'Have you so short a memory?'

'Garnet isn't going to take power again,' Ashiol insisted. 'I won't let him. This time I'm going to do it right.'

'Glad to hear it, my boy,' said Priest heavily. 'But I'm too old to make it through another battle of Kings. I don't have the soul for it any more.'

'But I need you,' Ashiol said in frustration.

'Need?' Priest repeated. 'What right have you to need anything from me? I'm tainted, boy, from the inside out. Those devils from the sky crawled under my skin, and turned me into more of a monster than I ever thought I could be. For all my crimes, I've never murdered in cold blood before, not like I did with Livilla's boys.'

'It wasn't you,' Ashiol said, baffled that Priest would even think so. 'We all know that.'

'Do you all?' said Priest in an angry rumble. 'Has anyone informed Livilla of this? Or my Bree, who trusted me more than life itself before the dust swamped my soul and took over my hands? I hurt her while that creature took possession of me, so badly that she would rather throw her lot in with the wolf bitch.'

Fionella the courtesa took out her frustrations on the trunk, throwing things in. 'You should go,' she said to Ashiol. 'He won't listen to you. He won't listen to any of us.'

'You'll leave with him, though,' said Ashiol.

She did not meet his eyes. 'I've lived in Aufleur my whole life. I've been a courtesa since I was fourteen... but yes, I will leave. Of course I will. Damson, too. My Lord Pigeon needs us.'

'I need you,' Ashiol said angrily. 'All of you.' He turned back to Priest, words tumbling over themselves in his urgency. 'Garnet must have made some kind of allegiance with those dust devils. It's the only explanation for how he got back here. Velody is in league with him. Poet, too. Velody is the one who gave your courtesa to Livilla — humbling you, punishing you for something that was out of your control. Hells, she gave you the tainted waistcoat in the first place. This is her fault, not yours.'

Priest gazed at him, his hand rocking back and forth to make curls of smoke from his cigar. 'But you, of course, will fix it all. Make everyone better. With tea and currant buns.'

Ashiol did not smile. 'Give me a chance. One chance.'

'I don't have any chances left, boy. I'm tired.'

No, it couldn't happen this way. Surely Ashiol could convince Priest to stay. He needed the old man at his side. 'I let you down, all of you,' he admitted. 'I stayed stupidly loyal to Garnet in the face of his cruelty. I should have taken him down years ago, become the Power and Majesty that the city needed. I should have stepped up when he died. I can't

change the past. But the future is ours, if you stand
with me.'

Priest glanced at Fionella, who looked back with one
unmistakeable expression of longing before she turned back
to the trunk.

'I have tickets to Bazeppe, leaving tomorrow afternoon,'
Priest said finally. 'You have until then to secure the support
of the other Lords and Court. If they are with you, I will stay.'

'And you'll swear allegiance to me as Power and Majesty?'

'I swore to Velody. To Garnet as well, come to that. I have
no wish to die forsworn, boy.'

'Velody and Garnet *died*. Your oath was severed by that.'

'Prove to me it won't do further damage to my soul and
I'll consider it. Now get out of here. We have packing to do.'

6

ONE DAY AFTER THE IDES OF BESTIALIS

NOX

'*D*on't go out again,' said Delphine.

She wanted Rhian found more than anyone, but Macready had been searching the streets all day. He came back from the ruined theatre looking like a man half-dead. He didn't look much better now, hovering between the kitchen table and the door.

'Another hour, lass.'

'You need to sleep,' she told him sternly. 'Velody is looking. Crane and Kelpie are looking.'

She needed to sleep, too. She felt stretched thin all over. And she wasn't going to admit that it would be easier to fall asleep with him beside her. Really. She wasn't that attached.

Mac took a breath, like he was coming up for air. 'I remember what it was like for Heliora that first year she was Seer. She went half-insane with it. Did a lot of crazed things. You think Rhian can get through it unscathed? After everything she's been through?'

Delphine narrowed her eyes at him. 'Are you lecturing me about looking after Rhian? I want her found as much as you do, and you're no good to her if you end up in a gutter.'

Were they here already, with Delphine playing the nag to a wayward husband? It didn't suit her.

'I'll manage, so I will,' Macready said, and she could see that his thoughts were already out there. He was barely listening to her. 'Stay here in case she returns on her own. Do you remember how to send a message?'

Delphine rolled her eyes. He'd spent weeks going over and over how she could communicate with the other sentinels via old Tom, the cat who'd started lurking around the shop ever since Ashiol came into their lives. Sentinels could use the animals associated with any Kings, and she'd got the knack by her second lesson, though he kept reminding her of the techniques anyway.

'I can use mice now, too,' she said sweetly. 'And — what creature does Garnet hold again?'

She wished she could take the snipe back when she saw the look on Macready's face.

'Gattopardo,' he said hoarsely. 'If one of those turns up, bar the fecking doors against it.'

And then he was gone, the kitchen door swinging behind him. Leaving Delphine behind, like she was some kind of housewife. What was she supposed to do, make soup?

She stalked up to her room. Fine. She could get to sleep without a cranky Islandser in her bed. No problem at all.

∼

IT WAS NOX. Velody climbed the Lucretine hill, her feet bare on the stone-lined streets, searching for Rhian. She couldn't help remembering the last time Rhian had gone missing, on the day of the Lupercalia, with the stink of leather and wine in the air. They found her later, dishevelled and broken, and nothing in her life had prepared Velody for how helpless she had felt to know that Rhian had been raped.

This was different. Velody had powers at her fingertips now. She could find Rhian, and ensure no one hurt her ever again. All she had to do was open her animor to the sky...

'Lady,' said a voice out of the darkness. The taste of his power was familiar a moment before his voice was. Warlord.

He wore a gold silk shirt that made his skin even darker in contrast. The Creature Court lived underground. Honestly, where did they get their clothes? Velody had never seen a shirt made quite that way before, with slash cuts in the sleeves. Did he send home to Zafir for sartorial care packages?

'You look better,' she said finally, 'than the last time I saw you.' Drained, bleeding, exhausted, damaged, but still fighting.

Warlord gave little away in his expression. 'We have missed you.'

'It's good to be home,' said Velody. 'Have you seen Rhian — our new Seer? Since the theatre?'

He shook his head slowly, eyes fastened to hers. 'I have not. Have you truly returned, Lady?'

'I hope so,' she said.

'I mean, are you still our Power and Majesty? Is he?'

Velody had not thought about it. Everything was chaos since she and Garnet fell through the ceiling of the Vittorina Royale. She didn't even know if he was still in the city, or if he was in any way the same person she had got to know in the broken city of Tierce.

'What do you want from me?' she asked.

Warlord laughed hollowly. 'You ask me that, Lady? You have made us oathbreakers, all of us. We are obliged to serve you and Garnet both. Perhaps we should be grateful Ashiol never asked us for a third oath...'

Velody blinked. 'Has Ashiol not been the Power and Majesty?' If it was Bestialis, she had been gone three months. 'What has been happening while I was gone?'

'I do not know much. The sentinels have kept Ashiol away from the rest of us. I suspect he ran mad. It would not be the first time.'

'I need to speak to him,' said Velody. 'And Garnet. I can't answer your question until we *talk*.'

Warlord looked unimpressed. 'If you are going to be Power and Majesty, it will not be because of a conversation, Lady. It will be because you draw more loyalty than your rivals. Because the Lords and Court choose you, as we chose you before.'

Rhian. That was what was important. The politics could wait, couldn't it?

'Who do you choose?' Velody said impatiently. 'Or is this you hanging around in the hope of another bribe?'

Warlord's eyes flashed. 'Your blood saved my life a few months ago. But Garnet was our Power and Majesty first. I will follow the King who shows the greatest strength. Sentiment has no place in these decisions.'

'Forget sentiment,' Velody said. 'And to hells with strength — as if *strength* is the most important thing a leader offers. Tell me which King you would prefer to have in charge.'

He smiled suddenly, the warrior facade cracking just a little. 'You. But I won't follow you if you plan to lose to Garnet.'

'I don't plan to lose to anyone,' Velody said, and continued walking up the hill.

'Do you love him?' Warlord called out behind her.

Velody spun around. 'What did you say?'

He was searching for something in her eyes. 'The way you returned, both of you. It bleeds through your animor. You and Garnet taste of each other.'

'That's... disturbing.' Velody realised why he was asking. 'Livilla was Garnet's lover, wasn't she? Are you hoping that I'll take him off her hands?'

The thought of it alarmed her. Sex with Garnet had been... of the moment, about building up their powers and giving them both the strength to escape. Velody hadn't had any time to think about whether it meant more than that, but the fact that he had bedded half the Court (that she knew about) made him an unlikely boyfriend. Things with Ashiol were complicated enough without them sharing a lover.

Warlord's smile was thin. 'Loving Livilla is like loving the wind. She is impossible to grasp, to possess. Garnet is the same, you will find.'

'And Ashiol?' Velody asked without thinking.

Ashiol. Why hadn't he taken the leadership of the city? She had relied on him. What had he been doing with himself? He was so pleased to see her alive. Her mouth still felt bruised by the kiss he greeted her with on her return. Once he realised she had returned with Garnet, though, he looked as if he hated her.

'You have a fight on your hands, Lady,' said Warlord. 'Unless you plan to frig them both into submission. A valid leadership method, it could be said, but you're mistaken if you think they won't try the same thing on you.'

'I have to find the Seer,' said Velody. 'Garnet and Ashiol can take care of themselves.'

She was startled by a memory — not her own — of Garnet and Ashiol together, when they were lovers: *red hair, black hair, bodies hot to the touch, arms and stomachs, skin against skin.*

'I'm sure they can,' said Warlord, and he stepped back into the shadows, leaving her alone in the street.

~

MACREADY MADE it as far as the Gardens of Trajus Alysaundre before he needed to rest. He was dizzy with adrenalin and lack of sleep. Delphine was right, though he would never admit it to the lass's face. He leaned against one of the crumbling stone walls, breathing hard. Rhian was lost in the city, maybe hurt, maybe under siege from the futures. Vulnerable.

(Vulnerable, eh? Then what had that tryst with Ashiol been about? Not such a shy and retiring little camellia, was she now?)

Since Rhian became the Seer, Macready had a new awareness of her, his sentinel's senses able to pick her presence before she entered a room. Sometimes when they practised her fighting skills, he almost caught a glimpse of her thoughts. It had been like that with Heliora too, when they crossed swords.

It wasn't enough, not nearly enough, to be able to track her. Velody had a better chance. Didn't stop him looking. He blamed himself for taking Rhian to that damned theatre (he had no right to be angry at her, time he acknowledged that) and that meant he had to be the one to find her.

Crane approached him, through the park. They nodded at each other.

'No sign?' Macready asked.

Crane shook his head. 'Some of the injured from the theatre were taken to a hospice near the Palazzo. The Duchessa asked her own dottores to treat them. But no one there has seen anyone who looks like Rhian.'

'Feck,' Macready said, too tired to even put emphasis on the word.

'Have you seen her yet?' Crane asked.

There could be only one 'her' Crane was referring to. As far as the lad was concerned, all the light of the sun and moon shone out of the arse of Velody, their former Power and Majesty.

'Aye.'

'Is she the same?'

Apart from the fact that she came back hand in hand with Garnet?

'She seems no different,' Macready said shortly.

Crane shivered. It might have been the chill nox with winter around the corner, or it might have been something else. 'Three of them. It's a long time since we've had three Kings.'

'Aye. The sentinels are practically outnumbered, so we are.'

'Will there be a challenge all over again?'

'How the feck should I know?' Macready dashed his hand over his forehead, noting the lad's hurt look but not saying a word of apology. 'Depends, does it not? On who gives way. Who's weaker.'

'Or who is stronger.'

'Come on,' said Macready. 'Let's sweep the Arches.'

'Do you really think Rhian would go there alone?'

'We don't know what the feck she'd do. But if she's down there, I sure as hells hope she's alone.'

TOPAZ WAS THINKING. She hadn't done much but think since Himself and his Garnet friend took their leave. She was surrounded by noise and chaos as the lambs practised their new stage trick, changing back and forth into creature form.

The Lady Livilla lounged on a fancy couch, watching the lambs play. Topaz got up her nerve finally and crossed the room to her, ignoring the dirty look from Bree. She went down on one knee, having seen enough aristo plays to know that would go down well. 'Lady?' she asked quietly.

Livilla reached out a hand, brushing over the close-cropped fuzz of Topaz's hair. 'Yes, dearling?'

Topaz could still feel the lizard shapes hot and wild inside her skin, wanting to come out. 'Did you do this to me?' She deliberately kept accusation out of her voice, allowing the curiosity to take rein instead. She wanted to *know*.

'Not to you,' said Livilla, and there was something almost human in her voice. Less false and brittle. A moment between all the stagecraft.

'But to them?' Topaz pressed, looking across to the other lambs. Belinny transformed her hand back and forth from a bear's paw, looking delighted with herself.

'It would have happened sooner or later,' said Livilla. 'I pushed it along, that's all.'

'Cos you wanted us with you and not those others?'

'Do you want to leave me for your Orphan Princel, Topaz?'

'Not now. Not ever. But I don't know as how you're any better than him. How can I know?'

'All you can do is serve,' said Livilla. 'And hope. If I am a bad mistress, Topaz, you can leave at any time. I hope you know that.'

'Really?' said Topaz, grazing her lip with her teeth out of nervousness.

Livilla's fingers locked around her wrist and she smiled a wolfish smile at her. 'No,' she said. 'Not really.'

~

ASHIOL CIRCLED THE CIRCUS VERDIGRIS. It was close enough to the river that he could hear the sounds of the docks. Nox would be over in a few hours and what did he have to show for it? Priest had set him an impossible task, and would leave if Ashiol didn't get the support of the others. Poet was already wrapped up in Garnet. Ashiol hadn't been able to find Warlord, and didn't have the balls to ask Livilla to make her choice. She always took Garnet's side.

In human form, not even bothering to play Lord, he dropped onto one of the tiered benches of the Circus.

Two sleek brighthounds ran the length of the green arena and back again, yapping at each other, play-fighting.

'How did you find me?' said a soft voice.

Ashiol glanced up and saw Rhian perched on a bench a little above him. He should have felt her from a mile away, but he always had trouble reading animor when his thoughts were muddled. It was an excuse for how he had thought Rhian was Heliora only a few days ago. He had gone so far as to fuck her without realising who it was in his arms. The madness of the last few months had left him now, he was sure of it. But he had to deal with the results.

He had been hallucinating, but what was her excuse? What had she been thinking? Had he not heard her protests, just as he hadn't seen that she was Rhian and not his dead lover? Had he taken her against her will? He had no frigging idea.

'Believe it or not, I wasn't looking for you,' he said. 'I was looking for him.' He nodded in the direction of the brighthounds: Lennoc, the newest Lord of the Court. 'Lief used to run here at nox. I was hoping his hounds followed the same tradition.'

'It's no good, you know,' Rhian said, sounding far away.

'You'll never get them all to choose you. The battle won't be won that way.'

'But it will be won?'

Ashiol had a lot of practice with these conversations, though Rhian was not, would never be, Heliora. He concentrated on remembering who she was, on not letting the hallucinations get a foothold again. This was *Rhian*. A background presence in Velody's household, an annoyance more than anything. Velody had been near obsessed with keeping Rhian and Delphine safe, and it held her back from accepting her place in the Creature Court.

Later, once Velody was dead, Rhian joined the sentinels in guarding Ashiol as his madness ran its course. He remembered she had even let him escape once, for a few precious hours in the sky.

She was the new Seer. It was perhaps understandable that he had hallucinated that she was Hel, his friend and bedmate, former Seer of the Court. But Ashiol could not for the life of him imagine why Rhian let him think it was true.

'I didn't say that.' She took a deep breath and exhaled. It wasn't yet cold enough at nox for them to be able to see her breath in clouds, but it wouldn't be long now.

'What are they planning?' Ashiol asked, though he knew the futility of the question. 'Poet and Garnet. They have something planned for Saturnalia. What is it?'

Rhian looked at him, her eyes glazed. 'You have to get on the train.'

He stared back. 'That's your advice? Time for me to run away? Back to my mother's estate with my tail between my legs?'

'I didn't say that. You don't listen very well to people, do you?'

'I'm not going anywhere,' he said sullenly. 'Priest is the one packing up his courtesi and linens and turning tail in the hope that Bazeppe might be shinier than what we have here. I'm not catching a train this or any other nox.'

No matter how much he might want to.

The brighthounds had stopped prancing and stared up at them both. They blurred together, shaping into a stocky man with a shock of white hair. He nodded warily at Ashiol and said nothing.

'Lennoc, Lord Brighthound,' said Ashiol. 'Will you swear allegiance to me as Power and Majesty?'

'You'll do a better job, will you?' Lennoc crossed his arms belligerently. 'Why you? Why not Velody or Garnet?'

'Because I'll bite your throat out right now if you don't,' said Ashiol, not even bothering to sound like he meant it.

Lennoc paused, considering. 'Works for me.'

He shaped himself back into hound form and bowed his heads before scampering off into the darkness. Ashiol couldn't resist shooting a look of triumph at Rhian.

'Try that on Livilla, see how far you get,' she said cynically, sounding so like Hel that for a moment he thought he had lost his mind all over again.

'Why did you do it?" he asked on impulse. 'Why did you let me believe you were her?'

Rhian looked sad. He had viewed her as a weakness, Velody's weakness. It had never occurred to him that she might also be his.

'You were safe,' she said finally. 'I knew I couldn't damage you. But I did, didn't I?' She stood up. 'Get on the train, before Saturnalia. The answers are there, not here.'

He watched as she walked away, and made no move to stop her.

'Ash,' interrupted a new voice a few moments later. He looked up and saw Kelpie glaring at him. 'Tell me that wasn't Rhian.'

'Clearly it was.'

'We've been combing this bloody city for that wench. Velody's climbing the walls, Macready's bitten pieces out of the furniture, and you just let her wander off again!'

'I'm not the Seer's keeper, Kelpie.'

'That's not what I hear.'

Ashiol rolled his eyes at her. 'Shut it.'

If he couldn't get all of the Lords on his side, he could at least try for a majority. Livilla or Warlord? Rhian had a fair point about Livilla.

'Where can I find Mars at this time of nox?' he asked.

Kelpie raised her eyebrows. 'That depends on whether he wants to be found.'

'He'd be found for you, wouldn't he?'

'Fuck you.'

'Kelpie —'

'No, seriously, Ashiol. Fuck you. I won't be used. I've been loyal as all hells, but you can't make me turn over people's secrets so you can launch some kind of takeover bid against the other Kings. Do you even remember what "sentinel" means?'

'Garnet used you. Abused you. Broke all the rules about what sentinels were.'

'Yes,' Kelpie spat. 'And you're supposed to be different.'

She turned and walked away from him. He watched her go.

Aye, that was what he was supposed to be. Different from Garnet. It was a fact worth remembering.

7

TWO DAYS AFTER THE IDES OF BESTIALIS

DAYLIGHT

*V*elody returned home at dawn. There had been no attacks from the sky that nox, thank the saints. Exploding a theatre was obviously enough to keep it quiet for a time. She met Crane and Macready at the end of her street. They looked as tired as she felt. Macready was swaying on his feet.

'Thank you,' she said. 'For trying. I know you can't have a lot of trust in me right now.'

'Don't say that,' Crane said indignantly. 'You're — we're not going to suddenly stop being your sentinels.'

'I don't see why not,' Velody said. 'I stopped being your King. I wasn't here. And now you have loyalty to three Kings to juggle.'

'Wouldn't be the first time,' said Macready. 'Don't fret about us, lass. We never expected to have you back with us at all.'

Velody hugged them both, impulsively. 'I didn't think I would make it, either.'

'Where were you?' Crane asked. 'I mean — I saw sandstone in the theatre.'

'Tierce, you said,' Macready repeated.

Crane flinched at that.

'I was in the sky,' said Velody. 'It looked like Tierce, but it was a shadow of the city I remember.' She remembered the original city now, clearer than ever before. 'I never saw... them.' The dust devils, vicious and fast and unlike anything they had faced before. 'Did they come back?' she asked.

Both sentinels shook their heads. 'Not since the sky swallowed you,' said Crane.

'I suppose there's a lot to catch me up on.' Velody managed a smile. 'Like how you talked Delphine into being a sentinel.'

Macready wasn't smiling. 'It was in her all along. All it took was —'

'Blood, sweat, yelling,' Crane chipped in.

Macready cuffed him lightly. 'Aye, that.' He was still sombre. 'There's something else you should know. About Rhian — and Ashiol.'

Velody frowned. 'He hasn't bothered her about this Seer business, has he? How has she been coping with it all?' Apart from going missing for a whole day after a near-death theatre experience.

'Let's go back to the house,' Macready muttered. 'Discuss it there.'

They headed up the back alley together. As they entered the yard, a figure on the doorstep stood up suddenly. Macready swore.

Velody fell forward. 'Rhian!'

Her friend looked ragged around the edges, more of a mess even than on that horrible Lupercalia nearly two years ago. At the same time, her eyes were bright and she seemed more alive, more Rhian, than she had been in years.

'Velody,' Rhian said calmly, 'you have to go to the train station, right now.'

'What happened to you?' Velody asked. 'Are you... have you been all right?'

Everyone was being so *strange* about Rhian. Velody had missed something vital, she knew it.

'If you don't get to the station now, Priest will leave the city,' Rhian said, still sounding so serene.

'The futures came to you?' Macready demanded, sounding oddly attacking.

Rhian paused, then nodded. 'Priest is catching a train, with Fionella and Damson.'

Velody barely knew the names of the courtesi. How did Rhian know them? 'Where is he going?' she asked.

'The clockwork city,' said Rhian.

'Bazeppe,' said Macready. 'Feck, the early train leaves in an hour.'

'I'll go,' said Velody. 'The rest of you need to get some sleep.'

'No,' Crane said suddenly. They stared at him. 'No more going off alone, Velody. It's not fair to any of us.'

'It's morning,' she pointed out. 'I think I can resist the urge to hurl myself into the sky again.'

'I'll go with you.' Kelpie appeared at the gate, arms folded. She arched her eyebrows at Velody. 'Or don't you want my help?'

'I'd welcome it,' said Velody. She poked Crane in the chest. 'Sleep. Thank you for your help this nox. You, too,' she added to Macready.

'All part of the job,' Macready muttered, his head down so that he would not meet Rhian's eyes.

Velody had no time to think about everyone's strange

behaviour. She and Kelpie headed south at a quick pace, matching each other.

'It's bad when the Lords start leaving the city,' Velody said in an undertone. 'Right?'

'Right,' Kelpie confirmed. 'Rats leaving a sinking barge and all that.'

'I should have paid more attention to Priest. After what happened with the devil that possessed him...'

'You weren't here,' said Kelpie. There was an uncomfortable pause. 'I don't mean that like it sounded. Not in a bad way. You can't expect to have sorted things out when you were somewhere else.'

'They didn't do a great job without me, did they?'

Velody was half-joking, but Kelpie turned a serious face on her. 'No, they really didn't. I never liked you much. But things are worse when you're not here.'

'Even if I brought Garnet back with me?'

Kelpie's face closed over and she turned away. 'Don't know how that's going to turn out. I cried when the sky took him. Felt like a failure. But it was a relief, too.'

'It might be different this time. He might be different.' But Velody couldn't promise that, could she? 'I don't know,' she sighed. 'I don't know who he is, not really. Everything he said and did while we were trapped in that place could have been a lie to make me trust him. I haven't even seen him since Ashiol tried to drown him in the Lake of Follies. Perhaps he caught a train, too.'

Kelpie shivered. 'Not him. He doesn't back down. Not ever. Especially with people he loves.'

They walked the rest of the way in silence. The morning sunlight was clear and bright by the time they reached the Aurian Gate. Despite the daylight, Velody felt something lift off her shoulders as she crossed through to the other side. 'Oh,' she said softly. Her animor was still there, pulsing in her veins. She could shape herself into little brown mice if she had to. But the intensity of it was gone.

'The sky's different outside the city,' Kelpie said quietly. 'Isn't it?'

That was it. The sky over the city was something else entirely. She was free out here, just as she was trapped when she was within the bounds of Aufleur.

'Perhaps we should all get on the train,' Velody muttered.

'You don't mean that,' said Kelpie.

'How do you know?'

'Because you're stronger than any of those stupid men.'

Velody laughed. She couldn't help it. She was still laughing when they stepped onto the station platform and saw Priest sitting there, a courtesa on either side of him and a large trunk at his feet.

'Wish me luck,' said Velody.

Velody stepped forward, her buttoned-up boots making a little noise on the platform. A memory came unbidden: of her brother Sage coming out of the steam, of Cyniver waiting at the side for him to notice her, of that last visit home before everything ended. Every temptation to step on a train and let it carry her away was gone in that moment. Aufleur would suffer the same fate as Tierce if they didn't stay to fight. Garnet and Ashiol would be at each other's throats — Garnet's homecoming had proved that. They needed her.

The gull courtesa, Damson, slid over to the other side of her Lord as Velody approached, making room for her. Priest looked unsurprised at her appearance.

'My Lady,' he said with courtesy. The absence of 'Power' or 'Majesty' was tangible.

'Why would you leave?' she asked. 'You, of all people?'

'I seem a fixture among the Court, do I?' Priest asked. 'If

that is the case, dear demme, you have not been paying attention. I have nothing holding me here.'

'Nothing but an oath,' Velody said.

'Two oaths,' he corrected her. 'Both broken by death. Or cancelled out by each other.'

'I'm not dead,' she reminded him.

Priest looked her over. 'You died. It is enough.'

'Are you so sure about that?' she said. 'Enough to risk becoming an oathbreaker? You know what happened to Dhynar Lord Ferax.'

'If anything, it is Garnet who has the prior claim,' Priest said, sounding entirely comfortable. 'Perhaps you should raise the subject with him.'

'Garnet isn't here right now,' said Velody. 'Only me. Look me in the eyes, Priest, and tell me that you are willing to walk away from the city, from the Court, from your Power and Majesty.'

He met her gaze placidly. 'I have done it before.'

'Why Bazeppe? Is that where you come from?' She knew he wasn't from Aufleur, but had never detected a regional accent of any kind.

'I hear things,' said Priest. 'They can use a man like me, I think.'

'Why?' she said. 'Why leave? It can't just be hurt feelings.'

Priest shook his head. 'You Kings. Mad, impatient children. No one in this Court has ever paid any attention to important matters. To the words spilled by Seers, or by the Smith. You have no history, no interest in learning anything, just sky, fight, frig, over and over again.'

'What do you know?' Velody demanded. 'What do you think you know that makes you better than us?'

'I know that the End of Days is upon us. I know that the salamander has joined the ranks of the Creature Court. I know that a devil climbed inside my skin and no one noticed until I started murdering children.' He blew out a long breath of a sigh. 'I know that if I stay, this city will kill me. Perhaps elsewhere I can be a great man again.'

Velody could hear a screech in the distance. The train came rattling into sight, around a bend.

She was caught by another memory, her earliest memory perhaps. Sage, sitting up on the wall at the south station in Tierce, dangling his legs. 'Ever seen a steam angel, mouseling? Watch as the train rushes in. If you stare at the steam long enough, you can see people in it.'

Little Velody, barely four years old, stared valiantly into the steam until her eyes were sore and red from the dust and did not see a thing. Sage laughed all the way home.

Dead, he was dead, the sky took him years ago. There was nothing left of her family. He would never have called her mouseling — it was a nickname of the Creature Court. Even her memories were corrupted by this place.

'This, I believe, is my train,' said Priest as the engine slowed, filling the platform with dense smoke and steam. Velody stared into the steam for a moment, looking for the answer.

Priest moved his head slightly and Velody followed his gaze. Ashiol stood on the edge of the platform, wind blowing his long black coat around him. He was staring into the steam as well. Velody turned her head and saw Garnet at the other end of the platform, posed just as dramatically. They stared at each other, no eyes for anyone else.

'Go,' she said softly.

'Majesty?' Priest was surprised enough to let the title slip out.

'Who am I to stop anyone from escaping this life? Go, Priest. Have my blessing. I hope you find what you're looking for.'

Velody felt tired, so tired. She thought coming home

would solve everything, but she was back to this, fighting over every moment, every conflict.

Priest hesitated only a moment, then he stood, scooping his enormous trunk up as if it weighed nothing. 'You are a true King, Velody,' he said. 'Good luck.' He stepped onto the train, Damson and Fionella with him.

The whistle blew, and more steam filled the station.

'What are you doing?' Ashiol demanded, striding towards Velody. 'We have to stop him.'

'Are you deliberately trying to weaken the city?' Garnet demanded, approaching from the other side. 'Do you want us to become a floating graveyard like Tierce?'

'Being a King isn't only about gathering strength, or fighting the sky,' Velody snapped. 'It's about looking after our people.'

'Priest can't run away,' said Ashiol between gritted teeth. 'You can't let him go.'

The train began to pull out of the station.

'You're one to talk,' Velody yelled at Ashiol. 'You've been trying to run away since you got here. You gave this city to *me*.'

Gone. The train was gone. Priest was gone.

'You left,' Ashiol retorted. 'Sacrificed yourself to the sky — what's that but another form of giving up? At least he—' he nodded to Garnet '— didn't mean to get himself killed. You both left me here. This is my city now.'

'And how have you used the time, Ashiol?' Velody hissed. 'What grand changes have you wrought? You never even took their oaths!'

'If Mama and Papa could stop fighting for a moment,' Garnet said, sounding far too amused. 'Let's work this out like seigneurs. Velody has allowed Priest to escape. That leaves us with four Lords. I have Poet's oath.'

Ashiol hesitated. 'I have Lennoc's.'

'You have Livilla,' Ashiol and Garnet said in unison, then looked at each other in surprise.

'Interesting,' said Garnet.

'Warlord says he will follow me,' said Velody. 'It comes down to Livilla's vote.'

'Vote?' Garnet said dismissively. 'The Creature Court is not a democracy.'

'Nevertheless, we have a choice,' said Velody. 'We can try to fight to the death over who leads the Court, or we put the decision in Livilla's hands and find an answer without spilling blood.'

Ashiol and Garnet looked at each other. 'Fight to the death,' they agreed.

PART III
RATS AND CUBS

8

POET

Some might reckon I deserved what I got, being daft enough to trust Tasha. You might even have put together that Madalena was more likely to have been torn apart by a demme who changes into a lion than a Lord who changes into birds. Aye, I was gullible, but that's beside the point. I was already lost. I was sick for months, through Aphrodal and Floralis, sweating and feverish, drowning in crazy dreams. Tasha didn't send me back to the theatre; she tended me, whispered motherly words into my ear. By the time I was right again, I was used to doing what she said, even if it was just opening my mouth for the soothing syrup, or turning my head so she could take the soaking pillow out from under me.

I was hers. There was naught for me back at the Vittorina Royale. I'd been gone too long and without Madalena to be sentimental about me, I'd have been replaced within a week. Not much point going back to Oyster, either. The only family I'd ever known was the Mermaid Revue.

Once, before my fever broke, I saw Bad Cravat sitting in a corner of my room, watching me. He was on his own, which was unusual. Tasha normally didn't let anyone else in unless she was there too, so either she was with me or I was alone.

Garnet, his real name was. I remembered that. He was a mite taller than he had been, but fitted his fancy clothes no better than before. He'd be of age in a year or two, maybe. He was drunk off his face. I was hazy, but I could smell it on him. He muttered to himself like he didn't expect me to hear him. I was just there. All manner of nonsense about skies and blood and burning that made me think he had more than gin in his cup.

I stirred, and he looked at me in surprise. 'You're awake.'

My throat was too dry and hot to do more than croak. He brought me honey water, dripped it into my mouth, fumbling with the glass.

'Welcome back to the land of the living, little rat.'

'I dream of rats,' I said when I could push out the words. 'Big white ones. Clambering everywhere. I dream that all the time.'

'Doesn't surprise me,' said Garnet.

That small amount of talking was enough to wipe me out. I closed my eyes again, and when I opened them, he was gone.

I got stronger after that, slowly. Tasha babied and cosseted me like I'd always wanted from Madalena. She called me her Poet, which I didn't understand, but it was a better name than Boy or Baby. She delighted in my memory, packed with a lifetime of overheard plays and pantomimes. As I recovered, she made me recite stage verse to her until my voice went dry again.

I'd do anything to please her. Anything.

If the fever had harmed my voice, I have no doubt she'd have thrown me to the street. Or perhaps not. She knew a secret about me, after all. Something even I didn't know yet.

One morning I woke up and couldn't think straight. My

mind was in a bunch of tiny bodies, all paws and tails and noses, running in a hundred different directions at once.

You see where I'm going with this, don't you?

I climbed the walls, clung to the wooden eaves, hid under the bed, and when I realised what was happening — I was rats, big white rats, dozens of them — I was so shocked that I fell back into my human body and crashed to the floor, bruised and bloodied and panicked.

Tasha came in, but I was screaming and crying and grabbing and she got bored fast. She shoved me down and walked away. 'Deal with it,' she snapped as she left.

Three bare-chested seigneurs stood in the doorway looking at me. Garnet and the two others, one dark, one golden.

'What's happening to me?' I yelled at them.

Garnet came, pulled me up on the bed, found another of the seemingly endless pairs of pyjamas that Tasha liked to dress me in.

'Rats,' he said with a sigh. Not drunk this time. 'Either of you pricks got a good way to explain it to him?'

'I can't change in front of him,' said the dark one. 'Cats might send the poor bugger completely over the edge.'

The golden one shrugged. He unbuttoned his shirt, kicked off his breeches, and then... changed. I had seen stage tricks before, and this was no trick. I was too close to fool myself this was anything other than a fellow shaping himself into a large furry creature. He was gold and brown and lithe, and his pelt slithered over his muscles as he padded towards me. My fingers stilled on the pyjama buttons as I gazed in a mixture of horror and awe at the amazing creature.

He licked my face, and the other lads cracked up at my horrified expression.

'Nicely explained, Lysh,' the dark one said, shaking his head.

Garnet sat by me, one hand caressing the furry head of his friend. 'This is Lysandor. He's also a lynx. See his tufty ears?' He tugged at the pointy tufts of hair that looked a bit like devil horns. 'I'm Garnet. I'm gattopardo. A bit like our friend here, but bigger, with spots. Better looking.' Lysandor the lynx snorted and Garnet cuffed him lightly. 'The smart-arse back there is Ashiol. Plain old house cats.'

'Fuck you,' said Ashiol, without any heat. 'What's your name, lamb?'

'Poet,' I said in a low voice.

Lysandor was warm. I wanted to bury myself in his fur and go to sleep.

'No,' said Ashiol. 'What was your name before you came here? Before Tasha got her talons into you?'

'Poet,' I said again, rebelliously.

'Knows his own mind, doesn't he?' said Ashiol, sounding almost impressed.

'I'm surprised he has any mind left after what she did to him.'

'Shut your mouth,' Ashiol said. 'He doesn't know.'

I wasn't stupid. They were talking about me like I wasn't there, which happened a lot back at the Mermaid and the Vittorina Royale. I'd learnt to understand what adults said, even when they weren't saying anything at all, and these were far from adults. I sat up straighter. 'Where are we?'

'We're safe,' said Ashiol, and this time it was Garnet who snorted. 'Underground,' Ashiol added, giving his friend a dirty look.

'Still in the big city?'

'Under it,' said Garnet. 'What do you remember, little rat?'

I ran my hands through my hair. It was longer than ever before. The stagemaster hated it when our hair fell in our eyes — he docked the wardrobe mistress's pay if she didn't chase us around with her snippers every month — even the demmes. Long hair was no use to a lamb, and even if you made it up to the better roles, short hair made it easier to slap a wig on, and avoid lice. But these boys all had longish hair, and now I did, too. I liked it.

'I've been sick,' I said.

'Aye, but do you remember what made you sick?' Garnet pressed.

'Stop it,' said Ashiol.

'You can't approve of what she did.'

'It's done now, and she's our Lord. It's none of our frigging business to approve or disapprove of what she does.'

'I never realised you were such a good little servant, Ashiol. Like you were born to it.'

Their faces were ugly as they sniped at each other. I ignored them, scratching Lysandor behind his ears. I didn't know if he wasn't changing back from lynx form because he couldn't or because he wanted to stay out of the argument.

'Is this why I'm sick?' I asked, interrupting them. 'I mean... is this part of the sickness? Is it catching?'

I had a horrible vision of all the lambs back at the theatre turning into creatures, crawling around and nibbling at the stage machinery, while the stagemaster howled and yelled until he turned into a giant bear or a walrus or something.

Definitely a walrus.

'You're not sick,' said Garnet. 'I mean, not really. Once your body adjusts, you'll be fine.'

I tugged more firmly on Lysandor's ears. 'You're saying this is normal? It's not going to go away?'

The two lads looked at each other, and I knew the truth. This was it. Forever. I was never going back to the Vittorina Royale.

White rats.

9

COURTESO

*I*t was a while before I found out about the rest of
it. Tasha was keeping me hidden, I figured that out
pretty fast. The lads — the cubs, she called them — were
always getting summoned away for one thing or another. I
wasn't allowed outside the den. It was a stone building, like
one of the sea cottages back home, but always dark unless
there were oil lamps burning.

If I asked too many questions, Tasha would leave me
without a lamp. I never minded. Maybe it was the rat in me,
or all those years climbing around backstage, but I had
pretty good vision in darkness. Sometimes, when they were
gone and I was feeling itchy-footed, I'd go exploring. There
were tunnels all around us, but most of them led nowhere, or
to ruined buildings and rockfalls. Once I found my way into
a massive tunnel with a canal running through it, and
followed it far enough to see a cathedral as fancy as any
theatre. I knew I was underground by then. I just didn't
know why.

One nox — Tasha and the cubs said 'nox' when they were
awake and 'daylight' when they wanted to sleep, though I

could never figure out how they could tell the difference —
Lord Saturn found me.

I felt him coming before I heard him. I did that with
Tasha and the cubs — an early warning system that let me
scamper back to the den and act like I'd never been
anywhere. This was different, I knew. It was like something
crawling over my skin.

He stepped into the den, all tricked out in his fancy top
hat and morning coat, and stared at me. I tried to hide, but he
lashed out his hand, pulling me out from behind our little
stove. Madalena's murderer.

'My word,' he said, staring at my dirty face. 'I know you.
You're the theatre boy.'

'Poet,' I said sullenly. 'My name's Poet.'

'I don't care what she named you, wretch, what are you
doing here?' He stared into my face as if trying to see some
great truth.

There was a knife near the stove — Lysandor had been
slicing bread before Tasha got the call and went swooping
out with the cubs in her wake. I didn't even think. Everything
came rushing back, all my old anger. I seized the hilt and
drove the blade hard into the man's chest.

That was it, then. I was a killer now.

Saturn looked confused rather than angry or hurt. He
reached down and prised my fingers from the hilt, then drew
out the knife and flung it hard against the nearest wall. There
was no blood. What was he?

He stared hard at me, and it was as if he had a hand inside
me, fingers prodding at my bones, squeezing my heart so
hard I couldn't breathe.

'Stop it!' I yelled, and did the only thing I knew how to do
when cornered. I exploded into white rats.

It was a mistake, because he was hawks, and they had the
better of me. When he changed, I panicked, scurrying and

cringing, and those beaks came down, terrorising me back into my human form, skinny and shuddering.

I heard the rustling of clothing, and then Saturn wrapped a blanket around my shoulders. 'Tasha,' he said in a disgusted voice. 'She should never have done this to you, boy.'

'I didn't have nowhere to go,' I snivelled. 'Not after what you did to my...' But there was no word for what she was to me. 'Madalena!'

'Madalena?' he said, and I hated him for the lack of recognition in his voice. 'The actress?'

'She wasn't no mask,' I said scornfully. 'She was the stellar. *Our* stellar. She looked after me. You made her play the Angel in our revue. And you killed her.'

'Killed her? She went back to that little town, didn't she? I saw she was no longer in the show, but I never thought...' His voice went chill. 'Dead, you say?'

'Ripped apart,' I said softly, not sure what to think. He sounded genuine but he'd always been an actor and a liar, hadn't he? 'By animals.'

Saturn looked sadly at me and finally I knew the thing I had been trying not to know for so long.

'Come with me,' he said. 'I'll get you home.'

I pulled on the shirt and trews — Tasha gave them to me. Everything I had was hers, really. Even the little mug I drank my tea out of. I laced my boots.

'Lord Saturn,' said a voice at the doorway. 'What are you doing?'

Garnet. It was Garnet, and my heart hurt to see him, because he'd always been my friend, more than the others.

'I am taking this boy,' said Saturn. 'You won't stop me, courteso. Your mistress has done badly by him — he should never have been brought here.'

'You can't just take him,' Garnet snapped. 'He's ours now. He's *family*.'

'Yours?' Saturn said in disbelief. 'Will he still think so when I tell him what you did to his mother? All of you?'

I looked at Garnet then and saw it in his eyes. Gattopardo. Lynx. Lioness. Maybe even plain old house cats. 'Madalena,' I said softly.

'I brought your theatre company to Aufleur, to the Vittorina Royale, as a gift for Tasha,' Saturn told me. 'She has a liking for grandiose gestures, for elaborate gifts. It was a mistake. She is easily bored, and she was jealous of the actresses. I got so angry at her, after all the trouble I had gone to. We fought...'

'She told you not to come back,' Garnet drawled. His eyes looked sort of... dead. Cold. Different from how I was used to seeing him. 'And you went straight out and consoled yourself by seducing that actress you *promised* her you didn't even fancy.'

'I didn't know she knew about that,' sighed Saturn.

'She always knows,' Garnet hissed. 'There are no secrets from Tasha. You know what she's like. How could you do it?'

'Am I really the one on trial here?' Saturn flung back at him. 'After what she did to that poor dame?'

'You're not taking him,' Garnet said, resolute. 'Poet is ours.'

Saturn got taller and wider and brighter all at once. He let out a cry like a dozen hawks. Garnet fell as if struck in the chest.

'When you are grown and a Lord, you may challenge me, courteso,' said Saturn between clenched teeth.

He held his hand out to me and we left together.

Saturn took me along the tunnel with the canal in it, past the cathedral and on into a large space like a dockyard, only with no ships in sight.

You know it as the Haymarket.

'My Power!' he called. 'Majesty!'

A shadow fell over us. I looked up, to the balcony above, and saw a shape. At first I thought it was a monster, and then I thought it was a Camoiserian paper dragon, the kind that the dancers carry through the streets. It wasn't any of those things. It was a snake, as thick as the canal itself, and it slid down the poles to the floor and slithered towards us. I was so scared I couldn't do anything but clutch at Saturn's coat.

The snake rolled itself into a coil and shaped itself into a man. He had a soft stomach and a bald head, and he looked at me like he knew everything I'd ever thought.

'I didn't realise you had a taste for children, Saturn.' His tongue still had something of the snake to it, a thin lisp.

'Tasha took him,' Saturn said. 'She brought him over as a courteso despite his age. She goes too far, Power. She will challenge you next.'

'Not I,' said the snake man, smiling. 'You, perhaps. She is ambitious, but she knows her limits.' He peered down at me and I got that feeling again, like something was poking around my insides. 'I'm surprised the lad survived it. Are you well, boy?'

I resisted the urge to correct him, though I was not happy about being 'Boy' again. 'I was sick, seigneur. I had a fever.'

'She can't be trusted,' Saturn said. 'She murdered this boy's mother — a daylight dame — because I had a dalliance with her.'

'Indeed?' The snake man looked far from surprised. 'That should teach you to keep your cock out of the daylight, should it not?'

'Majesty!' shrieked a voice, and Tasha strode into the yard. 'The Lord of Hawks has stolen my courteso. Give him back.'

She was blazing and beautiful and, even knowing what she had done, I was drawn to her. I understood how Lord

Saturn could love and hate her at the same time. She was power, down to the flesh and bone.

The cubs stood behind her, arms crossed, muscles on display.

'A child,' Saturn said, his voice dripping with disgust.

'Mine,' Tasha retorted.

'He wasn't ready. What did you do to him?'

She arched her eyebrow. 'If you are going to take him from me, you must expect a fight.'

'Excellent,' said the snake man. 'That is settled, then.'

Saturn looked at him in horror. 'Power and Majesty, you can't be on her side in this.'

'You presume much, Lord Saturn,' said the snake man easily. 'I expect you to work for your privileges, like anyone else. The boy is one of us. How it happened is irrelevant. Tasha Lord Lion cannot let an insult like this pass. If you want him, you must fight for him.'

Saturn looked down at me. I let go of his coat, unsure what I was supposed to do.

Owls fluttered into the yard from every direction, white snowy creatures flapping and gliding down to form a bright white shape: a big woman with pale hair and dark eyes. She stood beside Saturn, as careless of her naked breasts as the columbines who changed their costumes backstage.

'You were not invited, Celeste,' said Tasha with a glare at the newcomer.

'Where my Lord needs me,' the pale-haired woman said with an easy smile.

'Play on,' commanded the snake man.

I hung back, at the edge of the canal.

The fight was swift and vicious, and I was hardly aware of what it entailed. They flung handfuls of light across the canal, ducking and weaving to avoid each other missiles.

Then Tasha was a lion, tearing and biting, and Saturn flashed into a storm of hawks.

Garnet changed first, hurling his two gattopardo bodies into the fray, and the hawks tore at him, claws and beaks drawing a hundred points of blood. Lysandor shifted into his furry lynx form and bit birds out of the air, spitting them broken onto the floor. Celeste screamed into owl form, savaging his eyes and throat.

Ashiol was the last to change. He looked at me, head tilted a little to one side as if trying to work out if I was worth it. Then he was cats, and the hawks tore chunks out of him, too. Fur flew. Blood splashed.

I closed my eyes because I couldn't bear it any more. A large, slippery hand grabbed me at the back of the neck. 'Watch them, little cub,' said the snake man. 'This is for your benefit.' He smelled of cheap imperium.

I wanted to say that I was a lamb, not a cub, and I wanted to go home, but the words caught in my throat. The snake man — the Power and Majesty — squeezed my neck until I opened my eyes and stared.

They fought, tearing themselves to pieces. Lysandor broke first, rolling aside and into his human body, nursing too many wounds. Celeste reformed her body and then fell apart into owls again, unable to hold it all together. Ashiol slunk away one bloodied black cat at a time.

Garnet was cornered by several hawks, biting and snapping, but then one pecked hard at his hind paw and he went whining into the corner, his whole body in convulsions.

Tasha shifted from lioness to human, rolling in the blood that smeared across the concrete floor. She laughed, tilting her head up to the ceiling, exposing her throat to the hawks. 'Go on,' she said with great relish. 'Savage me.'

Saturn shaped back into his human form. He reached a

hand down to her and she tugged him down on top of her instead, laughing as he kissed her neck.

'An important lesson, little rat,' the Power and Majesty said with relish as the two made love before us, in a bed of blood. 'You are of the least value of anyone in this Court.'

That was nothing new for me, was it? Bottom of the frigging pecking order.

Saturn and Tasha rolled together, petting and biting like the animals they were.

The cubs regained their breath, and then Garnet came over to me, holding out a hand. 'You don't have to,' he said, and he looked as guilty as Saturn.

'Aye, I do,' I said, because I understood them now. I took his hand and let him lead me back to the den.

PART IV
TOURNAMENT OF KINGS

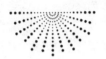

10

TWO DAYS AFTER THE IDES OF BESTIALIS

DAYLIGHT

*V*elody could smell the steam and coal dust from the train clinging to her skirt as she let herself into the kitchen. Crane followed her in, unapologetic about trailing her since the station.

'What are you going to do?' he asked, but she ignored him, stumbling through to the workroom.

Delphine and Rhian weren't even pretending to keep busy. Delphine was tucked into a chair, foot rocking impatiently back and forth. Rhian sat still, staring at nothing. They both started up when Velody entered.

'What happened?' Delphine demanded.

Velody's legs were wobbly. 'I have to fight,' she said. 'This nox.'

'Who?' Crane asked.

'Ashiol. Garnet.'

'Both of them?' Delphine demanded. 'You can't do that on your own — it's crazy.'

'They're not together — none of us is on each other's side,' said Velody. 'The three of us have to duel to prove who is to be Power and Majesty.'

'But that's ridiculous,' said Delphine. 'The Creature Court chose you. Months ago.'

'I've been gone,' said Velody. 'The Lords and Court only swore to me back then because Ashiol stepped aside for me. He's not doing that any more. He's so angry. He wants us to fight to the death.'

'But we do the fighting for you,' Delphine said earnestly. 'The sentinels. That's what the swords are for, right?'

Velody looked at her in alarm. 'You're not going to fight them in my place, Delphine.'

'More to the point, she can't,' said Crane.

'But our job is to protect Velody,' Delphine argued.

'To protect all of the Kings,' he corrected. 'That includes Ashiol and Garnet.'

Delphine was furious. 'The rapist and the psycho? I don't think so. I'm on Velody's side.'

'We can't take sides, Delphine.'

'He's not a rapist,' said Rhian.

Delphine turned on her. 'You don't get to talk about this. Don't talk about anything.'

'Dee,' said Velody, shocked by the violence in her voice.

'Oh, don't you dare take her side. You don't know anything of what she's been up to while you were away. Remember how we cosseted her, did everything to protect her, turned our lives upside down because she was sick, because we loved her, because she was so afraid of men...'

'Delphine, stop it,' said Rhian.

'No,' Delphine howled. 'Because either he's a rapist or you're a liar. You've been lying for nearly two years, about men, about everything!'

Rhian trembled, her hands pressed to her mouth.

Velody gave Delphine an accusing look and went to Rhian. 'You're speaking nonsense, Dee.'

'Ask her, then,' Delphine demanded. 'Ask her what made her fall into bed with Ashiol Xandelian the second you were gone.'

Ashiol? Ashiol and Rhian? Of all the combinations, that one had never occurred to Velody. She frowned at Delphine, and then looked at Rhian. 'But she can't...' Rhian could barely stand to be around men. Her attack had broken her mind, made her so afraid of life, of men, of people.

'Unless she's a liar,' Delphine said in grim satisfaction.

Tears ran down Rhian's face. Velody reached out a hand to comfort her.

'Don't touch me,' Rhian shrieked.

There was a burst of heat where Velody's fingertips brushed Rhian's arm. Velody stepped back, startled. There were black flames running over Rhian's skin, just for a moment, and then they were gone. Had Velody done that, or Rhian? What powers did the Seer have?

Rhian stood up, panicky and taking quick, shallow breaths. 'I have to go.'

'Run away again,' Delphine said cruelly. 'Why not? Make us all look for you, worry about you, over and over, because you're too fucking selfish to admit you have been playing us for fools.'

Rhian walked slowly to the staircase.

Delphine leaned in as she passed her. 'He thought you were Heliora,' she said sharply. 'That makes you the rapist.'

Rhian gave her an odd smile. 'I know.' She kept going, up the stairs to her room.

Velody blew out a long breath. 'What the saints has been going on around here?'

Delphine collapsed into a chair. 'So,' she said to Crane, as if nothing had happened. 'If we're not allowed to protect or help Velody in this battle, what are the sentinels supposed to contribute?'

'We make sure no one cheats,' said Crane.

'Oh, fun.'

~

ASHIOL PREPARED for battle on the roof of the Palazzo. It was a long time since he had let himself fall into a meditative trance. All the anger and annoyances and grief piled in on him, making it almost impossible to still his mind.

Then there was Kelpie at his side, which made it doubly hard because she couldn't shut her fucking trap.

'What the hells do you think you're doing?' she demanded.

'I'm taking the lead,' he told her. 'You wanted this.'

Kelpie sat on the clay tiles, knees up to her chin, staring at him as if he were a stranger. 'You're too late. You chose Velody. You made them all choose Velody.'

'And then she chose Garnet.'

'Is that what this is about?' Kelpie laughed at him, though there was little humour in it. 'After all you've been through, you'll let jealousy make your decisions for you? Can you really not forgive the demme for bedding someone other than you?'

He met her eyes, unfriendly. 'Are we still talking about Velody?'

Kelpie stared back, bristling with anger and defensiveness and all those other emotions Ashiol associated with her. Only more so than usual. 'Apparently not.'

Of all of them, he had thought Kelpie would be on his side. Kelpie was always on his side.

'I didn't think sentinels could take sides against the Kings, but here you are, choosing her over me.'

'I'm not choosing anyone,' Kelpie snapped. 'Don't you dare accuse me of not doing my duty, not ever. I've walked through death and out the other side for you — not just for Aufleur or the Kings, but for *you personally*, Ashiol Xandelian, and I'd do it again in a second. Question my loyalty and I'll stab you in the throat.'

'This is sweet,' he said, impatient with her. 'But I have a battle to prepare for. You're not helping.'

Kelpie stood up, shaking out her coat. 'You've had months to let yourself become Power and Majesty, and the mere thought of it had you in pieces. You've been drunk or drugged or mad or all three ever since the dust devils took the Seer down and Velody was swallowed from the sky. What the hells makes you think anyone will follow you?'

'I'm not Garnet. And I'm not Velody. I can do this.'

'You should have done it years ago,' she said coldly. 'We believed in you then. There's not much left of that.'

'I'll prove you wrong,' he told her.

Kelpie stepped forward, as if she was about to touch him, then stepped back again, out of reach. 'I really hope you do.'

~

MACREADY SHOULDN'T HAVE COME. That much was clear. But it didn't seem right to leave Garnet's return unacknowledged.

The sentinel sat in the mouth of the narrow tunnel, his feet up on the curved wall. He didn't have to wait long.

Footsteps sounded along the canal path and then stopped.

'What the frig are you doing here?' Garnet asked in a voice far more pleasant than his words. That was the way of him: all manners and serenity until you pissed him off, then he'd bite so hard you'd never stop feeling the teeth in your skin.

Macready yawned. 'Being a sentinel. Keeping a watchful eye over my stray flock of Kings. That's the right word, is it not — flock? Sounds better than herd, or gang, or murder. Like my new swords? Look elegant with the uniform, do they not?' He smacked the skysilver blade of his knife back and forth against his palm. It barely tickled.

'I see you like them,' Garnet said, getting edgier by the moment. 'Will you let me pass?'

'You haven't been here in years,' said Macready, meeting the King's eyes for all the cove tried to avoid looking directly at him. 'Tasha's den. Wouldn't have thought it was home to you any more.'

'It's not,' Garnet grated. 'But I received a less than welcome reception at the Haymarket.'

'Ah, that explains it, so it does,' Macready said lightly. 'Livilla took that death of yours rather personally. Shame she's holding you responsible. Still, you know demmes. A bunch of flowers, a flask of ciocolata and she'll come running back to your manly arms.' Macready still had not moved his legs. He unfolded his left hand, stretching it, wiggling the low stump where his ring finger had been once upon a time. 'Mind you, if she doesn't play ball, you can blast your way in there, leave her bruised and bloody like the old days. Not like you to back down from a challenge, our Garnet.'

'I have little patience for chatting with the staff,' Garnet said, teeth gleaming in the darkness. 'Get the fuck out of my way, Macready.'

This would be a good time to get out of the cove's face, so it would, but Macready had never known when to give up.

'Aye, the big battle. Should be fun to watch. Especially as you came back here with half as much animor as you're used to.'

Garnet betrayed himself with a twitch.

'Thought so,' Macready said with satisfaction. 'Used to

have Velody's under your belt, didn't you? Ashiol's, too, for a good long while. Now it's just you. The question is, laddie buck, do you think you're hard enough?'

The pain blasted into Macready's side, sending him rolling and crying out as it flashed against his skin, muscles, spine. He ended up with his face in the dirt, barely breathing, lungs full of some unspeakable cack.

'As you can see,' said Garnet, stepping over him, 'I still have juice to spare.'

'Aye,' Macready managed, coughing and hacking and really not ready to get up anytime soon. 'Very impressed, so I am.'

'This will do nicely.' Garnet's voice sounded from further down the tunnel where it opened up into a wide gallery with a sandy floor and a single intact building where once there had been several. 'Just like old times.'

Macready winced as he pushed himself up a little way. 'Ah, nostalgia,' he managed. 'The greatest thing in the world, so it is.'

~

VELODY WORE PURPLE AND GOLD. Delphine dressed her as if for an all-saints parade, draping her with paste gems and gilded links. The dress was a dropped-waist shift that trailed ribbons and feathers like a gaudy peacock.

'I'll get blood on it,' Velody warned her.

'I don't care,' said Delphine. She held out her knives, their hilts wrapped in rose-coloured leather. 'Take these.'

Velody smiled. 'And that would be cheating.'

'Crane won't tell.'

~

CRANE WAITED IN THE KITCHEN, chin on his hands. He looked up as Velody approached. 'Ready?'

'As I'll ever be,' she said with a deep sigh. Fighting Ashiol and Garnet together. There was nothing about this that she wanted.

The streets were quiet as Velody walked up the Lucretine with Crane and Delphine behind her. She could feel the nox taking over; not just the darkness and the shadows, but the strange other world that made her invisible to those of the daylight. She took Lord form, and the glow of her skin lit the street as she walked up to the crest of the hill. Lampboys passed her, and not one of them looked twice in her direction. Velody did not exist to them.

Garnet, Ashiol, Garnet, Ashiol. This wasn't a duel. It was a hunt.

Where are you?

Garnet was in her head. It was such a familiar voice and yet so alien that Velody almost tripped and stumbled.

None of your business, she hurled back.

He laughed. *You know you don't want to hurt me.*

Is that what we're doing here? Seduction rather than battle? This was your idea, Garnet.

Not mine, Lady. Ashiol's the one who wants to eat both our hearts out. I wonder why that is. Jealousy, perhaps.

Was he after an alliance?

She had considered the danger she would be in if Ashiol and Garnet teamed up against her — and had briefly considered whether Ashiol might listen to her long enough to put Garnet down. It had not occurred to her that Garnet would try to use her against Ashiol, but it was obvious now. He saw her as a minor player in this game and Ashiol as the prize. Either that, or he was working hard to keep her and Ashiol apart for his own protection.

What would Ashiol possibly have to be jealous of? she asked.

Don't you know?

Images burst into her mind: a jumble of limbs, of heat, of sex, and they weren't her own memories but Garnet's. Memories of her own naked body, of Ashiol's, the taste of their animor mingled with his, and above it all Garnet's laughter, thick and rich and pleased with himself.

I am going to kick your arse when I find you, Velody thought in his general direction.

No, you won't. You love us both.

Not right now. Really not.

'Velody.'

She was so busy in her head with Garnet that she wasn't aware of Ashiol until he was almost on top of her. He practically gleamed in the darkness — he wore leather and silks, his hair freshly washed, his skin edible.

Was it Garnet in her head making her think of frigging instead of fighting?

Cats on heat, both of them. Velody had to be the sensible one. She was a mouse. She was cunning and clever, and tidy, and... possibly tidy was not going to be useful at this particular moment.

We don't have to fight, she tried to say directly into his mind, but Ashiol was keeping her out, his defences high. He shook his head and smiled. 'Stay out, little mouse.'

'Not so little.'

'So I hear.'

'Base insults? Does it come to that?'

'No. I don't have time for insults. I've wasted too much time trying to make you into a Creature King. You were just a demme all along. Ready to tumble on her back at the first sight of a pretty face.'

Anger poured off him. He wouldn't be Ashiol if he didn't taste of anger. But he felt genuinely hurt as well. Velody was startled by that. His jibe at her morals was almost funny.

'Are you seriously judging me for who I bed? Is there anyone in the Court who hasn't had a taste of you?'

Oh, that anger of his — she had forgotten how it felt when his animor flared with it.

'You knew what he was,' Ashiol spat. 'You knew what he did. You let him in and you brought him back. Did you think we would thank you?'

Velody shook her head slowly, careful to keep a good distance from him, ready to transform in an instant if he attacked her. 'I didn't know anything about Garnet except what you told me, and I'm not sure I trust you any more. I don't know who you are, Ashiol. You're the one that turned this into a fight.'

That's the demme, Garnet said in her mind. *We'll take him down together. He can't fight us both at once, not if we team up.*

Then what? Velody demanded.

Garnet laughed in her head, filling her up. *Then the city is ours.*

Yours, you mean. It was her own fury she could taste now. *I'm sick of you both thinking that you're more than me, that what I believe doesn't count for anything. I was a better Power and Majesty than you ever were, Garnet.*

Prove it, little mouse. Let's see the colour of your claws.

Ashiol blurred in front of her. Velody leaped towards him, attacking rather than defending. She was angry enough at him that her animor leaped ahead of her, hot and lashing out.

He went chimaera, and she did, too, muscles expanding outwards, wings unfurling. She sank her teeth into the side of his neck and her claws into his chest. He raked his claws down her back and they rolled, bestial and fierce, on the cobbled street.

A noxcab rattled past, barely missing them, the black horse hooves coming within inches of Velody's wings. She hissed and let out a mighty shriek, slamming Ashiol back on the ground, pinning him down.

You're hot when you're murderous, Garnet said.

Shut up! Velody sent, concentrating on her body and Ashiol's, keeping her weight on him, keeping him down. If she could only come up with a plan, but the chimaera didn't think; it fought and it bit and it lashed out.

Pain cut through her as he freed his claws and thrust them into her thick hide. They rolled and wrestled and she found herself under him, then on top again, bleeding in too many places. Battle-rage was scarlet and bright in her mind, but she hurt, and it was all she could do to roll back and protect her throat from his snapping jaws.

She became aware of voices behind her: Delphine and Macready and Crane.

'You can't let him do this,' said Delphine in distress.

'Feck that,' said Macready. 'We need her to win fairly. She has to, or all this is for naught.'

Velody could feel others nearby. Warlord was watching, and there was a sniff of Livilla, and Poet... Where was Poet? Why had he sided with Garnet? It made no sense to her.

Ashiol dug his claws harder into her and Velody howled, shifting back into Lord form. Ashiol changed, too, his body covering hers. How did he end up on top?

He stared at her, breathing hard, and for one moment Velody wondered if this was sex rather than a fight to the death. The fact that it was so hard to tell pretty much summed up the Creature Court.

Not to the death, not that, it's not what I'm supposed to be doing, I am not that Power and Majesty, I never will be!

She could feel Ashiol hard against her stomach, and for a moment, just for a moment, he let her inside his head, inside his thoughts. All she saw was a mess of heat and hurt and memories. Saints. He really believed that she and

Garnet had teamed up against him, that they wanted his death.

'This isn't right,' she gasped. 'This isn't how we're supposed to be.'

There was pain, deep into her gut, a burning, roiling sensation, and his hand was — a claw, he still had a claw, he had gutted her, and he was crying, why was he crying? What had he done to her, what had she let him do?

Delphine screamed and landed on Ashiol, plunging her skysilver dagger into the side of his neck. He choked on his own blood, sliding sideways, slumping to the cobbles.

Velody's vision swam. She saw Garnet over her, leaning down, a horrible smile on his face.

'Sweet,' he said. 'A marriage made in hells. You know the story, don't you? It was an old musette favourite. The angel lay with the devil, and the devil lay with the saint, and they made a marriage all together, bathed in blood. And they went away, never to bother us again, as long as we light their candles and wear their garlands and sing, sing, sing.'

Velody slid into unconsciousness, not able to listen any more.

I know the stories, Garnet said in her head. *I know what we are supposed to be. I know the truth.*

11

TWO DAYS AFTER THE IDES OF BESTIALIS

NOX

*M*acready dragged Delphine away from Ashiol's bloodied body. 'Crane, get to him first,' he ordered.

Garnet stood a little away from them all, smiling like a bloody stained-glass saint. 'No,' he said calmly. 'I am the Power and Majesty. I say you will not let them live.'

'We're the sentinels of the Kings and that isn't a fecking order we'll obey,' Macready said in a growl. 'Kelpie, see to Velody. Crane, take Ashiol.' Delphine was limp in his arms, shaking madly, crying, gasping for breath.

'The oath, I think,' Garnet said sweetly.

Warlord stepped out of the shadows. 'To the victor the spoils. I pledge allegiance to Garnet as Power and Majesty.'

Poet, too. 'I pledge allegiance to Garnet,' he said, eyes bright as he stared at Garnet.

Lennoc was there, his face unreadable. 'I pledge allegiance

to Garnet, Power and Majesty of the Creature Court. Long may he reign.'

'Bastards,' Macready said in an undertone. Garnet wouldn't stop fecking smiling and it made Macready's left hand ache, where his ring finger used to be.

Livilla walked down the street dressed in rich blue robes with white trim, like she was the saint of everything. A trail of children followed her, clinging to her cloudy skirts, giving off the stink of newfound animor.

'I suppose you want me, too,' she said, head tilted to one side. 'Or have you oaths enough, my King?'

'I always want you, honey sweet,' said Garnet, reaching out a hand. She allowed him to kiss it, watching him carefully the whole time. 'How can I resist you and your little monsters?' he added.

'It will be different this time, Majesty,' Livilla said in a stern voice.

'Of course,' he replied, sounding utterly sincere, and they kissed for a long time.

Holding hands, Garnet and Livilla stepped over Ashiol's and Velody's bodies and continued together down the hill. The other Lords and Court followed them in a stately procession.

'Sentinels,' Garnet called behind him, as if it was an afterthought. 'If you heal those two, you may consider yourselves banished from the Creature Court.'

'That's not how things are done,' Macready yelled after him.

They looked back, all of them, Garnet, the Lords and Court, blank-faced.

'Imagine how much I care,' Garnet said.

Velody was making a low noise, not quite a whimper. Her body shuddered and there was blood, too much blood. Ashiol had stopped moving some time ago.

'Then I'm not a sentinel any more,' Delphine said, shucking off her skysilver sword and tossing it to the street with a clang that made Macready wince. She leaned over Velody, thrusting her wrist to her mouth, trying to make her feed. 'How do I do this?' she wailed finally.

Crane got to her before Macready did. He sliced into Delphine's wrist with his steel knife and let her drip the blood slowly against Velody's lips. Delphine buried her face in Crane's chest as she did it.

I should be doing that, Macready thought. He should be helping Delphine, but he couldn't move. He'd been nothing but a sentinel for twenty years. It was in his blood and his bones, and he was damned if he would let Garnet take it away from him.

Still holding Delphine, Crane cut his own wrist and put it over Ashiol's mouth. Their choices had been made. The Kings would be saved, and Macready had not picked a side.

He didn't have to pick a side. Crane and Delphine saved him from that choice. Ashiol and Velody would live.

A little way down the hill, Garnet stood watching them, the Lords and Court arrayed behind him. 'Take off your sword,' he called to Crane.

'Is Ash alive?' Kelpie asked in a whisper.

Like Macready, she was still on her feet, not moving one way or the other. Like Macready, she would rather die than give up being a sentinel, but that wasn't an option available right now.

Ashiol looked bad. He wasn't responding to Crane's attempts to feed him. The cobbles were sodden with his blood.

'Kelpie, take my sword off,' Crane said, not moving from where he knelt.

'You don't have to do this,' she said hopelessly.

'Take it off,' the lad snapped.

Not a lad any more, oh no. More of a man than Macready, so he was.

Kelpie slid Crane's skysilver sword from his back and laid it on the cobbles beside Delphine's. She was crying, tears sliding down her face, her breath coming in short bursts.

Ashiol gave a choking gasp, and began to suck on Crane's wrist. Alive. Holy feck, alive. Powerless, but saved.

Kelpie squeezed her eyes shut and started walking down the hill towards Garnet. Away from them. *Oh, lass.* Macready watched her go, understanding her choice. He had not made his yet.

Velody fed properly now, suckling at Delphine's wrist. Crane let his skysilver knife join the sword on the cobbles and returned his attention to Ashiol, not even looking at Macready and Kelpie. As if they had no decision to make, as if it was obvious what they would do.

Crane took charge, saints help him. He drew Delphine's skysilver knife out of the side of Ashiol's neck and put it with the others. No blood ran free. For now, Ashiol was as mortal as the rest of them and the skysilver could not touch him.

Kelpie looked back at Macready only once, and he saw the despair in her face. She was not choosing Garnet over Ashiol. She was choosing to keep her oath the only way she could, just as Crane and Delphine kept theirs in their own way. He understood. Better than she might think.

Macready hated Garnet. Hated him. The thought of leaving Ashiol and Velody in the street to follow that colossal arsehole was revolting to him. But these swords were his. He didn't know how to function without being a sentinel. He couldn't give it up.

He had served Garnet before. He could do it again. Couldn't he?

Velody cried out, a low, quiet sound like she was struggling with a bad dream.

Garnet spoke to Livilla and she sent several of her child courtesi to scamper up the street and pick up the fallen weapons. They were careful only to touch the leather-wrapped hilts. One lad was too small to lift Crane's sword properly and dragged the tip awkwardly on the ground. The sound scraped Macready's heart.

'Mac,' Delphine said in a small voice, so small. She had finally noticed that he hadn't chosen a side.

Feck. Feck. Feck.

Ashiol would live. Velody would live. They didn't need him to give anything up. Macready could stay on the inside, keep an eye on Garnet. A dozen justifications for his choice rose up in his throat, choking him.

One of Livilla's lambs watched them. She was dark-skinned demme on the edge of adulthood, her hair in short twists against her scalp, her eyes wide and watchful. The thought of what the Court would do to her was enough to resolve him to this: the final moment of letting go. Macready took his sword off and held it out to the little lass, hilt first.

Giving up his blades the first time Garnet had demanded it was a sacrifice, and it had burnt in his gut. Losing those original skysilver blades to the dust devils was another loss, another wound. This time it was oddly freeing. No more. He could walk out of Aufleur any time he wanted. He could go home to the Isles, visit his sisters and those tribes of babbies they had between then. He wasn't going to do any of those things, but he could if he wanted to.

'The Creature Court,' he said loudly to Garnet, 'can suck my fecking balls.'

Garnet smiled like ice, and turned away. The Court went with him, down the side of the Lucretine towards the Arches. Kelpie went with them, and so did the skysilver blades, grasped in the hands of the courtesi children.

Ashiol shuddered wildly and sucked in a breath, then another. He rolled over, spitting blood clots onto the ground.

'You,' he muttered to Delphine. 'No more stabbing me.'

'Stop making me,' she retorted. 'Velody is mine and you can keep your grubby hands off her. No more fighting.'

Ashiol laughed weakly. 'Have you met us?'

'I don't have to be on your side any more,' Delphine told him with some satisfaction. 'I'm not a sentinel.'

It hurt Macready how much she relished her own words.

Ashiol blinked. He looked at Crane, then Macready. 'What happened?'

'Garnet gave us a choice, and we chose you,' Macready said in a flat voice. 'You'd better be fecking worth it, that's all I can say.'

'Where's Kelpie?'

Macready avoided Ashiol's gaze. There was no reason why he should be embarrassed about Kelpie's choice, except that he had almost made the same one.

Velody groaned and came awake, her whole body shuddering. Ashiol turned to her, one hand sliding over her ripped dress to rest upon her bare stomach. 'Velody...'

She shrank away from him, reacting hard. 'Don't touch me. You tried to *kill* me.'

That gave Ashiol pause, but only for a moment. 'I didn't want that. I was confused. You were on Garnet's side.'

'When have I ever been on anyone's side but yours?' Her eyes flashed. 'Hands off.'

Ashiol lifted his hand away and sat up slowly, rubbing his bloodstained fingers through his hair without seeming to notice. There was a ragged cut and scrape on his leg that hadn't healed, probably caused by something mundane like falling hard onto the edge of a paving stone.

'You brought him back,' he said. 'Garnet. This is what he does to us.'

'He wasn't the one with claws in my stomach,' Velody snapped back.

'What do we do now?' asked Crane, sounding his age for once.

'No fecking idea,' Macready muttered.

The nests. Would they be able to get into their nests without skysilver? Would they still be able to share a fraction of the Creature Kings' instincts? Or were they mortal already, shut out of the Court forever?

Velody stood, with Delphine's help. 'Duel to the death,' she said to Ashiol in a withering voice. 'You utter child.'

'Resolved the issue, didn't it?' he said.

'Aye,' Macready said sharply. 'You got what you wanted, my Lord Ducomte. You can waltz off into the sunrise now you've successfully made someone else Power and Majesty. Good candidate you picked for it, too; a fine nox's work.'

He was angry at them all, at the world, at this saints-forsaken city.

A shadow crossed Ashiol's face. 'It's done now,' he said.

Macready laughed without humour. 'As ever, we're the ones who live with the consequences, my King.'

There was no fight left in Ashiol. 'I have no more call upon your loyalty,' he said. 'You're free of it, all of you. I wish you well.'

He turned and walked away, limping, over the crest of the hill.

'We can't let him go like that,' Crane said in a low voice.

'Fecking well should,' Macready muttered. 'He's a cat, they're practically immortal.'

'He's human right now.'

It would take at least a day for the sentinel blood to fade from Ashiol's body, and his animor to return.

'Aye, and a Ducomte with a Palazzo to live in,' snapped

Macready. 'My heart bleeds for him. How will he manage to survive?'

He turned to Velody, sliding an arm around her waist. 'Let's get you home, lass. Nothing else we can do now.'

The sky could fall, the city could be swallowed, and there wasn't one of them could do a blasted thing about it.

12

THREE DAYS AFTER THE IDES OF BESTIALIS

DAYLIGHT

*V*elody could hardly breathe, could hardly think. She had done this. Once again, she had wrought destruction on the Creature Court. She could no longer remember anything good or right she had done since she stepped into their world.

The sentinels were shattered, all of them. Kelpie turned to Garnet's side. Ashiol was gone. Velody didn't even have her animor, not as long as she had the taste of Delphine's blood between her teeth.

It was early morning when they let themselves into the house, which was quiet and still. No fire burned in the stove.

'Rhian must be asleep,' said Delphine, leaning against Macready. 'What do we do now?'

'You were happy enough to give up your swords,' Macready muttered. 'You tell me.'

'The next big festival is the Pomonia,' Delphine said,

sounding horribly gleeful about it. 'You can hold the green satin while I cut ribbons.'

Macready swore at her and stamped his way upstairs. They heard a door slam above.

Velody came very close to telling Delphine not to tease him, but shut her mouth. Who was she to comment on their relationship? Macready wasn't her sentinel any more.

Delphine didn't seem to care that she had upset her man. 'At least this whole wretched game is over,' she said, shrugging. 'We can go back to our lives.'

'If you believe that, you're stupider than everyone thinks you are,' Crane said angrily.

Velody had never heard him be so rude to anyone.

Delphine put her hands on her hips, giving Crane a dirty look. 'Take out the rubbish, will you, Velody? I think we have our full complement of sponging, non rent-paying guests.' She flounced up the stairs after Macready.

Crane looked faintly ashamed of himself. 'Sorry,' he said to Velody.

'Don't worry about it,' she told him. 'We've all said and done things worthy of regret this nox.'

It was all so huge. Velody had no idea how to deal with this, no way to understand it.

'Has this ever happened before?' she asked. 'Kings and sentinels exiled from the Court?'

'It happened to Ashiol,' Crane reminded her. 'Reinforced with enough damage to make him stay away for five years. But when Garnet made sentinels give up their swords before, we were still *sentinels*.'

Velody rubbed her stomach. The skin was smooth over the wound that had almost leaked her life away on the cobblestones. She really thought she was going to die this time around, and part of her had welcomed it, reaching out for her lost family, hoping for peace and rest.

If she had wanted peace and rest, she should have stayed in the empty remains of Tierce and let the sky take her.

'Do you think Garnet will come after us?' she asked Crane.

'If you stay in the city, then yes, sooner or later. He doesn't bluff.'

'What are you going to do?' she asked. 'You can stay here. Don't worry about what Delphine says.'

Crane shook his head slowly. 'No, I don't think so. It's time I had a go at this real world thing. The daylight life. I don't think I can do that if I'm living here.'

He had been a part of the Creature Court his whole life, had lost everything because of Velody.

'Crane, I'm —'

'Don't,' he said, cutting her off before she could apologise. 'We all made our choices. I wish I'd been strong enough to walk away from Garnet last time. This is for the best.'

'I'm still sorry.'

He gave her a flicker of a smile. 'Do you think it's too late for me to find something real?'

Velody had spent months of her life in a timeless unreality. She could smell that false Tierce every time she lost track of where she was.

Reality. If it was an option for any of them, it was for this bright-eyed young man with his whole future in front of him.

'It's never too late,' she said, and meant it.

Delphine wasn't sure how to do this. The supportive, caring, domestic partner wasn't a role she'd ever had to play. She couldn't pretend to be anything but glad that this whole wretched, violent mess was over. She never wanted to be a sentinel; only took up swords when she had no choice. Macready, she was pretty sure, felt differently.

She opened her bedroom door and looked at him. He lay on her bed, so exhausted and broken that her heart turned over.

Oh, no. No going soft. Not this demme.

'If you're going to feel sorry for yourself, you can sleep at the foot of the stairs,' she said firmly, closing the door behind her.

He opened his eyes and looked at her. 'Make me.'

There was a thrum in his voice that made her skin prickle. This was the annoying thing about Macready. He spent the last couple of months making himself indispensable to her. There weren't many men who could make her wet with a word or two, said in a certain voice.

Delphine pulled her dress over her head and knelt on the bed next to him. 'Or, you know, you could make yourself useful.'

'Got anything in mind?' Macready reached out, fingering the soft cotton of her breastband with his damaged hand.

If they didn't have sex, they might have to have a conversation about what they had done, what he had lost. Delphine was happy to put that conversation off until the world ended.

'Frig me like you mean it,' she said, her voice catching just a little. 'I can make you forget.'

Macready gave her a cynical look. 'No offence, love, but I don't think you're *that* good at it.'

Oh. A challenge.

Delphine gave him a shove back onto the bed. 'You're going to regret saying that.'

～

ASHIOL LIMPED BACK to the Palazzo. He didn't want to speak

to anyone. Rage burned deep in his chest. He hated Velody, hated Garnet, hated Kelpie, hated them all.

He climbed in the window to his rooms with more difficulty than usual and headed straight for the bath, where he sponged off blood and prodded with distaste at the long cut on his leg. It was nearly dawn. It would have to stop bleeding soon.

'My Lord Ducomte?' he head from the other room.

'Fuck off.'

Armand the factotum entered with his usual 'something smells bad in here' expression. 'My Lord —' He broke off when he saw the wound. 'Can I get you anything?'

'Aye, you can get the hells out of here.'

Armand rolled his eyes with prissy patience and began pulling bottles and jars out of the cupboard at the back of the room. 'Beeswax tincture, and henwort to staunch the blood. You'll need a leaf poultice to clean the wound or you'll end up with a fever.'

'Might be fun.' Ashiol let the factotum fuss over his leg and smear it with some cack that felt oddly good. 'Did you want something?'

'Her high and brightness needs you,' said the factotum, making it clear by his voice that nothing could be of less use to Isangell than her troublemaking cousin.

'You could tell her I'm asleep,' Ashiol suggested.

The factotum glared at him. 'I can undo all this work in under a second.'

Ashiol was calm for the first time in months, damn it all. His mind felt clear. Velody was not in league with Garnet. Garnet had the Creature Court. No one wanted anything of Ashiol... no one except Isangell. 'Fine,' Ashiol muttered. 'I'll see her. But I need a drink first.'

'I'll send up a vat of wine, shall I?' the factotum said with surprising sarcasm.

If he kept that up, Ashiol might start enjoying his company.

~

THE DUCHESSA'S rooms were filled with trunks and maids. Ashiol, well fortified with two shots of imperium warming his stomach, watched as they went back and forth with armfuls of frocks and shoes and other fluffy items. 'Are we moving house?'

Isangell emerged from her bedroom, arms full of papers, looking harried. 'Please don't assume I have a sense of humour right now, Ash. This is all your fault.'

'What am I being blamed for now?'

She looked more tired than she should, shadows under her eyes. He was used to his cousin being loving and forgiving, not this... vibrating anger that was more like himself.

'I am preparing for my visit with the Duc-Elected of Bazeppe to negotiate a marriage with one of his sons,' she told him crossly. 'Because the cousin who was *supposed* to stand in as my consort so I could establish my rule in this city before giving myself over to marriage has consistently let me down.'

'Oh,' he said. 'That.'

'The City Fathers are pressuring on me about these spates of bad luck in the city this year,' said Isangell. 'The theatre collapse was the last straw for them — and I've spent enough time with their eligible sons to put me off local flavours of wedding cake. This way, at least, we can forge stronger bonds with Bazeppe.'

'I didn't think you were serious about that.'

'I don't see any other option,' she said sharply. 'Oh, don't blame yourself for a moment — it's all my fault.' She went back to her packing, giving further instructions to several maids. Just when Ashiol thought she was done with him, she added: 'Mama warned me. No one thought bringing you here was a good idea, or that it would solve all my problems. No one but me.'

Now he felt bad. Bad, bruised and far too sober. Seven hells of a combination. 'Isangell —'

'No, let me finish.' She dismissed the maids with an impatient wave and waited until they were all gone before she spoke again. 'I put you in this ridiculous situation, expecting you to be strong for me, to play the hero. But that's not what you do. Everyone could see it but me. I understand now. I've looked past the veil of that Creature Court of yours. I saw your friend die. I might not be able to see everything that happens in that nox of yours, but I do know that nothing in this world matters to you like being a... Creature King.' Her face was calm. 'I don't blame you for it, Ashiol. But I have to stand on my own two feet, and stop pretending you can be what I hoped. If that means I change my plans and acquire a husband to play public consort earlier than planned, then so be it.'

Nothing in this world matters to you like being a Creature King. Her words were a cold knife to the neck.

Ashiol had lost his chance to beat Garnet at his own game. Velody was unforgiving, and after the stunt he'd pulled he didn't blame her. He'd tried to kill her. He was an idiot.

He could still feel that slow burn of anger, the desire to kill the Lords and Court, one by one. To kill Garnet. It had regressed somewhat since the fight with Velody, but the bloodlust was still there. He did not know if it was part of his madness, or a reaction to Garnet's return, but he knew he could not unleash it again, not without killing someone he loved.

They didn't need him. The Lords and Court chose Garnet. Ashiol couldn't blame them, either. He'd had his chance, when Velody was swallowed by the sky, and he'd wasted all that time being weak. Being useless.

'Let me come with you,' he said impulsively.

Isangell looked at him. 'Aren't you needed here?'

'No,' he said, almost laughing with joy at the revelation. 'I'm not. You can't go alone. This is too important. You need support, and I've given you little enough of that. Let me do this.' The Creature Court were better off without him.

She hesitated, as if not sure whether to believe him. 'Pack your things, then. We have a train to catch.'

PART V
DEMOISELLES ALWAYS
MEAN TROUBLE

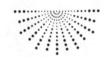

13

POET AND LIVILLA

I was the one who brought Livilla to Tasha. Didn't see that coming, did you?

Three-quarters of a year had passed since I first fell sick (since Tasha made me hers) and I hadn't returned to the Vittorina Royale.

Saturn took an interest in me still, and Tasha allowed it. That was part of a deal between them. He took me with him sometimes when he went out during daylight. He bought and traded books, supplying dusty leatherbound volumes to the city librarion as well as private collections — at the Palazzo, or in other fine houses. He made me practise my reading and writing, reminding me that someday I might want to know how to read a script if I wanted the theatre life back. I humoured him in that, trying to mimic his perfect copper-plate handwriting.

'Knowledge is power,' he told me once. 'Books have longer memories than people do.'

I knew he was wrong. Power was blood and heat and claws and Tasha's smile of triumph when someone did exactly what she wanted. Books had nothing to do with anything real.

~

THE FIRST TIME I saw the sky fall, I was so busy trying to figure out the trick of it, I almost got myself killed. Even after I saw Garnet's arm slashed and blackened from a cloudwight, I remained convinced that it was all some grand performance.

Only question was: who was the audience?

Eventually it became as normal to me as a pantomime. After a battle, the cubs were always wired, bright-eyed and fierce. They swapped war stories, teasing each other over who had slaughtered more devils, who had flown higher or harder, who was the best.

Tasha loved them at these times. She lolled on cushions, laughing throatily as they attempted to outdo each other. The prize, of course, was her. When one of them suitably impressed her, she dragged him into the bedroom for a personal reward.

When Tasha wasn't watching, the mood among the cubs was darker and their cups ran deeper. Sometimes Garnet wouldn't return straight away from battle. He'd turn up hours or days later, high as a kite, jumping at shadows or laughing hysterically at nothing. More than once, one of the other cubs distracted Tasha while the rest of us went to drag him out of some seedy bar. I didn't understand how he could be part of this life when he hated it so much.

One nox, Tasha made Garnet stay home with me because his arm was wounded, and I saw the impatience in his face, the frantic movement of his foot bouncing back and forth, and I realised that he hated to be left behind even more.

It gets into your blood, this sky of ours. It captures your soul.

They wouldn't let me fight yet. Not even Tasha was that much of a monster. They teased that they might train me up to dance the sky, but I knew they thought of me as a pet rather than truly one of them.

Also, I suspected that Tasha thought if I spent too much time in the city above, I might run away.

~

It was a bad season. Nox after nox, that familiar tug came and Tasha and the cubs went running out to save the city. Garnet's arm didn't heal well, and on the third nox in a row of being left behind, he cracked.

'Come on, little rat. Let's see what's out there.'

We scampered along tunnels, emerging from the lock where the canal ran out of the side of a hill.

'Stay low,' said Garnet, already fierce and bright eyed, like he'd taken something. Perhaps he had and I'd missed it. 'Don't want the lioness to know what we're about.'

We both shifted into creature form and ran up the slope together, my rat bodies keeping close to the paws of his gattopardo. He had a limp to him, but I knew better than to notice. He was still angry about that hurt.

Being outside made my skin tingle. I had been underground so long, and had no idea how much I'd been craving the sky. It called to me. To Garnet, too. As we crested the hill, he let out a sound halfway between a growl and a cry of triumph.

The sky was full of lights and colours and shapes swooping back and forth. Garnet's eyes glowed with it.

A nearby bush exploded into flames and sparks. Garnet

leaped towards it rather than away, savaging the bush with his teeth. Something bright and cold squirmed in his jaws and he took off into the sky, dragging it with him.

I was alone. Part of me wanted to go after him, to see what it was really like up there. To please Tasha, and make her realise how useful I was. To be part of the family. On the other hand, this was the first time I'd been alone and free in the best part of a year.

I scampered back to where my clothes lay near the lock, and changed into boy shape. I didn't know where I was, but this was a main street, and Aufleur was easy enough to manage if you worked around the hills. I followed the street until I spotted a familiar piazza, and kept going.

All the way to the Vittorina Royale.

The shops and houses along Via Delgardie were lined with boughs of green. It was Saturnalia. Had I really been underground so long?

Finally I found myself standing in front of the theatre. It was too late for the lanterns to be lit, and the whole place was smaller and grimmer than I remembered.

Aye, I was such a wise old man at ten years old.

I crept around to the alley where Madalena was found, and let myself in at the back, making my way past the dressing rooms and scenery. It smelled like home — of gin and cosmetick and the detritus left by a heedless audience. I made it to the stage, and found it set for the last scene of a saints-and-angel, with satin orange-blossom wreaths tossed over every prop. No one was about.

For so long this had been my world — the Mermaid back home, and then the Vittorina: layers of facade pretending to be grand and exotic.

I'd always thought the theatre was my future. My dreams had been shaped by it — I wanted to be a mask, a songbird, a gaffer, a harlequinus, a tumbler...

My new world was smaller, or it had been until I realised what the sky had to offer.

Standing on that stage, I remembered a song Madalena used to sing to me. It was a number from the old days, she told me, when she and my mam dressed up as urchin boys and sang their guts out, turning the audience from laughter to tears on the change of a verse. I sang it there and then, remembering the steps, running through the old routine. My voice knew how to project to the gods. I could do this. I could live this life.

Halfway through, a creature padded into the theatre, then another. I half-expected a gattopardo, and my voice faltered, but it was two half-grown wolves, ragged and matted. Come to bring me home, no doubt. I didn't know how many Lords and Court were out there — I'd only met Tasha and the cubs, Saturn, Celeste and the snake man they called Power and Majesty.

I finished the song, then slid off the edge of the stage. 'Are you one of them?'

Two pairs of deep, miserable yellow eyes stared back at me, and then they shifted into each other, forming a naked demme only a few years older than myself — old enough to be a columbine, near enough. She was half-starved and shaking. I didn't have the words yet for what she was — I'd heard the others talk about animor, courtesi, and the meanings hadn't settled into my head like something that mattered — but I knew she was like me. Like Tasha and Garnet and the rest. I could feel it.

I reached out my hand to her and she flinched back. I recognised her then, though she had grown in all directions since I saw her last. Liv. Saints, it was Liv. There were bruises all down her side. Someone had beaten her.

'Is this your first time?' I asked her.

She said nothing, but shivered all over. It reminded me of that fever I'd had, though she was cold and not hot.

I had a choice. I could take her backstage and throw her on the wardrobe mistress's mercy, hoping the daylight world could comfort her. But those bruises made me think that maybe she needed something else, a new life.

I took her to Tasha.

Livilla. I hadn't even known that was her proper name. She was just Liv to me, the one who wasn't as pretty as Ruby-red, and didn't talk as much as Kip and Benny, and could sing a bit when she thought no one was looking but clammed up when she had an audience.

She was broken and sad, and skinny and ugly enough that Tasha didn't see her as a threat. At first, Livilla withdrew from the rest of us, but the cubs treated her like a princessa and eventually she warmed up.

No one at the theatre had ever thought she was anything special.

On the third day of Saturnalia, Ashiol brought her a sugar pig from the market, and Livilla sucked every crumb of sweetness from it, rolling it around on her tongue like she'd never had such a feast.

On the fourth day of Saturnalia, Garnet and Lysandor brought paper sparrows to make her smile, and heaped her lap with them.

On the fifth day of Saturnalia, I snuck back into the Vittorina Royale and stole her a dress. It was red and shiny and I thought maybe it belonged to Adriane, if she was still there and a stellar and not off having babies or whatever. When Livilla smiled at me, her mouth was red and shiny, too.

The older boys became quite stupid over her — enough that it began to irritate Tasha — but Livilla liked me best. I enjoyed someone else being the pet for once. She let me brush her hair and fetch things for her.

On the seventh day of Saturnalia, Tasha discovered that Lysandor was bedding Saturn's courtesa Celeste, and all the seven hells broke open.

14

POET AND SATURN

*E*veryone knew how it worked. The cubs shared Tasha's bed whenever she wanted. Saturn shared her bed too, when the two of them weren't feuding. Tasha could have anyone she wanted, as many as she wanted. But she didn't share. Even I understood that.

I woke up that day to the sound of screams, and discovered that Livilla had crawled in with me again. She felt safer with me than the cubs, who were older and wanted more from her than comforting warmth. My first thought was that Madalena was having another of her fits, then I remembered that Madalena was dead.

The screaming didn't stop when I sat up and looked around.

'Is it her?' Livilla asked.

She never said Tasha's name, nor 'my Lady' or 'my Lord' like the cubs. She still hadn't been up on the rooftops with us, not yet. All she knew was that we were different, and that no one was going to hurt her here. (I hadn't admitted to her yet that maybe that part wasn't true — she'd learn soon enough.)

When I nodded, she made a small noise and burrowed deeper in the blankets. I didn't blame her.

I crept out into the main room and saw Lysandor, naked and bleeding. Three long claw marks had laid his belly open and he whined like a wounded animal.

'And you,' Tasha blazed at Ashiol and Garnet, who hung back out of the way, making no move to help Lysandor, 'did you know about this betrayal? This disgusting breach of trust? Did you know he was frigging that bloated owl-wench?'

They protested their innocence, but we all knew they were lying.

'Come forward,' said Tasha. Both obeyed. 'Put your hands on him,' she ordered.

Ashiol did it first, hesitating only a little. Lysandor cried out at his touch. Garnet gritted his teeth and did the same.

Tasha smiled horribly. 'Hurt him, and I'll believe you.'

Ashiol closed his eyes and sank his fingers into one of the wounds in Lysandor's stomach, making him writhe with pain. Garnet kept his eyes open and drove his fingers in harder, forcing his friend to scream. His face didn't show revulsion or pleasure. Just... nothing.

I stumbled away, out of the den, thinking of Madalena and how I'd lived all year with the animals who tore her apart because she bedded Tasha's sometime lover. It was the one thing I managed *not* to think about, most of the time. I wanted to be sick, but it wouldn't come up. I pressed my head against the cool stone of the tunnel and waited to stop shaking.

Some time later, I realised Saturn was standing over me. I didn't know how long he'd been there. Celeste was with him, but she stayed in owl form. I didn't blame her. If Tasha was that mad at me, I'd want to be able to make a quick getaway, too.

'Well, boy,' Saturn said. 'Are you ready to accept that the demme is a monster?'

I thought of him and Tasha drenched in each other's blood and rolling around on the floor of the Haymarket. Half-killing each other was their only way of loving.

'We're all monsters,' I whispered. Truest thing I ever said.

'Are you so desperate for a family? Go back to your theatre.'

'I need to be here.' I was miserable. 'I don't belong anywhere else.'

'Boy,' said Livilla, behind me. She wore an old shirt of Ashiol's and nothing else. Her feet were bare on the dirty tunnel floor.

'Poet,' I corrected, angry at her for not bothering to remember. I wasn't Boy any more. He didn't exist.

'Poet,' she repeated. 'I — what happened to Lysandor?'

'He broke the rules,' I said, staring at Saturn, who walked past me and into the den. I didn't know if he was going to punish Tasha or join her in making Lysandor scream.

Livilla came to sit next to me and let me rest my head on her shoulder. Celeste shaped back into human form and sat with us, her pale skin gleaming in the near-darkness.

'Lord Saturn wants Lysandor,' she said quietly, miserably. 'He wanted me to seduce him away from *her*. Everyone thinks Tasha has too many courtesi, too much power.'

'Because of us?' Livilla said.

I shared her disbelief. She and I were hangers-on, everyone knew that. We weren't warriors like Ashiol and Garnet and Lysandor. We weren't even allowed to fight the sky yet.

Celeste shook her head. 'He wants to break up the cubs. The other Lords fear them. The three of them are just so... powerful together. Powerful for Tasha.'

'That's because we're a family,' I said.

The two demmes exchanged a look like I was a child and didn't know any better.

Saturn had tried to take me away before, but this was different. Garnet was already on edge. He needed Ashiol and Lysandor to keep him on his feet, to keep him strong. Tasha needed all of us — she wasn't as strong as she pretended to be. She was just like Madalena. She screamed and fought when she thought people might have stopped loving her for a moment.

She was screaming now.

Celeste stood, and Liv and I followed her, creeping back to the den. Tasha hurled objects at Saturn — plates and cups and bronze lions. His cane lay on the ground near the entrance and I picked it up.

'Jealous,' Tasha shrieked. 'All of you. Trying to destroy what I have, trying to peel my warriors from my side. You will never make my boys stop loving me.'

'They don't love you,' Saturn scoffed. 'You're a vicious wench with a murderous streak and you drag them down to your level. You hide behind them because it's easy, because they protect you. You are nothing without your army of corrupted children.'

Tasha slapped him, claws out, and blood streaked hard against his face. 'Get away from me,' she hissed. 'Never touch me again.'

Saturn considered her, his beautiful face taking in all possibilities as he looked her over from top to toe. After great deliberation, he punched her in the face.

Everything went red. Garnet and Lysandor lunged for Saturn, with only Ashiol cool enough to hold them back.

I got there first.

Saturn turned, looking at me in bemusement. Blood blossomed on the front of his very white silk shirt. He opened his lips and blood flecked there too, filling his mouth. Only then did I notice the gleaming skysilver tip of his cane sticking out of his chest. It had been driven directly through his body from behind.

Let me rephrase. *I* drove his cane into his back. *I* killed him. It was me.

Saturn fell to his knees and slumped sideways. Celeste threw herself upon him, holding fast. She didn't scream as demmes always do in the theatre. She was silent, grasping her Lord, daring any of us to come close enough to touch.

Tasha stared down at Saturn. Blood ran out of her nose from where he had hit her. To my surprise, she stepped back, and made no objection when the cubs moved between her and the fallen Lord, as if protecting her.

A rushing sound filled the cave when Saturn died. It hummed in my ears, along my veins and flesh. It made my skin feel bright. Celeste rocked with it, light filling her body and glowing out of her face. Some lashed out at the cubs. Livilla felt it and straightened up, looking pretty for the first time since I'd known her.

My stomach was hot and then cold, and I was taller, stretched thin. The rats inside me woke up and wanted to dance.

Finally, Celeste stood, still glowing all over. She leaned down and lifted Saturn's fallen body into her arms as if he weighed no more than one of his hawks.

'Congratulations, Lord of Owls,' said Tasha in a sharp voice, pushing the cubs aside to face Celeste.

Celeste bowed her head briefly, dislike evident on her face, and walked away.

I wanted to say something, but what was there to say? I had killed him, and I didn't know why, not really, just that I had felt so hot all over when he punched Tasha.

'Well,' said Tasha when Celeste was gone. She looked at

Lysandor. 'Planning to abandon me for that trollop now she has a Lord form?'

'No,' said Lysandor, looking at the ground. 'I know where I belong. I'm not going anywhere.'

Tasha passed by Livilla, touching her hair, a rare moment of softness for her. Then she came to me.

'Well, my darling Poet,' she said, resting her hand on my head. 'Look at you. I think it's time we let you fight the sky. What do you say, my cubs?'

Garnet glanced at me, and I couldn't tell if he was disgusted or despairing or proud. Maybe all three.

'I don't know if there's much left for us to teach him,' he said finally. 'May as well let him fly.'

PART VI
THE REIGN OF GARNET

15

THREE DAYS AFTER THE IDES OF BESTIALIS

*T*opaz did not understand these people. They were performers of the highest order, that much was obvious. Preenfeathers, the lot of them. This Garnet saw himself as the stellar, and the rest of the Court were willing to let him take centre stage.

She had thought the Haymarket was Livilla's place from the way he backed down last time the Lady threw him out, but now Garnet swept in and made it very clear that he was the King of everything.

Topaz stayed quiet and nudged the lambs to do the same when they got fidgety. She was busy watching, and noticing things. Like that all the other courtesi were older than them, and that the other Lords only had a few each.

Mostly, she watched the Orphan Princel, the cove that the Creature Court called Poet. *Himself*, though he wasn't their stagemaster any more. He was the most interesting person to look at, and not only because he was the one Topaz knew from before this world swallowed her whole. Back at the Vittorina Royale, he was the stellar. He was the money, too — they all knew that though he didn't like it spoken about.

Here, Poet followed Garnet around like he was a stage-hand. He acted aloof and casual, but his body snapped to attention when Garnet spoke to him. Well trained, Topaz reckoned.

The other coves who were Lords — the white-haired one and the Zafiran — stood there all growls and folded arms, acting tough.

Then there was Lady Livilla. Topaz couldn't tell about her. She acted like a leading lady, silently swooning when-ever Garnet graced her with a look, but there was something else there.

'Your loyalty will be remembered,' Garnet said now, all grand and puffed up with himself. 'The past is forgotten. Let us move forward from this day. It is a new reign. A new time.' He waved a hand at Livilla. 'Clear my rooms for me. I'm home to stay.'

'Where will my children sleep?' she asked, making no move to obey him.

'Oh, that's another thing,' said Garnet, in a very casual voice. 'You have far too many courtesi, Livilla. It's unseemly. I want you to give the children back to Poet.'

The Lady blinked. Topaz stared at her anxiously. Would Livilla give them up? Would he make her do it? The lambs had nowhere else to go, but Topaz was damned if she would let them be passed around like lost parcels.

'No,' Livilla said clearly.

Garnet laughed at her. Topaz didn't like him at all. 'You gave me an oath, Lord of Wolves.'

'To serve you as Power and Majesty,' Livilla agreed. 'But my courtesi are my own. I owe them allegiance and protec-tion.' Her voice faltered only on the word 'protection'.

'It's unlike you to be so rebellious,' said Garnet, as if she amused him. 'It doesn't matter. You can't have a dozen cour-tesi. It's not allowed.'

'Who says?' Livilla demanded, her voice rising. 'Is it tradition? Is it written down somewhere? We thought women couldn't be Kings and along came Velody, proving us wrong.'

'And look how that turned out,' said Garnet.

Interesting. He was trying to keep his anger under control, but his neck had gone red and the flush crept up towards his face.

'There's a difference between saying women make bad Kings and women can't be Kings at all,' said Livilla firmly.

'Is that what you want, Livilla?' he mocked. 'To be a King? Is that what this gaggle of street rats is all about — a grab for power?'

The Lady's expression was gentle beneath her harsh cosmetick. 'I can see how you might think so. The fact remains, there is no rule that says I have to give up the children.'

'You will obey me!' Garnet thundered. There was a power in his words that shook the floor of the Haymarket and made Topaz's bones rattle in her chest.

Livilla took a deep breath. 'No,' she said. 'Not this time.'

He shaped so fast. Topaz gasped and stepped back. It was like his body peeled into two, becoming a large spotted cat with gleaming teeth, ready to pounce.

'Topaz, *now*,' Livilla said sharply, and Topaz could feel what her mistress wanted of her.

She shifted, too, letting her moist human body fall into tiny, tight, hot lizards, licking and spitting and spreading out between Livilla and the gattopardo.

Garnet's eyes flashed, and she could practically feel the confidence rolling off him.

Topaz burst into flames. The fire burned along the skin of each of the lizards, a glorious warmth that tickled her down to her toes.

The gattopardo leaped back, keeping its distance from the

flames. Topaz wanted to laugh. So much for big scary
Garnet. She could feel something else that she needed to do,
and slowly shaped her small bodies back into one. She didn't
go human, though. Instead she became one large, powerful
lizard, flames running from the crest of her head to the tip of
her tail as it whipped back and forth.

Livilla gasped and then started to laugh, a glorious sound
of genuine surprise.

'Garnet, dear, meet my salamander,' she said happily. 'I
think we'll be keeping our rooms above the Haymarket,
don't you?'

∽

'IT'S NOT YOUR FAULT,' said Delphine to Macready.

A sweet lass she was, trying her best, but she had no idea.
Kelpie was gone, wrapped up with that bastard Garnet, and
of course it wasn't his fault, it had been Kelpie's choice every
step of the way.

But Macready couldn't forget the look on Kelpie's face as
she walked away, as if it *wasn't* her choice. As if she couldn't
possibly do anything else. That bastard Garnet.

Delphine came to the window, and wrapped her arms
around his waist. Odd, that. Usually it was him doing the
comforting. He couldn't find it in him to care about the
reversal.

Since they gave up their skysilver, Macready didn't care
about much of anything. He shared Delphine's bed, and that
resolved the situation of where to live, but what else did he
have? Who was he now?

Velody showed no sign of needing protection. Ashiol had
vanished — left the city from what they said at the Palazzo.
Crane went off spouting some noble cack about finding a life
for himself. Macready couldn't do anything for anyone.

He didn't exist.

Delphine wormed her way around to his front. 'It's not over,' she said firmly. 'You know it isn't. And even if it was, would that be so bad? You could have a normal life.'

'And what would I do in that normal life?' he scoffed. 'Join the army? The vigiles? I'd make a fine lictor, I'm sure, if they took men my age.'

'You could love me,' said Delphine.

He looked at her slowly. He had no idea what she saw in his face, but it must have been something bad because she panicked. 'I didn't say that. I take it back.'

'You can't take it back,' he said softly.

'Yes, I can! I can do anything. Shut up.' Delphine tried to slip away from him, but he grasped her waist. 'I don't want it,' she said firmly. 'It's ridiculous.'

'Love?'

'Anything. I don't want you.'

Macready nodded slowly. 'I don't want you, either.'

She slid her hand down the front of his trews, something she often did when she wanted to change the subject. 'Good. As it should be.'

'I don't know how to live in the daylight, Delphine,' he said in a low voice, trying to keep a brain in his head despite her wandering fingers. 'It's been too fecking long. I don't have a trade, I've nothing to offer you.'

'Thimblehead,' she said, moving her hand slowly and enticingly. Even with this alarming turn of conversation, he was growing hard against her palm. She really was bloody good at the art of changing the subject. 'I'll teach you to make ribbons.'

He laughed, and gasped as her fingers wrapped around him, tugging in no uncertain terms. 'Aye, that sounds like a grand life. Satin strips and silk thread.'

She giggled, and managed to slip her frock half off with

only one hand. Now there was a skill. 'Oh, you have so much to learn.'

Macready seized hold of her, taking her to the bed and climbing on top of her, hands pinning her to the bedspread. 'Is that what you think?' he growled, burying his face in her throat.

'That tickles,' she whispered, and he kissed lower. 'Oh...'

His mouth was on her breast now, teasing and sucking until she lost her words entirely and descended into moans.

He could change the subject, too.

~

RHIAN WALKED.

The air was crisp and cool, rasping in her throat as she set one foot in front of the other.

This city. She had so loved this city, when she was young. When she was strong and bold, and could climb the hills without bothering to catch her breath.

She walked these streets so many times without thinking about it: the paths from home to the Forum, from home to the docks. Nothing much had changed in her time — nearly two years now — of self- imposed exile. But the city looked different, felt different.

The buildings loomed over her.

She had been pretended for so long, that she was afraid of her attackers (her victims). Pretended she was afraid of what men could do to her, instead of admitting her fear was about how easily she could destroy them.

Even when the Creature Court burst into her home with their wild language, odd clothes and stories of the sky, she had been able to hold it all together, to preserve the story (not the whole story) that she was attacked. That her odd behaviour, her panic attacks and terror, all stemmed from that imaginary assault.

The truth was so much harder to admit. This city had nothing in it to frighten Rhian, except herself.

Walking in the fresh air helped to quell the voices: the frantic chorus inside her head of Seers dead and gone. But when she reached the hidden entrance to the Arches (the Creature Court called it the Lock) and climbed down into the damp, buttressed underground tunnel, the voices rose up again, fierce and demanding.

So that was why Heliora had spent little time down here. Rhian assumed it would be better, away from the sky, but the wall stank of Creature Court, of their wretched animor. It made her dizzy.

As she walked, she came up with a refrain in her head, repeated over and over, fierce enough to keep the voices at bay.

Velody's fault, it's all Velody's fault, it's all Velody's fault.

She tripped several times in the darkness, and once nearly fell into the enormous canal in the central tunnel. After that, she let the voices themselves guide her steps. They knew the way, and she did not.

Eventually, even in the darkness, Rhian found her way to an old grocer's shop, with lamps burning in the upstairs window.

You don't have to do this, Heliora's voice said, emerging clearly out of the messy chorus of Seers.

Yes I do, Rhian replied, and knocked.

After a short while, it opened. She felt a wave of Garnet's animor before she could focus on enough detail to see it was the Power and Majesty himself, standing in the doorway. 'Can I help you?' he asked with exaggerated politeness.

Rhian clenched her fists, holding herself together, determined not to fall apart here in front of this man. 'I'm the Seer of the Creature Court. Don't you think we should talk?'

Garnet hesitated, and then smiled, stepping back so as to usher her up a narrow flight of stairs. 'Poet, my dear, we have a guest.'

This was a warm, elegant room, but their host provided enough frost to make up for that. 'Mistress Rhian,' Poet said, nodding warily.

'I think I should warn you,' Garnet said, obviously the only one enjoying this. 'Your predecessor was less than helpful when it came to serving her Power and Majesty.'

'Yes,' said Rhian, glancing carefully around the room before choosing a chair to sit in. 'But Heliora didn't like you very much.'

Poet laughed at that, a sudden surprised bark. 'You're not wrong.'

Rhian was here. Anything was possible. Heat flared in her hands, and she pressed her palms hard against her knees, attempting to calm it down. 'I came to you because I need to understand my powers. I think we can both learn something useful from the voices in my head.'

Garnet looked intrigued. 'Voices? What do they say about me?'

Heliora was shouting at her. The others too, a cacophonous muddle in her head. Rhian resisted the urge to press her hands to her ears. 'The city will be saved if you make the sacred marriage,' she told him.

Poet was watching her intently. Garnet too. 'And what do you know of this sacred marriage?' Garnet said finally.

'Not enough,' Rhian admitted. 'I think the older Seers in my head know about it, but the knowledge is so old and their voices are weak. I thought you could help.'

'I'm hardly an expert on hearing voices,' said Garnet.

Poet muttered something indistinguishable, covering it with a cough.

'I think the Seer might have a purpose other than seeing the futures of the Creature Court,' Rhian said, pressing on. 'Why else would I be able to hear the Seers of the past? If we can learn from them...'

'I have learned everything I need to know about the Creature Court, past, present, future,' Garnet said dismissively. 'I don't need you.'

He was lying. She had said something that drew him in, something of value. Wisps of smoke uncurled from the palms of her hands as Rhian stared at them. She had made the right choice. If it all went wrong, she did not mind Garnet of all people getting hurt.

She met his eyes. 'We are going to help each other. We are going to save the city.'

'No,' Garnet said simply. 'You would not come all this way to give me a prophecy, not when you could have given it to your Velody. You think you can use one fragment of future as coin to bargain with me? It makes no sense.'

Oh, he was smarter than Rhian thought. That wasn't good. Poet was watching Garnet as if he might bite her.

'I came to help,' she said again.

Garnet leaned in, dangerously close. 'No, you didn't. Tell me what you really want.'

You can't do this, Heliora hissed. *You cannot trust him with our secrets.*

Rhian ignored her. She met Garnet's gaze, and for once did not care if her hands burst into flames and her body dissolved under the weight of this strange power she had been infected with for so long. 'I have learned much about the Seers of the Creature Court,' she said finally. 'Enough to know that they made a mistake when they let the futures come to me. I was not supposed to do this. I am not a Seer.'

Garnet seemed amused. 'What do you expect me to do about that?'

'Take it back,' she breathed. 'I am the last of the Seers, and they got it wrong. You are the Power and Majesty. If anyone can take it away from me, it is you.'

Garnet seemed to consider it. 'Tell me everything you can discover about this sacred marriage, and I could be persuaded. History fascinates me, after all.'

Everything she told him, he could use against Ashiol and Velody. Rhian knew that. But the weight of the futures pressed down against her and it was wrong, she had to get rid of it before she started destroying people.

She sighed, and nodded her assent.

16

LUDI PLEBEII

FOUR DAYS AFTER THE IDES OF FORTUNA

Time passed. The month of Bestialis became the month of Fortuna. Life without the Creature Court was strange for Velody, but survivable.

She started sewing again, festival smocks at first, but then she sent her cards to former clients and accepted two dress commissions looking ahead to the month of Saturnalis. She went back to working during the day and sleeping at nox.

The hardest times were when the slow rain seeped in through the cracks in the ceiling, or the sky erupted into the lights and colours that signified a battle. Velody would stand at her bedroom window watching, wanting to join in, wishing she could be part of it all.

Sometimes Macready would come in and sit in a corner of the room, not saying anything, just being there. Delphine never acknowledged the difference between one nox and another, and gave a very good impression of having completely lost all of her sentinel instincts.

Rhian was never there for those noxes. That was the strangest part. After so long not being able to leave the house, Rhian now absented herself on a regular basis. The first time Velody found her room empty, she had a major meltdown, but she had grown used to it now. It was normal — as much as anything to do with Rhian these days counted as normal. She didn't work. When Delphine prompted her about the berry fronds and bleeding-heart for Ludi garlands, Rhian looked at her blankly, as if the words made no sense. Eventually, Delphine found another florister to supply what she needed to fill the council order.

On the last day of the Ludi Plebeii, four days after the Ides of Fortuna, with a wintry chill stinging the air, Crane returned.

Velody felt him coming. That, at least, hadn't changed. She ran to the door, grinning all over her face as he let himself in the back gate. 'You're here.'

'I told you I would be,' he said, reflecting her grin with his own. 'Didn't you get my last letter?'

She hugged him, letting his familiar smell enfold her. 'I thought your mother might want to keep you.'

'She was pleased enough to see me,' he said. 'I was able to get in the winter's firewood for her, at least, and see to the roof of her cottage.' A shadow crossed his face. 'There was a cost whenever I petitioned the Power and Majesty to let me go home at this time of year. It wasn't always worth paying.'

Velody drew back from him, crossed her arms uncomfortably over her chest. 'I'm not the Power and Majesty,' she reminded him.

'I know that,' he said quickly, and there was an awkward moment between them.

Velody broke the tension, drawing him inside. 'There's soup if you want it.'

'Always.' Crane sat at the table, stretching out his long legs as Velody busied herself with fixing a bowl for him, with bread and oil and herbs. 'Any sign of Ashiol?'

'He went south with the Duchessa on some diplomatic mission, but that's done now. He'll find us when he's ready.'

The Duchessa recently returned to the city to preside over another run of sacred games, and they all assumed that Ashiol returned with her. Still, no one had seen hide nor hair of him.

'Good for him. I mean, he's neglected his daylight life for so long.'

Velody sighed. 'I don't like giving up like this. But it's not like any of the Creature Court is begging for my help. They chose Garnet to lead them.'

'They'll regret it, if they don't already.'

'I can't help that. I can't march in there and — what, challenge him to a duel? They don't want me!'

She sat near Crane, enjoying his proximity. She had missed him. The Macready/Delphine circus of fighting, making up and canoodling in corners was tiring to witness, and Rhian wasn't *here* even when she was physically present.

Velody missed Ashiol. She missed the certainty of him and her, linked by the Creature Court. Part of her even missed Garnet — the man she met in that other Tierce, the man she brought home, if not the man he became once he was here. There was an emptiness in Velody's life where the Creature Court used to be, and no amount of dressmaking could fill it.

'You've lost more than I have,' she reminded Crane.

He did not wear his steel sword. Macready didn't, either, although they hadn't given those up to Garnet. The swords belonged to another life, and were apparently best kept in her cupboard under the stairs.

Crane set his soup spoon down. 'As long as you still have time for me.'

'Always,' she said. 'Do you know what you're going to do now?'

Macready worked shifts at the dockyards and would often disappear for days at a time. Velody knew he was drinking more than he should, though he hid it from Delphine.

Crane hesitated. 'I'll think of something.'

'Do you want to stay here? The nests don't work any more.'

'I know they don't,' he said impatiently. 'Velody, I'm not your responsibility.'

'Of course you are. Garnet can take away your swords, but he can't take anything from me. Like my obligation to look after you, for example.'

'Don't you understand?' Crane said in frustration. 'I don't want to be your obligation. I want...'

Oh. That. Velody tried not to react awkwardly, but her shoulders stiffened as she realised what he was trying to say.

Crane saw it, he had to, but he pressed on anyway. 'I love you. I don't expect you to feel the same — but that's how I feel. I don't want you to see me as some stray you have to feed and house. I want to be something better than that in your eyes.'

She reached out and touched his hair in the old way.

'You can be anything you want,' she said. 'You're free of it. This should be the beginning of your life. A new start.'

The Creature Court had given them nothing tangible. Just loss and danger and bloodshed. But this daylight life they had now seemed no better. None of them had the hang of it yet.

Crane nodded. 'I'll find something on my own. But thank you for the offer.'

The fact that she hadn't responded to his declaration of love hung between them. Velody couldn't bring herself to acknowledge it.

'Thank you for the soup,' Crane said finally, pushing the

bowl away. 'I'll come by in a day or so, try to catch up with Macready. If that's all right?'

Velody nodded. 'You're welcome here any time, Crane. I have missed you.'

He smiled sadly. 'That's all right, then.'

~

LIVILLA HAD TRANSFORMED herself into the princessa of the Haymarket quite successfully, with the lambs as her court. Topaz loved that it was her own strength, her fire, that protected Livilla and the lambs from those who thought they could order them around.

From a position of power, Livilla was benevolent, granting Garnet the Haymarket rooms below her own, on condition that no one came up to the balcony without her permission. She was, it turned out, the mistress of diplomacy, preserving her own power without making Garnet look weak to the rest of them.

Livilla enjoyed everything that went along with being the Power and Majesty's consort, and saw no reason to give that up.

Topaz was still figuring out what it meant to be a salamander. She'd never heard of them before. The other lambs loved to practise shaping and unshaping into their creatures, but none of them could do what she could — shape into one large creature or many small versions. They were all one or the other.

Livilla never answered when Topaz asked about it, just acted all mysterious. Topaz was starting to suspect that she didn't have the faintest idea.

She stared at herself sometimes, when she was alone in the room she shared with Bree. There was a long mirror propped against one of the walls, with a crack in the corner.

Topaz would stare at her body, trying to figure out how her firm, brown skin could change into all those lithe, scaly little legs and tongues. When she shaped herself small and then big, it felt so right that it filled her head with crazy-making joy. It was better than singing on the stage, better than clean sheets, better than the taste of ciocolata melting on her tongue.

Better than anything.

The lambs all adapted to being in service to Livilla — it was another role to play, and they got more rehearsal time than they were used to. Niloh and Zeb got into it most, bringing stolen food and other gifts from the city above in attempts to please their new mistress.

Topaz rarely went above. Why should she? There was nothing up there but people and things. This was their home now. The lizard part of her liked it underground, the dark dampness of it all. She craved sunshine, but it was winter and there was hardly any to be had, so better to stay down here in the dark.

Seven days before the Kalends of Saturnalis, Niloh brought Livilla a flagon of hot coffee she'd pinched from a stall vendor while Zeb distracted him by pretending to steal a handful of chestnuts. Livilla smiled at both of them like they were sunshine and light. She allowed them to pour her a cup, then summoned Topaz over.

'Take this to Garnet, with my compliments,' she said in a low purr, handing Topaz the mostly full flagon.

It was always Topaz that Livilla sent to Garnet with messages or gifts. Topaz reckoned she didn't trust him not to snatch one of the other lambs and hand them straight over to the Orphan — to Poet.

There had been many gifts: little tokens of food or drink. All props adding to the show that Livilla was subservient to the Power and Majesty, instead of holding him at bay with her powerful fire-lizard. There was no reason why this gift should be any different. But it was. Topaz could tell. She had not seen Livilla add something to the coffee, but there was a brightness in her eyes, an excitement that was out of place.

That was when Topaz knew she was being sent to Garnet as an assassin.

She carried the flagon carefully down the stairs, her feet heavy, and knocked on Garnet's door before entering. Perhaps he would be asleep and then she wouldn't have to...

'Come in, baby firetrap,' he called in a merry voice.

Topaz kept her eyes downcast as she entered the room. She glanced up briefly to see that Garnet was naked in bed, his skin shockingly pale against dark green sheets. A demme shared the bed with him, but she lay with her face to wall, body held stiffly as if she couldn't wait to leave.

'A gift from Lord Livilla,' Topaz said politely.

She was a mask. She had always been a mask. She could act as if this were any other token of Livilla's 'respect'.

'Another crumb from the table of our landlady,' Garnet said in one of those voices men liked to use when they were pretending not to be as cruel as they were. 'Is she not kindness itself, Kelpie?'

The woman in his bed shrugged one shoulder and said nothing.

'Sit up, sentinel,' Garnet said sharply.

Kelpie sat up. She didn't look right. Something about her eyes. Topaz had seen beaten women before — the stellar in the musette she worked before the Vittorina Royale was a right bastard to the columbines, leaving them blue and streaky all over when he was in a drinking mood. The sentinel had that look, though there wasn't a mark on her.

Garnet took the flagon. Topaz couldn't help wondering how it would happen, what it was, how fast it would be.

'Well?' he demanded. 'Cups, woman.'

Kelpie slipped out of the bed, looking more uncomfortable with her nakedness than anyone around here ever did. She found a cup and returned to the bed with it. Garnet poured for himself with great ceremony, eyes on Topaz.

'My mother always made the best coffee,' he said conversationally. 'She was a cook, you know. Head cook of a fine manor house. The Baronne himself said she was a saint in the kitchen. He liked to start his day with a small cup of coffee prepared by her hands. There's something about that smell, the way it infuses a kitchen.'

He handed the cup to Kelpie without looking at her. 'Drink.'

I am a mask, I am a mask, I am a mask. Topaz didn't want this. She had no problem with offing this vicious cove, but how could she let a demme, another of his victims, die from it?

Garnet smiled, and Topaz knew then that she had failed. Some twitch of her face had given it away.

'Now,' he commanded.

Kelpie looked at the cup and then up at Topaz, and oh saints and devils, she knew, too. She knew there was something about that cup. Quick as a ferax, she threw the contents down her throat, swallowing hard.

Topaz wanted to scream a warning, but it was all too fast. She bobbed her head, taking her leave.

'Wait,' Garnet said in a low, threatening voice.

Kelpie shook. At first Topaz thought it was fear, but then her face twisted up into an ugly mess and she fell to the ground.

Topaz ran. She ran and ran, feet pounding up the stairs. She was so scared she changed into salamanders halfway up, leaving her dress behind as she scampered up the balcony and into her room where she slid miserably under the covers, shaking and shuddering more wildly than Kelpie had.

She was a murderer.

Eventually she changed back, and cried so hard she almost threw up her guts onto the pillow.

Livilla came later, her hand stroking Topaz's short hair. 'Is it done?' she asked quietly.

Topaz hated her and loved her all at once. She shook her head tightly. 'He gave it to —' and then she was crying again, so hard she could barely breathe.

'Ah,' Livilla said, sounding mildly regretful, 'he doesn't trust me yet. That's worth knowing.'

She patted Topaz as if she were a well-behaved pet and went away again, the smell of perfumed smoke lingering in the air.

17

FORTUNA

SEVEN DAYS BEFORE THE KALENDS OF SATURNALIS

NOX

*D*elphine was stuck being the good partner again, because Macready was falling apart. He never said as much, did his best never to show her any weakness at all, but she could tell. She was an expert on falling apart.

He stayed over less frequently, and when he did come around, he smelled like a distillery. Sometimes he'd be gone already when she woke up in the morning. It wasn't the job exactly — he shrugged it off when she asked about it, like it didn't matter what he was doing. The point was, he wasn't being a sentinel.

She wondered if he'd even come back to her at all if she didn't share a house with Velody; somehow he could still pretend he was here to protect her if he was sharing a bed with Delphine.

They were hardly making love any more, except sometimes when he fumbled for her in the middle of the nox, and then she had to bite her lip not to complain when he buried his face in her breasts, stomach, like he was trying to dig his way inside her and never let go.

When he wasn't here, she still felt smothered. This wasn't what she had signed up for. The memory of how Macready believed in her when she was so empty tightened around her throat like a rope. Obligation. Duty.

This nox, she sat up waiting for him. It was stupidly late, and she needed to go out early in the morning to buy the proper linen to braid into Serenalia wreaths. Still, it had to be done. They had to talk. Had to end this.

She heard the back gate creak, and stood at the window to watch him cross the yard. Macready had his own latchkey now. When had that happened?

Delphine waited, but he didn't come up to her room. Eventually she padded downstairs herself, her bare feet making no sound on the stairs. She could see him sitting at the kitchen table. At first she thought his companion was Velody, and the old jealousy rose up inside her. Even this, even trying to break up with him, had Velody smack bang in the middle of it. Then the woman moved her head and held a hand out to him, and she saw that it was Rhian.

Macready let his head drop to the table, utterly despondent, and Rhian put her arms around him. Rhian, who couldn't bear to be touched. Macready's shoulders were shaking. Was he crying?

Delphine held her breath, wanting nothing more than to go back upstairs and forget she'd seen them. But then she felt the unmistakeable presence of the Creature Court close by. No matter how hard she tried, she couldn't entirely put it aside, the instincts of a sentinel. Clearly the sky didn't agree with Garnet forcing them to give it up.

One of them was lurking out there, dangerously close. From Macready's and Rhian's reaction, they could feel it, too.

Delphine stepped into the kitchen and took some grim

satisfaction in the guilt and embarrassment that crossed Macready's face as he and Rhian broke apart. He dashed one hand quickly over his eyes.

'Who is it?' Delphine asked in a low voice, keeping this strictly business. 'Can you tell?'

'Garnet,' said Macready. He made for the door. 'You two stay here.'

'You're as vulnerable as we are,' Delphine said sharply, and then wished she'd bitten off the words when she saw the look on his face. 'I'm not porcelain, you know,' she added, which was slightly better.

'Stay here,' Macready repeated, sounding more confident than he had in ages. He darted out into the nox.

Delphine waited, not looking at Rhian, and when she heard Macready's cry her heart almost burst into pieces.

'Mac!' she yelled.

It was raining. The kind of cold, bleak rain that told you there was snow in the mountains nearby. The wetness soaked through Delphine's skimpy robe as she ran out into the yard, to the alley, with Rhian behind her.

'Macready!' she screamed again.

For one horrible moment she couldn't see him, and then he lurched through the rain and the darkness with a body in his arms. Kelpie, it was Kelpie. Was she dead?

They got her inside and laid her out on the kitchen table.

'What happened to her face?' Delphine gasped in alarm.

Kelpie was barely breathing. Her face was like puckered grey silk. Her body went into a seizure, jerking wildly on the table.

'Get Velody,' Macready ordered.

Delphine practically flew upstairs, dragging Velody's quilts off the bed. 'Get up, we need you!' she cried.

Half-asleep, Velody came without asking questions. As soon as she saw the state of Kelpie, she went for the cupboard under the stairs to fetch Delphine's steel dagger from the blade collection.

'The Creature Court don't have an immunity to poison, do they?' asked Rhian. She paused in a really creepy way, as if listening to something inside her head. 'They don't.'

'Velody's blood will still make her stronger,' Macready said frantically. 'She's more likely to survive this.'

Velody nodded. 'We have to try.' She sliced open her wrist, letting the blood well over the blade.

It was wrong. They were all wrong.

Delphine's hand lashed out, knocking Velody aside. 'Don't.'

'We don't have much time!' Macready protested. 'Look at her.'

'Yes, *look at her*,' Delphine said, sure now that her guess was correct. 'Look at her skin, Mac. She's practically glowing.'

The greyness of Kelpie's skin had a metallic tinge to it. Her eyes, staring unseeing at the ceiling, gleamed in a familiar way.

'Oh, saints,' said Velody, holding her slashed wrist to her chest as if afraid the blood would leap into Kelpie's veins. 'It's skysilver. Someone fed her skysilver.'

Macready blew out a shaky breath. 'That's why she's still alive. It would have killed a King... or someone with King's blood in them. Feck, if you'd given her your blood, she'd be finished.'

'You're welcome,' Delphine said, more snarky than she intended.

'So what do we do?' Macready demanded.

Rhian sighed. 'She's going to have to sweat it out. There's nothing we can do except wait and hope.'

~

THE REST of the nox and the day that followed were utterly miserable. They took turns sitting by Kelpie, mopping her brow and arms with wet cloths, trying to stop her hurting herself when she went into seizure. Her fits grew less intense as the day went on, but perhaps that was because she was getting weaker.

They moved her to Velody's bed. Kelpie's skin felt warmer, more mortal now, though she still shook wildly from time to time and cried out in her sleep.

Days passed. One morning, Delphine went in to take Macready's shift and found him slumped exhausted in a chair.

'You need more rest than this,' she said impatiently.

'I'll be all right,' he muttered.

She thought disloyally that he preferred this — that Kelpie being sick was an emergency that made him feel alive again, useful and complete. He had seemed more himself these last few days than for the whole of Fortuna.

'We're done, aren't we,' she said softly.

'She's getting better.'

'No. I mean, yes, of course she's getting better. She's going to be fine. But I don't think we are.'

Macready let out a very long sigh. 'Aye,' he said, meeting her eyes just for a moment. 'We're done.'

Delphine leaned over and kissed him swiftly on the top of his head, and left the room before she could change her mind.

18

FORTUNA

TWO DAYS BEFORE THE KALENDS OF SATURNALIS

NOX

The sky was falling.

Five days after they brought her inside, Kelpie still hadn't opened her eyes, and the sky was falling.

Velody left the house in Via Silviana, heading for the Lucretine. She walked up and over the hill until she reached the Gardens of Trajus Alysaundre. The sky was calling to her, luring her to fight it. Her whole body ached with staying on the ground. Flashes of scratchlight arced across the blackness.

'Coming back for more?' said a musical voice. 'Really, Velody, isn't that a little pathetic?'

She turned and saw Poet stepping out from the trees. 'Funny, but I always thought you were on my side,' she said conversationally.

'That was naive of you. I've always been on my side. Everyone knows that.'

'Everyone's wrong. It was *his* side you were on. When he came back, you weren't surprised. Why?'

'Mirrors,' said Poet simply. 'Call yourself a real demme? Obviously you haven't spent enough time gazing at your own reflection.'

'He talked to you,' Velody breathed. 'When we were in Tierce.'

'I was the only one listening. The only one who didn't give up on him.' Poet lifted his pocket watch out of his coat and tossed it back and forth. 'Pretty, isn't it? I gave it to him, years ago. After the sky swallowed him, he was able to speak to me through it. After that, it was a matter of keeping my eyes open in the right places — and my ears, of course. He needed the right song to bring him home.'

Velody stared at him, remembering that song, the cabaret of monsters, and then the damage that had wrecked the theatre when she and Garnet came back through the cracks in the sky. There was so much blood, so much pain.

No wonder Garnet was so certain he would make it back.

'Has he rewarded you for that loyalty?' she demanded. 'You brought us through. You saved his life. What has he done for you?'

Poet got an odd smile on his face. 'What have *you* done for me, little mouse? I don't see gratitude shining out of any of your prominent parts.'

'He'll hurt you,' Velody insisted. 'Ashiol loved him, trusted him, and look what Garnet did to him.'

Poet was both amused and impatient, like she was a child performing a very dull trick. 'You can't protect us from everything, you know — or anything, as it happens. You're not our Power and Majesty.'

'I can still be your friend.'

A look of annoyance crossed Poet's face. 'Don't do that. We don't like you. This isn't a social club. It's death and war and blood and we don't have time to stand in a healing circle and chant happy songs.'

'You'd better be getting back to it, then,' she said.

Poet smiled at her. 'You miss it. You know you do. For all your prissy, saintlier-than-thou ways, you want to be dancing the sky and fighting and frigging with the rest of us. How much is it killing you that we don't need you any more?'

He shaped himself into rats, his body disassembling itself neatly and pouring away into the shadows before Velody could say, 'You need me more than ever.'

She said it anyway, in the silence, and felt stupid for it.

The sky opened up in a bright burst and shapes flooded out, darting across the darkness, bright and glittering. Saints, they were dust devils. Velody flew into the sky without thinking, intercepting one only a few feet from the hospice on the Octavian. The devil grinned at her, eyes shining silver, and snapped its jaws in her direction. She reached out, protecting her hands with the glow of animor, and snapped its neck. It shattered into motes of dust that scattered down to the hill below and didn't reassemble.

'Nice work,' said a voice behind her.

Velody turned, and saw Garnet. He hovered before her, wearing a loose shirt that fluttered in the air.

'I didn't think we were on speaking terms,' she said, and then saw another two devils behind him, bearing down on them both. She dived for one as Garnet turned and seized the other, tearing the creature into pieces.

'These are more fragile than the last gang of dust devils we faced,' she said with a gasp. 'Keep them away from your new skysilver collection. That's how they get solid. They're almost impossible to kill in that form.'

'Thank you for keeping me informed,' said Garnet with a thin smile.

'Don't be so pompous,' Velody said impatiently. 'I don't want the city to get swallowed any more than the rest of you do.'

She turned and swooped back down towards the Gardens of Trajus Alysaundre. She could feel him following her. When her feet touched down on the grass, he wasn't far behind.

'What do you want from me now?' she demanded. 'Plan to rip me apart with your own hands? I think Poet's around here somewhere if you still prefer to make others do your dirty work.'

'Actually,' said Garnet, 'I want to marry you.'

Velody had thought the Court had no more surprises, but Garnet's words shocked her so deeply that she could no longer feel her arms and legs. 'You want to *what*?'

'Marriage. Hands joining, bands of bronze and silver. We can slaughter a sheep for the augury, if you like, though you have no father living to demand it.' Garnet paused and gave an odd little smile. 'Mine's still alive, I believe, but we don't want to invite him. Miserable old bastard, he'd only drink us out of wine and gin and try to grope the bridesmaids.'

'You're still crazy, then,' Velody said when she'd recovered her breath. 'I'd been wondering about that.'

Garnet shook his head slowly. 'I finally started listening to the voices in my head. Well, other people's heads. Our new Seer has been most useful in that regard.'

'Rhian,' Velody said quietly. Oh saints, was that where Rhian had been going? To *Garnet*? Velody didn't ask, didn't wanted to know, but this...

Garnet's smile became decidedly more predatory. It made Velody want to bite a piece out of him.

'Our last Seer was so obstructive,' he said. 'Heliora wouldn't do a thing I wanted, no matter how nicely I asked.

This one can't get enough of the Court and our amusing little ways. So helpful and instructive. A real trooper.'

The thought of Rhian in Garnet's hands after everything Velody did to protect her... it had her boiling over. He smiled more fiercely the angrier she got, as if he could feel it. Well, perhaps he could.

'You need to leave her alone.'

'Oh no, little mouse. She's mine now, not yours. Did you know that the Seers have the voices of every other Seer in their heads? I didn't, not until our Rhian explained it to me. We've been working together, listening to what those voices have to say. There's a history there, the whole past of the Creature Court, and it's fascinating. We've had it wrong for so long.'

'Is that what's brought on the sudden desire for matrimony?' Velody said, hardly able to believe it.

Garnet nodded, looking so smug. 'Power and Majesty,' he said, as if testing out the words, 'such an odd concept. Why have more than one King if we only need one leader? All it does is create paranoia, strife, internal battles.'

'Only when there's no trust,' Velody said sharply. 'Ashiol and I managed fine on our own until you came back.'

'But it was close to the surface, his fear of what you could do,' Garnet chided her. 'He turned against you so fast, almost as if he always hated you, don't you think?'

She shook her head, refusing to believe it, though she could still feel the anger pouring out of Ashiol and the painful burst of his claws twisting in her stomach. It was true that he had turned against her far too easily.

'Power and Majesty,' Garnet said again. 'We've been working, Rhian and I, to see into the past instead of the futures. And we discovered the truth. The Court were never supposed to have one King over all the others. The Power and Majesty was a *pair* of Kings. A sacred marriage.'

Velody laughed. 'You expect me to believe that you would share power with me, equally?'

'Why not?' Garnet's eyes were bright, his voice fierce and, oh saints, he was serious.

'Why me?' she said finally. 'You've loved Ashiol longer. Don't tell me with your history that you're hung up on marrying a demoiselle instead of a seigneur.'

'Believe me, I have no wish to implant little baby gattopardi in your womb,' said Garnet. 'Ashiol's gone, and he's not coming back. Leaving the Creature Court is his pattern; he can't be relied upon.'

'You exiled him!'

'A mere excuse. He could have stayed; he could have fought me. He gave up, then and now. I want you, Velody. Partner, lover, King.' His face softened and, oh, he looked like that vulnerable madman she had begun to like in the empty city of Tierce. 'We could be beautiful together. We might finally win.'

'Win what — the sky war? There isn't a victory line, Garnet. It doesn't stop. All we have is survival.'

'That's because we've been doing it wrong, don't you see?'

Velody couldn't believe him. He was mad, or trying to trick her. There were no other options here. 'More lies. I don't trust you — I can't. The idea of marriage is laughable.'

Anger flashed across his face. 'You think you're too good for me?'

'I think you goaded Ashiol and I into half-killing each other, and I believe you'd do it again in an instant — not even to protect yourself, but to amuse. I think you're fucked up. I think you waited until Ashiol was gone before you told me this, because you're scared we'll band together and exile you.'

'Ashiol isn't the marrying kind,' Garnet sneered.

'Neither am I,' Velody said simply.

She turned and walked away from him, more slowly than she would have liked. She wanted to run.

As she left the park, she could have sworn she saw a white tail whisk away into the shadows. The bushes had ears, then. Little rat-shaped ones. She had to talk to Rhian.

~

MACREADY SLEPT on the floor of Velody's room since the break-up, not wanting to leave Kelpie's side while she still suffered from her fever. It temporarily solved the problem of where he was going to live now that he wasn't a sentinel or a live-in lover.

Delphine acted no different now that they were no longer whatever they had been. It was as if it had never happened. He didn't know whether to be heartbroken or relieved.

Macready was still drinking more than he should, and still hiding it. There were two flasks secreted under Velody's bed that no one knew about.

'Mac,' said a voice in the darkness.

He awoke with a grunt to see Kelpie upright in bed, the light of an oil lamp flickering against the walls.

She gave him an odd smile and stretched the muscles in her shoulders and arms. 'How long?'

'Forever,' he said, breathing out in a rush. 'Oh, lass.'

'I'm all right.' She pulled away from his gaze, her eyes not meeting his. 'It was stupid.'

'No.'

'I wanted to hold on to —'

'I know. Lass, there's nothing you need to say about it. Dead and done. Only not dead, thank feck.'

Her hair fell around her face, a rare thing for Kelpie, like she was trying to hide behind it. 'Wouldn't blame you for hating me.'

'You think giving up the sentinels was a decision that came easy to me?' Macready demanded. Her face closed up and he fell over himself to assure her. 'No, I meant nothing bad by that. I could never hate you for your choice. Hells, lass, I could never hate you at all, don't you know that? I don't want to hear another word about it.'

Kelpie smiled, a rarer thing. 'The good news is that the poison came from Livilla and was meant for Garnet,' she said, faking lightness.

'Eh, is that not the best news I've heard all year,' Macready teased. 'It's a fine, fine thing when a woman that vicious takes against a man we loathe. Chances are high she'll succeed next time.'

Kelpie nodded slowly. She was too thin, he'd have to do something about that. None of that fecking herbal soup they were always eating around here; the lass needed meat on her bones.

She tilted her head to one side. 'Do you hear shouting?'

Oh aye, he did at that. Never a good sign around here.

Kelpie slid out of bed in only knickers and a breastband. Macready averted his eyes as she flashed her hipbones at him. Someone had brought her old clothes back from the laundry down the street and left them neatly folded on the dressing table. She pulled on her trews, cinching the belt a notch or two tighter than usual, and dragged a shirt over her head.

'Let's go see who Delphine's screaming at this time,' Kelpie said.

~

IT WASN'T DELPHINE. Delphine was nowhere in sight. Macready knew from the top of the stairs that it was Velody. Her voice went straight to his skin, every time. His King.

Kelpie stumbled, weaker than expected, and he gave her his arm as they made it down the stairs together.

Velody stood in the kitchen, red-faced and yelling like a fishwife. At Rhian, of all people. 'How could you do it? I have to hear it from Garnet of all people?'

'You don't belong to the Court now,' Rhian said, and it didn't sound like her voice. She was cold and remote and broken in all new ways. What the feck had Garnet done to that lovely lass? 'You walked away.'

'I crawled away bleeding,' Velody spat. 'Are you honestly saying you owe him greater allegiance than me? After everything we've done for you?'

'What *have* you done?' Rhian retorted. 'Could you protect me? Could you stop this happening to me? This was always going to happen. It's not about you, Velody. It was never about you.'

'Mac,' said Kelpie in a low, warning voice.

He saw it. A flicker of light running along Rhian's shoulders and arms. Not animor. Something else. He could smell smoke in the air.

'You can't trust him, Rhian,' Velody continued. 'That man will use you and spit you out. Look at what he did to the sentinels.'

'Don't bring them into it,' Rhian said impatiently. 'You're just annoyed that Garnet knew something before you. Do you have any idea what I've been going through?'

'He said you have their voices in your head. Why didn't you tell *me*?'

'Why didn't you ask? The world moved on while you were gone, Velody. We had to live without you. It's not fair to complain that we got good at it.'

Velody was silent for a moment and then reached out a hand to Rhian. 'I'm still the same —'

'Don't touch me,' Rhian barked, stepping back against the cupboards, making them shake. 'Stay away.'

'I'm listening now. Tell me what's happening to you.'

'What was always happening,' said Rhian, her voice breaking on the words.

The kitchen door banged open and Delphine and Crane barged in, arms laden with shopping baskets. Whatever the lad had been up to since he and Macready had lost their swords, he had no qualms about playing footman to the lasses.

'What's going on here?' Delphine asked, the laugh still caught in her voice.

Macready had missed that sound. It was a long time since she'd been so merry around him. *Hardly a surprise, miserable bastard that you are.*

'You might as well all hear,' Velody said sharply. 'Mac, Kelpie, please join us.'

Slightly shamefaced, the two sentinels entered the kitchen.

'What's up?' Macready asked with false jollity.

Rhian was hugging herself. That odd light had gone from her, but the smell of smoke still hung in the air.

'Garnet wants to marry me,' announced Velody in a grim voice. 'And now I think we all need a drink.'

PART VII
OATHBREAKER

19

TASHA AND GARNET

Tasha let me fight the sky properly, at last. It scared the cack out of me, but I did it. The thought that kept me going was that I had killed Saturn and that made me as wicked as the rest of them. Most of the time I tried to forget that I was the worst of the monsters, but in the sky it was an odd comfort. It meant I could take care of myself. I could be something, someone who mattered.

Things were different with the cubs. With Garnet. After Saturn, he fell apart, drinking hard and taking every potion and powder he could get his hands on. He gave up. Total despair. Ashiol and Lysandor were run off their paws trying to keep it from Tasha: how bad things were, how far he had fallen. It was my fault, and I knew it. I was sick about it. Something about me and what I had done to Saturn was killing Garnet slowly, from the inside.

Liv and I tried to help the others cover for him, but we weren't much help.

Livilla decided she was in love with Ashiol, but whenever Garnet crooked his finger at her, she went to him instead, kissing and making up to him. She was trying to make

Heliora, Ash's pet sentinel, jealous, I think. Everyone knew Heliora was after Ash. The cubs were all of age now, but they still acted like boys.

One nox, something changed. Ashiol found Garnet off his face in the middle of a skybattle and sent him home. Somewhere between the Forum and the Arches, Garnet sobered up and then some.

I got back ahead of him, Livilla half-carrying me as a scorchbolt had torn a layer of skin off my back. I was sick and sleepy, dazed from the pain, but Livilla wasn't allowed to heal me until Tasha came back and decided whether I deserved it or not.

Garnet entered like the pantaloon in a harlequinade, puffed up with power. He ignored me and strode straight to Livilla, drew her up off the couch and kissed her until she could hardly breathe.

'What happened to you?' she asked. 'You feel —'

'Sick, hot, weak, marvellous, tremendous?' Garnet teased her. 'I've never felt better in my life.'

He danced her around the rooms, humming a song he'd picked up somewhere.

'You quenched someone,' Livilla said, pouting at him. 'You didn't share!'

Garnet mimicked her sulky expression. 'Ask our lovely Tasha if there was a death call this nox.'

'You've eaten someone,' Livilla protested. 'You must have.'

'Me?' he laughed. 'I'm naturally talented and wonderful, you know.'

As he danced past me, I felt the throbbing pain in my back ease. I stared up at him in alarm. 'You're not supposed to —'

'Leave Tasha to me,' Garnet carolled, kissing Livilla again, rougher than before. 'Call that a gift from a little brown mouse.'

I thought he had finally run mad.

Tasha knew what he'd done before she even stepped over the threshold. She was alone, no sign of Ashiol or Lysandor. She must have left the battle early, as soon as she felt Garnet healing me.

'Get up,' Tasha demanded, dragging me out of bed so that I fell on the floor. 'This is what I do to disobedient boys,' she added, eyes fixed on Garnet as she pressed her palm against my back, burning a handprint of animor between my shoulder blades.

I screamed, too shocked with the pain to do anything else.

'Stop it,' Garnet snapped, dragging her away from me. 'I did it. Punish me.'

'Believe me, I will,' Tasha snarled, baring her teeth at him. 'I am your Lord and you will not forget that. Cub.'

Garnet shoved her hard, knocking her to the floor. 'For now, perhaps,' he said, standing over her. 'But I won't be your courteso forever. I'll be a Lord and then a King, and you can never be anything more than you are now. *Woman.*'

Tasha screamed soundlessly at him and shaped herself into the lioness. She pounced and bit, and he let her tear at him, laughing helplessly though the pain must have been overwhelming.

'You can't kill me,' he said finally, pale and shuddering under her teeth. 'You don't dare quench anyone. Not if you don't want to end up like Samara.'

We all knew the story of the female Lord who tried to be a King and burst apart from her own power. Women could not be Kings.

Tasha shaped herself back into a person, golden and naked, pinning him to the ground. 'I can kill you without quenching you,' she gasped.

'No, you can't,' said Garnet. 'You don't have it in you to hold back. You can't trust yourself.'

Tasha turned away from him and punched the wall in anger, enough to scrape her knuckles bloody. 'You are mine. You will not speak to me like I am the dirt under your finger-nails. I own you, boy.'

'Aye, you do,' Garnet said, and there was blood in his mouth now. 'But we are here because we love you, not because you own us. I want you to swear an oath that you will not raise a hand in violence against one of us again.'

His eyes were serious. Had he meant this all along?

Tasha laughed hollowly. 'Who do you think you are?'

Garnet stood up then, which was a surprise to me, even through my haze of pain. He shouldn't have been able to do that, shouldn't have had it in him with his body torn and bitten raw, but he had managed to boost his power somehow. He wasn't a Lord yet, but he wasn't far off being Tasha's equal.

'Swear the oath,' he said dangerously. 'Or I will leave and take them with me when I become Lord. They love me more than they love you.'

Livilla and I both avoided Tasha's penetrating gaze. It was true. Tasha was glorious, but Garnet was *ours*. If we had to choose, we would choose him, even if we hated ourselves for it.

He wouldn't make us choose, would he?

'I will destroy you for this,' Tasha whispered.

'You can try,' Garnet replied. 'But I'm not Saturn. I won't go down so easily.' He pressed a hand against his chest and blood oozed through his fingers. 'Swear the oath, Tasha. You will not deliberately harm any of your courtesi. Not a hair on their heads.'

'You're a fool,' she whispered.

Garnet raised his voice. 'Poet. Livilla. We're leaving. Celeste Lord Owl will take us in.'

'You can't threaten me,' Tasha spat.

'On the contrary,' said Garnet. 'You are the one with something to lose. You owe *everything* you are to us. Swear the oath, Tasha. No more pain from your hands to our bodies. We have suffered your tantrums long enough.'

Her eyes blazed at him, but she swore the oath.

Garnet fell to the couch halfway through, and I saw an expression flicker across Tasha's face as she considered ending him once and for all. But she didn't. She promised not to hurt any of her courtesi with her own hands from that nox onwards.

Ashiol and Lysandor came in later, punchy and high-spirited from the battle. None of us told them what had happened. At least, Livilla and I never did. I think Garnet kept his mouth shut, too, even from his closest friends.

Tasha brought a cage into the den, and coils of skysilver wire from the Smith. If one of us displeased her, she would order us to bind one of the cage's bars in tight skysilver coils, smirking as it burned our palms and fingertips. Even Garnet did it when she told him to, though he knew she couldn't enforce the order. He seemed to enjoy it, or was good at pretending so. Once the bars were all wrapped in skysilver, the cage made an effective prison for recalcitrant cubs. I don't think Ashiol or Lysandor ever knew why she had changed her methods of inflicting pain.

20

TASHA AND LYSANDOR

Two years later, Tasha broke the oath.

The cubs were nineteen now. Tasha was the most powerful Lord of the Court. Livilla and I added to her numbers, but it was those three young men with their fierce, devastating animor that showed the rest of the Court that Tasha was someone to be reckoned with.

Ortheus the Snake King, our Power and Majesty, adored her. She replaced Saturn as his favourite. Perhaps it was knowing she could never be a King that made him trust her so greatly, but it didn't matter why. She stood at the snake's side and served him well.

Argentin, the other King of the Court, tolerated Tasha with something like amusement. She spent years trying to seduce him and he merely laughed at her. Of all the Court, he was the only one who acted like a monk. If his taste was demmes, young boys, or Ortheus himself, we never saw it.

Tasha allowed both Kings to order her courtesi around as much as they chose. She took particular delight in letting the Power and Majesty hurt or punish us in ways she no longer could herself. Once, Ortheus ordered Garnet to be beaten bloody on the floor of the Haymarket. Ashiol expected Tasha to protest, or offer some kind of bribe to prevent it, but she did nothing.

Garnet grinned through the pain, knowing she had bested him, and yet... he had beaten her, too. She had to go to such lengths to hurt him.

It was only a matter of time.

Heliora was Seer now, new and raw. The first time she fell into the futures, it was Ashiol's job to frig her back to her senses. He did it because he had to, because Ortheus had ordered him, and because he cared about Hel, just a little. Tasha allowed it — she never saw Heliora as a threat, just as she never saw Livilla as a threat. Maybe because neither of them was likely to become a Lord. Heliora was stuck being a Seer for the rest of her life, and no one thought Liv had any ambition.

It was Celeste who provoked Tasha's jealousy and her hate; Celeste who had become a Lord upon the death of Saturn and drew Lysandor's eyes everywhere she went; Celeste who was loved.

I don't know if Ortheus knew all this, if he planned events to unfold the way they did, but one nox he called a Court for us all to hear Heliora speak the futures — and nominated Lysandor to be the one to frig her back to her senses afterwards.

Everyone tensed, except Tasha, who thought the idea was amusing.

Ashiol glared with suppressed fury. He loved Lysandor, but Hel was his to protect. Heliora herself, preparing for her visions, didn't look happy. Lord Celeste blazed with anger, though she didn't show it on her face.

Garnet reached out, quite casually, and took my hand. He held Livilla's on his other side. For comfort? To know exactly where we were? I had no idea, except that he watched the whole Court with the alert eyes of a gattopardo ready to pounce.

'No,' said Lysandor. He stood up.

'I am your Power and Majesty,' said Ortheus, who had not been defied in a long time. 'You will do as you are told, cub.'

Tasha flinched at the use of that name.

Lysandor gave an odd sort of smile. 'I believe the Seer would be better eased from her burdens by someone whose body she trusts. She should be honoured for the unique role she has, not passed around like a meat dish for everyone to taste.'

'Indeed,' said Ortheus. His head moved back and forth, small darting movements, as he weighed up Lysandor's stance, the cadence of his voice, the weaknesses he might betray. 'Have you any further advice for me, *courteso?*'

'I apologise for my inability to perform your request, my Power,' said Lysandor. Even Garnet winced at that one. To say 'request' when all knew it was an order... We would be lucky if Lysandor got out of this alive.

'How charming,' said Ortheus. 'How polite.' He never raised his voice. That was part of what made him such a chilling master. Like the snakes he could shape himself into, he was calm right up to the moment he struck out. 'You know I will punish you.'

'I expected as much, my Majesty,' said Lysandor.

Ortheus laughed. Many of the Court relaxed, laughing along with him, or at least smiling. I didn't smile, nor did Garnet or Ashiol. Livilla laid her head on Garnet's shoulder, shivering.

'You amuse me, courteso,' said our Power and Majesty. 'But I don't believe for one moment that you refuse the Seer's body out of some doomed sense of honour. Tell me the truth. Why will you not fuck her?'

Lysandor met the Snake King's eyes. 'I love another,' he said simply.

Celeste breathed out, and for a few seconds that was the only noise we heard. That, and each other's heartbeats.

'There is no law, after all, that we should all mate like animals,' commented Argentin lightly. Argentin rarely spoke except to add weight to the words of our Power and Majesty.

Ortheus didn't laugh this time. He was intrigued, as if Lysandor had said something he really couldn't understand. Then he shrugged, just once. 'Cat. Come and sit by the Seer. She will need you shortly.'

As Ashiol crawled forward to Heliora's side, Ortheus looked at Tasha. 'Discipline your boy.'

Tasha could not appear weak before the Court. As she strutted towards Lysandor, my eyes were on Garnet. He looked half-sick, half-delighted with himself, his eyes unnaturally bright. He gripped my hand so hard it hurt. I wondered if he was on something, but I hadn't seen him take a single powder or potion since the nox he'd forced Tasha to make that oath. Power was a better drug, it seemed.

Looking at him then, my eyes locked on his face as Tasha made Lysandor scream, I realised this was what Garnet intended all along. He knew that, sooner or later, her oath would conflict with Tasha's service to the Power and Majesty. Garnet was responsible for what was happening right now. He had turned Tasha into an oathbreaker.

Our walk back through the tunnels was slow and uncomfortable. Lysandor was healed enough that he could leave the Haymarket on his own two feet; he limped a little on the uneven ground. Tasha's anger was tangible, bouncing off the walls around us.

We were a few steps from the den when we felt the sky boiling above us, the beginning of a battle.

'Go, all of you,' said Tasha, eyes fastened on Garnet. 'We will follow.'

'What's going on?' Ashiol asked, but Lysandor tugged on his arm, knowing better than to question Tasha in that kind of mood.

Livilla and I, knowing the truth, exchanged glances and followed the cubs up through the pipes into the city. Neither of us looked back, and I know we both expected that we would not see Garnet again. He had gone too far.

The battle distracted us. The sky was so bright with screechlight and gold flashes that it could have been daylight. We ducked and weaved through the threads of power, small wounds opening in the sky faster than we could seal them off. I was new enough to fighting that it took me over completely. I exulted in the battle, buzzing with the glee of it as I dodged death and burning over and over. There is truly no feeling like it in the world. Nothing as good, nothing as terrible.

No, that isn't true. There is something more terrible.

I felt it that nox. A loss I couldn't begin to explain, or understand.

Ashiol was hit by it first. He almost fell out of the sky, and I thought he had been hurt. He let out a cry that pulled us to him, Lysandor, Livilla, me. We were in animal form, circling around him in our many shapes of rat, wolf, lynx. Ashiol shaped back, human instead of black cats.

Lysandor's mouth fell open in shock. I still didn't feel it, not really. The sky was so alight with fiends and animor that I was dazed. Then the sky actually shook, and I reached out for Tasha, as we always did when we were sick or hurt or scared.

She wasn't there. Saints and devils, she wasn't there. There was nothing but a void where she used to be. Darkness and nothingness.

We fled the sky, all five of us, though some of the Lords screamed about our cowardice, and there would be punishment from the Power and Majesty later. We couldn't think about that.

Tasha was gone, Tasha was gone, Tasha was gone.

We slid down through the pipes and tunnels, dropping onto the sandy floor of the den. Garnet sat there, knees tucked under his chin, covered in blood. I don't think he was even aware that we were there, not at first.

Tasha was a crumpled figure on the sand, her human torso twisted half in and half out of a pair of lioness's back legs. There was blood on her, too.

Livilla let out a cry and went to our Lord, throwing herself on her body. 'What have you done?' Her eyes were glassy and her skin pinker than usual; what little she had quenched of Tasha had hit her hard. 'Garnet, what have you *done?*'

'What do you think?' Lysandor said in an awful voice. 'He's done exactly as Tasha taught us. Lived her lessons fully.'

I hated Lysandor in that moment, that bastard blaming her for her own death.

'I win,' said Garnet, looking at Ashiol as if he was waiting for applause.

Everything Garnet did had an audience in mind, and, with Tasha gone, Ashiol was the most important member of the audience. Box seat. Toffee apples. Curtain call.

'Congratulations,' said Ashiol slowly. 'Lord.'

I looked at Garnet, trying to see it in him. He was always good at keeping his power under wraps, only revealing the full extent of his abilities when it suited him. It was a useful skill in the Creature Court. He stood up now, unfurling his animor, and oh, yes. A Lord.

Ashiol had realised before the rest of us, acknowledged it, and yet he still took command.

'All right,' Ashiol said. 'We need a plan.'

'No plans, no tricks,' said Garnet, horribly calm. 'It doesn't matter what the rest of the Creature Court think. I'm going to look after all of you. I can do that now.' He shone, brighter than ever before, pale as an angel.

'Of course you are,' said Ashiol impatiently. 'Now. Here's what we're going to do...'

~

WE BURIED Tasha in the Angel Gardens without telling anyone. Ashiol was right about that part. It didn't matter that Garnet was a Lord; once the rest of the Court knew that Tasha was gone, they would fall on us. The other Lords had hated her for having so many courtesi, for being Ortheus's favourite. Our Power and Maesty would not extend that favouritism to us, we knew that much.

Once the digging was done, and Tasha lay buried under the earth, we sat around, dirty and scared. They would find out. Of course they would find out.

Only Garnet was unconcerned. He made a stone to mark her, imprinting the shape of a lioness on a fallen piece of masonry. 'It's just us now,' he said. 'We'll keep the family together. I promise.'

Ashiol and Lysandor looked at each other, and said nothing.

21

TASHA'S CUBS

The sickness started soon after. The five of us curled up in Tasha's bed, not wanting to be alone. I awoke in darkness to hear Livilla sobbing, and it was a short while before I realised it wasn't an ordinary bad dream. She had the sweats, a high fever. Lysandor wasn't looking good either. He shivered as he and Ashiol talked in low voices about how to smuggle Livilla to a daylight dottore.

'I know one,' I said. They looked at me, and now wasn't the time to mention how hot my skin felt, or how everything blurred before my eyes. 'If he's still there. He worked at an apothecary across from the Vittorina Royale. He was a bit of an old crook — I think we can... well, not trust him, but if we pay him enough he'll keep his mouth shut.'

'Garnet, go along with Poet to grab the fellow,' said Ashiol flatly. 'We can see to his silence later.'

'Is that an order?' Garnet challenged him.

'For fuck's sake, we don't have time for pawing the ground,' Ashiol growled. 'Argue the point later. Punish me if that's what you want. Livilla needs our help.'

Garnet scowled, but jerked his head at me and we left

together. We heard Lysandor coughing as we scrambled up into the city. Livilla wasn't the only one who was sick.

~

WHEN WE REACHED THE APOTHECARY, it was empty and no amount of pounding on the doors roused anyone from the apartment above.

Garnet pressed his fists angrily against the cool glass of the windows. 'You haven't sworn an oath to me yet,' he said, staring in as if the cure for Livilla might appear before his eyes. 'Will you be my courteso?'

'Of course,' I said, surprised he had to ask. 'Where else am I going to go?'

'Back to your theatre?'

Garnet looked across the street to where the Vittorina Royale queened it over every other building. There were broadsheets plastered all over the boards at the front, advertising this year's Saturnalia revue. A small fragment of my old life holding steady between those walls.

'I don't want to go back,' I said, despite the small twitch in my stomach at the thought of it. 'You're my family now. Of course I'll swear — we all will.'

'Ashiol won't,' Garnet said, his eyes cold. 'He'll come up with some excuse. He won't swear allegiance. He can't stand the idea of me being above him. He won't take orders from me.'

'He might surprise you,' I said.

Garnet laughed shortly. 'You, who watch us with those beady little eyes of yours, taking in every weakness and foible, you believe he will kneel to the son of a servant?'

I could make no such observation. The sickness had gone to my head, making it ache dreadfully, and I couldn't see very well. But I had watched enough of Ashiol and

Garnet together. There was love there, as well as
competition.

'You needn't worry about me,' I said. 'I'll swear.'

Garnet brushed his hand over my cheek, then leaned
down and kissed my forehead. 'Thank you, ratling.' He
turned back to the window. 'Is there anything in here that
can help Livilla?'

'Poultices maybe,' I said dubiously. 'Something to bring
the fever down. Pastilles to soothe her throat...'

Garnet smashed the glass with his fist, spraying blood
and glass everywhere, and cupped his hands as a stirrup to
lift me inside. 'If Ash does swear, then I'll finally know
whether I can trust him,' he said thoughtfully. 'That's
something.'

As I stood on the glass-strewn floor of the apothecary,
passing items out to Garnet, I felt her coming. Closer and
closer, bringing something dark and awful with her. My
headache sharpened, the pain stabbing me between my eyes.

'She's not dead,' I breathed. 'Garnet, Tasha's not dead.'

Garnet's hand shook as I passed him the last of the poultices. 'She's dead,' he said in a terrible voice. 'I know
that much.'

He scooped me back out of the window, set me on my
feet, and we turned to face her.

Tasha. It was our Lord and yet not our Lord. She walked
on unsteady, grey-white feet. I stared, trying to bring her
into focus through the pain in my head. There was a stench
about her — that familiar scent of her skin and hair and
animor mixed with dirt and blood. There was something else
there, too, a wrongness. If I had been in animal shape, I
would have turned tail and fled whimpering into the
darkness.

'Not fair,' Garnet said in a broken voice.

Tasha laughed, and it was then that I knew it wasn't really

her — the sound was cold and wrong. Tasha was always warm. Some days, the heat of her knocked us to our knees. She wasn't here; it was a semblance of her presence.

I could see her in sharp focus, but nothing else around us. My skin was burning up. As she moved closer to us, I fell to my knees, unable to keep upright any longer. The poultices lay scattered on the ground and I stared mindlessly at them.

'You made me this,' she said in a throat that was no longer made for human words.

'No,' said Garnet, close to tears, or something.

'Oathbreaker,' Tasha hissed. 'Because of you. My blood brought me back. You brought me back, traitor boy.'

She reached out to touch his face and I was overwhelmed by the stink — not of her body, which had hardly had time to rot, but of the power clinging to her. It was like animor, but wrong, turned inside out and upside down. Topsy-turvy, I thought hysterically, remembering that it was Saturnalia again. A festival of things turned upside down.

A bad festival for me. Madalena died, and Tasha dragged me into the Court, and I killed Saturn, and Garnet killed Tasha. The daylight people thought that Saturnalia was a time for joy, but I knew better. How could a festival in the coldest part of winter be a happy thing? It stank of death.

'Don't let her touch you!' yelled a voice. Many voices.

Saved, we were saved. It was Ashiol, and he'd brought help. I let myself slump to the cobbles, overwhelmed by the sickness that Tasha had brought with her. It was up to them, now. The cubs and whomever they had brought with them. All I could do was die.

~

I WAS cold when I awoke, so cold that I thought I had died

after all, but then I heard Livilla's soothing voice and I slipped back into sleep.

Next time I awoke, Ashiol was there, sitting at the end of my bed, telling me how the Lord Priest had saved Garnet's life, that they hadn't been able to stop the Tasha-shade. She haunted the streets still. As I lost consciousness again, I heard his whispered confession: he and Lysandor had promised allegiance to Priest in return for saving my neck, and Garnet's.

'He'll hate me for it, won't he?' he asked.

I closed my eyes. He didn't need me to confirm what he already knew. *He'll come up with some excuse.* Garnet's prediction had come true and he would never forgive Ashiol for it.

22

THE LAKE OF FOLLIES

*S*aturnalis became Venturis and Tasha's shade stuck to the city like greasepaint. The Creature Court didn't only have the sky to fight any more. Livilla came to my bedside, grey and twitchy, telling me about the daylight children who died from the plague that began the nox Garnet quenched Tasha. They called the sickness the Weeping Fate.

Garnet visited me sometimes. He recovered from whatever it was Tasha's shade had done to us, faster than the rest of us. He hardly even coughed any more.

He said nothing, did nothing on these visits, only sat with me. I opened my mouth more than once to tell him it wasn't his fault, but never spoke the words.

Garnet laughed when he told me that Ashiol and Lysandor had sworn allegiance to Priest, but the laugh sounded hollow. Normally I would look to his eyes for the truth of it, but the fever damaged my sight too badly for me to read him that way. The world was blurred.

I could still hear Tasha. It wasn't a loud sound, but a faint echo that drifted through the Arches from time to time. She was miserable and broken and dead, but she wouldn't lie down. Every time I thought that the silence might last, she started up again. Whether I was asleep or awake, I could hear her.

'You hear her, too,' I said. 'Don't you?'

Garnet fell silent. I wanted to yell that I couldn't see him, it wasn't fair not to use words. Then he reached out and took my hand in his, skin cool against my warmth. 'It can't last.'

~

IT LASTED FOR A MARKET-NINE, and then another. Tasha's voice sounding in our ears; Tasha's shade trailing sickness and death through the streets of the city above.

Ortheus demanded that the Seer give him answers, that she tell him how to banish Tasha once and for all. Heliora tried, she really did. She wore herself ragged, throwing herself into the futures over and over, until blood flecked in her eyes and on her lips. Ashiol carried her bodily out of the Haymarket, prepared to fight the Power and Majesty himself to keep her from destroying herself. Priest supported his new courteso, letting Ashiol keep Heliora safe in the Cathedral. Ortheus didn't challenge them.

There were no answers. People died. People died. People died.

'They blame us,' Garnet said once, pacing back and forth on the sandy floor of the den. 'All of them. The Lords and Court think this is our fault.'

'Your fault,' said Livilla in a clear voice. She was distracted since Tasha's death, taking more potions and powders than usual. It was angel dust today, which made her alert and feisty. 'They blame you.'

Garnet growled deep in his throat, but didn't pounce on her.

'Ortheus says we should stay out of it,' was my only

contribution. Our snake of a Power and Majesty had sent Argentin to my bedside specifically to tell me that the ghoul trailing contamination through our city was no concern of mine.

'Ortheus can't solve this problem,' said a voice, and I didn't have to stare at the familiar silhouette in the mouth of the tunnel to know it was Ashiol. Lysandor stood at his side.

'What are you two doing here?' Garnet demanded in an unfriendly voice. 'I thought you served a new master now.'

'We're not done with the last one yet,' Ashiol said grimly. 'I don't give a frig what Ortheus and Argentin have declared. Tasha was ours. It's up to us to release her. The Power and Majesty would have done it by now if he knew how.'

Lysandor cleared his throat. 'Celeste lets me read Lord Saturn's old journals. He copied down theories about how the Creature Court worked, the history we've lost, even what lies beyond the sky. Saturn talked to the Smith, to the Seers... I've been trying to learn if anything like this has ever happened before.'

'If it happened in Saturn's lifetime, Ortheus would know,' Garnet said scornfully.

'Maybe,' Lysandor said hesitantly. 'Saturn had this theory about the cleansing properties of the Lake of Follies. There are stories about it vanquishing devils in the old days.'

'And how do we convince our dear departed Lord to get her feet wet?' asked Garnet.

I could hear the edge in his voice. We were in dangerous territory when he felt control slipping from him.

'Poet,' said Ashiol, sounding so bloody sure of himself.

'Me?' I replied, startled to be called upon.

I was the youngest of them, could barely stand up after my first brush with Tasha's shade, and — though I had admitted it to none of them — I could barely fucking see. I had only been out of bed a few days, finally able to walk on my own two feet provided I squinted to check how close the walls were. There had been a few embarrassing tumbles.

'Tasha always loved your voice,' said Ashiol.

Livilla laughed sadly. 'Well, of course,' she said. 'That would do it.'

~

THERE ARE two feast days in Venturis in honour of Saint Carmenta, the oracle who announced the end of the skywar and led the people of Aufleur out from their underground city to start life anew. Or, as the Creature Court call her, that lying bitch. The daylight folk celebrate her through songs of hope.

The last time I sang for Tasha was the nox before the first day of Saturnalia: a carol about plums and sweet coffee and toy soldiers. She fell asleep with her hand resting on my hair, smiling as if she were a child under the spell of a lullaby. Those moments we had together were rare, but there are days when I can't push them out of my mind. She loved me; I know she loved me. More than my mam, who left too young. More than Madalena, who was stuck with me and didn't always pretend to be happy about it.

Tasha chose me: I could never forget that.

In forgiving Garnet for what he had done to Tasha, I betrayed her as surely as I betrayed Madalena for forgiving my boys for their bloody work.

There was a little pavilion at the Lake of Follies that the priests used during summer festivals. I didn't know how the cubs got hold of it, but it was floating out there now, in the middle of winter, waiting for me under boughs of winter greenery and cotton bunting.

I couldn't see far in front of my face, just the grey darkness that comes not long before dawn, and the flicker of the scarlet and purple ribbons that fluttered around the poles of the pavilion.

What kind of repertoire do you call upon to lure your Lord to her destruction once she has become a ghoul of pestilence and plague?

I sang the songs that she always liked: sad and angsty ballads, war songs, childish rhymes that said nothing and meant everything. Then, feeling alone and vulnerable — the others were around somewhere, but not within touch; they could have abandoned me for all I knew — I sang the songs that I liked best: my favourites from the Mermaid and the Vittorina Royale, comedy routines to music, character pieces.

Just as I was close to giving up, the chill air making my voice stutter and catch in my throat, I heard from across the shore the same song reflected back to me in a singing voice I hadn't heard in years. Livilla; she had a peach of a voice, untouched and still halfway innocent. it wasn't strong, but it was sweet.

I closed my eyes, because darkness was better than the blurred lantern light, and I heard another voice, and then another. All of Tasha's cubs, singing for her. For a few minutes, it felt like we were inside each other, all limbs of the same body, connected in a way we had almost forgotten about. Tasha was gone. Our family would never be held together the same way again. But right now, on this nox, we were beautiful.

She came for us. We all felt her. I could sense Livilla's revulsion, Garnet's guilt, Lysandor's fear. Nothing from Ashiol; nothing but walls put up to keep the rest of us out.

I kept singing. The others fell away. I couldn't see her; didn't want to see how she looked now, if she was even really here, or just spirit.

An ugly stench overwhelmed me, but I kept singing. A

darkness of fear and despair swept over me and my skin heated up. I couldn't survive another bout of whatever illness she carried with her. The thought of losing what little eyesight I had left...

I heard the others talking, as if they were close to me, though I knew by the feel of their animor that they were on the shore, nowhere near.

Lysandor: What's this going to do to the lake?

Garnet: Poison it, obviously.

Ashiol: It's an ornamental fucking lake; it's not like it's the city reservoir. We can afford to lose the lake.

Livilla: I can't see him, I can't see Poet. What will she do to him?

Garnet: I doubt somehow she's going to join him for a duet.

I started singing again, to drown out their voices. After a few moments, Livilla joined me. I had missed the sound of her voice. Why hadn't Tasha ever asked her to sing?

Too late to ask that question now.

The floating pavilion swayed under my feet. The creature that had once been Tasha was getting nearer. I sang harder, louder, deeper. Thirteen years old and it was the performance of my fucking life.

Sight or no sight, I knew the moment she set foot into the lake. It was hard to miss. The water's temperature dropped suddenly, fiercely. Frost ran up the poles of the pavilion and the wind-stirred ribbons froze solid.

I forgot all the words to all the songs in the world. There was nothing else. My voice faltered. In the silence that followed, I heard Livilla's thin voice getting stronger — a sad song from the cabaret that sometimes formed part of the Mermaid Revue. It was Madalena's favourite, she sang it when she was drunk, and I didn't even know the title because we called it 'Madalena's brandy song'. It was about wanting to be loved, wanting to be the stellar on someone else's stage, not another player in the chorus.

Half the words weren't words at all, but silly sounds that weren't so silly when sung by a mournful drunk, or a demme on the shore of a lake tinged with the frost of a dead woman's shade.

Jazz is good like that. Songs for every occasion.

Tasha, or the thing that used to be Tasha, waded deeper into the water.

Nothing happened. There was no scream, no cleansing. What was left of her body didn't shatter like glass under a mallet. The water around me and the pavilion merely grew colder under my feet, and my breath fogged the air, and she was getting closer, closer.

It would be nice to say that we banished her with love, that the power we had from being together was enough to conquer her. It would be nice to say that we gathered the strength to send her to a better place; that we held hands and chanted a song with meaningful lyrics and turned her to dust. That would be a story worth the telling, wouldn't it?

Instead, she reached the pavilion and dragged her grey body onto the frosted platform. I backed up as far as I could go, and cried out as she lunged for me, her hands grabbing. She felt like bone and plague all at once, and just being near her was enough to make me struggle for breath.

Garnet rose up behind her, dripping wet, and snapped her neck. She didn't seem to notice, her thin fingers still clamped around my throat, her fingertips drilling into me like spikes of ice. This close, I could see her, could see the grey patterns on her face, the broken skin, the shadowy shapes inside her that animated this thing that was no longer Tasha. It was as if the nox itself leaked out of her.

The sun should have risen half an hour ago.

Light, orange and crackling, bright and hot, flashed past my eyes. Ashiol yelled, and Lysandor, and I felt myself burning as the flames took hold of everything — me, Garnet, the Tasha-thing. The pavilion broke under our feet, submerging us all in the cold, contaminated water.

It tasted like death, and I was happy to drown in it.

Livilla found me, and we came up out of the water together, her sodden strands of hair stuck to both of us. She buried her face in my chest, and I stared through my misty vision to see whatever it was she didn't want to see.

The cubs, all three of them, in their animal forms. The lynx, the gattopardo and the cats clung to the wreckage of the pavilion, shadowy shapes tearing and gnawing at something in the water. It was a moment before I realised what it was that they were doing. They were eating her, piece by piece.

LIVILLA and I made it to shore and sat there shivering as the sun finally rose over the city. One by one, the cubs joined us, naked and man-shaped again. They flopped down on either side of us, breathing hard.

'Thank you,' Garnet said in a low voice, his eyes closed.

Ashiol leaned over in that casual, thoughtless way he had and dropped a kiss on his forehead. 'We're family,' he said. 'We'll always be family.'

But Tasha was gone, and Ashiol and Lysandor had sworn allegiance to Priest. Garnet was a Lord, and the rest of us were courtesi. It would never be the same again.

WHEN WE RETURNED to the Arches, we stayed together as long as we could, but then we broke apart to go our separate ways. Ashiol and Lysandor trailed up the canal path to the

Cathedral, while Livilla and I followed Garnet back to
our den.

'Nothing has to change,' said Ashiol as we parted, but
Garnet turned away from him.

Back home, Livilla burrowed into the covers of Tasha's
bed. I sat in the chair that was mine, the one with the
squeaky leg that showed I was the lowest in the pecking
order. I could take Ashiol's chair now, but I didn't want to be
so bold.

Hands came over my face, cool and gentle. I blinked,
looking through the glass of a pair of spectacles. The room
came into sharper focus than before.

'They were in the haul from the apothecary,' said Garnet.

I was pretty sure that wasn't true. He had to have gone
back for them specially. But I wasn't going to complain about
the kindness.

I leaned back, letting my neck rest against his hand.
'Thank you.'

'You won't leave me,' he said, and there was barely a hint
of question in his voice.

'Never,' I vowed.

Garnet sighed. 'You're lying, Poet. Everyone lies, whether
they know it or not.'

I felt the imprint of his hand on my neck long after he
walked away.

PART VIII
LAMB TO THE SLAUGHTER

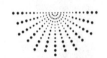

23

FORTUNA

ONE DAY BEFORE THE KALENDS OF SATURNALIS

NOX

Topaz was worried about some kind of vengeance after she delivered the cup of death into that bastard Garnet's hands, but there was no assault on the stairs. She and the other lambs were left alone. Livilla stayed in her rooms, rarely stepping out.

Fortuna was almost done and the Lord Livilla still knew nothing about what that man of hers had in mind for the Saturnalia revels.

Sometimes the sky changed colours and Garnet called the Lords and Court to join him, but Topaz and the lambs were made to stay home. Too young, Livilla insisted. Bree sneered and tossed her head, proud she was the only one allowed to accompany their mistress into the sky. Topaz had no idea what happened in that dratted sky, but she was pretty sure she lost nothing by staying where it was safe and warm.

The last nox of Fortuna was the worst. Livilla and Bree were gone for so long, and the lambs were more restless than usual. They huddled up to Topaz, craving her warmth. She did her best to heat their hands and feet without bursting into flame. It was getting easier to control her heat, though it still didn't feel natural.

Livilla screamed. The lambs all exchanged a fearful look, and then scampered as one to the balcony.

The whole Creature Court was there, what was left of them, gathered in the Haymarket below. They were a mess, charred and smelling like thunderstorms, hair stuck up in all directions, burns on their skin and clothes. Garnet stood in the middle of them all, his hands around Livilla's throat.

Topaz felt the heat rise within her. The lambs needed their lady; how else were they to survive this mad world that they had been hurled into?

'So this is it,' Garnet said, voice loud and hateful. 'Can't poison me with your drink or your cunt, so you'll let the sky do it for you?'

Livilla glared at him. 'I did nothing to that damned sky,' she managed to say. 'It wants you dead, and why not? You've been dead once already, and you escaped. Shouldn't the sky be angry at you? Shouldn't it want your blood?'

Topaz's heat prickled her skin from inside out. Smoke curled out from under her fingernails. She climbed up on the rail of the balcony.

'None of you touch me,' she cautioned, even as the other lambs made to grab hold of her.

'Little salamander wants to play, does she?' said Garnet, without even looking up in her direction.

'Let her go,' commanded Topaz.

The heat was pressing heavier against her skin, like there were coals alight in her belly. She stood up on the balcony rail.

'Do not speak to me, courtesa,' said Garnet, disgust evident in his voice. 'You are less than nothing.'

Topaz broke into lizard form. She spread out in her many bodies, running at full tilt over the curve of the balcony and down the sheer drop of the wall. Her lizards fanned out as she hit the floor and burst into hot, scorching flames all over.

The Court scattered like the animals they were. Only Garnet stayed, his hands still clasped around Livilla's throat.

'I am your Power and Majesty,' he raged, shaking Livilla, and Topaz could feel it, the anger of him, the power pressing down around them all. He was strong enough to crush the lizards, body by body. He would hurt her if he could. Topaz was supposed to bow and scrape to him like all the others. Too bad no one had ever stopped to explain all the rules to her.

She burned hotter and hotter, until her eyelids had to fall closed to protect her eyeballs from her own flame. 'LET HER GO,' she thundered, and felt the city shake with the wonder of her words. She could see nothing, but she felt it, all of it, the moment of his capitulation.

Livilla breathed once, a shaky gasp. 'Topaz,' she said, in the gentlest voice Topaz had ever heard from her. 'Enough.'

Topaz let go of the flame and felt the cold of the concrete seep into her lizard skin. She looked up and saw that Livilla stood nearest to her. Garnet stood away from them both, his face blistered and scarlet.

'You are not of the Court,' he said in a voice that shook and swayed. 'Swear an oath never to turn your flame on me again, salamander, or you will leave this place. I will have order here.'

Topaz found the thought that belonged to her demme body and crawled into it, forming arms and legs, shaping herself whole. 'I serve my Lord,' she said, when she had a throat.

Livilla gave Garnet a triumphant look. 'You were always such a rebel, lover. Can't you appreciate how glorious she is?'

'She can be as glorious as she likes as long as she swears an oath to me,' Garnet spat.

'Make us,' Livilla challenged. Eventually, Garnet walked away.

'He's going to kill her,' said Bree later, when they were alone in their room. 'He's going to kill all of us, and it'll be your fault.'

'I can't help what I am,' said Topaz.

'Livilla Lord Wolf was loyal before you came along,' the other demme said in a sulky voice. 'To all the Power and Majesties, even Velody, and she hated her *way* more than Garnet.'

'I think she wants something different now.'

'You make no sense,' Bree huffed. 'This is how it's supposed to be. Courtesi obey Lords, and Lords obey Kings, and the Power and Majesty rules them all, and we fight the sky. There's an order to it.'

Order. That was what Garnet said.

'It never made any sense to me,' said Topaz. 'Maybe it's time it all came crumbling down. Make something new.'

'It will be over Livilla's dead body,' Bree warned. 'She can't fight him. She never could. My old Lord, Priest, always said she was too soft for Garnet and one day it would get her killed.'

Topaz breathed deeply, trying to give herself over to sleep. 'Reckon she's stronger than you think she is.'

They had to hope so.

Later, when Bree was sleeping, Topaz awoke with the scent of Livilla's perfume and cigarette smoke wrapped around her like a thick curtain. Her mistress sat at the foot of her bed, legs crossed like a child.

'Topaz,' she said quietly, her eyes gleaming in the darkness, 'our Power and Majesty is not one to let these insults of ours stand. He will move against us soon.'

'My Lady,' Topaz said. 'Do you want us to leave this place? The lambs? Or all of us together?'

'Goodness, no!' Livilla seemed offended by the idea. 'These are my rooms. This is my territory. But we can't carry on like this. We need to find out exactly what it is the bastard has planned for Saturnalia. For leverage, you understand.'

Topaz understood that Livilla didn't like anyone knowing something that she did not. 'What do you want of me?'

Livilla smiled fiendishly. 'Poet is his weakness, sly thing that he is. And you are Poet's weakness. Find out what he knows.'

Topaz knew better than to point out how badly it had gone last time Livilla tried to use her as an instrument for her own political manoeuvres. She was uncomfortable with the thought that Livilla might not count that one as a failure. Still, she had promised to serve.

'As you wish, my Lord,' she muttered.

～

THE DAYLIGHT WAS harsh on Topaz's eyes after so long underground. It was strange to breathe the ordinary air, to walk the streets. She could run and hide, maybe sneak onto a train out of this place, or just walk and walk until her shoes gave out. Who needed shoes? She could be out of Aufleur by the next noxfall.

But the rest of the lambs were with Livilla, and Topaz didn't trust her to do right by them. She wasn't all that sure Livilla knew the difference between right and wrong, let alone anything else.

The Vittorina Royale it was.

It was a shock to her, the sight of the ruined theatre. She had half-forgotten what had happened that nox, and how bad was that? Bart had skipped her mind entirely; Bart and the cruel wedge of golden stone that pounded the breath out of him.

Topaz curled up on the pavement outside the ruin, allowing herself to feel utterly miserable. They were happy here. Their first chance of a real life. She stayed there for some time, until she felt a familiar presence approach.

'Hello, lamb.'

The Orphan Princel — *Poet* had found her, not the other way around. Himself stood there all fine in one of his pretty suits, with a scruffy boy and a sulky young man at his heels.

'What did you want us for?' Topaz blurted, staring at her hands. 'Why did you bring us here?'

Why had Bart been here, to be crushed by pieces of a city that didn't exist?

Himself rubbed his nose, pushing up his spectacles. 'Let me buy you a cake,' he suggested.

Only he could take such a ragged pair of imps into a fancy tearoom and be greeted by smiles and approving looks rather than, you know, being chased out with a broom.

It was called the Gardenia, and was all white walls, cane furniture and tiny teacups. Topaz slouched in her high-backed chair, feeling like a rat in the custard bowl. Her only consolation was that Poet's boy was as uncomfortable as her. His other courteso refused even to come inside, claiming he was guarding the exits.

'Livilla let you out for the day, did she?' Himself asked.

Tisane arrived in swan-shaped pots, with silvery net scoops to catch the leaves. Cakes came next, tiny feathery things made of air and sugar. Topaz didn't want to touch them.

'We go where we please,' she said stubbornly, staring at her knees. 'She don't lock us up.'

'She needs you close, though, doesn't she,' said Himself thoughtfully. 'Her secret weapon.'

Topaz didn't like the tone of his voice. '*You* could have had us if you'd paid us a moment of your time when everything was falling to bits.'

'I know that. As you rightly surmise, I regret it now.'

'Tough,' she muttered, rather liking the luxury of being rude to him.

The boy was eating, shovelling in cake after cake. There would be none left for her at this rate. Not that she wanted them.

'I remember what it was like,' Poet said. 'Being a courteso for the first time. Not wanting to leave the side of your mistress. Doing anything, forgiving anything, just to catch her approving smile.'

Topaz couldn't imagine him as a lamb. He was always so refined and sure of himself. 'Don't sound much different to how you are now, with him,' she observed. When Poet's sharp gaze fell upon her, she distracted herself by seizing a cake from under the hand of the boy and biting into it. Puff and sweet crumbs, oh yes. It tickled her throat and she fought not to cough.

'Not stupid, are you,' said Poet. 'I'm not stupid, either. Livilla wants to know what Garnet's up to. Were you expecting me to unfold like a stage trick?'

Topaz shrugged and took a mouthful of tisane, which was sticky and sour. She was no spy. Livilla knew that. Poet should, as well.

Poet leaned forward, hissing unpleasantly through his teeth. 'Tell your mistress this. I brought him back after she gave up on him. He's mine now.'

'I don't reckon anyone belongs to anyone in this Court of yours,' Topaz observed.

Poet folded his arms, glaring. 'Eat your cake.'

~

THEY RETURNED UNDERGROUND TOGETHER, Poet and his silent courtesi with Topaz, clambering down underneath the street. Topaz hated this part, the way that the tunnels smelled of cold earth and dampness. They emerged into a maze of underground shops and buildings. She realised she could see in the dark now. They always had lanterns in the Haymarket, so she hadn't noticed it, but the dark streets of the Shambles lit up under her new eyes, even in human shape.

'I'll walk you home,' said Himself, returning to his usual stately manners. 'Dangerous people around here.'

Topaz preened a little, letting flames lick around her ears. 'More dangerous than me?'

He laughed suddenly, looking her over. 'I'd forgotten that. You are dangerous, little lamb, because you don't look it at all.'

It was best that they underestimated her. Topaz put her fire away. 'I'll walk you home,' she said with mock gallantry.

Poet was nicer when he laughed, like a real person. She couldn't afford to like him. Livilla had plans for him, she reckoned, and anyone who got on Livilla's bad side had to be in big trouble.

'This is mine,' he said as they reached an old shop with a rusted sign showing cabbages and apples hanging in front of it. Soft orange light gleamed out of the upper windows. 'If ever you need to leave that wench of a Lordof yours, bring your lambs here. I'll look after you.'

'Better than last time?' Topaz said cynically.

Poet gave her an odd sort of smile. 'Better than last time,' he promised. Then he stilled and his eyes went strange. She could tell that he was no longer thinking of her at all. 'What's she doing back here?' he murmured.

He turned and went inside the shop without another glance in Topaz's direction, and his courtesi went with him.

She should run back to Livilla, but she'd learnt nothing yet. She followed them inside.

Topaz found Poet at the top of a narrow, dark staircase, one hand resting on the boy's shoulder. He shifted slightly to show that he knew she was there.

'You're safe here,' said a familiar voice. Garnet. She'd know him a mile off. 'They won't find you.'

'I'm so tired,' said a woman. Her voice was familiar, but only just. Topaz couldn't see her in the room.

'We should be looking after you better. Do you know how valuable you are?' Garnet's voice was like honey.

Poet stood still, as if he wanted to blend into the walls and floor. Topaz could barely feel his power, let alone see him among the shadows.

'The flames are getting hotter,' said the woman in a low, low voice. 'The heat in my skin. I can't stop it. I get so angry. I've never been this angry before. When I lose control... I don't want to hurt anyone.'

'You can't hurt me,' said Garnet. He was amused at the thought of it.

Topaz stared at her own hands, barely visible in the dark. Flames under the skin. Was there someone else like her?

'Come in, Poet,' Garnet said suddenly, his voice sharp. 'Don't hide in the shadows like an interloper. We are your guests.'

Poet stepped forward into the light of the room. 'Didn't want to interrupt,' he said. 'I'd hate Mistress Rhian to be startled. It's such a bore to clean up the mess afterwards.'

Rhian. The Seer, then. Livilla spoke of her dismissively.

'I have such terrible dreams,' Rhian said. 'Of Saturnalia, and a sacrifice. Are you really going to —'

'Enough,' Garnet commanded. 'I have no secrets from Poet, but there are some things that should never be spoken aloud. Not until the time is right.'

Topaz felt a shiver. Did he know she was there? She could feel the heat of his animor, and Poet's, shining out of that room like a beacon.

She had to get out of here. She turned, stumbling on the steps as she went.

Her human body was too big and clumsy for this. She felt a hand in the small of her back, pushing her hard down the stairs. She shaped herself into her real form, burning and cool-skinned, lizard feet scrabbling on the steps as she rushed down.

They were everywhere, Poet's people, all around her, leaping in from the darkness. She felt the shadehound snapping at her heels, the weasels sliding between her feet, and she burned brightly, her flames bursting free to keep them at bay, all of them.

None of them could touch her. She scattered into several lizard bodies, making for the door, but fierce silver threads held her back, wrapping around her feet and limbs, a different kind of burn tangling around her.

This one hurt.

She couldn't see, and there was no heat to the burn, just pain, pain, a tangled net of crossed threads binding her forms together. Topaz howled, slithering, biting, but it was too late.

She was trapped.

24

NEPTUNALIA

THE KALENDS OF SATURNALIS

DAYLIGHT

*T*here were many things wrong with the sight of Livilla on Velody's doorstep. Apparently she didn't spend the daylight hours hanging upside down by her ankles somewhere (or, to be fair, curled up in a basket).

Livilla wore a glittering cocktail dress that most definitely did not suit the occasion. She posed, as ever, like she expected a chorus line of men to carry her from place to place, lighting her cigarette and kissing her feet. She also looked worried. That was new.

'I suppose you'd better come in,' said Velody, standing aside.

She was alone in the house. Delphine was out doing something stupid to prove how over Macready she was, and Rhian was simply gone. The Seer came and went as she pleased, and while Velody would never get used to that, she had grudgingly accepted it. The world was different now. Everything was different. Rhian and Delphine had, after all, accepted what she'd had to do when she was Power and Majesty. This was no different, except that it was Rhian and it was all Velody could do not to wrap her in a quilt and drag her home from wherever she was.

Livilla graciously stepped into the kitchen, glancing around once as if wondering how people could actually live in such a hovel. 'I need your help,' she said.

'Shouldn't you ask your Power and Majesty for that?' Velody couldn't help saying. 'That's what he's there for.'

Livilla turned on her, unsmiling. 'My Power and Majesty has abducted a thirteen-year-old courtesa and is holding her prisoner in the cage. You know the cage I mean.'

Velody kept her face as composed as she could. 'What is it you expect me to do? Go to war against Garnet for the sake of one courtesa?'

'I expect you to live up to your promise,' Livilla snapped. 'Heliora believed in you. Ashiol believed in you. You were supposed to change everything for us, and what have you done so far?'

'You walked away from me,' Velody accused. 'You turned your backs and ran to Garnet the first chance you got, every single one of you. You left me bleeding on the ground. Why should I be loyal to you after that?'

'Because,' said Livilla with a shrug, 'you're nicer than me.'

Hard to argue with that.

'I can't fight Garnet alone,' Velody warned.

'Well, then,' said Livilla. 'We'd better get Ashiol back, hadn't we?'

~

VELODY HAD VISITED the Palazzo several times before, as the Duchessa's dressmaker. This was altogether different. She was passed from secretary to secretary, none of whom was prepared to answer her question about the whereabouts of the Ducomte d'Aufleur.

It was hard to tell whether the presence of Livilla helped or hindered. Her casual, moneyed air did make Velody feel more confident about being here, but on the other hand there was the possibility that Livilla might start screaming randomly or breaking things and that was enough to make anyone nervous.

'I don't see why Ashiol should be the one to live in a Palazzo,' Livilla drawled during one of the many gaps between secretaries. 'He doesn't appreciate it. Not in the least.' She moved to the window and let the thin muslin of the curtain swish over her hand. 'All these fine things. This would make a dreamy dress.'

Velody laughed suddenly. 'I thought I was the only one who wanted to strip this place of its furnishings and make them into frocks.'

They shared a startled look of mutual appreciation.

A young, rather stuffy factotum in a bright cravat stepped into the room and regarded Livilla with distaste. 'Demoiselles, I regret to inform you that the Ducomte is unavailable indefinitely.'

Livilla let the curtain fall from her fingers. 'Do I remember you? That spotty little face seems familiar.'

The factotum screwed up said face, which was indeed rather mottled. 'It would be for the best if you left, demoiselle. Immediately.'

'No,' Velody said quietly. The man had barely acknowledged her presence. 'I'm afraid we can't leave until we've spoken to the Ducomte.'

'The Ducomte is away,' said the factotum between his teeth. 'He accompanied my mistress to Bazeppe on a diplomatic mission.'

'Your mistress returned for the games,' said Velody, still

calm and reasonable. 'Word in the marketplace is that the Ducomte returned with her.'

'I cannot be expected to respond to what is said in the marketplace,' he sneered. 'The Ducomte is not available to you.'

Velody despaired, just for a moment. This ridiculous petty bureaucracy was so unnecessary. She needed Ashiol, and if this ridiculous man wouldn't give him to her, she was going to have to try another way.

She reached out blindly for the nearest object and her hand closed around the cool surface of a vase. Animor swelled up under her skin. Velody had barely used it for so long, but there it was, an old and reliable friend.

'You stand there, so smug and self-satisfied,' she said. 'As if keeping me from the Ducomte is some kind of achievement. The city could fall and burn if you don't help me. It's my job to save it.'

The glass of the vase crumbled into powder. The floor rippled under their feet. Plaster peeled from the ceiling. The glass-drop beads of the chandelier above their heads began to pop, one after another.

Livilla giggled.

'How... are you doing that?' said the factotum with a gulp.

Velody smiled. 'I very much wish to see the Ducomte. If you won't bring him to me, I'll have to call him. I think he'll recognise the tone of my voice.'

The window broke, one pane at a time. Livilla threw up her own animor and the glass hovered around her like a cloud of interesting flies.

'You could warn a demme before you do that,' she grumbled.

'No time,' said Velody, eyes on the factotum. 'I'm sorry, did you say you were bringing Ashiol to me right away?'

He turned and fled.

'Being thrown out of a Palazzo by a horde of lictors will be a new and exciting experience,' Livilla mused, clearing away her halo of broken glass with a flick of her wrist.

'At the very least,' said Velody. She sat down to wait.

Ten minutes later, the Duchessa d'Aufleur entered the room. She was alone. No secretaries or lictors to protect her. No Ashiol, either.

'Is this how you behave in your world, dressmaker?' she demanded of Velody. 'If you cannot have what you want, you break things like a child throwing a tantrum?'

'That's a pretty accurate summary,' said Livilla.

Velody stood up. 'I'm sorry your factotum was distressed, high and brightness. I'm sorry your room was damaged. But my cause is more important than correct paperwork and I trust you understand that.'

Isangell stared at them, every inch the Duchessa. She seemed more confident for her trip away. 'I understand that you believe your cause is just. But those of us who have to live in the daylight world do not take kindly to visitors who track mud and broken glass through our homes like ill-bred peasants.'

'I need Ashiol,' Velody said simply.

'You cannot have him,' said the Duchessa, just as simply. 'He did not return to Aufleur with me.'

This was a blow, but Velody rallied. 'When will he return? He is needed here.'

'My cousin is not returning from Bazeppe.'

The words fell like screechbolts around Velody. 'Never?' she asked, trying to keep her voice steady.

'He believes that the place is healthier for him, and I agree. I am to marry the son of the Duc-Elected of Bazeppe, and Ashiol will remain there as my emissary. An ambassador between our two cities.'

The Duchessa's voice was cool, as if she was dismissing

one of Ashiol's mistresses on his behalf. Livilla began to laugh, softly, in the background.

Velody felt hot and cold all over. 'He is needed here,' she said.

She couldn't take Aufleur back from Garnet without him, and what was her other option? To join with Garnet and take part in his ridiculous sacred marriage? No, that was beyond imagining.

'Ashiol will not survive Aufleur,' the Duchessa said firmly. 'I know that now. There is something about this city that tears him into pieces. He is glad to be useful elsewhere.'

'Useful?' Velody said furiously. Useful. As if anything was more important than Ashiol being here, fighting the sky, dragging Garnet from power, saving the souls of the Creature Court. Useful.

'Thank you for telling me,' she said finally, forcing her anger down, resisting the urge to flay the Duchessa's skin from her body. 'I won't bother you again.'

The Duchessa nodded. 'I enjoyed your dresses very much. I will recommend you to my friends among the Great Families.'

'So kind,' said Velody, and left the room in a rush, dragging Livilla behind her.

Ashiol wasn't coming back. It was just Velody, four wounded sentinels and the craziest of all the Lords. Oh, and a mad Power and Majesty who wanted to marry her.

'What do we do now?' Livilla asked as they walked away from the Palazzo. She smiled toothsomely at a passing maid-servant. 'If you want to burn the place to the ground, I know some people.'

'Not today,' said Velody, her mind working fast. 'We're going to have to do this without him.'

25

NEPTUNALIA

THE KALENDS OF SATURNALIS

DAYLIGHT

'*S*he's a spy,' said Macready. Of all the Court, the last one he was prepared to trust was this venomous bint.

'Dearling,' said Livilla, 'if you're going to accuse me of vile things, at least wash your hands first. I'm as trustworthy as they come.'

Macready and Kelpie had worked a shift at the docks today. Kelpie had rope burns on her palms from a careless moment, but otherwise fell into the life of a working cove far more comfortably than Macready. He was almost embarrassed by how long he railed against earning an honest living. He still drank, but not so much he had to hide it. It made a difference having Kelpie working at his side. Like maybe this new life made some sort of sense.

Now here they were, back in Velody's kitchen, talking about the Creature Court all over again. Livilla sat there all smug and full of herself. Crane was hunched against the back wall, looking about as happy to be there as the rest of them. Delphine managed to sit as far from Macready as possible without making it look deliberate. Clever lass.

He missed her, but not as much as he'd thought he would. Letting her go was a fecking relief in the end. Someone else's problem. Unless it was he who was someone else's problem now.

Velody looked the same as ever: calm and steady and expecting them all to jump when she snapped her fingers. Of course they would. She was still a King if not the Power and Majesty. Even if the old rules were no longer supposed to apply.

'Where's Rhian?' Delphine spoke up, the first thing she'd said since they'd all gathered together. 'Should we start without her?'

Velody looked uncomfortably at Livilla.

'The Seer is not on your side,' said Livilla. 'Just so you know.'

'Don't you mean "our" side?' Macready said sharply. There she was, proving his point already. 'Rhian wouldn't throw her lot in with Garnet. That's crazy talk.'

'Livilla's sanity is not the issue here,' said Velody with a sigh. 'I believe she's telling the truth. About Garnet, and her captured courtesa. About Rhian. Something bad is coming, we know that. It might be sooner than we thought.' She took a deep breath. 'It's time for me to take the city back from Garnet.'

Macready wanted to argue further about Rhian, but they had moved on. Fighting Garnet. He felt himself spark up at the thought of it, though practicalities took over soon enough.

'He has the other Lords,' he reminded her.

'I know,' said Velody. 'But I have the sentinels. Also, I

actually want to keep the city in one piece. I no longer know what Garnet's motivation is.'

'We don't have our blades,' said Crane suddenly. They all looked at him. He coloured a little, but continued. 'We don't have our blades. Ashiol is gone, and Garnet is crazy. We're right where we were before the Floralia.'

Macready gave him a light shove on the shoulder. 'We have Velody now, lad.'

Usually he and Kelpie took turns to be the cynic. It wasn't Crane's job.

'And that's enough, is it?' The lad sounded angry now. 'We're not Creature Court any more. We walked away. We chose that. It's not honourable to try to get it back. We lost the fight.'

Macready let his hand fall, staring at him. 'Got something better to do, have you?'

'It's all very well, this honour of yours,' remarked Livilla. 'But Garnet has none.'

'You were happy enough to throw your lot in with him until he stole one of your toys,' Kelpie said sharply.

Livilla's eyes went cold. 'And these are your precious sentinels, Velody? So very compassionate when it comes to the needs of a vulnerable child. Topaz is a person, not a toy. And she is *mine*.'

'Don't you act the high and brightness with us, love,' said Macready. 'You haven't been a saint over the years, have you? If there are lads and lassies in danger, it's because you brought them into the Court.'

'I saved them,' Livilla said huffily. 'Devils only know what Poet had in store for those lambs.'

'And you have such a history of keeping your courtesi safe,' Macready said, and watched hatred flash in her eyes. Good to know he still had the touch.

'You're not helping, Mac,' said Velody.

'And you're trusting too easily.'

'It's what I do. Are you still angry at me for bringing him back?'

'Apparently.' He sat back and folded his arms.

'I need Topaz home,' said Livilla, starting to sound desperate.

'Why?' broke in Kelpie. 'Because you're worried about her? Or because you need your secret weapon?'

Macready glanced at her. 'What are you on about, love?'

'Topaz. She's the salamander, isn't she?'

Macready blinked. That was a word he hadn't heard in a long time. 'Salamanders don't exist.'

'This one does. I've seen her. She controls fire. She can shape herself at any size. And she's loyal to you, Livilla.' Kelpie's voice shook only a little. 'She carried the poison cup directly to me. The one meant for Garnet.'

'Why do you let them ask all these questions?' Livilla flung at Velody. 'They're not our equals. They're dirt. No wonder you never get anything done.'

'I tried demanding that everyone follow me blindly,' said Velody. 'It didn't work out well. Now I listen. Is Kelpie right about this Topaz of yours?'

'She holds Garnet at bay with that little demme,' Kelpie said scornfully. 'He was afraid of her.'

'Exactly,' said Livilla. 'So who knows what he will do now he has her in that damned cage.'

'I know,' said a voice.

Macready looked up and saw Rhian. She seemed taller, her wide shoulders filling the doorway. She was blazing bright, as if she had swallowed sunlight and it shone out of her skin. The room smelled of smoke. Then she blinked rapidly and stumbled into the kitchen, herself again.

Delphine darted forward to help her. Macready hung

back so as not to get in her way. 'Quite an entrance,' he noted.

'What do you know, Seer?' Livilla demanded of Rhian. 'What has he done to her?'

Rhian pushed Delphine carefully away, keeping a distance between them. 'I know what Poet and Garnet have in mind for the salamander demme,' she said clearly. 'They're going to kill her on the Kalends of Saturnalis.'

'It's the Kalends today,' said Velody.

Rhian nodded. 'That's right.'

'You look pale,' Delphine accused. 'And all bony — have you been eating?'

Velody stood up slowly, looking at her friend. 'If you're here, it's because he wants you to be here. He wants you to tell me what they're planning to do.'

'That's not true,' said Rhian. 'He doesn't know I'm telling you his secrets.'

'How can you still be so naive? He's using you. He uses everyone. It's how Garnet operates.'

'As opposed to you, who only wants the best for us all? Saint Velody, the queen of everything.' With that retort, worthy of Delphine, Rhian turned around and walked right back out of the house.

'You can't let her leave,' Livilla insisted. 'Not if she can help us save Topaz.'

'I'll go,' said Macready, and darted out the door before anyone could debate it. He caught up with her in the alley. 'Rhian, lass! Don't huff off like that right when we need you.'

'Keep your distance, Mac,' she flung back at him, still walking. 'Velody's right. You can't trust me.'

'Hogshit,' he said, and took her hand in his. It was warm, but no one got set on fire. Good result. 'Why did you come back?'

'This is my home.'

'Haven't noticed you around much.'

'Do I have to defend myself to you, too? We were all so understanding when Velody got swept up in the Creature Court. Why has no one got the same patience for me?'

'To be fair, Delphine wasn't all that understanding with Velody...'

Rhian had no time for jokes. 'They both have their roles — Velody, Delphine. You, too. Why can't any of you see that what I'm doing is important?'

He kept holding her hand. 'No offence, my lovely, but it looks a lot like you're collaborating with the Power and Majesty who threw us all out of the Creature Court.'

'Threw you out?' Rhian snorted. 'Garnet can't do that. You did it to yourselves.'

'Will you listen to what you're saying?' Macready said in disbelief. 'Velody and Ashiol were *this* close to death.'

'Their choice,' she insisted. 'I don't have time for all this game playing and duels. The futures have no patience for such things, and neither does the Seer.'

Oh, it was never a good thing when anyone started talking about themselves in the third person.

'This is pretty much what it's always been like in the Court,' Macready said carefully.

'I know that. Do you think I don't know that? I know everything, Mac. I have a dozen voices in my head, all telling me the same things, and some days I think I'm going to explode with them all.'

Rhian let go of his hand and leaned against the nearest wall, her chest rising and falling with the effort of it. She looked not just weary but old. Far too old for a lass like her.

'I can see how that would not be easy,' Macready tried.

'You don't see anything. I have it all inside my head. And it's so important!'

'Why?' he asked gently.

'Because I'm the last Seer!' Rhian's voice rang out across the alley and she looked horrified. 'I don't think I'm supposed to tell anyone that. So many secrets... I can't keep them all straight.'

'What do you mean, love?'

'I mean, this is it. I'm the last one. There won't be any Seers after me. I don't know what it means — if the city will fall, or if I'm going to be doing the job forever, or what. But it's hard and it's heavy and I don't know what to do with it.'

She slid down the brick wall to the ground. Macready sat next to her. When he took her hand again, she let him.

'How long have you known?' he asked.

'Since the nox Garnet came back. Everything crashed in on me and I saw so much... I'm still trying to make sense of everything I saw. I came to Velody today because I saw that I did. I went to Garnet because I saw that, as well. I know everything I'm going to do, and it makes it easier in some ways. At least I don't have to make any decisions.'

'How do you know the future you've seen is a path and not a warning? You can't let it rule your feet and hands, lass. Fate is something to be fought against. You don't walk into it like a —'

'Like a lamb?' Rhian said cynically. 'I'm so tired. The voices in my head won't be quiet, even for a moment.'

She leaned against him, and he let her, wondering when she had last used touch as comfort.

'Can't help noticing you're not burning me to a crisp,' he said lightly after a while.

'I can control it more now, the heat,' she said. 'Garnet — being around him helped, I don't know why. Ashiol, too. I think because they're both so used to having so much power in their skin. I can almost... borrow control from them.'

'Can you see inside their heads?' asked Macready, alarmed at the possibility.

'Sometimes. I'm not sure if it's their thoughts or my anticipation of events.' Rhian sighed deeply. 'Two minutes from now, you're going to try to kiss me.'

'I wouldn't do that,' he protested, his cheeks flaming with embarrassment. Damned Seers.

Rhian smiled, as if his sense of honour made her sad. 'And yet.'

'What's going to change in two minutes?' Macready demanded. 'Are you planning to hit me with a rock or will I randomly take leave of my senses?'

'You do have a flattering tongue on you.'

'It's not that, love. You know it wouldn't be right.'

'What's right means so much to you. You're the last honest man in the world.'

'Oh, I hope that's not true,' he said fervently.

They sat together for some time. The silence wrapped around them like a blanket. Once Macready was sure that two minutes and then some had passed, he said, 'See? We can change the future.'

Rhian turned to him, her eyes so dark and melancholy though she was smiling. 'You can,' she said.

It took every ounce of control he had not to kiss her. The future was not going to make him its tool. He reached out, though, and touched her face. 'Fighting is the best thing we have. It keeps us sane and in one piece. Sitting still and letting the bad things happen — that's what kills your soul.'

'I lied,' Rhian said softly. 'You were never going to kiss me.'

He leaned in towards her.

A very definite sound of a throat being cleared filled the alley, louder than any thunderclap.

'Velody wants to know if you're coming back,' said Delphine. Her eyes were bright and cold.

26

NEPTUNALIA

THE KALENDS OF SATURNALIS

DUSK

*V*elody had never seen Rhian so sad. Scared, panicky, climbing the walls with misery, yes. But not this quiet melancholy.

Rhian stared at the tabletop, avoiding the eyes of them all as she explained the situation in a low voice. 'After Ashiol left the Court, Heliora refused to see the futures on Garnet's behalf. Once he gave up on her, he consulted every fortune-teller and card-reader he could find in the city. They all said the same thing: death by fire. That's why the salamander frightens him.'

'We can fight it,' Macready said determinedly. He was hovering protectively close to Rhian. 'We can beat him.'

Velody wondered what made him so sure.

'Just as long as we start by saving my lamb,' Livilla reminded them all.

'What about the other children?' Velody asked. 'They're safe from Garnet, aren't they?'

Livilla gave a little frown. 'He knows to keep his distance from my rooms.'

They all stared at her.

'Because the salamander lass is there to frighten him away?' Macready said finally. 'I'm pretty sure that threat doesn't work any more. What with him having her locked up.'

~

TOPAZ AWOKE IN A CAGE. She could still feel the harsh lines of the net that captured her. It had left a pale web of scars across her brown skin. Her hands shook as she levered herself up into a sitting position. Her foot brushed the side of the cage and she pulled it back with a yelp. More pain; she couldn't take more pain, not now.

She tried to bring the flames up, but her body hurt too badly for her to concentrate.

'Good morning, salamander. I trust you slept well?' said Garnet in an overly cheerful voice. 'Look, we brought some friends to keep you company.'

Topaz looked around, fearing the sight of the other lambs imprisoned alongside her. She only saw one: little Freddy, shackled to the wall. No skysilver near him, but his creature was a bear, so he couldn't change into many smaller forms in order to escape the cuffs. Her heart turned over when she realised how bruised he was.

'He runs with a limp,' she remarked aloud. 'Was he the only one you could catch?'

Freddy's face lit up. 'It was keen, Topaz,' he said, his chin crusted with blood from a split lip. 'Belinny's slingshots worked a peach. Told you it'd be worth stealing one of those shiny swords to break into bits.'

Topaz swallowed a startled laugh. Garnet's face looked hard and displeased.

Poet came in a short while later, several scratches on his arms and face. 'Little bastards,' he muttered. 'Shade almost lost an eye.'

'Maybe if you'd protected us lambs like you promised, we'd be on your side now,' Topaz yelled to him. No point in being polite.

'I wouldn't worry,' said Garnet, tending to Poet with a light cuff around the temples, then tugging him closer by his hair to examine the small wounds. 'They'll fall into line when their leader is sacrificed. The lake will run red with blood, and the lambs will either flee or serve me as they should serve the Power and Majesty.'

Topaz went very still. 'You have Lord Livilla?'

'You, Topaz,' called out Freddy. 'They want to sacrifice you! I told 'em we'd see 'em hanged first.'

Topaz shook her head quickly. 'Get word to the others, Freds. They're not to do anything foolish, not for me. Better you all run while you can.'

'You show great confidence,' said Garnet. 'The boy will tell his friends nothing unless they join you both in custody.'

Topaz stared hard at Freddy and then pushed him with her... Livilla and Bree called it "animor", though she thought of it as her fire. Freddy jolted as if he was about to throw up, then shaped himself into hundreds of tiny lizards. He skittered across the floor and was gone in an instant.

Poet and Garnet stared at Topaz in amazement. 'What the fuck was that?' Poet said.

'I made him into a salamander,' Topaz said boldly. 'Sacrifice me all you like. Do it twice if you want to. I'm not the only one, you know. We can all do it. I taught them.'

Poet and Garnet exchanged hurried words. 'I told you she

was valuable,' Poet urged. 'She's changing the way the Creature Court works.'

'Too late for that,' said Garnet. 'Keep her unconscious until the ritual. The sky needs blood.'

~

'SACRIFICE,' Livilla said bitterly. 'So wrong. We don't take part in *rituals*.'

Delphine stared at her in dislike. Why was this wretched woman even allowed in their house? 'That's just for the plebs and peasants of the daylight world, is it?'

'Frankly, yes,' sneered Livilla.

'Bollocks,' said Macready. 'The Creature Court can't scratch their backsides without some kind of fecking ritual. You bite and kiss and flirt with each other instead of baking honey cakes and tearing the guts out of an animal. It's all the same.'

Delphine was silent. She didn't need Macready's help in this conversation, and the last thing she wanted was to feel grateful to him. He had been kissing Rhian. She didn't want to think about that.

'Our ways aren't empty,' Livilla said sharply. 'They're to prove loyalty, to make our power stronger. Executing a barely blooded courtesa is beyond anything Ortheus would have done. Anything Garnet would have done before your Velody brought him back.'

'Oh ho,' said Macready with a laugh. 'Her fault, is it? That he doesn't fancy you any more?'

Livilla hissed between her teeth.

Delphine felt her own cheeks colour, damn it. Was that it? She'd thought they ended it because they had nothing left to give each other; because she was a fucking failure as a nurturing lover and he was a selfish wreck. Not because Macready liked someone else better.

Velody and Rhian returned from upstairs. Rhian was so pale you could almost see through her to the staircase beyond. How could Macready fancy her? She didn't even know what to do with a man. Though that was a lie. Anyone who could tumble with Ashiol Xandelian wasn't a shrinking violet. What else was a lie? How long had this Macready and Rhian thing been going on?

'Rhian doesn't know where the sacrifice will take place,' Velody said.

'So what are we going to do?' Crane asked.

Delphine made a rude noise. 'How can she not know? She saw it, didn't she?'

'I'm right here,' Rhian said mildly.

Delphine met her friend's gaze, finally letting herself feel something. Anger. Resentment. 'If you saw it, then you know where it happened.'

'No. I'm sorry. It doesn't work like that.'

'By all means, tell us how it does work.'

'Delphine,' Velody said firmly, 'stop being a bitch. We don't have time for it.'

'I saw Topaz's body falling into water,' said Rhian. 'Believe me, I've tried to see it more clearly. But that's all I know.'

'The sluice,' Kelpie said grimly. 'In the Haymarket. It's swallowed its share of dead bodies.'

'The lake,' Livilla suggested. 'Garnet's always had a thing about that lake.'

'Come to that, there's a whole fecking river wrapped around this city,' Macready said. 'We'll have to split up.'

Delphine attempted to put the thought directly into Velody's head that if she was paired with Macready she would push him into the river.

'I can keep an eye on the Haymarket without being spotted,' Crane volunteered. 'There's an old nest near there.'

Velody nodded. 'Take Delphine with you. Kelpie and Macready can stake out the lake. Livilla and I are best suited to search the river.'

She reached out one hand and Delphine watched in mild disgust as two small brown mice detached from the skin of Velody's arm. One ran to Delphine, and the other to Macready.

'If you see any sign of the sacrifice being readied, send it back to me,' said Velody.

Delphine looked at the mouse and nudged Crane. 'That can be your job.'

He grinned and scooped up the small creature. 'Fine. But you have to kill any of the Lords and Court we run across.'

'No problem,' she said sweetly.

~

DELPHINE HAD BEEN PERFECTLY fine with never setting foot in the Arches again. The wet, musty underground smell got to her every time. She'd had to burn several outfits because no amount of washing could get rid of it, and if she hadn't learnt the trick of washing her hair in mint and lemon, she would have been tempted to cut it even shorter.

Crane led the way down through winding tunnels (crawling; she would have been fine to avoid all future crawling as well!) to an alcove deep in the walls that surrounded the Haymarket.

'I didn't know there were any nests down here,' she said as they squeezed into the small space together.

'The Silver Captain made this one as an experiment,' said Crane. There was really just enough room for one person, and Delphine was practically on his lap. 'To see if he could do it without Garnet noticing. We would never have moved against him, but Cap wanted to gauge the Power and Majesty's moods so he could pick the right moment to plead for our blades back.'

Delphine shifted uncomfortably as a corner of rock dug into her back. 'Why didn't it work?'

'Cap died.'

'Oh. Sorry.'

Delphine felt like she couldn't turn around at the moment without putting her foot in her mouth. Though that was more acrobatic than she could contemplate right now. Crane smelled like wool and dried barley. The warmth of him was strangely comforting. Every time he shifted, even slightly, Delphine felt the planes of his body against hers.

There was one part where the wall was thin and they could actually see into the Haymarket. It was deserted.

'Are you glad to be doing this again?' Delphine asked, raising herself up on her toes to see better. The gap wasn't quite a window, and if she looked too closely everything blurred.

'I'm not glad that Garnet's trying to sacrifice a child.'

'That's not what I asked.'

Crane sighed, a deep and weary sound for such a young man. 'No, I'm not glad. Macready and Kelpie are born sentinels. It's been a struggle for them to live without it. But I... was getting used to the idea.'

'I know what you mean,' said Delphine.

'I would never walk away — I mean, I'm loyal to Velody. I left the Court because my duty was to her, and to Ashiol.'

She reached out to pat his shoulder and her hand closed around his upper arm. 'You don't have to explain anything. Velody's lucky to have you.'

'She doesn't want me,' he muttered.

Delphine remembered all those puppy-dog looks of his

whenever Velody entered a room. The poor dearling. Velody's taste in men was kinglier than Crane.

'I know what that's like, too,' she said.

Crane shifted and she felt his woollen cloak rustle against her. She was wearing hers, too, for the first time in months.

'You?' he sounded amused. 'I thought you could have anyone you wanted. You got Macready easily enough.'

'And lost him all over again.' That came out more bitter than she had intended. She wasn't going to dwell on Macready. Not now, not ever. 'How long do we have to hide out down here?'

'Hours,' Crane said. 'Until we're sure the sacrifice won't happen here, or we hear from the others.'

Hours jammed together like dormice in a pot, feeling sorry for themselves. No, that wouldn't do at all.

'We'll have to find something to do to pass the time,' she said.

~

DUSK WAS FADING INTO NOX. Velody glided high over the river, her chimaera form a dark shadow among many. Occasionally she caught a glimpse of Livilla in her creature form, or a shadow she thought was Livilla. The Wolf Lord was dangerously good at avoiding being seen, even if you knew to look for her.

There were a few spots here and there along the river that were secluded enough to stage a sacrifice, but there was no sign of Garnet or the rest of the Court at any of them. Perhaps they'd been wrong. Perhaps Rhian had misled them, or made a mistake. A body, falling into water... It could be anything, anywhere.

Ashiol was gone. He was really gone. He hadn't just left the Court that exiled him all over again; he left Velody behind to clean up the unholy mess that remained of the Court. She still couldn't comprehend it, that he willingly stayed away. What was in Bazeppe to keep him there?

The new moon was barely a sliver of light in the sky. A shadow flitted past and Velody almost ignored it. But no, there it was again. A bat. It swooped over the city then plunged down, south of her position. Towards the lake.

Velody turned in the air to look for Livilla, and saw the silhouette of two slender wolves streaking through the sky above her.

Had Warlord let himself be seen deliberately? Was he choosing his old loyalties to Livilla, or even Velody, over Garnet? Or was it a trap?

Velody sped as quietly and swiftly as she could over the city. Time to find out.

~

DELPHINE AND CRANE were wedged into the small nest for hours. Or maybe it only seemed that way. The Velody mouse had not only failed to pass on any exciting messages but was now asleep in Crane's pocket. All right for some.

Delphine tensed as pain jolted through her calf. 'Mmmph,' she said, trying not to cry out.

'What's wrong?'

'Cramp. Owwww.'

'Shhh.' He moved against her, and they both jostled for space as he tried to help her stretch it out. 'Better?'

'No, ow!' she said crossly, though it did feel better when he did that. 'Harder.'

Crane rubbed her calf until the knots of tension went away.

'Okay, fine,' Delphine grumbled. 'You're good at that.'

'An old trick.'

He struggled to straighten up again and their bodies pressed clumsily together. Oh, to hells with it. Delphine was bored and depressed and pissed off at Macready, and what else did they have to do? She reached out and took his hands in hers, steadying both palms against her hips.

'What are you —' Crane started to say, and fell silent.

'Shh,' she said unnecessarily, and untucked his shirt, brushing her fingers over the bare skin of his stomach. He wasn't that young. If Velody was going to be all fussy about it, that was her problem. Delphine was far more inclusive in her tastes.

Crane stood very, very still as she explored him with her fingertips, up his chest and then down over the taut muscles of his stomach, to the line of his belt.

'If it'd make you feel better,' she said softly, 'you can still keep a lookout while we do this. I'm not precious.'

It was warm, very warm, in the nest. Delphine lifted Crane's hands under her own shirt and he got the idea right away, tugging her breastband up and groping her gently. A little too gently, but she could work on that.

They made the touching last longer than she had intended. A frig like this should be fast and frantic, a swift transaction, but they had time to kill. She lingered once she had his trews open, stroking and tugging him into hardness.

Crane was good at staying quiet. Muffled sounds only, when she did something he liked. He gave as good as he got, too. Young though he was, this wasn't his first time. Delphine found herself twisting on his fingers, gasping and muffling her own cries against his cloaked shoulder as he curled into her.

Breeches. Why had she worn breeches? She wasn't even a proper sentinel, and one of her own frocks would have been so much easier to slide up over her hips to let him inside.

Obviously the sentinel uniform wasn't designed for knee-tremblers. A shame, really.

They managed, peeling clothes back just enough to allow access, and taking the necessary time to get the angle right. Then he was fucking her, harder than she'd expected, against the rough wall of the nest, and neither of them paid the remotest attention to keeping watch.

It was her turn to muffle his cry as he came inside her, and she kept her hand pressed against his mouth as the heat surged through her all over again. Damn. She had needed that.

They stayed quiet for a long time afterwards, just breathing and touching, before they began to reassemble their clothes.

'Still quiet out there?' Delphine asked.

'No sign of anyone,' said Crane, shifting around so he could see out of the thin patch again.

'Good,' she said, buttoning up her trews. 'So let's go and steal our swords back while the going's good.'

He looked at her in astonishment, and then grinned like the sun emerging bright and fierce from behind a cloud. 'That is an excellent plan.'

27

NEPTUNALIA

THE KALENDS OF SATURNALIS

NOX

*I*t wasn't going to happen at the fecking lake.

Macready was certain of it. The place was full of revellers celebrating the Neptunalia. The water was covered in lanterns and paper boats, and its shore crowded with families, sailors and hot-bean sellers. Daylight folk all, and no room for the Creature Court.

'Freezing our balls off, and for what?' he grumbled.

Kelpie solemnly placed a paper admiral's hat on his head. 'Enjoy yourself, Mac. How often do we get to come to something like this?'

'Fecking waste of time.'

She tossed a bag of hot chestnuts at him. 'But it's not. We know it's not. The daylight festivals have a purpose — they keep the city strong so it can heal from the battles every morning. Without them, we'd be royally screwed, so suck it up and eat a nut.'

Macready hated chestnuts. Bits got stuck in his teeth.

'We'd be better off joining the others underground. Garnet's not going to sacrifice the lamb in front of all these daylight folk.'

Music burst across the lake. A parade of children dressed as fish danced along the pier, following a boy who carried a shining pearl on the end of a fishing rod. Flute-demmes and drummers heralded the arrival of the Sea-father, decked out in gleaming blue robes and a false silver beard.

'I think,' Kelpie said faintly, 'we need to stop making assumptions about what Garnet is capable of.'

The Sea-father stood up, shaking a staff from which hung many strings of shells. 'Happy Neptunalia!' he roared, and the crowd hollered at him, throwing ribbons and sweetmeats into the lake.

Holy fecking saints and devils, *Garnet* was playing the Sea-father, right here in front of the whole mother-fecking city.

'Call Velody,' Macready hissed.

Kelpie spoke urgently to the mouse she carried, before sending it skittering off into the streets.

'Bring forth the fish,' the Sea-father boomed. Several daylight folk dressed as sailors carried a large platter on which a huge moulded-paper fish lay as if ready for a feast. It was traditional to slash at the fish with a sword until it emptied its belly, scattering more ribbons and sweetmeats and nuts into the crowd.

As they watched the fish being winched up to the roof of the floating pavilion, Macready noticed that it was, in fact, large enough to hold a small person.

And it was twitching.

VELODY REACHED the edge of the crowd at the Lake of Follies

at about the same time as Livilla. 'Perhaps we got it wrong,' she said, seeing how many daylight folk were about. But, no. She could feel Garnet nearby, his animor alight and pulsing with energy.

Livilla smiled viciously. 'Trust him to make a spectacle of himself. Silly boy. He does so like to be the centre of every-one's attention.'

Macready and Kelpie ran over to them, looking like a couple of Neptunalia revellers with lopsided paper hats perched on their heads.

'The pavilion,' Kelpie got out.

'He's using the festival for his own ritual, sick bastard that he is,' Macready added.

Velody didn't see it at first, but then heard Livilla suck in a breath as she looked at the floating pavilion.

It was just like every other Neptunalia. The pavilion was hung with blue and white ribbons and paper fish. Children were dancing in costume. The Sea-father held his staff and sword, playing up to the crowd. But the sword gleamed in a way that was seductive and familiar.

'That's a skysilver sword,' Velody said.

'It's my fecking sword,' Macready said grimly. Delphine and Crane came running up, out of breath and grinning like idiots.

'There was no one in the Haymarket,' said Crane.

'We got the blades,' Delphine added, half-crashing into Velody as she came to a halt.

'We couldn't find your sword, Mac,' Crane said apologeti-cally. 'Or mine.' He handed Kelpie's skysilver sword and knife to her, and she slid them into their empty sheaths.

Macready gave Crane a hard look. 'Are you wearing the Silver Captain's blade?'

'We're at war, aren't we?' Crane said, looking abashed. 'No point in being precious about it.' He handed Macready's knife to him, and an unfamiliar sword with the hilt wrapped in white leather. 'I found Ilsa's for you. You were about the same height. It's better than nothing, isn't it?'

Macready grumbled, but took the sword.

Livilla let out a cry and ran towards the lake.

'Oh, hells,' said Velody, and followed her.

'Garnet!' Livilla screamed.

The Sky-father turned and waved cheerily. 'Hello, lover.'

'Stop this right now!' said Livilla, sounding more in control than ever before. Velody hadn't known she had it in her.

'But it's the Neptunalia,' said Garnet from behind his beard and blue hood. 'Have to have the Neptunalia.' He waved and smiled and flourished Macready's sword. 'Makes the crops grow, and the rain fall, and the fish bite.'

'Kill the fish,' the crowd started shouting. Because they were idiots.

'This is it, then,' said Livilla, her voice dripping with disdain. 'This is the kind of Power and Majesty you choose to be. You would murder children for your own entertainment. What happened to you, Garnet? Do you hate us all so much?'

He tilted his head to one side, as if she had said something terribly quaint. 'Did you only just notice, sweetling?'

'You take everything and give back nothing in exchange,' she yelled at him. 'You dared to make me think that I couldn't take power, that I was unworthy of you. You think you are so much better than all the others who went before you, but you're not. Just another paper soldier making children cry and bleed.'

'Pretty words,' Garnet said, and the air around him seemed to grow colder. 'I'll enjoy making you regret them, Liv.'

Velody joined Livilla at the lake's edge. *Don't do this*, she sent directly to Garnet. *Don't make me stop you.*

Garnet laughed and grinned around at the crowd. *Go ahead and try, little mouse. You haven't seen a fragment of what I can do.*

Nor you, me.

You don't have Ashiol to hold your hand any more.

I'll cope without him. You, though — they stopped believing in you when you sent him away, you do know that, right? They didn't want you back.

Shut up. You can't hurt me. I'm the Sea-father. All powerful, all wise. The fish is going to die, wriggling on her little hook.

No. She's really not.

Velody stepped out onto the water. It held under her feet. She walked steadily across the surface of the lake, her ragged grey dress blowing around her legs in the breeze.

The crowd, knowing a spectacle when they saw it, clapped and cheered.

Garnet gave a cry of triumph and malice, and thrust the skysilver sword directly through the body of the fish.

Velody and Livilla stopped pretending at that point and flew directly at him, both their bodies colliding hard with his. Animor smacked against animor with a sound like thunder rolling across the sky. Livilla punched Garnet once in the face and he struck her back, his power lashing out in tendrils.

The Sea-father's court threw off their disguises as fishermen and mermaids, revealing Poet, Warlord, Lennoc, and their courtesi. They joined the fight, dragging Velody away from Garnet.

The sentinels crashed along the pier, swords and knives flashing, and the Creature Court turned on them with snarls and bites.

Velody swiped Lennoc across the eyes with a flash of animor and threw herself at Garnet again, knocking him to the unsteady floor of the pavilion.

Delphine swept past them both, her sword shining like a beacon, and made it to the swinging, broken paper fish. Crane was with her, helping her lift the fish down. They broke it open and lizards poured out of it, some shiny with blood, others trailing smoke behind them.

'You really think I give a frig about the salamander wench?' Garnet gasped with laughter as he rolled on top of Velody, his power hot and vicious against her. 'It's not a true sacrifice unless I'm giving up something that I love.'

~

TOPAZ COULDN'T BREATHE. The heat under her skin felt like it had to burst out somewhere, anywhere. Water pressed around her tiny, scrabbling bodies and there was pain, so much pain everywhere. It hurt worse than the net, worse than the cage. They had forced her to swallow a potion of some kind that made her dizzy and slow. She had expected to die.

Lizards couldn't swim. These lizards couldn't, in any case. She shaped herself back into human form with the last of her strength, and hands grabbed her, pulling her out of the water.

'She's still bleeding,' said a woman's voice, and then something hot and salty pressed inside Topaz's mouth. She only realised later that she was drinking blood.

Blood! These people were crazy. Life had been so much better when she was poor and living on gruel; at least no one had ever filled her mouth with blood. It tasted good, that was the worst of it, and she found herself lapping, drinking deeply.

The burning sensation in her stomach stopped. The heat died away. Panicked, she stared at the two who had saved her. Sentinels. The sentinels who had walked away. 'What did you do?'

'The skysilver wound wouldn't heal without it,' said the man, taking back his bleeding wrist and wrapping it tightly with a bandage from his pocket.

Topaz had no animor. This was worse than the drug. She tried to shape herself back into salamander form, but couldn't. 'Take it back. Take it back!'

'It's all right,' the blonde woman said, as if Topaz was somehow stupid. 'We have our blades, we'll protect you.'

'But who's going to protect her?' Topaz wailed.

'What do you mean?'

Another voice broke in over them, one Topaz would know with her eyes closed, even here in the dark with her animor quiet inside her body. Poet, the Orphan Princel. He stood on the bank of the lake, looking down at the three of them.

'Topaz was never the sacrifice Garnet wanted,' said Poet sadly. 'She was the bait.'

28

NEPTUNALIA

THE KALENDS OF SATURNALIS

*N*ox Some of the crowd had fled when the battle began between the Creature Court. Others still watched, as if they thought it was some kind of organised spectacle. They ate chestnuts, or drank bean syrup from paper boats.

Velody, bruised and battered from her fight with Garnet, found herself held down by Warlord and Lennoc, each of them pouring all of the animor they had into keeping of her arms pinned to the floor of the pavilion.

'What are you doing?' she demanded hoarsely. 'This isn't right. Did you know he meant to do this when you pledged your loyalty to him?'

'That's how loyalty works,' said Lennoc. He could barely see after what she had done to him in the fight, but his hands were still strong and steady. 'We serve Garnet, whatever he chooses to do. He is our Power and Majesty.'

'I could tear you to pieces,' she threatened.

She could, even with their power so directed in keeping her down. She could go chimaera. She could make their animor burst out of their bodies. She was a King and they were Lords.

'If you were willing to hurt us, you would have done it by now,' said Warlord in that rich voice of his. 'You are weak.'

Velody could feel her animor uncurl within her body. It was desperate to hurt, slash, kill, to be free. She could barely contain it. Maybe she should just let it go. That was what Ashiol would do. She had done it before, allowed the animor to make the decisions for her.

She had pledged never to be like Ashiol; and besides, he was a coward and he wasn't here.

Somewhere, Livilla screamed. Velody knew it was Livilla: she could feel the wolf-animor in the pain and outrage of the cry. The crowd began to protest, muttering amongst themselves. The Sea-father's script was no longer familiar to them.

Garnet rose slowly above the lake pavilion, glowing bright like a Lord. The blue hood of his costume had fallen back and his beard had slipped away into the waters of the lake. He held Livilla by the throat, the skysilver blade gleaming as he threatened her with it.

'What, such distress?' he roared at them all. 'I thought you people were used to sacrifices. You love to cut the entrails out of sheep and deer and poor little birdies. The blood runs thick across the floor of this fucking city. How is this any different?'

'He's going to kill her,' Velody whispered. There was no bluff about Garnet's stance, or the hold he had on Livilla. 'I thought you loved her,' she snapped at Warlord. 'How can you let him do this to her?'

Warlord's grip on Velody loosened, his animor fluctuating a little. 'Garnet loves her too. He's trying to scare her into joining us.'

'Because Garnet has always been so kind to those he

loves!' Garnet loved Ashiol so much he'd almost killed him. Velody could see that memory in Warlord's eyes. 'He will *kill her*,' she repeated.

'She betrayed him,' Warlord said, but Velody felt another waver in his animor.

'He took her courtesa, threatened to sacrifice her to the sky. He set Livilla *up* to betray him. She can't change sides with no air to breathe, even if she wants to.' Velody sent one sharp pulse of animor stabbing out at Warlord, testing his grip, and then at Lennoc. 'Get the hells off me. No one has to die this nox.'

Garnet laughed from where he floated in the air above them, a long and melodious sound. 'Do you think I can't hear you, little mouse? You're so very wrong. Someone does have to die. It's part of the deal.'

What deal? she sent silently at him, but he didn't reply.

'What deal?' she demanded of Warlord and Lennoc. Both of them shook their heads, not willing to speak.

'He's our Power and Majesty,' said Warlord.

'He's a fucking lunatic,' declared Velody.

'The two concepts are not exclusive.'

Lennoc snorted. 'We're all fucking lunatics,' he said. 'But we swore an oath to him. We can't go back on that.'

'You swore an oath to me,' she said furiously. 'You wanted to change the Creature Court. Did you really want *this*?'

Delphine and Crane hurried over, half-carrying a young demme between them.

'Topaz says she was never the sacrifice,' blurted Delphine.

Crane had wrapped his cloak around Topaz but she shook it off impatiently. 'It was always Lady Livilla he wanted,' she gasped out. 'Please — my animor — it's my job to protect her! You have to give it back.'

'If the sentinels gave you their blood, there's nothing else we can do until it wears off,' said Velody.

'The sentinels were *supposed* to give her blood,' said Warlord. 'Getting the salamander out of the equation was Garnet's first thought.'

Saints, Velody had been so busy trying to find Garnet, she had forgotten to think like him. He really was this crazy. She freed herself from Lennoc and Warword with a single burst of power, and took to the sky, flying towards Garnet and Livilla.

Stay back, little mouse, or I'll burst her head open, Garnet sent into her thoughts.

I don't believe you. It's trick after trick. You want something from me, or you wouldn't have gone to all this trouble.

It's not always about you, Velody. This city is on the edge of falling into the sky and I'm the only one who can save it.

Talk to me. I can help you. We should be working together.

No. Look at them. They followed me until you turned up, batting your eyes and making them distrust me all over again. I'm the only one who knows how to save us.

How? How do you know?

Livilla struggled out of his grip just enough to speak. 'He made a deal with them,' she snarled. 'Isn't it obvious? He made a deal with the dust devils.'

Velody didn't know what to believe. 'Is this true?' she asked Garnet.

He laughed again. 'Your little Seer friend isn't the only who hears voices in her head. I know the truth. I have always known. They tell me what we have to do to save the city, and it's *hard*, and there will be sacrifices. Real blood-draining, bodies-falling sacrifices. But we will be free.'

'How many sacrifices will they ask for before it's not worth it any more?' Velody demanded.

Garnet smiled. 'It's always worth it.' He looked past Velody, past all of them, to a lone figure at the edge of the lake. 'Listen to her, if you won't listen to me.'

Rhian stood there wrapped in a heavy green shawl, looking sad. 'Bazeppe will fall before the Ides of Saturnalis, and Aufleur will follow,' she said.

'No!' Delphine yelled at her. 'That's just one of your stupid futures — it doesn't mean anything.'

'What do we do to change it?' Velody asked.

'We can't change it,' Rhian said in an awful voice devoid of emotion. 'That is the future; it's all the futures.'

'But there must be something we can do.'

'Something I can do,' said Garnet sweetly. 'Ashiol's gone, and you walked away, Velody. I'm the one who's going to save us from our fate. Starting with the first sacrifice.'

He released Livilla, letting her hover under her own power for a moment, and slashed at her with the sword faster than she could move.

There were screams. Velody felt numb as the blood arced through the air.

Livilla looked startled, a line of red across the front of her throat. Then she fell, her body crumpling as it hit the lake.

'So much prettier when she's silent,' said Garnet with satisfaction.

Animor washed over them all, thick and rich and real. It tasted like wolf and perfumed smoke, and Velody was giddy with the power of it before she remembered to be sickened. Saints, he had done it. Sacrificed someone that he loved, again. How long had he been listening to the voices from the sky?

Light poured from the lake in a bright burst, turning the sky blue with its intensity before the nox closed in once more. Livilla was powerful, and the taste of her lingered in the air.

Warlord lay on the pavilion, his head down and his body still, grieving even as he quenched the lost Lord. Velody could see the strands of power that he dragged into himself, as if wanting to keep as much of Livilla as he could.

They were all quenching her, and there was so damned much of it. How had Livilla not become a King?

Garnet's laughter fell over them all, and he took off across the sky with trails of Livilla's animor dragged in his wake.

Velody couldn't breathe for a moment. She didn't know what to feel. She watched Macready wade across the lake to reclaim his sword, and she was still numb.

Macready called to Kelpie and Crane and the three of them ducked under the water, searching. Macready came up with a string of pearls, finally, but no body.

'There's nothing to bury,' he said flatly. 'The lake took her.'

Velody still felt nothing.

Topaz started to scream. She was a small figure, sodden and wrapped in Delphine's cloak. She had no power and presence in this sad scene, muffled as she was by sentinel's blood. Still, she screamed. Poet was by her side, and Delphine, but Topaz shoved them both away from her.

'You, this is your fault,' she sobbed at Poet. 'You let him do this. You were supposed to protect us!'

Poet looked at her, dazed, and she smacked him on the shoulder, in the stomach, crying so hard she could hardly breathe.

Delphine tried to touch the child, who slapped her hand and bared her teeth. 'Don't touch me. None of you. You think you're so special! Not one of you is any use. What do you do but rip at each other and show off all the time? I hate you all!'

She ran away into the darkness, and was gone.

Velody walked into her kitchen. The sentinels trailed

after her, squelching in their wet clothes. Only Rhian
was dry.

'That little demme was right,' Velody said. 'We're useless.
We can't even protect...' She pressed her hands to her mouth,
not sure if she was going to throw up.

'None of us liked Livilla,' Macready said gruffly. Kelpie
elbowed him. 'What? Afraid of the truth? She annoyed the
hell out of all of us. You especially. She was a crazy bitch who
didn't give a damn about any of us —'

'Shut up,' snapped Delphine. 'Just shut up. Is that how
you'll talk about me when I'm dead?'

'I'm sure I could think of a few more original words.'

'No one else is going to die,' said Velody.

Macready laughed unpleasantly. 'Do you not listen to our
Seer? We're all dying. Bazeppe first; and when the clock-
makers have vanished off the face of the earth, it's our turn.'

'Why don't you have a drink?' Delphine said sweetly.
'Make it all go away.'

'Oh, you're a fine one to judge,' Macready said, his voice
rising. 'A real expert on making the pain go away, aren't you,
lass?' He leaned in towards her, his face hard. 'I can still smell
him on you,' he hissed.

Delphine looked as if he'd hit her. 'I'm not the one who
went looking elsewhere,' she replied.

Velody didn't have time for this, for any of it. She didn't
care about the stricken expression on Delphine's face, and
she really didn't want to know why Crane looked like he'd
been caught stealing from the poor box, or why Rhian was
refusing to look at anyone.

She could feel their emotions, all of them, prickly and
savage, beating against her skin, and she wanted none of it.
She stretched her back, so tired that her body protested even
that movement. She wanted to break into a thousand pieces,
run away from this rabble of sentinels and sleep the calm,

unhurried sleep of a heap of mice. But there was work to do. Always work to do.

'I'm going to Bazeppe,' she said. They didn't hear her at first, so she raised her voice. 'I said, I'm going to Bazeppe. I'm going to find Ashiol and bring him home. And... if we save the city, then that future is broken and Aufleur will be safe.'

'No,' said Macready, turning away from Delphine, returning to thoughts of duty. 'It doesn't work that way, lass. You're needed here.'

'To stand by and watch as Garnet murders the Court, one by one?' Velody asked. 'I don't think so. We need *Ashiol*.'

'What the hells do you think he can do that you can't?' Macready asked, his voice cracking. 'He abandoned us. He walked away from all this —'

'We all walked away,' Velody snapped at him. 'We all gave up. I can't fight Garnet without Ash.'

'Ashiol doesn't want to fight Garnet.' Kelpie spoke up from the doorway, breaking her usual stony silence. 'He doesn't think he can.'

'Well, he's better than that,' Velody declared. 'We can do anything, we can survive this, we only need something to believe in. Something bigger than our own petty concerns. If you can't believe in me, then... I'll create something you can believe in. For that, I need Ashiol.'

Garnet had given her the answer. He had worked so damned hard to keep her and Ashiol apart.

'The sacred marriage,' said Crane, and his eyes met Velody's. Her heart turned over a little at the tone in his voice — as if he was working so hard not to be hurt.

'Perhaps,' she said. 'I don't know. But I have to try. If Ashiol and I working together frightens Garnet so much, it's the only thing *left* to try.'

'I'll come with you,' Kelpie said unexpectedly. 'If you want me.'

Velody nodded. If there was a musette melodrama breaking out between Macready and Delphine, Delphine and Crane, Macready and Rhian, then Bazeppe looked like a pretty fine option.

'Thank you,' she said to Kelpie. 'I would be glad to have you.'

PART IX
THE STAGEMASTER

29

LOYALTY

'Poet,' whispered a voice, down low. 'Poet, wake up.'

Nearly three years had passed since the death (and then the other death) of Tasha. The other cubs matched Garnet's Lordship in the months that followed his rise in status, frighteningly fast, as if it were a competition between them.

A year ago, Garnet became a King, and then Ashiol, and then Lysandor.

More recently, Ortheus and Argentin were killed in a skybattle that ended a hair's breadth before the city was eaten whole.

I was sixteen, and Garnet... Garnet was Power and Majesty.

My bed was in the cupola up high in Priest's cathedral. I didn't want to go to him; at first I refused to choose another Lord when Garnet became a King. But a courteso can't survive on his own in the Court. Sometimes stupid loyalty really is stupid. I was still skinny and not the most powerful; the other courtesi thought they could frighten me into choosing their various Lords as a master. I was beaten bloody more than once.

Eventually, Garnet snarled at me, bit me lightly on the back of the neck, leaving marks. 'I can't protect you now, ratling. Old oaths don't matter.'

'I don't want to be your courteso,' I blurted to Priest when I placed myself at his feet. 'When I'm a Lord, I don't want to have courtesi under me. It's a stupid system. It doesn't work, and it only brings... pain.'

Priest blinked slowly, then lit a cigar. 'You stay out of my way, boy, and I'll stay out of yours.'

We got along all right, after that. He had no interest in frigging me, and I had no interest in frigging his other courtesi, all pretty young demmes.

Six years in the Creature Court and I was still alive; that made me a veteran.

We weren't a family any more, not as we had been. The Kings lived separately: Lysandor with Celeste in the Eyrie; Ashiol in his own territory, the museion; Garnet in the Power and Majesty's rooms above the Haymarket. Livilla was there too, in the apartments below which she shared with Mars, a courteso she inherited from Ash. She liked to play the part of consort to Garnet's Power and Majesty, but they fought dreadfully sometimes, and everyone knew she fucked Ashiol any time she could. It didn't seem to bother Garnet, but then Ashiol went to *his* bed on a regular basis, too.

'Poet,' the voice hissed again.

I muttered in complaint, but someone shoved my spectacles onto my face. I blinked until he came into focus. Lysandor.

'What do you want?' I asked.

He looked miserable and tense. 'I wanted to give you a chance. I know you have Priest to protect you, and he probably thinks he can —'

'What are you on about?'

'We're leaving. Me and Celeste.'

The second he became Power and Majesty, Garnet stopped hiding his dislike of Lysandor's attachment to Celeste. He hated any loyalties the Court had with each other outside formal oaths. If you play the tyrant, it's easy to assume everyone's out to get you.

'Leaving where? You're not abandoning the Court?'

'We have to go,' Lysandor said miserably. 'Garnet's getting more unstable, don't you see that?'

'You swore an oath,' I said furiously. 'Do you want to end up like Tasha?'

'I want to get out of this fucking city with my head still attached to my body,' Lysandor flared.

I sat up, peering at him in the near-darkness. 'Go. Don't tell me any more. If he finds out I knew, he'll kill me.'

'Is a monster like that really worth your loyalty?'

Anger flashed inside me. No one insulted Garnet to my face, not even one of my oldest friends. I wouldn't accept it.

'You loved him before I did,' I flung at Lysandor. 'You belonged to each other before I came along. How can you give up on him now?'

'Celeste is pregnant.'

Now that was a shock. 'She can't be. That doesn't happen.'

Livilla was convinced a year back that she was pregnant to Ashiol, but it came to nothing, and that was the closest thing to a scare anyone in the Creature Court had in years. Whatever it was that fuelled our power kept us barren, for the most part. Almost all the Lords and Court (and Kings) took the lack of pregnancies as an excuse to act like the animals they were, bedding anything that moved.

'I don't know,' Lysandor whispered. 'It's not supposed to happen, but it *has*. So don't you see? If Garnet finds out, it'll be one more thing someone has that he doesn't. He'll kill her because of it, or me, or both of us.'

'It won't be that bad,' I said, because my first reaction was that it couldn't be. But he rolled his eyes at me and I had to admit he was probably right. 'You didn't tell anyone else about this, did you?'

Lysandor hesitated. 'I wanted to give Livilla a chance to escape, too.'

I stared at him in horror. 'For fuck's sake, we're not lambs any more. She'll never take your side against Garnet. She'll tell him!'

Screams cut through the silence outside. Livilla had already spilled the news.

Lysandor shaped himself into lynx form and hurtled down the spiral staircase. I pulled on breeches and shirt and followed him, meeting Priest on the stairs.

'Such a commotion, dear boy,' Priest said, his tone not quite light enough to belie its warning tone.

'Garnet's about to slaughter Celeste, my Lord,' I said breathlessly.

'Well, then. Let us proceed towards the show at a reasonable pace.'

Loyalty is a terrible thing. These were my friends, my family, but the only people I technically owed allegiance to were Priest Lord Pigeon, and our Power and Majesty.

We proceeded at a reasonable pace, by Priest's standards.

By the time we got there, Celeste stood up to her knees in the canal that ran through the Haymarket, blood everywhere, her white dress soaked through with that awful redness. She had always been the cool, intelligent one: sarcastic, reserved. Now, she screamed like a wild thing, her hair exploding around her into bright white feathers. Livilla's wolves nipped at her ankles.

Garnet was in a fury, his own shirt drenched in Celeste's blood. He held a knife between finger and thumb, one of the sentinel's knives, the hilt wrapped with leather and the blade gleaming skysilver. The sentinels lined up on the bank of the canal, flat-faced. Celeste would get no help from them; their allegiance was to the Kings.

She would get no help from me, either, though I liked her.

Lysandor leaped into the water, growling at the wolves until they backed off.

Celeste clutched her white dress to her skin. I couldn't see where the blood was coming from, but it made the canal run pink.

'May you die alone and unloved,' she shrieked at Garnet, shaking with fury. 'You have no right to be Power and Majesty. You give us nothing and take everything!'

'Lysandor,' Garnet said, recovering his breath and his dignity. 'Silence your woman. She talks too much.'

The lynx let out a fierce cry and leaped for him. Garnet shaped himself into his gattopardo, and tore at the lynx before Ashiol stepped in their way.

'Stop this!' he yelled. 'We're supposed to be family. We're brothers!'

Garnet threw himself back into human shape, gasping for breath. 'Not any more,' he said. 'Not now.'

The lynx stared at him.

'Go!' Garnet yelled. 'You'll be back. You have nowhere to shelter. You have nothing but this. Nothing but me. Leave and you will be an oathbreaker. You wouldn't *dare*.'

Lysandor sent out his final message so furiously that we all heard it inside our heads. *Anywhere but here. Any fate but you.*

Celeste burst into blood-stained owls and flew away down the canal. Lysandor turned and ran after her.

I never saw them again.

~

LYSANDOR LEFT ME A LEGACY. I didn't discover it until I returned to my cupola in Priest's cathedral. A familiar carved chest lay at the foot of my bed. Saturn's chest.

I opened it slowly, breathing in the smell of sandalwood shavings and linen. Saturn's clothes. I pulled out fine white cambric shirts, silk cravats, waistcoats and coats and breeches. A pair of boots that would never fit me, but the rest... A top hat, carefully cushioned by the other garments. A fob watch made of actual clockwork — a rarity in Aufleur, where mechanism was banned. Several volumes filled with sketches and tiny, perfect handwriting. Then, in a compartment right at the bottom of it all...

Gold ducs. Hundreds of them. More money than I had ever seen. No wonder his Lordship could throw so much at the stagemaster long ago.

There was a key in there, wrapped in a note in Lysandor's handwriting. *This opens a security box at the temple of Juno Moneta. We've taken our share, but Celeste says Saturn would want you to have the rest.*

Then a line written in an unfamiliar hand that must be Celeste's: *Lord Saturn said once that we took you away from your people and someday we would have to give you back. It's your choice now, Poet. Stay, or go. But remember who you are.*

Who was I? It was an impossible question.

~

IT WAS several market-nines before I got away from the Arches during daylight for long enough to visit my new security box. There was more gold there, stacked in so deep I could hardly see the end of it, and ownership papers not only to the Mermaid Revue but to the Vittorina Royale herself. Sheaves of paperwork. The company would have gone bust years ago, but Saturn kept on supporting them, propping them up. A strange sort of loyalty to a theatre troupe he turned upside down as a failed Saturnalia gift to his lover.

Saints, he was still paying their wages. The bill was regularly siphoned out of this security box, despite the fact that the man who'd owned it was years dead.

The theatre wasn't my life any more. My life was fighting the sky, serving Priest, keeping Garnet sane. I had nothing else; needed nothing else. My voice was a conduit for animor; my performances for a private audience only. Tasha and Saturn and Lysandor were gone, but I still had Ashiol and Livilla. My Lord Priest. Garnet, Garnet, Garnet.

I took the papers home, hid the key, ignored it beautifully for a month or two. But when the end of the year came around, I dressed myself in Saturn's best suit and boots and hat, tucked his pocket watch inside my coat, and took myself to the Vittorina Royale to see their Saturnalia revue.

It was going to be so easy. I would hand the ownership papers and the key to the account to the stagemaster. I would make a gift of the theatre to the company that had once been my own; my best, my brightest, home. All in all, it was an excellent plan.

Their columbines were sloppy, their costumes ragged, their pantomime recycled and creaking at the edges. It was the worst performance I had ever seen. The cabaret of monsters was slapdash, and the harlequinade was a joke. I recognised only a few faces among the masks, the tumblers, the songbirds or the columbines. They had no stellar, and no one that I could see stood out as being worthy of that name.

They had lost their heart.

Afterwards, I slipped backstage, past the spruikers and crew and up to the stagemaster's studio loft. The smell of cheap imperium hit me before I'd even opened the door. The stagemaster, my old stagemaster, lay drunk on the desk, snoring.

The loft was exactly the same, though there were no posters on the walls with sketches of the current troupe. He was surrounded by ghosts of the past, beautifully inked and lettered and frozen in time. He hadn't bothered to watch the show. Why should he, unless the old toad was on the lookout for a new mistress?

The Mermaid Revue was poor in the old days, an illusion of paper masks and cheap cosmetick, but honest. Now they had nothing to believe in, nowhere to go. No one to lead them. This old man had lost hope, had lost heart, and failed them all.

I leaned over his stinking body, speaking in the clear, projected voice that he'd begun teaching me when I was five years old and we were the best thing about our boring seaside town.

'You had everything. The best job in the world. You even had a gracious benefactor sending you gold every year, no questions asked. How did you manage to fuck this one up?'

He snorted in his sleep, as if breathing was a difficulty.

'I have a vision,' I told him, enjoying the way that my voice bounced off the walls. 'A vision of the Vittorina Royale as the finest theatre in the city, home to a renowned company. A glory and wonder to behold.'

I leaned in. 'Two very good friends gave you to me. I think they saw it as my redemption, a way out of the life I stumbled into so long ago. They think I'm not a monster, that there's still hope for me. But they're wrong.'

His neck snapped so easily under my hands.

'It'll be easier without you,' I told him. 'We're going to be spectacular. You'll see.'

Backstage, the company were weary, half-starved and entirely unsurprised by how bad they'd been. This was normality for them, it seemed.

A harlequinus dancer lifted his long neck to stare at me and I realised it was Kip, my old friend. He didn't look entirely pleased to see me. That columbine leaning up against his arm with too-thick cosmetic and cheekbones to die for, was that Ruby-red?

'Oy, who the frig are you?' one of the gaffers called out.

I gave him a superior look. It didn't matter that I wasn't of age. I channelled Saturn, Ashiol, Garnet and Tasha as hard as I could. I might be a courteso in the Creature Court, but in this theatre I could be a fucking Lord. I could tear this poor excuse for a company to pieces if I chose to, but that wasn't what I was here for.

'I am the Orphan Princel,' I said grandly. When I placed my hand inside my coat just so, it brushed Saturn's pocket watch and it was as if I could hear the voices of the dead speaking through it. The stagemaster, Madalena, my mother, Lord Saturn himself, showing me the way forward.

'I am your new stagemaster, and your salvation. Rehearsals begin this afternoon. Those who arrive on time will eat supper. Those who do not may find employment elsewhere. It meant something once, to be a part of the Mermaid Revue, and it will mean something again.'

There have been many memorable performances in my life — those on a stage before hundreds of eyes, and those in the darkness or a blazing sky that have saved my life. This wasn't my finest, but, of them all, it is the one that makes me happiest to recall. It was the beginning of my life starting again.

Lysandor would have been disappointed that I began my

new life without letting go of the old. But it wasn't as if he cared enough to come back and check on what I'd done with his gift.

As with any mask, my best performance will be the next one. Right around the corner. Not long now.

30

HIMSELF

*T*ierce fell two years after that. It was the beginning of the end for us — for the Creature Court as I remember it best. Heliora told us it was going to happen, and there was a moment when we thought — all of us — perhaps we could go and stop it. That we could be heroes after all.

We looked to Garnet to see what we should do. He walked away, up into his rooms alone, and drank himself into unconsciousness.

'At least he still has a soul,' Livilla said to me, when no one else was listening. Then she laughed. 'Not sure I do. Who gives a frig about Tierce really? We have our own city to worry about.'

Garnet didn't emerge for several days, so I took my life into my own hands and went in after him. Made him drink water and one of the healing tisanes we used in the theatre to keep our voices fresh and our heads clear for performance.

He sighed, and leaned into me. 'Have you ever had to make a terrible choice, little rat?'

I thought of the stagemaster of the Vittorina Royale and the way his throat felt breaking under my hands. One of many dreadful things I had done, but that choice had been so simple and mundane. I heard the voices of the dead every time I closed my eyes and slept with Saturn's pocket watch beneath my pillow.

'Yes, my Power,' I said.

'Good,' he muttered. 'Let us be monsters together, then.'

I wanted to give him something: a keepsake, a treasure. Some token to show him that he wasn't alone, that no matter how many times Ashiol and Livilla broke his heart, there was someone who would always be his.

I only had one treasure, apart from the faded playbill, that meant something only to me. I stroked Garnet's damp hair back from his face, and made him cup his hands, then dropped the Saturn's watch into them. The chain slithered against his skin, and for a moment I felt lighter, as if I'd done the right thing.

Garnet sighed again and smiled at me. The best of smiles. 'It's beautiful.'

'It's yours,' I said in a quiet breath of a voice, meaning something else.

He drew me close and kissed me, his mouth brushing my forehead and then my lips. 'I will never forget,' he said softly, 'that you stayed. My Poet.'

I wanted to be warmed by those words, but his face crumpled as he remembered that the ones he loved best didn't love him enough.

Garnet had bad dreams after that, worse than ever. They tormented him. It's hard to remain sane on so little sleep, especially in a world like ours, where death must be constantly fought against. I had no courtesi to worry about (nor ever would, that was my promise to myself; we all have to choose our own methods of staying as human as we can) and I would sometimes visit him in the Haymarket when Livilla or Ashiol were sleeping elsewhere. I curled up as rats at the foot of his bed and kept him company so that someone would be there when he screamed himself awake.

Yes, I was in love with him. That must be obvious by now.

'Poet,' he whispered one day in the darkened bedchamber. 'Do you hate me?'

'Never,' I sighed, shaping back into human the better to talk. 'Hush, don't be stupid.'

'The bitch Heliora won't see the futures for me.'

'I know. Doesn't matter.'

'Of course it matters, Poet. Everything matters. I've been to every fortune-teller in the city. Hacks and charlatans, most of them. And yet... twelve of them have said the same thing to me. It must be true.'

'What must be true?'

'I will die by fire.'

That woke me up. 'You won't die. I won't let you.'

'Sweet boy,' he sighed, and reached down to grasp my hand. He tugged me to lie beside him, the blanket tangled between his body and mine. 'We screwed you up good and proper, didn't we?'

'I wouldn't worry about that,' I said, watching his chest rise and fall in the dim light. 'I was never going to amount to much.'

MY LIFE SEPARATED into two halves, both nocturnal. At the Vittorina Royale, I was the lord and master, the Orphan Princel, stagemaster. Some of them feared me — when I was displeased, I could channel Tasha or Garnet pretty damned effectively. Others looked up to me.

There were new performers every year: pages and scrappers learning the trade, scrabbling to get a chance on stage. I saw myself in every single one of them. I chose the best, the ones I thought might turn out extraordinary, even if they were considered odd or unusual.

Then there was the other nox, the one that lit up the sky after the theatres had closed. Even after I became the Lord of Rats, Garnet and Ashiol and even Livilla still thought of me as a lamb, the youngest one, not worth worrying about. They were at war, the three of them, and each thought me neutral.

When Garnet started torturing Ashiol, punishing him in public and in private, locking him in that dark room and using the net or the blades to show him just who was Power and Majesty, Livilla chose a side. Suddenly her love for Garnet was eternal. She stopped running to Ashiol when Garnet was in a temper with her; instead, she amused herself with her courteso, who at least treated her like she was important. I knew she was frigging Mars long before anyone else did. I don't know why people tell me these things.

It bemused me, the way the Lords and Court and Kings opened themselves to each other so easily. Did they have so little regard for their safety that they would let a wolf, snake, panther into their bed for the sake of a quick tumble? I remembered the cleverness of Argentin and took no lovers from the Creature Court. Why should I, when there were so many eager young seigneurs (demmes too, but rarely, and less often as I grew into myself), desperate to catch the eye of the oddly young stagemaster of the Vittorina Royale, each hoping I would give them a part in our latest pageant.

Every one of them wanted to be a stellar, and who was I to deny them that dream?

Sometimes I even brought my more enthusiastic callers down to the Shambles, to the cozy grocer's-shop apartment that I took for myself once I was a Lord. It was easy enough to dodge the rest of the Creature Court as I had the Shambles to myself, and a glass of doped imperium after the fact ensured that my lovers never found their way back down into the tunnels.

It added to my mystique, I like to think.

On my eighteenth birthday, I was feeling nostalgic. I bought oysters at the docks and wandered along the embankment, eating them until my mouth dripped with salt water and lime juice. It was a strange life I had made for myself, though, to be fair, I knew of no sensible alternative.

I would never return to my seaside town, I knew that then as now. We would hardly recognise each other, Oyster and I. For a moment, I wondered what it might have been like if we never left. If Madalena was there to play mam and give me a new shirt to celebrate the day, or at least buy me a pot at the alehouse.

Certainly I would not be stagemaster if I had stayed there. But what would I be? Perhaps I was always meant to be a monster even if my life was mundane. I might drink too much and beat my unsatisfied wife. Perhaps I might have died of a cold before I turned ten. There is no sense wondering about such things. The futures are endless possibilities, and all we have is who we are from one moment to the next.

RETURNING to my warm nook above the grocer's shop, I found Livilla waiting for me, drunk on my most expensive imperium. From the smell of her, she'd found some herbal remedies to ease the passage of the drink.

'What's all this, sweetling?' I asked, trying not to show how annoyed I was by her presence. No sleep for me now if I had to cart her across the Arches and dump her back in Garnet's bed.

'He doesn't love me,' she said into her glass.

Oh, one of those mornings indeed.

'If you wanted love in the traditional way, you should have chosen worthier objects,' I said, which was true and yet applied to me as well as her.

'I should be everything to him. I should be everything to *someone*,' she said, the last of her drink slopping out of her glass and onto my expensive rug.

I relieved her of her glass. 'Is it Ashiol or Garnet making you miserable?'

'Both of them.'

Ah, and wasn't that that a fine problem?

'They'll never love anyone the way they love each other,' I said, and threw a blanket over her. 'Something we all have to live with.'

I had a choice: to drag drunken Livilla home, or to wait and deal with cranky, hungover Livilla sometime in the future. I chose the latter.

The other choice would have found Ashiol healing from his latest punishments in Garnet's bed. The outcome, with a miserable Livilla thrown into the mix, would almost certainly have been different. But how was I to know that?

WHEN LIVILLA WOKE, groaning and complaining before she even opened her eyes, I forced her to eat bread and honey, which she threw up in my kitchen. I sponged her face and dressed her in a suit of my own, vaguely recalling the times I tended to Madalena as she recovered from her cups.

Livilla said little about Ashiol and Garnet, though it was clear from her melancholy that the two had at least temporarily reconciled from their latest fight and neither had a thought to spare for her. It was tempting to ask whether she preferred it when Garnet had Ashiol chained up as punishment for some imaginary rebellion, but she was too miserable for sarcasm and I took pity on her. Silence suited us both.

We reached the Haymarket eventually, and when Livilla stared at the steps with an utter lack of recognition as to how to use them, I helped her up as far as the balcony.

The doors flew open and Garnet burst out, looking worse than Livilla. He was wide-eyed, terrified, and hung over the balcony rail as if the sky itself were after him.

'What have you done?' asked Livilla in a deadened voice, and it occurred to me that her misery was not at all about how much either of the cubs loved her, or how much they loved each other. Something had happened here, and I was too distracted with my own life to notice.

'He's dead,' said Garnet in a gasp. 'I've killed him.'

He was naked, and smelled of sex and animor, too much animor. He shone like a beacon, the power pouring out through the motes in his skin.

I couldn't feel Ashiol. Not at all.

I ran to the door of the room and saw him sprawled on the bed, his body unnaturally still. I heard the sob that caught in Livilla's throat and stuck there. I could hear Garnet's heart beating louder and louder, too fast.

'You'll have to make them think you meant to do it,' I said, when I had a voice.

This was nothing. Garnet had killed Tasha. He was one of the beasts who ripped Madalena to pieces. What was one more beloved corpse?

I made my way to the bed and stood over Ashiol. He didn't breathe or move, and there was no animor in him. He was empty, like someone had carved out his insides, taken everything that made him himself.

This is what happens to the people Garnet loves, I thought, traitorously, and laid one hand on Ashiol's bare chest.

He woke up, and started screaming with a pain and anger I'd never heard, not from any of them.

He was still empty.

~

GARNET AND ASHIOL were trained and punished by some of the harshest monsters the Creature Court had produced and yet no one ever hurt them as deeply as they hurt each other.

While Garnet buried his anguish in every potion he could get his hands on, and Livilla stayed at his side to lick up every fallen drop, it fell to me to cart Ashiol to the people of the daylight who might care for him.

Mars helped. He was Livilla's courteso now, but he had served Ashiol once. He said little to me as we carried Ashiol's inert body up through Saturn's old Eyrie and towards the Palazzo on the top of the hill. Garnet had drugged Ashiol to dampen his screams, dosing him with so much poppy juice we were lucky he hadn't killed him all over again.

'I didn't know it was possible,' Mars said, breaking his silence as we laid Ashiol on the Palazzo steps. 'To drain a man of animor. A King...'

'There is much the Power and Majesty can do that we could never understand,' I said.

We walked away and left Ashiol to be found by his daylight family and their servants. He lived, though it wasn't long before we heard that he had left the city.

Mars had a point. No one had ever heard of a King being drained of his animor. It was possible to give and take animor, to share it when your Lord needed greater strength, to bestow it when your courtesi were wounded... but this was unheard of. The only conclusion we could reach was that Ashiol had given it up of his own free will, but that hardly fitted with the facts known.

I went through Saturn's books again, hunting for some answers as to what powers Garnet had, and what he had done to Ashiol, but they provided little.

There was one book missing. I counted and checked several times to be sure. I knew it; had once deciphered several pages of inane theories about creatures that lay beyond the sky and how we could communicate with them. I didn't know what the rest of the volume held. But I found a single fine red hair in the chest and knew who had stolen it from me.

Apparently, my capacity for forgiveness is infinite. It's important to know these things about yourself.

PART X
THE CLOCKWORK COURT

31

FOUR DAYS AFTER THE IDES OF BESTIALIS

DAYLIGHT

*T*he train journey south brought memories crashing in on Ashiol. He kept flashing back to that day five years ago when he awoke, still half-drugged, miserable, broken, to find himself in a private carriage en route to Diamagne. Three blank-faced lictors were his only companions, charged by his Grandmama the old Duchessa with ensuring he arrive alive at his stepfather's estate.

(No, not stepfather; his brother's estate. Diamagne was dead by then, there had been a letter, but Ashiol was so caught up in Garnet and his madness that he hadn't even sent a card of consolation to his mother.)

Ashiol spent most of that journey trying to figure out how to steal one of those axes that the lictors carried, or how to escape them long enough to throw himself off the train.

The smell of smoke and steam, the coal dust and the constant noise — rattle bang, rattle bang, rattle bang — were the same. It was even the same fucking train line. Heading south. He was running away from Garnet again, all over again. Garnet was back from the dead and Ashiol was still running, tail between his legs, choosing some form of survival over doing what he should have done years ago.

He should have put Garnet in the fucking ground and ensured he stayed there.

Last time, Ashiol abandoned Heliora, Livilla, Poet, everyone he loved. He was sick and wounded, empty of his animor, thinking of nothing but how to end it, how to get another drink, how to find some kind of oblivion. He told himself he had no choice. The betrayal was too great.

'Forgive me,' Garnet breathed, kissing the marks that the net had burnt into Ashiol's shoulders, down his back. 'I was angry.'

Ashiol closed his eyes, feeling the imprint of Garnet's mouth slowly trailing down his spine. 'You have to trust me. I'm not going anywhere. I'm not going to take anything from you.'

Last time, Ashiol was a wreck, powerless, his life at an end. The train journey represented failure.

This time, he wore a respectable suit and sat in the first-class carriage opposite his cousin, the Duchessa d'Aufleur. Isangell sat upright, formal in her travelling attire, a little suit with a long skirt reaching to her ankles, her blonde hair concealed under a cloche hat.

The blank-faced lictors were the same. There were maids, equally blank. Ashiol never bothered to learn their names. They were interchangeable.

He made occasional attempts at conversation, but Isangell gave short, clipped answers. She still didn't trust that he was doing this for her and not some other Ashiol-specific reason. Besides, the very fact that she was travelling so far to find a husband was his fault. He couldn't blame her for hating him right now.

Garnet's mouth was in the small of his back, his hands splayed over Ashiol's hips. 'Never again,' he whispered. 'I'm sorry, I'm sorry...'

Ashiol gasped softly at the touching, fingers, mouth, light pressure here, and then there. 'I always forgive you, bastard,' he said, and then there were no words, there was just Garnet, mouth, tongue, lips, lick, lick, lick, fingers warm and urgent and everywhere...

When he came it was with a scream, and the pleasure dissolved into something else, something bad and dark and fierce that latched on and ripped him into pieces.

Ashiol blinked, back in the carriage, staring guiltily at Isangell. 'What did you say?'

She gave him an acid look that said *I knew you would be no help whatsoever.* 'Have you ever been to Bazeppe?'

'No. Mother used to send there for her dresses, or to have Diamagne's clocks mended, and sometimes she went for... some kind of season? She took Bryn there to find himself a wife. She preferred to avoid Aufleur if she could.'

'Aunt Augusta has good taste. Bazeppe's costumiers are said to be the best in the world,' Isangell said primly.

'You don't have to do this,' he said in a low voice. 'It's too soon.'

'I was always going to have to find a husband, Ashiol,' she said, sounding very much like her mother. 'Silly to postpone the inevitable.'

'So what are we looking for?' he drawled. 'Some older man who will take the reins of the city from you and tell you not to bother your pretty head? Or a young fop who'll be so busy trying on apricot cravats and buggering the footmen that he won't get in your way?'

Isangell stared at him, half-shocked, then burst into peals of laugher. 'Oh, they both sound such charmers. I'm glad you're here to put it all into perspective.'

~

IT WAS LATE in the day when they arrived at the station just north of the city walls. Isangell stood, pale and swaying as she contemplated what lay ahead of them. Ashiol took her arm.

'You're worth more than any of them put together,' he said in a low voice. 'Don't convince yourself otherwise. You're offering some lucky arsehole the chance of a lifetime.'

She squeezed his hand gratefully and then released it, the mask of formality coming down. 'Please walk a few steps behind. I don't want you to spoil my entrance.'

For once, Ashiol did as he was told.

There was a metallic tinge to the air as they stepped out onto the platform. The city of Bazeppe smelled like coal dust and machinery. Steam swirled around them, thick and masking everything from view.

It cleared to show a retinue of lictors in scarlet and gold livery lined up like toy soldiers on the platform. They saluted as Isangell approached. A gentleman in a bottle-green striped suit and top hat stepped forward to make a formal bow. He had a bristly moustache, and his monocle almost popped out as he straightened.

'High and brightness, you honour us with your presence. I am Jenkingworth, Minister of Mechanism, and on behalf of the Duc-Elected Henri of Bazeppe, I welcome you to our fair city.'

Isangell bowed her own head graciously. 'I am glad to be here, Minister.'

The station gates jerked open as if pulled on strings and Minister Jenkingworth led them towards an unlikely contraption. 'If you would like to take your seat, high and brightness?'

Ashiol reached out a hand to Isangell before she could

move. 'What the saints is that?' he asked, curbing his tongue against more violent swearing.

Minister Jenkingworth smiled broadly. 'Why, Seigneur Ducomte, that is an automobile. One of Duc-Elected Henri's personal fleet, as it happens. His pride and joy. It took a long time to source the racing-green paint, but the effect is rather splendid, don't you agree?'

'Isangell,' Ashiol said in a low voice, 'you can't step into some random mechanised cabriolet you know nothing about. It looks dangerous.'

'Nonsense,' Isangell said defiantly, and allowed the Minister to hand her into the machine. 'We don't want to insult Duc-Elected Henri,' she added, smiling brightly.

Glaring and grumbling, Ashiol followed her. The whole damned city smelled like metal and thunderstorms. The hairs on the back of his neck spiked up and it was all he could do not to snatch Isangell up and abduct her back onto the train and away.

'What marvellously impressive factories,' Isangell said as they jerked along in the 'automobile', which had a growl like a wounded panther. 'The smokestacks are so very high.'

'We pride ourselves on our industry,' the Minister said, as if it was the culmination of his life's desires to explain the history of Bazeppe to a pretty young demoiselle. 'Our clock factory is the finest in the known world.'

'Goodness,' said Isangell, while Ashiol tuned out the educational ramblings.

The lands around the city were flat enough that you could see much further than you could from the shambling urban hills of Aufleur. The buildings were taller, for the most part, and there was a pale greyness to them. Steam was everywhere: funnelling out of factory stacks, rising from the urban outline and clouding the air around them.

Ashiol roused himself long enough to hear Minister Jenkingworth promise Isangell something called a 'princessa clock', which was apparently all the rage with the demoiselles this year.

Isangell demurred and told him that clockwork mechanisms were considered unlucky within the city bounds of Aufleur.

'Good gracious, how do you live?' the Minister said in surprise. 'No, no, I'm sorry, that was dreadfully rude. Religious compunctions are the backbone of society, of course.'

Ashiol was reminded of the endless tick, tick, tick of his stepfather's clock collection. Diamagne would have loved this fellow.

After a circuitous route designed to show Isangell the glories of the city, with Ashiol gritting his teeth at every bump and jolt in the road, they arrived at a wide tree-lined avenue leading up to a grand Palazzo. There were statues everywhere: along the road, and the stone edgings of the Palazzo, and overlooking them from the roof. They gleamed metallically in the wintry sunshine.

Finally the inhuman rattletrap juddered to a halt, almost flinging them out in the process, and Ashiol could breathe again. He stepped out, and allowed Minister Jenkingworth to help Isangell, relinquishing his own role as consort with a combination of resentment and guilty relief.

As they walked towards the Palazzo, every statue came to life, saluting in jerky, automated fashion. Ashiol jumped and swore, while the Minister blithely pretended he hadn't heard the stream of profanity. Fucker.

'Don't mind our saints,' the Minister said, leading Isangell forward. 'They don't bite, ha-ha, though you wouldn't want them to, would you. Don't fancy a pair of bronze choppers sinking into your leg.'

Bronze. The statues — the saints — were bronze, but articulated: an army of clockwork men with faces as flat and emotionless as those of Isangell's maids and lictors. Ashiol was so busy staring at them, he almost missed the appearance of Duc-Elected Henri, who emerged from the large doors to hold out both his hands to Isangell. He was every bit as sartorially splendid as the Minister of Mechanism, in a bright purple coat and red boots. Both his moustache and beard rivalled Minister Jenkingworth's for bushiness.

'My dear demoiselle Duchessa, how splendid, how lovely, what roses you have in your cheeks, I had no idea what a tulip you are, the very pink of health, excellent, excellent...' The man appeared never to breathe between words, let alone sentences. He turned on Ashiol with the same degree of gush. 'My word, Ducomte Ashiol, is it, I know your mother the Baronnille so well, excellent madame, such impeccable taste, the most educational dinner conversation, quite an elegante, we do miss her these days, you must give her my very best wishes, very best.'

They were ushered into the main foyer, through doors that steamed and hissed as they opened and closed.

'Automation — a curse and a blessing,' Duc-Elected Henri said gaily. 'The entire mechanism broke down once and we had to go in and out of windows for a week; rather bracing but hard on the knees, don't you know.'

Automation. It was everywhere. The Palazzo gulped and spat steam and smoke like it was some sort of mad, hissing dragon creature. The cats inside Ashiol wanted to run away, but he had to stay at Isangell's side, had to prove to himself that he was here for a reason. That he hadn't fled Aufleur like a coward.

This is where I am meant to be. I owe her this.

The taste of iron clung to the back of his throat, but he forced himself to accept port from Duc-Elected Henri and, if not to make polite conversation, at least to glower in the corner with a semblance of civility.

'I am delighted, beyond delighted, terribly honoured, that you have chosen to seek a consort among our humble people,' Henri was saying, so earnest and polite. Ashiol entertained himself by wondering what noises the Duc-Elected would make if all his fingers happened to get broken, one by one, in some kind of dreadful accident.

'It seemed a politic choice,' said Isangell. 'Our own city is so inward looking, with the Great Families dancing around each other in the hope of some slight crumbs of power. I do not want a husband whose agenda is separate from my own.'

'Quite wise, quite wise,' said Duc-Elected Henri, his head bobbing with enthusiasm. 'We have a small reception for you this evening, discreet, merely a few notables who wish to make your acquaintance, some refreshments. I trust you are not too tired from your journey to attend?'

'Nothing would give us greater pleasure,' said Isangell.

Ashiol, naturally, was not consulted. Silence seemed appropriate, especially if kidnapping Isangell and taking her home were not an option.

'Marvellous,' said Duc-Elected Henri, and laughed merrily as a huge clock in the corner exploded with noise to chime the hour. Echoes were heard throughout the Palazzo. There were clocks everywhere, ticking, chiming, so fucking delighted to be in synchronisation with each other.

Isangell smiled politely.

Ashiol estimated the measurements of the windows, in order to determine which would be easiest to jump out of.

32

FOUR DAYS AFTER THE IDES OF
BESTIALIS

NOX

*A*shiol was well experienced with torture. Actual torture, with nets and blades and all manner of orchestrated cruelties. He had been beaten bloody; had every drop of power drained out of him. Right now, he would gladly trade a long nox with Garnet's tortures in exchange for the evening he had to endure in the Palazzo of Bazeppe.

Everyone was so *interested* in him, and there were few aristocratic niceties in this city of clockwork and metal. Its people touched constantly, hands brushing arms, kisses against cheeks and wrists. Ashiol had spent too long in the Creature Court, where touch meant an exchange of power or comfort or blood. He wasn't used to it meaning nothing.

The air smelled of thunderstorms and tin. It set Ashiol so far on edge that he jumped at every sound. The music crushed around him, and the people as well. So many people in a ridiculously small reception room.

He had expected Isangell to be the centre of attention, not

himself. The few public receptions he had not been able to avoid in Aufleur were peopled with seigneurs and demoiselles who gave him a wide berth. His reputation was good for something, after all. No one here had any such qualms. They tugged at him, cooing and gossiping, and dragged him into dance after dance. The steps were overly confusing, and though he matched his partners' movements well enough, it was clear that Ashiol was being in some way utterly hilarious.

So many of the women had their hair cut short; not in the flapper bob he was used to from home, but mannishly short. Was it the fashion, or fear of being dragged into machinery?

The food was brought up from the kitchens on jerky little elevating platforms. Steam puffed constantly out of a large metal water pot, kept piping hot for the servants to serve fresh tea at a moment's notice. Even at supper, the people of Bazeppe drank tea as if it were their patriotic duty.

The Duc-Elected of Bazeppe — who, it transpired, had been elected to the position without contest for the last twenty years — had three sons. Ashiol didn't think much of any of them. They obviously spent far too much time inside reading books and talking politics or some shit like that. He couldn't tell the difference between the three, except that one was particularly irritating — either the plump one or the one with spectacles.

Ashiol had made the mistake of wearing the outfit laid out for him by the Palazzo servants: some kind of embroidered jacket thing over a waistcoat, and breeches that were far too tight. It felt as if there was metal in the cloth, pressing too close around him.

Not any daylight metal he knew, nor skysilver. Something new. It made his skin itch.

'I've never been to Aufleur,' said a buxom dame wearing a seigneur's suit of clothes. A pearl-edged pocket watch hung decoratively from of her cravat and Ashiol couldn't take his eyes off it. This whole city was as bad as his late stepfather, counting time in hours, minutes, seconds. How did they get anything done?

'Are they all like you back home?' the dame asked.

'I hope not,' he said fervently.

A hand slid over his sleeve. 'Excuse me,' said a melting voice. 'May I borrow the Ducomte for a moment?'

Once more, Ashiol was not consulted. On the other hand, nothing could be worse than this. He allowed himself to be led away.

The melting voice belonged to a man in his early twenties, whip-thin and energetic, in one of those gaudy suits. 'Sorry to be so forward,' he said with what could only be a flirtatious smile. 'But you looked like you were about to drown yourself in the punch bowl.'

'I considered it,' Ashiol admitted.

The young man held out a hand and shook Ashiol's vigorously when he ventured it in that general direction. 'The name is Troyes. I'm to be your personal secretary while you're in Bazeppe.' There was no mistaking the way he lingered on the word 'personal'.

'And what exactly does that mean?' Ashiol asked, giving little away.

'It means I'm to provide you with anything you need,' purred Troyes. 'What do you need, Seigneur Ducomte?'

'Fresh air,' Ashiol said without thinking.

Home. I need to go home and put my feet under Velody's table and run on the rooftops and save the world. I don't think you can offer that.

'Done,' said Troyes, whipping out a small book and making a note inside with a scratchy feathered pen. 'I'll have you moved to a room with a balcony — somewhere at the back, overlooking the oak grove. Not too high up.' He smiled a dazzling smile. 'You seem the athletic type. I'm sure you'll want to make use of the grounds.'

~

DAYS PASSED: a jumble of receptions, suppers, breakfasts and other formal occasions, all measured out to the second by the hundreds of noisy, ticking clocks. Factory visits, parades, ceremonies... clocks.

There weren't as many parades and ceremonies as Ashiol might have predicted. He didn't notice at first, because the latter half of Bestialis was traditionally quiet, but then it was the Kalends of Fortuna, and no sign that there would be any celebration of the Pomonia. No green ribbons, holly crowns or sacrifices in honour of the beginning of winter. Now he came to think of it, Bazeppe had only held a single parade in more than a market-nine, and Ashiol got the impression it was especially to honour their ducal guest. Even the everyday rituals were sparse compared to what he was used to.

The ticking didn't stop even when Ashiol was alone in his room. There were clocks on the walls, on the bedside table, and in the corridor outside. He could have asked Troyes to clear the room of clocks. His 'secretary' was nothing if not brutally efficient in any task given to him, whether in or out of Ashiol's bed. But Ashiol couldn't help his suspicion that Troyes was watching him carefully and he was loathe to give too much information away.

He could live with the clocks.

The balcony attached to his room saved his sanity. It provided the closest thing he could get to silence. He liked to go wandering in cat form at nox, climbing trees and running for miles. Sleep found him sometimes before he even reached his bed. He'd fall asleep as a pile of black cats, warm and purring, only to awake naked on the balcony or by the fire in his room, with a blanket tossed over his body. He wandered what Troyes thought about his behaviour, but couldn't find it in him to care.

The evening of the Kalends of Fortuna, a particularly gruelling poetry reading at which Ashiol had spent an hour trying to make conversation with one of Isangell's prospective husbands (and considered it a great triumph that he hadn't bitten the twit's throat out), he retreated to his room and his balcony. The first snowfall covered the skeletal tree-shapes of the grove and he closed the glass doors behind him, leaned against the snow-dusted rail and breathed in the cool nox air.

Guilt set in. However irritating the chatter and amateur dramatics of the nobles of Bazeppe might be, at least they filled his head. Only here, when it was cool and silent, did he remember everything he had left behind. Garnet. Warlord. Livilla. The sentinels. Velody.

It was more and more difficult to avoid thinking about Velody.

Stars gleamed between the misty shapes of the clouds. It was a long time since Ashiol had been able to look at a nox sky without fear or tension. The sky over Aufleur was coloured with the constant threat of death, blood, devils. Bazeppe's was calm. A greenish black, lit as it was by so many flickering gas lamps, but it was peaceful to gaze up and see nothing that wanted to eat you alive.

A white shape flickered near his field of vision and Ashiol turned his head to see pale owls gliding overhead, their wings catching the breezes beautifully. Even that was a peaceful sight. The owls called to one another, disappearing into the silhouetted bare trees of the oak grove with only a hoot or two breaking the silence.

Ashiol breathed. He could live here. He could forget about Garnet, and Velody. The ticking clocks were worth putting up with, surely, in return for this kind of inner peace. No wonder Priest saw this city as a sanctuary. It was so far from the politics of the Creature Court, from everything dangerous.

A city that wasn't doomed. Must be nice.

A woman walked out of the oak grove. She was the colour of moonlight all over: pale hair, pale skin, a lush figure contained within a long white gown. Her feet were bare. Ashiol gazed at her for a long while, wondering why this scene was familiar, like something from an old story someone had once told him.

The woman turned her head and for a moment Ashiol thought she was staring directly at him, though she shouldn't be able to see anyone from that distance. The room behind him was dark.

She crossed the lawn towards the Palazzo, stopped right underneath Ashiol's window and looked up. 'My Lord Ducomte,' she said in a voice laden with sarcasm, familiar and cutting. 'Or should I call you King?'

Ashiol's fingers gripped the railing. Motherfucking saints, it was Celeste.

'Lord of Owls,' he said with a dignity that belied the panic in his head. 'Are you well?'

'Aye,' she said, and there was that smile, a half-crease that had completely enraptured Lysandor and drawn him away from Tasha, from Garnet, from all of them. 'I am well. I never thought you would come here. I did not think you would still be alive, in truth. Men like you don't grow old.'

'Is —' Ashiol's voice broke a little, because he wasn't sure if he wanted to hear the answer.

'Lysandor,' said Celeste, and her face glowed like the moon this time when she smiled. 'He is also well.'

Something Ashiol had not known he had been holding

tight inside himself all these years cracked open. 'Can I see him?' he asked.

Celeste grinned and held out her hand.

Ashiol leaped off the balcony, landing on hands and knees on the grassy earth. He took Celeste's hand and they went into the grove together.

33

THE KALENDS OF FORTUNA

NOX

Celeste took Ashiol to an old factory warehouse at the edge of the city near the train station, one of few factories in the area that did not belch smoke from its smokestacks.

'Is there a Court?' Ashiol asked, looking around at the size of the place. There were several enormous rooms, still filled with their original equipment. One space even larger than the Haymarket was half-full of tables, chests and bedrolls. It looked very much as if people lived here.

'Of course there's a Court,' said Celeste, sounding as if she thought he was stupid. Just like old times. 'The sky falls here as well, you know. Aufleur is not a unique flower. Bazeppe never had an underground city, but we make do. The roof of the Emporium is reinforced with skysilver, which gives us the protection we need; and besides, we have friends to help us in our battles.'

There was a groaning sound, not far away, and then

Ashiol heard the ticking of a clock, and another, loud enough
to fill the warehouse with noise. A nearby door opened to
admit two of the bronze statues from the Palazzo, or something very like them. A harried-looking demme with wild
hair accompanied them, and an old man, and Priest, and
Lysandor.

Ashiol was so busy staring that he couldn't even acknowledge the presence of Priest. He couldn't take his eyes off the
man he still thought of as a brother. When Lysandor left with
Celeste — how long ago? Six years? Seven? — he and Ashiol
were both so young and broken. Now, Lysandor was every
inch a man: a grave-looking seigneur in a wool suit, his gold
hair trimmed short. He had a beard, in the manner of so
many men in Bazeppe.

'What's this?' the demme said in a strident voice.
'Bringing chaps in off the street now, Celeste? I hope he has
useful skills, or you can throw him back where you
found him!'

She wore trousers, had a smear of what must be oil on the
side of her neck, and smelled of wolf.

'Nonsense, Peg,' said Lysandor, his voice wary but warm.
'He's an aristocrat; he can hardly be trusted to tie his
own shoes.'

Ashiol laughed at the familiarity of it, of Lysandor
mocking him, and the laughter broke a tension of sorts.
Lysandor came forward. They clasped and shook hands in
the Bazeppe fashion, then hugged hard. Lysandor smelled of
smoke and metal, like everything in this city. He smelled like
he belonged here. But underneath it all was the comforting,
familiar scent of lynx. *Brother*.

'You made it,' Lysandor said in a muffled voice. 'I have so
much to tell you.'

Ashiol looked over his friend's shoulder to Celeste. More
people were coming through the doors now, including a

small demme with bright silver hair who cried, 'Mama, mama,' and ran to Celeste, begging to be picked up.

Celeste held her child closely and her mouth tightened just a little. 'If you make him go back with you, I'll kill you,' she said, quite calmly.

'I wouldn't do that,' said Ashiol, staring at the impossible child.

'Really?' She arched her eyebrows. 'You wouldn't even try?'

'My boy,' Priest said warmly, rescuing Ashiol from Celeste's sharp gaze.

Ashiol clasped his arm in greeting. 'I'm glad you're here.'

The Pigeon Lord nodded, and smiled.

'Come, stand in the warmth,' said Lysandor, smacking Ashiol on the back. 'Did you come here on your own?'

'He's staying at the Palazzo,' said Celeste, still gripping her silver-haired child as if she thought that Ashiol would snatch her away.

'Of course,' said Lysandor, leading the way to a boiler that pumped warm air into the space. 'Ducomte and all that. Have some warm cider. It's been too long.'

Ashiol looked around at the people who made themselves comfortable in the warm part of the warehouse. Some were interested in him, staring openly, but others had started up their own conversations. It was more casual than the crowded receptions of the city aristocracy, and had nothing of the tensions he expected from a Creature Court.

'You're happy here,' he said to Lysandor.

It was more of a statement than a question, but Lysandor launched into an anecdote about his daughter — his *daughter* — and it seemed this wasn't the time for complex discussions about the nature of their different Courts.

Later, as Ashiol sat against the wall with a mug of cider in one hand, watching Lysandor tuck the little demme into a

makeshift cot at the back of the warehouse, Celeste came
over to sit near him.

'Do you live here?' he asked, still not understanding.
There was no evidence of anything but a nomadic existence
— many of Lysandor's friends had bedrolls or swags
with them.

'Only when the sky is unfriendly,' she said. 'Some of us
have managed to reinforce the roofs of our homes with
skysilver, but the protection is better here.'

'And is the sky unfriendly this nox?'

'You're getting old if you can't feel it,' Celeste said
cynically.

Ashiol looked around. There were half as many people as
before, and the walking bronze statues had vanished as well.
Priest was gone, and his birds with him. How much had
Ashiol been drinking? He hadn't even noticed. He stretched
his animor out to the sky, but the heavily shielded roof made
it hard to have any awareness of what was happening
outside.

'We work in shifts,' said Celeste. 'It's rarely bad enough to
require all of us up there, especially with the saints on
our side.'

'Saints,' said Ashiol. 'Is that what you call them, the
mechanical men?'

'Clockwork saints. Did you never wonder why clockwork
is banned in Aufleur?'

Aufleur had so many odd conventions and traditions;
Ashiol had honestly never thought about it. He tried again to
get a sense of the skybattle, but even once his animor
extended beyond the skysilver roof, nothing felt familiar.

'I feel blind,' he said in frustration.

'It will get better if you stay here long enough,' said
Celeste. 'Lysh and I were the same at first — our bodies were
attuned to Aufleur; anything else felt numb and pointless.

But our animor adapted. It still doesn't feel the same as Aufleur. Less intense. It doesn't make you so...' She trailed off, looking uncomfortable.

'Crazy,' said Ashiol.

'I didn't say that.'

'They really fight the sky, these... clockwork saints?'

'I'll show you.'

She glanced back at Lysandor once and then led the way out of the Emporium and into the empty street. Ashiol looked up, and saw nothing at first. It was like being dosed with sentinel's blood, all his senses dull and useless. Finally he saw pale grey lines streaking across the sky, then a few dashes of colour here and there. There were creatures in the sky, and clockwork saints, fighting side by side. It all seemed so ordinary, and businesslike.

'This is what it's supposed to be like,' said Celeste. 'The Clockwork Court don't rip each other to shreds over it all. We don't just survive. We live. We thrive.'

'Who is your Power and Majesty?'

Lysandor, he thought, unless there were more Kings here. These people all felt so lacking in animor, although they fought the sky with as much power and ability as any of his own Court.

'I am,' said Celeste.

He looked at her in surprise. 'You're not a King.'

'We don't use those titles.'

'But... you're not a King.'

She shook her head at him, like he was a child refusing to learn his letters. 'Leadership is about more than power and brute force. I was chosen to lead this year because the people trust me. It doesn't matter that Lysandor could beat me in a duel. He doesn't choose to. None of us choose to.'

'What if someone else thinks they would be a better leader?'

'Then they can run for election in the autumn.'

'*Election?*'

'It's called civilisation, Ashiol. We are not animals. We don't have to be monsters.'

'Because these clockwork saints do all the work for you?'

'That's part of it. It's another life. A better life. Ask Priest how different it is. How different he feels. Aufleur was killing him. It is better here. Better for all of us.'

'And if this life of yours is so perfect, why do you look so afraid whenever Lysandor looks at me?'

'Because he loves you. He has always held a sadness inside about leaving you, and Garnet. Despite everything that monster did to us, he thinks of you as family.'

Ashiol could hear the bitterness in her voice.

'I didn't think we could have children,' he said. 'The nox you left... all that blood. I thought you had lost the child.'

'Our miracle,' Celeste said softly. 'Lucia was the sign, the first sign, that life didn't have to be the way the Creature Court dictated. This is our family now. Our home. Don't break it. Stay with us, Ashiol, or walk away as you choose, but take nothing that is mine.'

'I promise,' he said, but how could he promise that? This was Lysandor, and Ashiol had been missing him for so long, like a lost limb. Perhaps together they could save Garnet, bring him back from the brink.

The skybattle had ended. The warriors came back in groups: creatures, humans, Lords, all glowing with animor accompanied by the clockwork Saints. One saint was surrounded by falcons, which changed quickly into the form of a slender young man who gave Ashiol a guilty grin before heading inside the Emporium.

'Troyes,' Ashiol said beneath his breath. 'So he *was* a spy.'

'We're not entirely original,' Celeste said sweetly. 'Will you stay, Ashiol? We have so much more to show you.'

It was peaceful here, in a way Aufleur had never been. There were no complications. No one who wanted anything from him, except for him not to destroy what they had. It was a better way to live.

'I'll stay for now,' said Ashiol finally. 'I have nowhere else to go.'

Celeste hugged him and the scent of feathers filled his senses. 'We are glad to have you here.'

~

'WHAT DO YOU THINK?' Isangell asked him over breakfast the next morning. 'Roget or Niall?'

'Which is the one who keeps talking about historical theorems?' Ashiol asked, biting into the largest pastry in the hope that it contained meat. No such luck, and the flakes exploded all over his shirt.

'Michel,' said Isangell. 'I've already discounted him. He smells of peppermints.'

Ashiol shrugged. 'Whichever one you like most, or dislike least.'

'Very helpful.'

'Matchmaking was never my forte. If you wanted an opinion, you should have brought your mother.'

'Beast,' she laughed, and threw the napkin at him. 'I have to be home before the games begin. The priests and proctors are unnerved enough that I have been away from Aufleur for more than a market-nine. And I will have to commission several dresses for Saturnalis —'

'We're going back, then.' Ashiol straightened his back.

'Aren't you glad? It's no secret you're not enjoying yourself here. The servants are all half-afraid of your temper, and the number of marriage proposals I've received on your behalf has dipped strongly since the first few days.'

'That doesn't mean I want to go back.'

He had work to do here. Lysandor and Celeste barely trusted him yet, and he had so much to learn from them and their odd clockwork saints. He had to talk to Priest, really talk to him.

'You could stay without me,' Isangell said quietly.

Ashiol had been trying to think of an excuse to do exactly that, and stared at her with suspicion. 'I could? Why?'

'Whether I betroth myself to Roget or Niall, I will need a representative here, to arrange things between our families. A sort of ambassador.'

'And I'm so known for my diplomatic skills.'

'Aufleur was killing you, Ash. I'm the one who brought you back, and it... I feel bad about that now. I didn't know what you were coming back to. You need to stay away from that world, from the Creature Court. If you don't want to return to the Diamagne estate, then why not make a home for yourself here?'

'Aufleur was killing you' ran around in his head as he thought it over. Celeste had said the same thing of Lysandor.

'You sound like Grandmama,' he said finally. 'Only she was under the impression I was running rampant in the streets with criminals and drunkards.' Isangell knew the truth, or as close as anyone of the daylight could know.

'I leave in two days,' she said. 'If you want to remain here in Bazeppe, say the word and I will arrange it.'

'You don't have to protect me, you know.'

Isangell gave him an impatient look. 'Someone has to.'

PART XI
THE CABARET OF MONSTERS

34
POET LORD RAT

I broke one of my most important rules after Ashiol
left us. I took courtesi.

Halberk was first. He stepped off the boat from Inglirrus
a full-grown man with no idea of what animor was, or why
he had a tendency to transform into a bear when the moon
was high. He was one of the rare ones whose power came to
them far from the city bounds, with no one to show them the
way. Animor is weak outside the cities, but can still find you.

From Saturn's books and my own observations, I have
come to realise that those with animor are drawn to Aufleur
or Tierce or Bazeppe whether they know it or not. But
perhaps I am wrong. Perhaps our three cities are not so
special, and the world is full of coves and demmes who
change their shape as easily as breathing.

Halberk had embraced his monstrous nature. He liked to
kill women, sometimes slowly, sometimes with terrifying
speed. I found him a market-nine after he arrived in the city,
after my hunt for a missing actress turned up a trail of blood-
soaked petticoats. It would have been easier to kill and

quench him than to tame him. Believe me, I considered it. He was a wild animal with no idea how to behave.

I swarmed him, beat him senseless with my slender arms bolstered by bright animor and forced him to surrender. Then I bought him a new suit of clothes and a tankard of beer, and he followed me like a pet lamb.

He was a soldier waiting to happen. Once I showed him how to fight the sky, he never killed another demme, though I had to watch him carefully in the months when the sky was quiet.

Zero was another matter. Livilla found him only a day or so after he came into his powers, and dumped him on my doorstep. When I asked her what the fuck she meant by it, she shrugged and smiled. 'He doesn't match my set, dearling. Besides, he reminds me of you.'

Zero was quick and smart and knew how to applaud when I was practising a new song. I kept him, and would have put him on the stage if he had an ounce of talent for anything but trouble and shaping himself into weasels.

Garnet did not mock me for changing my mind and taking courtesi, though I half-expected him to. He made one veiled comment — that it was lucky I hadn't sworn an oath on the matter — but left it alone. Perhaps he was glad I was no longer alone. Or perhaps he simply didn't care very much about what I did.

~

I HAD ALLOWED myself indulgences such as friendship outside the Creature Court: I paid for a room in a boarding house so I could see Kip and Ruby-red sometimes, pretend I was another member of the chorus instead of the boss who paid their wages.

That had to end. The last Saturnalia before Garnet died

and Velody changed everything... it was getting worse. Garnet needed all of me, and I could no longer trust him to forgive my weaknesses without using them to hurt me.

I kept the theatre. I remained the stagemaster. I even finally, *finally* let them call me stellar, something I had resisted for the longest time.

The sky dipped closer, taking its toll, sliding under our skin.

Garnet grew angrier. Colder.

I sent my friends, my oldest friends from the Mermaid Revue, away on a train. I found the lambs, and offered them coin to be my new Cabaret of Monsters. I readied myself for the end.

Someone was going to die. Stupid. I thought it was me. I was prepared for it.

~

THERE WAS ONLY one thing I could not forgive Garnet for. Dying was the cruellest trick he ever played on me.

It was Ashiol's fault. He was back in the city and we all knew it. His return had Garnet rattled. It was an ordinary skybattle on an ordinary nox, but one careless mistake led to another.

The sky swallowed Garnet, and the world ended.

~

ASHIOL, Velody; Velody, Ashiol. I thought she was the cheap trick, the distraction, and that Ashiol would come back to us when he realised how much he was needed. But he turned out to be a constant disappointment, and she was the future.

Finally, I put Garnet behind me. Mourned in private. Continued with my life.

~

IN THE YEARS Ashiol was gone, I grew up up in every way imaginable. It hardly hurt at all when Halberk died. It's easier when you don't love the people you're trying to protect. You can feel failure without wanting to die of it.

~

WHEN THE UPSTART Ferax Lord went the same way as Tasha, I saw the loss in the eyes of his hounds and let them into my own corner of the Court. My life, such as it was, continued.

But then the song started. So quiet at first, hardly an undercurrent of sound, a note here and there. Then, gradually, getting louder and louder. It followed me everywhere, through the city.

It was loudest in the Killing Ground. I wasn't supposed to go there, but I trespassed more than once, trying to find the source of the song that filled my head.

The most obvious possibility was that I was going mad. It would happen eventually; why not now? I had my first vision of the future the nox that we took down Priest, when he was possessed by the sky. A future which had Garnet in it. If this was madness, I didn't want to be sane.

~

THEN CAME THE PERFORMANCE: a mad circus on the sands of the Killing Ground, the whole Creature Court coming together to heal the city. In the midst of it all, I heard the song louder than ever before, and caught sight of something I had never expected to see for the remainder of my lifetime. Garnet's face, staring out of a mirror. He had one finger pressed to his lips to silence me. Our little secret.

The song was his, the voice was his, and how had I ever thought any different?

Mirrors, it was all about mirrors. I saw him in every reflected glass, every shiny surface. The song he sang was the song of the Bestialia, and so I turned to my own Cabaret of Monsters. After Livilla, I had developed the knack for spotting them: children who would belong to the Court someday. I'd been collecting them for months; now I pushed them to be something beautiful.

Like Tasha before me, I planned to bring their powers out a little early. Where was the harm? They were destined to be ours. I only wanted to ensure that they were mine, and his. They would sing the song to guide Garnet home.

Courtesi, our courtesi.

~

I HAVE NO REGRETS. How can I have regrets? It all worked as it should. Livilla is dead, but Garnet still lives and loves me.

The future is ours.

~

I KNOW I am in the cage. I recognise the scent of it. Nothing else smells like sky silver.

My throat is raw from telling my story.

'You wished me to speak; I have spoken nothing but the truth. Am I allowed to know my captor's name? Why am I here, and why is it dark? Ashiol, is that you?'

'No,' says a low voice, a demme's voice, and while I can feel her animor, I don't know who she is. I only know that I am inside the cage.

She strikes a light and holds a lantern up to my face. I know where I am now. This is my old dressing room underneath the ruined Vittorina Royale. The stellar's dressing room. Behind the sharp stench of the skysilver bars is the smell of mould and damp. How did they get the cage here? They must have burnt their palms raw. Never underestimate children who travel in a pack.

'Topaz,' I say. I remember her. More than any of the lambs. Her solemn, dark little face. Bright eyes. She wanted it, wanted the stage, more than any of them. Of course she is the salamander. She is the best of my cabaret of monsters. Her voice has more power in it than mine ever had. 'What did you give me?'

'Dalerian,' she says, looking at me like I am the enemy. 'It's a tincture using —'

'I know what it is.' I am quite the amateur apothecary these days. Someone had to be when Garnet and Livilla took too much of one powder or started keening for a potion they craved. 'No wonder I've been talking for so many hours.' I don't remember when it started, but my throat is rubbed raw.

'Days,' she says. 'We gave you the dose days ago. Too much, I think. You kept falling in and out of consciousness, but when you were awake, all you did was babble.'

She knows all my secrets, then. Much good may they do her.

'Why am I here?'

'Because Livilla is dead, and it's your fault.' Her voice is shaking. I remember that, the loss of your first Lord. Had it been anyone but Garnet who killed Tasha, I would have avenged her fiercely.

'I never meant for her to die. I didn't expect —'

'No,' Topaz says sharply. 'You expected him to kill me. You were going to *let* him kill me. You didn't give a damn. How selfish is your love that you can stand by and let him do these things to other people?'

'We're all selfish when we love,' I tell her. 'What are you going to do with me?'

'I'm going to hurt Garnet.' She means it, she really does. Her eyes are bright with the fire of the salamander.

I laugh. Maybe it's the drugs or the tiredness or the pain in my throat, I don't know, but the whole thing strikes me as deeply hilarious.

'You think you can hurt Garnet by killing me? He won't bat an eyelid. He doesn't love me back.'

Saying it aloud doesn't hurt as much as I thought it might.

Topaz tilts her head at me, confused. 'Why do you say that like it's some kind of triumph?'

'Because he doesn't love anyone. Not me, not Velody, not Liv. Only —' And there I stop because, oh yes, it does hurt, after all.

'Only Ashiol,' said Topaz. 'That other King.'

That sums Ashiol up, doesn't it? *That other King*. The runaway. The traitor. The one who isn't Garnet, isn't Velody. The one we don't need.

'Yes,' I whisper. My body is sluggish from the potion, but I recognise the burn now, the feel of the skysilver cuffs at my wrists. Topaz has learnt from the best. 'He only loves Ashiol.'

And Aufleur, of course, this fucking city that takes everything and repays nothing. Garnet loves Aufleur, and Ashiol, and I am nothing to him.

Topaz blows out the lantern and I hear muttering in the darkness. Three voices, or four.

'Where are the rest of you?' I call out. It takes a while before she answers.

'You don't need to know that.'

'I know that the sacrifice for the Kalends was a taste of things to come,' I tell them. Here they are, the final secrets, spilling out, and I don't even have the dalerian to blame for it as the potion has long since worn out of my system. 'Garnet has been listening to the dust devils, to whatever lives beyond the sky. It was my fault. I gave him the watch; I didn't know... He thinks he's made a fucking bargain with them, and if the city is going to survive past Saturnalia, it's going to take seven hells of a sacrifice.'

Silence, and more muttering.

'What kind of sacrifice?' Topaz asks.

'Where are the rest of your lambs?' I counter. 'Are they safe? He'll be coming for them first. They're easy meat.'

How long have I been wanting to tell someone, to warn them all?

'Courtesi, Lords, sentinels, Seers, Kings. Maybe even the daylight folk. I don't know who they are. But I know he thinks that he has to make sacrifices to save the city from falling into the sky. He thinks they will keep their bargain.'

Topaz is so still in the darkness. 'Livilla?'

'Livilla was the first. More to come.'

She leaves me after that and I find myself crying, tears wet on my face. Not for my poor pitiful life, or the memories the dalerian has made me spill forth. I am crying for Livilla, who loved Garnet, and who was finally brave enough to stop loving him, to find something else to fight for. I always thought she was the weak one, but she was so much stronger than me.

My sister.

Garnet is wrong. I love him, but he is wrong.

~

On the Kalends of Saturnalis, my true love gave to me, a lake full of milk and honey.

On the Nones of Saturnalis, my true love gave to me, two lambs a-crying and a lake full of milk and honey.

On the Ides of Saturnalis, my true love gave to me, three

sentinels screaming, two lambs a-crying and a lake full of milk
and honey...

I DON'T FEEL like singing any more.

~

TOPAZ COMES TO ME AGAIN, later, in the darkness. I am
exhausted and sore, can barely move even when she unlocks
the cage. The potion has worn off, but its effects have not
completely played themselves out.

'I don't remember how you captured me,' I whisper.

'I slipped the potion into your drink.'

'No. I am not so foolish as to take a drink from your
hand, my little poisoner.'

'I did it.' Another voice; one so familiar that I am startled
into a coughing fit.

'Zero.'

Another betrayal. First the brighthound hid his powers
from me, and now my pet urchin sides with his own kind to
bring me down. Was Halberk really my most loyal courteso?
I should never have broken my own fucking rule.

'I'm sorry, my Lord,' Zero gabbles. 'But you're going to get
yourself killed if you stay at his side, that Power and Majesty.
He killed Livilla, he don't care about anyone, and I know you
can't see straight when it comes to him. I only wanted...'

He runs out of words, finally.

'You wanted to protect me,' I whisper in the darkness. Oh,
saints preserve me from this.

'We need you, Poet Lord Rat,' says Topaz, her voice
damnably confident. 'We need you to help us take him down.'

'It can't be done,' I croak. Not because it's impossible, but
because if they are relying on me to betray Garnet, they are
playing a fool's game.

Topaz reaches out and touches the side of my face, a gentle touch that reminds me horribly of Madalena. This demme knows all my secrets. All my weaknesses.

'It don't have to be the way it always has been,' she says. 'It can be different.'

Saints and devils. Another Velody. How will we cope?

I see Livilla's white throat with the slash of red across it. I see Garnet, knowing before he did it that he was going to make the cut. I taste the wolfish burr of Livilla's animor at the back of my throat.

'Time to make a choice, my Lord,' says Zero.

When did he grow up? He doesn't sound like the boy he was when I took him in.

I want to scream, or sing, or laugh. Anything but make the choice to, finally, let Garnet go.

'Show me how you take salamander form,' I say instead, forcing the words through my scraped throat. 'Show me your fire.'

Garnet is afraid of flame. Flame, betrayal and Ashiol. The one thing he is not afraid of is me.

That could be his undoing.

PART XII
THE SAINTS OF BAZEPPE

35

BONA DEA

ONE DAY BEFORE THE NONES OF SATURNALIS

DAYLIGHT

*V*elody leaned back against the cool leather of the train seat. It felt as if Aufleur was tugging on her skin, trying to restrain her from leaving. They powered away from the city so fast, she couldn't think straight.

Of all the people she might have expected to have sitting opposite her, Kelpie was one of the least likely. They had never been friends. Kelpie was the sentinel Velody never connected with. There was something about her that made Velody feel as if she herself was an unwelcome visitor.

It hadn't surprised Velody when Kelpie chose Garnet and the Court over her, though the fact that she turned her back on Ashiol at the same time was rather more shocking.

Perhaps that was why she was here now — to make amends to Ashiol.

'If you have something to ask me,' Kelpie said abruptly, 'just do it. I'm not made of glass.'

'Have you recovered from the poison?'

'That's not what you want to ask.'

'Isn't it?' Velody fell silent. She should ask Kelpie about her motivations for coming to Bazeppe with her, but that wasn't enough. 'Why don't you like me?' she said finally.

Kelpie stared at her. It was rare to see her entire face; usually she hid behind her hair or swords, or in the shadows. 'You haven't earned your place,' she said finally. 'You don't belong in the Creature Court. We're family, and you're not.'

'The others disagree.'

'They're stupid. We all know each other, inside and out. We start young, we grow up in the Court, that's how it works. I don't know you, and they all seem to... I don't know. They love you, and I don't get it. You're not one of us.'

'Why did you pledge your loyalty to me in the first place if you felt that way?'

'Because you're a King, and we don't get a choice about loyalty. Because it was the only way Ashiol was going to stay with us. If we made him Power and Majesty, he would run, we all knew that.' Kelpie smiled thinly. Her eyes looked so sad. 'He ran anyway.'

'And if you have to choose again, between the three of us?' Velody challenged her. 'If it was down to you, which of us would you have as Power and Majesty?'

Kelpie sighed. 'Maybe this time I'd run away. It seems like the thing to do. Maybe I'm doing it already.' She leaned her head back against the leather seat and gave Velody an unfriendly look. 'It's an unfair question. Sentinels never get to choose.'

'Do you think we can bring him back?'

'Depends, doesn't it? What's even in Bazeppe to keep him there?'

That, Velody thought, was a very good question.

~

THE SERVANTS at the Palazzo in Bazeppe were of a different mould to those at home. Velody had expected to have to lie her way through a phalanx of factotums and stewards to get to Ashiol. Instead, she and Kelpie were sent directly to a chatty under-secretary who proclaimed how delighted he was to show them to the Ducomte's office.

'Office,' Kelpie mouthed behind the under-secretary's back.

This made as little sense to Velody, but she pretended to be unconcerned. The under-secretary gave them a rambling lecture about this particular wing of the Palazzo and its historical significance, which allowed her to gather her thoughts.

Her animor sparked with life again once she stepped within these city walls. It tasted different here in Bazeppe, but good. Now she was inside the Palazzo, it truly awoke within her. Ashiol was here. She could feel the heat of him nearby. His animor was awaking, stirred by her own. She felt her skin prickle at his proximity.

'Troyes, these demoiselles are here to see the Ducomte,' the under-secretary said with a flourish as they entered a room in which a slender young man in a burnt-orange linen suit lounged behind a beautifully carved desk. 'I believe they are his...'

'Tailors,' said Velody, her gaze steady and uncompromising.

'Indeed,' said this new secretary, eyeing her with an unfriendly gaze. He walked with deliberation to the connecting door and knocked before opening it. 'Seigneur Ducomte? I'm afraid the lawyers have not yet sent up the draft contracts. But your... tailors are here to see you.' His voice made it clear that he didn't believe a word of it.

Kelpie hung back for a moment, but Velody seized her hand and pulled her into the office.

It was a gorgeous room, all green leather and carved wood. Ashiol sat behind a desk four times the size of his secretary's, and he had a view of the wintry landscape outside.

He stood to greet them. He looked so different. He wore a plum-coloured brocade suit with a beautifully cut sapphire-blue morning coat — respectable and debonair, but obviously designed for a man ten years older and thirty years more respectable than himself. His hair was combed, his face recently shaved. Strangest of all, he was at peace with himself. Had Velody ever seen him when he wasn't angry or afraid? She couldn't think of a single occasion.

'Mistress Velody,' he said politely, treating them as near-acquaintances. 'Mistress Kelpie. How kind of you to come all this way.'

'I couldn't entrust your shirts to anyone else, seigneur,' said Velody, as Troyes withdrew and closed the door behind him.

Immediately, Ashiol's face changed. The old anger surfaced, most of it directed at Kelpie. 'Changed sides again, have we?'

Kelpie stepped back as if slapped.

'Garnet almost killed her,' said Velody. 'Don't be horrible about it.'

Ashiol was unmoved. 'I've missed much.'

'That happens,' said Kelpie sharply, recovering a little from his first blow, 'when you *run away*.'

'You're a fine one to talk about running away.'

'I did my duty,' she flared, and then turned away from him with some effort, going to look out of the window. 'Cushy set-up you have here. Very nice. Do they pay you in honey wine and figs?'

'The Creature Court aren't the only ones I have a duty to,'

said Ashiol, but he wasn't looking at Kelpie now. His eyes roamed over Velody, dark and serious. 'Why are you here?'

'I came to bring you home,' said Velody.

Ashiol's face closed over, taking on that false formality he had shown in the presence of his secretary. 'I'm sorry you had a wasted journey. But I'm not going anywhere.'

Velody glared at him. 'Is that all you have to say to me?'

'I don't need new shirts.'

'Funny.'

He moved then, past Velody to the door. For a moment, he was close enough to touch her and her animor sparked hard. Didn't he feel it?

'Come on,' he said. 'If you want to know what's keeping me here, I'll show you.'

Velody followed him out, Kelpie trailing sullenly behind them. Ashiol led them down several flights of stairs and out into a wide courtyard lined with bronze statues. It was cold enough to make their breath steam, though there was sufficient heat rolling off Ashiol to keep all three of them warm.

'What are we looking at?' Velody asked.

Ashiol grinned, oddly carefree. Since when did he recover his humour that quickly?

When Kelpie stepped out into the courtyard, two of the statues moved, barring her way. 'Hey,' she protested.

One of the statues made a noise, all whirrs and chimes.

'Is it talking?' Velody asked in astonishment.

The other statue flipped up Kelpie's cloak and laid its hand on her swords. She stepped back out of range, fury evident on her face. 'Don't you dare! Ashiol, stop this.'

'It's not me,' said Ashiol, enjoying himself far too much. 'They don't want you to approach me armed.'

'Tell them I can kill you with my bare hands,' Kelpie said sarcastically, then ducked back once more as all the statues turned to look at her. 'That was a joke — eugh, what are they?'

'The clockwork saints,' said Ashiol. 'They're all over this city. These are the ones that protect the Palazzo. They're what the Creature Court of Bazeppe have instead of sentinels.'

'I've been replaced by a few hunks of articulated bronze?' Kelpie said in disgust. 'Lovely.'

'They're more than soldiers,' said Ashiol. 'They fight the sky. They're the reason Bazeppe is in no danger of being swallowed like Tierce.'

Velody bit back a reply. Rhian had said that Bazeppe would fall before Saturnalia, and Aufleur would follow. But just because the Seer said it didn't make it true.

'It's the clockwork,' Ashiol explained, his voice alight with enthusiasm. 'They don't bother much with festivals here. They don't need them. The clockwork holds the sky at bay.'

'But doesn't stop it,' said Velody. 'Doesn't end it. The Court of Bazeppe are trapped in the same everlasting war that we are.'

'No,' said Ashiol, shaking his head furiously. 'You don't understand. They break *all* the rules. They don't fight each other. They elect the Power and Majesty — they take turns, for fuck's sake. They've figured out the answer, the essence we were searching for when you took over in Aufleur. They've been doing it this way for years.'

'And how is that going to help us with Garnet?' Velody pressed. 'How is it going to stop the sky falling?'

There was an intense light in Ashiol's eyes. 'If I can figure out how it all works, if I can stay a little longer, I can save everyone,' he said.

'Can you do it by Saturnalia? That's how long we have.' Velody took a deep breath. 'Bazeppe is under threat, too.

Whatever is happening, whatever Garnet is up to, it will affect them.'

'The clockwork saints are the answer,' Ashiol said stubbornly. 'I know they are.'

'You won't come home with us, then?'

'No, I won't.'

She darted a quick look at Kelpie, who was still being held at bay, prevented by the clockwork saints from entering the courtyard because she refused to take off her blades. Velody stepped nearer him, telling herself it was necessary, and not just because her animor was screaming out to touch Ashiol and to be touched. 'Do you know what the sacred marriage means?' she said in a low voice.

He gave her an odd look. 'Is that a proposal?'

'Garnet knows more about the Creature Court than anyone — not only its future, but its past. Power and Majesty was never supposed to be one person, it was two. A pair of Kings, joined together.'

Velody stared up into Ashiol's face as he thought it over. 'That makes a lot of sense,' he said slowly. 'How did we not know about this?'

'I think the Creature Court have forgotten more about their own traditions and history than we ever guessed.'

'That I'm sure of,' he said firmly. 'It feels as if each Court, each city, only knew a handful of the secrets. Why did we never talk to each other? If Bazeppe had festivals too, and Aufleur had clockwork, how mighty would we be?'

Velody closed her eyes. He was so close, she could almost lean in and rest against his chest. She wanted to, so badly. He smelled like home.

What did Tierce have that the other cities didn't? No clockwork saints, she was sure of that — she would have seen some remains of them when she and Garnet were alone in that city, surely.

'My brother used to tell me stories of steam angels,' she said. 'Tierce was a city full of water, and they used steam to open temple doors and to push the boats. Do you think that was their secret? The steam?'

'Perhaps,' said Ashiol. She opened her eyes again and saw him gazing at her. 'Did Garnet want you to be Majesty to his Power?'

Velody almost laughed. 'I think he wanted to be the Majesty. But yes. He offered me that.'

Ashiol stepped away from her, marking a firm distance between them. 'Perhaps you should take him up on the offer.'

'You don't mean that.'

'Why not? By all means, let's follow the pointless, long-dead traditions of our people. What else have we to lose?' He was almost shouting now.

'You're such a child, Ashiol. If you and I could work together for half a day, we could take the Court back from Garnet,' she threw at him.

'I don't want it back.'

'Stop saying things you don't mean! It only wastes time.'

'If you want the sacred marriage from me, Velody, I can't give you that.'

She folded her arms defensively. 'I didn't ask.'

'I'm not stupid. Last time I opened myself up to a fellow King, he stole my power. I can't do that again.'

'Then what are we going to do?' she asked him softly.

Ashiol smiled. 'You are going to go back to Aufleur. I am going to stay here and find out the secrets of the clockwork saints.'

No, it wasn't right. She couldn't leave him here; couldn't trust him to keep himself alive, let alone save everyone else. 'It's not enough.'

'It will have to do.'

Ashiol turned and walked back towards the Palazzo.

Halfway up the steps, he made an impatient gesture and the clockwork saints moved back to their original positions, releasing Kelpie.

Kelpie blew out a breath. 'So what do we do now?'

Velody couldn't take her eyes off Ashiol's back. 'Will you wait for me at the train station?'

'What am I, a dame's companion?' Kelpie muttered.

'I have to convince him he's wrong, and he'll never admit that in front of an audience.'

'Fine. But don't blame me if he uses those clockwork saints on you.'

BONA DEA

ONE DAY BEFORE THE NONES OF SATURNALIS

DAYLIGHT

*V*elody followed Ashiol back up the various flights to his office. He turned around impatiently as they reached the door. 'Don't you understand a farewell when you hear one?'

The finely garbed secretary gave her a half-hidden a smirk. Velody ignored him. 'We still have things to discuss.'

'Oh, really?' Despite his obvious reluctance, Ashiol held the door open for her and followed her in. 'What do you have to say to me that you couldn't utter in front of Kelpie?' He widened his eyes and grabbed her hand mockingly, holding it to his heart. 'Velody, is this a seduction?'

'Let's not be too ridiculous.' She snatched her hand away, but not before his animor sent a surge of heat through her own. He tasted different with Bazeppe inside him as well as Aufleur, and she was starting to sense the power of this new city in other ways. She wasn't used to a playful Ashiol, let alone one who switched from humorous to serious in the blink of an eye. Had he reclaimed his youth, or found some different powders to swallow?

'I really don't see what else there is to say.'

'You've changed,' Velody accused. 'You're so different.'

'This is what I'm like when I'm not angry and scared all the time. I realise that it's new.'

'Why aren't you angry and scared? Is this city really so much better than Aufleur? A few days of clockwork saints fighting your battles for you and suddenly you're all serene?'

'I like to be looked after. Simple as that.'

'Is it that Garnet isn't here? Is that what makes you so happy?'

But no, Garnet was gone before and Ashiol never looked like this.

'Lysandor is here,' he admitted, and his face softened. 'He's fighting the sky, they all are, but they have the clockwork saints to help them, and they don't tear each other to pieces. He has a wife and a child, the closest thing to a normal life that anyone of the Creature Court has ever managed to pull together. Bazeppe has given me hope, Velody. I didn't realise how seductive it could be: the possibility of being normal. Mundane. Of balancing the daylight and the nox without sacrificing my own humanity.'

Velody folded her arms. 'You had plenty of opportunity for a normal life in the five years you were exiled from Aufleur. You didn't exactly settle down and start having babies, did you?'

Though, to be fair, she knew nothing of what he had done in that time. He could have impregnated dozens of milkmaids and shepherdesses.

His face clouded over, for one moment looking like the old Ashiol. 'That was different.'

'Was it? I thought you were unhappy because you spent that five years hiding from what you were supposed to be doing, and yet here you are, hiding again and apparently delighted about it.'

'You only want me back because I'm a better proposition for the sacred marriage than dear Garnet,' he said sourly. 'That's hardly flattering, Velody.'

'I never said you were a better proposition. I never said I wanted anything from you!'

'But you do. You want everything, and I can't give it. Why don't you stay?'

She looked at him in surprise. 'Here? In Bazeppe? What would I do — sew cravats for the Duc-Elected?'

'He has daughters as well as sons. I expect they need dresses from time to time.'

'That's not even funny.' She saw no humour in his face.

'Let Garnet get on with whatever he plans to do to keep Aufleur from falling into the sky. He wants the Creature Court so damn much. Give it to him.'

Did he have any idea what he was actually saying? 'Ashiol — Garnet is sacrificing children.'

He shrugged callously. 'Perhaps the people of Tierce should have sacrificed a child or two, if that's what it takes.'

Overwhelmed with fury, Velody shoved at his chest, too upset even to coordinate a slap across his face. He stumbled back a step and took hold of her wrists. Heat shot from his skin to hers.

'I can't stop him,' he said between his teeth.

Tears stung her eyes, which she hated herself for, just a little. 'You don't want to try.'

The proximity of him after so long made her heart beat faster. Their animor recognised each other. Being this close was almost like being within the walls of Aufleur again, only more intense because Bazeppe was beating at their skin, too.

'We can't fight him without you,' she said breathlessly.

He turned her face up to his. 'Liar. You know full well that when it comes to Garnet, I'm a liability, not a weapon.'

It would really be good if they could stop touching right now. The city's metallic energy was already coursing through Velody, and Ashiol was bright, from the inside out. She had missed him so much.

'Are you still angry at me? Is that what this is about?'

He gave her a very Ducomte expression. 'Angry?'

'You were so furious,' she said helplessly. 'About Garnet and me. About everything.'

'I don't remember,' he said, and the mask of his face was horribly perfect. 'Why don't we let it go? I'm sure none of that matters now.'

'You have to stop pretending,' Velody insisted.

He was so changed. Calm. Did she have any right to take him away from this life, this place, that made him a real person instead of a raving maniac?

Even if she preferred the maniac.

'Pretending to be sane?' said Ashiol. Finally, the mask cracked, if only a little. He still held her arm, keeping her close to him. 'Pretending I belong here? Or pretending I have something to offer beyond tilting at shadows?'

'We need you. I need you. Garnet...' Velody didn't know how to say it any other way. Surely there had been enough words that he could start believing her.

She could tell he was getting impatient now, though he kept it under control. His animor flared with it. 'You brought him back. You knew what he was. Or you would have done, if you believed me. Trusted me. But Velody always knows best. Velody, the kind, compassionate little mother.' His hand was tight, now, over her arm. 'You gave him the Creature Court. It's not my job to take his toys away from him, it's yours.'

'I can't do it alone.'

She should pull away, walk away. But she had to try. She couldn't go back to the sentinels, to Kelpie, without being able to say that she'd tried with every mote of her being to get him back.

She couldn't leave him to fall with Bazeppe.

'Yes, you can. Don't you get it, Velody? I'm a liability. I always have been. I'm not a leader. I didn't beat him last time. I gave in. Submitted to his will. How is that going to be helpful?'

The fury rolled off him, finally. If he was in cat shape, all his fur would be standing up. Velody liked him angry. He made so much more sense that way. Did that make her a bad person?

'You are stronger than you think you are,' she said.

Ashiol laughed in her face. 'I'm really not.'

'Everything you've learnt here, about the clockwork saints, about Lysandor and this Court — we can take the secrets of Bazeppe back with us. Use them to end the skywar and free Aufleur. If we could only work together, perhaps we could end it once and for all.'

An odd look crossed Ashiol's face. 'But what would we do with the slaves?'

'I'm sorry?'

'One of the early Ducs in Aufleur was shown a steam engine, hundreds of years ago. He ordered it destroyed, and declared, "What would we do with the slaves?" I believe they did something similar when clockwork crossed their paths.'

'There's never been slavery in Aufleur.'

'Just us. What do you think will happen if the skywar ends? Do you think Livilla will give up biting chunks out of underage boys and take up needlecraft? That the others will get jobs in wine bars or factories, settle down to being ordinary little daylight folk? You'll have a bunch of bored, disenfranchised monsters on your hands and it will be a fucking massacre.'

Velody stared at him. Part of her wanted to argue that they couldn't give up hope of ending the skywar because it provided gainful employment to the Creature Court, but there wasn't time for that, because saints, oh saints, oh saints, he still thought Livilla was alive, and she had to be the one to tell him otherwise. How had she forgotten?

Ashiol responded to her stricken look. 'What?'

There was no kind way to put it. 'Livilla's dead,' Velody blurted out. 'I'm sorry.'

This time, he released her. 'You should go.'

But no, not with that. She had to give him more than that. 'I need to tell you how —'

'No, thank you kindly,' he said, with a smile that was more of a snarl. 'That's not my world any more. I don't need to know.'

Livilla was a hero. Would he laugh if Velody said that out loud? Livilla had died to save her courtesa from Garnet's cruel sacrifice. 'Ashiol —'

'Get out!' he snapped. 'You've done your bit, properly simulated care and attention for my feelings, but I'm done with the Creature Court of Aufleur and with you. I'll end my days happily sitting in the shadow of the clockwork saints and there's not one fucking thing you can do about it.'

'Fine,' said Velody. She was tired of this, of stepping around the emotions and egos of everyone else. She wasn't the Power and Majesty any more and the job had still got harder. She turned to leave.

Ashiol went back to sit behind his desk, playing the stone-faced bureaucrat. He didn't say goodbye, didn't say anything. It was as if she'd already left.

Velody made it as far as the door, then spun back around. She couldn't help herself. She walked to Ashiol quickly and tugged at the sleeves of the sapphire morning coat, feeling the stiff fabric under her fingers. 'This doesn't suit you. You can't wear bright colours; you look like something that escaped from a carnivale.'

He couldn't say *this* was none of her business. Not if they were talking about clothes. Not that Ashiol said anything. He looked at her vaguely, as if wondering why she was still here.

Velody pulled off his coat and threw it on the desk. 'You're not a middle-aged Baronne: you shouldn't dress like one.' She reached down and started unbuttoning his brocade waistcoat. 'Not this, either. Not if you don't want children to point and laugh at you in the street.' The plum colour was rich and bold and had obviously been chosen by someone who wasn't Ashiol. Given a choice he would match black with black and more black, and that was as it should be.

Ashiol's eyes flashed, but he let her divest him of the waistcoat. 'Are you planning to strip me until I feel better about losing Livilla?' he said, with a hint of sarcasm that was at least better than the sheer nothing she saw in his face.

'Whatever it takes,' she said, and her voice trembled just a little. She saw Livilla again, falling. Damn him for not being willing to share his grief. He had to have sadness inside him or he was a monster, and Velody didn't believe he was a monster, not for a second.

'I didn't love her, you know,' he said. 'You don't have to comfort me.'

She stared at him, sitting there at his desk, pretending to be someone he wasn't. 'Liar.'

Ashiol made a grab for her, pulling her into his lap. She let him, not moving as he slowly ran his hands over her waist, breasts, neck. Finally, touching her. His fingers tightened in her hair and she let out a sigh. Finally, something real.

'Lying about what?' he asked, his voice sounding hoarse.

'I've forgotten,' said Velody, and kissed him.

He tasted of warm imperium and lemon-mint and her animor responded fiercely to him. They wound their arms around each other, kissing hard and rough, mouths wet and wanting. This and only this. If he refused to come home, there was no reason to pretend to be indifferent to him.

They said no more words.

Ashiol lifted her up onto the desk and removed her boots with swift movements, her stockings, the dress that still smelled of travel dust and train smoke. When there was nothing left but slip, breastband and knickers, he lowered her onto her back and ran his mouth over her, finding places to kiss and suck at her warm bare skin.

Velody reached up, unfastening buttons, dragging his shirt from him and letting it fall to the floor. It was an ugly shirt and it needed to die. Who had ever thought that design of collar a good idea?

They were going through the motions, almost politely, as if they had done this many times before. *An old married couple*, Velody thought, on the edge of hysteria, and then Ashiol bit her on the neck and the mild pain of it woke her up. She clawed at his face, pulling him to her so they could kiss messily, their tongues hot against each other.

She unfastened the plum brocade breeches that matched the rest of his suit. Plum brocade. How could anyone look at Ashiol and think plum brocade? She slid her hand inside, feeling the heat and hardness of him, the silkiness of his cock.

'Here,' she said breathlessly. 'With me. Not... wallowing in nostalgia or old wounds or anything.'

No grief allowed, not now, even if that made her the most selfish wench in the city. This was about something else. She would not think the word 'marriage', she would not, but they had to see what it would be like, the two of them, if there was an accord that could be reached. If they were stronger together than apart. They had to be, surely.

She was thinking too much.

Ashiol's answer was a growl, low in his throat, more like a lion than the street-cat he was. He ripped her knickers down to her knees and pressed his fingers inside her, making her gasp. She cried out as he stirred a deep wet warmth inside her cunt, and this time she closed her teeth over his shoulder.

He teased her, bringing her to the edge and back again, and it didn't take much of that before she was muffling her sounds against his neck. This would be a fine scene for those pretty secretaries to walk in on...

It was hard to care about that when Ashiol's hands were all over her, and the heat of him, of his blood, his animor, was swirling in her head. She had never felt as powerful as she did right now, her legs splayed apart on his desk and the weight of a mostly naked King against her body.

While she was recovering from the delicious work of his fingers, he stretched himself out on the desk like the lazy cat he was. His erect cock jutted from the opening in his breeches, but the look in his eyes displayed no particular urgency. A bluff, she guessed. It had to be. She leaned over him, fingers curling into the brocade that still covered his thighs, and paused deliberately. There it was, the gleam of impatience in his eyes. Ha!

She eased his ridiculous breeches down only a little way, leaving him nicely entangled. Just in case he wanted to run away or anything. (It seemed unlikely.) She crawled onto him, keeping her eyes fixed on his, looking for those little signs that, yes, he wanted her specifically, Velody, not just a warm body to frig.

His hand trailed slowly up over her hip and then he grinned suddenly and — oh dear. The cat that got the cream.

She was never going to be able to hear that phrase again without blushing.

She parted her thighs and slid onto him, slow and steady and filling herself with warmth. Ashiol's fingers found her spine and she shivered, rocking against him. Slow, painfully slow.

Her animor pulsed, and his. Everywhere they touched there was not just warmth but an unbearable heat, scorching power, and something else. Something she couldn't define yet.

Velody arched over him, gasping every time his hands found a new part of skin to touch, feeling him so deep inside her. Their animor surged against each other, overwhelming waves that shut out everything except the places where her body touched his.

Bazeppe unfolded into Velody's mind, not only the strange cityscape but all of it, everything that Ashiol had seen and heard while he was here: faces, names, the eerie calm that made him so different from his usual self.

He throbbed hard inside her and, oh, there was his anger, buried more deeply than usual, but she welcomed it because it was Ashiol, he didn't make sense without it. His hands were rough on her now, the outlines of his palms hot and wanting as she bucked harder, riding him into insensibility.

His anger bubbled up, dark and familiar, and Velody cried out at the deeper vibrations of him hard inside her, and then she was on her back, shuddering and fever-hot as he took control, heavy on top of her, eyes black as his chimaera. Her body gave up, finally, and she came with a howl, her animor barely holding her in human shape.

Ashiol stopped what he was doing, oddly still. He looked at her as if he had no idea who she was or why he was inside her. Velody slid her hand between them, feeling where they joined, smoothing her fingertips around the base of his cock.

'Let go,' she told him in the firm Power and Majesty voice she had been cultivating for so long. He shuddered and emptied himself inside her, warm and wet.

Ashiol dragged in a long breath of air and stared down at her. 'There's something wrong with this city.'

'I know,' said Velody. 'We'll deal with that later.'

BONA DEA

ONE DAY BEFORE THE NONES OF SATURNALIS

DAYLIGHT

*T*hey didn't sleep, not exactly. It was the middle of the day, after all, and one of those secretaries might take it upon themselves to burst in on them at any time. Still, neither of them was in any hurry to move. They curled into each other on the large desk, lightly touching, getting used to the idea of this.

'You didn't steal my animor,' Ashiol observed.

'No,' said Velody. 'You didn't steal mine, either.'

'Is this what trust feels like?'

'Don't get sentimental.'

'Hells of a trust exercise.'

'I have to tell you something.'

'Is someone else dead? Because I need a nap before any more comforting takes place.' There was an edge to his voice behind the humour.

'Thimblehead,' she said fondly. 'It's about Power and Majesty. About it being two people.'

'You didn't put on a red veil and wedding bracelets while I was resting my eyes, did you? The wedding doesn't count unless I slaughter a lamb for the augury...'

She smacked him lightly. 'I don't think the sacred marriage involves an actual marriage.'

'Well, that's a relief.'

'Does Bazeppe have one Power and Majesty or two?'

'One, I think. But they've been contaminated by democracy and vote them out if they aren't happy.'

Velody thought about that. 'Can I be in the room when you mention that option to Garnet?'

Ashiol laughed. 'Our people are too set in their ways. You know they won't accept a leader they have to elect.'

'You thought it would be a hard sell making them accept a demoiselle.'

'And they were so loyal to you, the second Garnet came back they put a man in charge again.'

She gave him a serious look. 'I think Garnet has a point. Two leaders, not one. It could be the thing that saves the city.'

Ashiol sighed, sitting up on the desk so that she could see nothing but his bare, muscled back. 'So marry Garnet. Or whatever it takes. One Power, one Majesty.'

'Garnet's crazy.'

He laughed at that. 'And you think I'm perfectly sane.'

'Not perfectly...' Velody leaned against his back, her mouth brushing against his shoulder blade. 'We're stronger together than we are apart. You know that.'

'Did you actually come here plotting to fuck me, form a partnership and save the Creature Court, possibly not in that order of priority?'

'My plan was to do it without the fucking.'

Ashiol laughed at that for quite a while. 'Is that how irresistible I am?'

'Apparently,' she said dryly.

He turned then, and kissed her. 'Can we save Garnet?'

'We have to save Aufleur *from* Garnet,' she reminded him.

'I know. Can we save him anyway?'

'I'm not sure.'

He frowned at her. 'Be sure, Velody. There's Bazeppe, as well. We have to figure out what's wrong with this place, protect Lysandor and his family.'

'Fine,' she said in exasperation. 'We can save everyone. Why the hells not?'

Ashiol smiled, an odd light in his eyes. 'How do you do that? You drag hope around with you like a tail.'

'Anything is possible,' she said. He leaned in to her, but she pulled away. 'I thought you needed a nap.'

'Later. Much later. I want to see if I can resist stealing your animor again.'

As they kissed, the slow heat of their animor building as their bare skin pressed against each other, a voice broke in on them.

'Velody, the train station. Quickly!'

A mouse sat on the window sill, speaking in Kelpie's voice.

~

'I NEED MEAT,' said Ashiol as he and Velody rattled along in the back of one of the Duc-Elected's blasted mechanical cabriolets.

'You should have eaten before we left,' said Velody, sounding like someone's mother. Possibly his, but that was a thought he must never, ever entertain.

'I mean it. Those wretched servants at the Palazzo put vegetables into everything. I haven't felt like myself in days.'

'You were willing to live forever in a city that doesn't feed you meat?'

'I told you, there's something wrong with this place. It's like there's a veil over everything. It's foggy.'

She coughed on the dark smoke being belched out by the vehicle. 'I'm not convinced that's fog.'

There was a train in at the station as they arrived, and steam billowed across the platform. 'That's not fog either,' said Ashiol. 'Do you see your steam angels? We're going to need all the help we can get.'

'I see Kelpie,' said Velody, quickening her step as she hurried to the sentinel.

Kelpie stood with her arms folded defensively. 'Coming with us now, are you?' she asked Ashiol.

He didn't have an answer for her yet.

The train pulled out of the station with a shriek and whistle. When the smoke and steam cleared, they saw Priest sitting on a bench, his back straight, hands placed carefully on his knees. He was alone, neither of his remaining courtesi in sight, and there was something very wrong about the expression on his face.

Velody went to him, sat beside him. Ashiol stood over them, with Kelpie hanging back just a little.

A faint flicker of a smile passed over Priest's face as he recognised them. 'We meet again, my Kings. Quite like old times.'

'Hello, Priest,' Velody said, her voice calm and measured. 'Did you find what you were looking for here in Bazeppe?'

'I did not,' he said after a long pause. 'But I still trust that I will. You came a long way to bring our cat home to Aufleur, my King. Was the journey worth it?'

'Entirely,' said Velody without a blush. Priest was drawn, his skin without its usual rosiness. 'Are you unwell?'

He let out a deep sigh. 'The word, my dear Power, is "doomed". There is nothing to be done for me.'

Kelpie made to say something, but Velody shushed her. 'Is there anything I can do?'

Priest did not turn to her. His fingers beat out a slow rhythm against the edge of the bench. 'Ashiol here was my courteso once, did you know that? He and Lysandor both. They traded loyalty with me to save their friend's life. To save Garnet. But it was a mere excuse.'

Ashiol hadn't thought about that time in years. Tasha's shade... it was an excuse, of course. To take a new Lord, any Lord, who was not Garnet.

'I don't know the details,' said Velody.

'Lysandor did the one thing that none of us had the strength for,' Priest went on. 'He left. Began a family of all things. A true family, here in Bazeppe.'

'He always was the creative one,' said Ashiol.

'Indeed.' Priest's voice was sluggish, like he was drunk. He didn't smell of alcohol, just a sort of stale perfume and cigar smoke. 'Lysandor will not evacuate with you,' he added conversationally. 'Nor Celeste. Too noble by half, those two, and their contentment in this city has made them soft. Though, if you can, you should save the child. She is unique.'

Saints, not that. Not Lysandor and Celeste, after being safe for so long.

'Save her from what?' Velody asked.

Kelpie let out a cry and drew her sword. Ashiol grabbed at Velody, pulling her off the bench and away from Priest. His skin was grey and his expression terrible. The wrongness was evident now. There was a grainy texture to him, as if he were made of sand. He exhaled, and part of his face fell away into dust. How had Ashiol not realised?

'They never let you go,' Velody whispered. 'The dust devils, the things beyond the sky...'

'Sadly, they did not,' said Priest, and there was a hint of the old timbre in his voice momentarily. 'I tried to run, but no train is fast enough for such a venture. I could travel no further, and now... I am sorry for what I have wrought.'

'Not your fault,' said Velody, though she choked on the words.

'You are too kind,' said Priest, and the rest of him fell fast, too fast. Even his clothes crumbled like dry leaves and blew along the platform with the dust that remained of him.

As he fell to nothingness, Priest's voice left one last message hanging in the air. *Ask Garnet about his choice.*

'Saints,' said Kelpie with a choking sound. 'I've never seen anything like that.'

'Did you hear that, at the end?' Velody asked Ashiol. 'What does it mean?'

Ashiol didn't have time to think about Garnet, or to grieve Priest. 'You said that Rhian predicted Bazeppe would fall, before Aufleur?'

'Yes.'

'I have to warn them.'

'And when you say warn them, you mean fight at their side to stop it happening,' Kelpie said, sounding weary.

Yes. Of course that was what he meant. Wasn't that obvious?

Velody reached out and touched Ashiol's hand. Her skin sparked against his, and for a moment he could think about nothing but their bodies, back in his office, the heat of her.

'Did you expect us to wait here at the station like good little demoiselles,' she said, 'while you fight and die for a city that isn't even ours?'

'Screw that,' Kelpie added, in case he didn't get the message.

Ashiol wanted to bundle them both onto the nearest train. Unfortunately, there wasn't one. 'Fine, then. Let's go.'

～

IT TOOK TOO LONG for Ashiol to find the Emporium where the Clockwork Court made their home. It annoyed him that it was Kelpie who finally pointed out he should stop trying to use his human brain about it. As soon as he went into cat form, he could feel the skysilver-reinforced roof shining out like a beacon.

Velody fell into her creature form as well, and they ran together. He could still feel the spark of her animor, though at least in this form he could be clear-headed without wanting to touch her all the time.

At the warehouse, Kelpie shoved at the door, which was wedged shut. She threw clothes impatiently at the two Kings and concentrated her energies on trying to get them inside.

Ashiol dressed himself quickly and joined her at the door, shoving animor as well as human strength into it. There was a creaking sound, and they were able to push it open just enough for Kelpie to slip through the gap. Ashiol heard a crash and then the door opened properly.

'One of those creepy clockwork soldiers,' she said, and Ashiol saw the stiffened body of one of Lysandor's saints. Its eyes were empty and there was no sign it had ever been able to move. Dust poured out of its articulated joints.

'Priest got here before us,' said Ashiol. 'Or whatever he brought here with him.'

He led the way past the teetering walls of packing cases to the main space, where the Court made their refuge. There were only a few of them clustered around the boiler, many looking half-asleep or distinctly unwell. Lucia was there, her bright gold curls standing out in the dim light. The child was being looked after by one of the demmes. Lysandor and Celeste were nowhere in sight.

'What happened here?' Ashiol demanded.

'And where were you?' replied a strident voice. It was Peg, the Wolf Lord of Bazeppe. Her clothes were charred and she smelled like power and death. 'Or aren't you one of us now? That would explain a lot.'

'We were dealing with Priest.'

She gave him an unfriendly look. 'A little late for that, don't you think? He's responsible for all this. That damned dust of his is getting everywhere.'

'It wasn't his fault,' said Velody.

Peg rolled her eyes. 'As if that makes a difference, pet. The clockwork's gone — every piece of it stopped working. That makes us sitting cubs. Lambs to be eaten.' She looked speculatively at Velody. 'You're a King, aren't you? They breed mice fierce in Aufleur.'

'Apparently so,' said Velody.

'Well? Get in the frigging sky. We need you. And the pretty boy.'

'What can I do to help?' Kelpie asked, stepping between Peg and Ashiol.

'A sentinel,' Peg said appreciatively, looking Kelpie over. 'Well, well. We could do with more like you, I can tell you that much. No dust in your joints. We need someone to help our silversmith mend the corner of the roof. This place is our only shelter.'

'If the city goes, it won't be shelter enough,' Ashiol warned.

'Aren't you a little ball of sunshine?' snapped Peg. 'We're not stupid. If the sky falls, we're all screwed. Mind if we labour under what little hope we have left?' She called another trousered demme over. 'This is Bett, she's in charge of work patrol this nox.'

'Hello,' Bett said to Kelpie. 'Come to join the workers, have you? No animor to be bothered about?'

'Not me,' said Kelpie.

'Good.' Bett took her arm and grinned. 'Stick with us. We're the ones who get things done around here.'

Velody took to the sky, not bothering to wait for Ashiol to finish arguing with the Wolf Lord. Everything smelled of dust and smoke. She stretched her animor, trying to see the battle clearly, but it was like being in a fog.

There were skybolts and thin streaks of scratchlight, crackling bloodstars and other familiar threats, yet none of them behaved as Velody was used to. As she dodged and weaved her way through the sky, blasting a path with her animor, it was as if she was doing it for the first time. Bazeppe was getting into her head, or wasn't enough inside her head. Nothing felt right.

A warm glow swept over her and, for a moment, the fog lifted. Celeste was there, blazing brightly as she fought a pulsing mass of gleamspray. Her proximity made Velody feel more clear-headed and she swept in to help the Owl Lord. Power and Majesty, she had to remind herself.

'Glad you're here,' Celeste said with a nod. 'Haven't seen it this bad for a while — and we're not used to managing without the clockwork saints.'

She ducked as a whistling shadowstreak flew over her head, then blasted it before it could get away.

'Anytime,' Velody said breathlessly. At least here she could be useful.

Though she could not escape the thought that all this was a distraction. While she and Ashiol dallied in Bazeppe, anything could be happening at home in Aufleur.

BONA DEA

ONE DAY BEFORE THE NONES OF SATURNALIS

NOX

'*Y*ou should be in the sky,' said Lucia, the little demme looking clearly at Ashiol with Lysandor's eyes. He was unnerved by her. Children in the Creature Court were wrong: pieces of two separate worlds that should not fit together.

'I know,' he told her. 'It's a long nox ahead of us, though.'

'It's the last,' she said, her voice freakishly adult.

He gave her a second look at that. 'Are you their Seer?'

'Bazeppe doesn't have Seers, or sentinels, we have no need —'

'Yes, yes,' he said impatiently. 'You have your saints; much good they are doing you now.'

'They are doing exactly what they are supposed to do,' the little demme told him, and then pouted. 'I want a pastry. Do you have pastries?'

'No,' he said, rocking back on his heels. 'I'm not much use, am I?'

'Not much,' she agreed frankly. 'Papa always made it sound like you were something special. I thought you'd be taller.'

There was a sound behind them: a creaking wheeze and a slow, familiar ticking sound, then another, and another.

Lucia clapped her hands. 'They're back!' she said delightedly.

Ashiol turned to see the clockwork saints on their feet again, slowly moving, rotating their joints to allow the dust to pour free from them. 'Amazing,' he said.

'There!' roared Peg. 'That bleeding sky can't keep us down for long, can it?'

Had the plan of Priest and the dust devils failed so easily?

'Don't go near them,' Ashiol warned.

'We don't have to,' Peg said, giving him an odd look. 'Time to give our fighters a break from the battle!'

She made several rapid-fire gestures at the clockwork saints, who returned her signs and took off, out of the door and into the nox sky.

'You trust them very easily,' Ashiol said in surprise.

Peg gave him an unfriendly look. 'The only traitor we've ever had in this Court was your man Priest. He's gone now. His attempt failed. Back to normal.'

Ashiol looked up to the rafters where Kelpie and the silversmith, Bett, were mending the skysilver layer in the roof. Kelpie seemed relaxed, laughing as they secured the panels. How long was it since she had been asked to do something that was of practical use and not in some way degrading to her sense of honour?

'Where do they come from?' he muttered.

'Silly,' said Lucia. 'The saints come from the same place as animor.'

To prove her point, she shaped herself into a small pile of puppies and cuddled back down onto her blanket.

Ashiol stared at her for a long time. In the many years since he had first tangled with the Creature Court of Aufleur, he had never once thought to ask where animor came from.

~

A GREAT SHOUT went up across the sky. 'It's the saints. The saints are back!'

Celeste laughed delightedly. She threw back her head to look at Velody. 'It's all right now,' she said.

The clockwork saints, a dozen or more of them, came tearing through the sky. Velody hovered there and watched as they caught skybolts and fought light tendrils with dazzling precision. 'They're good,' she agreed.

'Thank the angels. Now Lysandor can go back to Lucia,' Celeste said.

Indeed, several of the Lords and Court were flying back to the Emporium, many of them nursing injuries. Velody saw Lysandor among them, waving at Celeste as he went.

'They're just going to leave the saints up here?'

'Of course. They're far better at fighting the sky than we are.' Celeste blasted a cloudburst with her animor and it exploded close enough that a wave of cold air swept over them both. 'I usually stay out here most of the nox. Power and Majesty, you know. It's expected. But we can hold the sky with only one or two of the Court attending me and the saints at any one time.'

The sky had been raging only a few moments ago, but now it seemed clear.

'Is that it?' Velody asked. 'Is it over?'

'Seems to be,' said Celeste, and frowned. 'That's odd.'

The clockwork sentinels in the sky drew together in a formation and started to fly down towards the Emporium.

'Hey, come back,' Celeste yelled at them. 'You're not off

duty yet. The sky could bubble again.' She tried making her command signs at them, but not one even turned its head in her direction.

Velody felt a sudden cold wash of premonition. 'We have to —'

An explosion rocked the sky. Skybolts flew from the hands and eyes of the clockwork saints, striking the Emporium roof in one controlled blast. The building crumpled under the pressure, and collapsed.

Celeste started screaming.

There was chaos everywhere, dust and smoke and the sound of creaking metal. Velody's hands dissolved easily through the first layer of roof, but she leaped back with a jolt of pain when the skysilver reinforcement burned her. The place didn't even look like a warehouse any more, just mess and rubble.

A few members of the Clockwork Court had been thrown some way from the Emporium, or hadn't made it there before the explosion. The clockwork saints were nowhere in sight. If their intention was to destroy the Clockwork Court, why hadn't they stayed to finish the grisly business?

'You can get in there,' Celeste said urgently. 'You're *mice*. My daughter is under that wreck.'

Velody nodded and shaped herself into thousands of tiny bodies, each scrambling into the wreckage. It was hard going. The skysilver masked everything, and the few times she opened her animor up fully to listen for survivors, the reflected pain and screams and moans were too much for her senses to deal with.

It was dark and she had thousands of tiny throats choking up with dust and the smell of death. Every time she found a body, alive or dead, she sent a short burst of animor up and out of the wreckage like an arrow of light, alerting the rescuers. It went like that for hours.

Sometime near dawn, they found Kelpie. The sentinel's body was twisted and broken, and Velody thought at first that she was dead, but it was another demme's arm wrapped around her waist that showed no pulse.

Velody called together her many tiny bodies and found enough space to shape herself into Lord form. She used her animor to blast an opening into the air above, hurling back roofing and rubble. The clear air scraped against her human throat as she physically lifted Kelpie up and out of the crumpled Emporium and carried her away from the wreckage.

There was no sign of Kelpie's blades on her body and Velody could not bear to touch more skysilver, so she bit hard into her own wrist to draw the blood she needed.

Someone grabbed her shoulder. 'You can't stop,' Celeste said frantically. 'There are still survivors in there. We need you.'

'Go to hells,' said Velody, and forced the blood into Kelpie's mouth. 'She's mine and she matters. I've been saving your people all nox. This is my turn.'

～

ASHIOL COULD NOT MOVE. Every time he tried to stir, he felt skysilver burning into him. He tried to change, to shape himself into cats, but the cats refused to take his place. They didn't like being trapped in the dark.

He tried to send to Velody, but everything was muffled by the skysilver and he couldn't even sense her presence. Perhaps she was dead. Perhaps they were all dead.

Was this what it was like when you were swallowed by the sky?

He could sense other bodies and people around him,

moans and the occasional cry. Dying here would simplify matters immeasurably.

Time stretched out, endless and numb around him. Nothing to do but think, and keep breathing. Thinking was one of the things Ashiol preferred to avoid. There was no escape under here from Livilla. He had adored her so much once upon a time. More than that, they were family.

He could hear her singing, that sweet voice before she went all husky and controlled. She was like Poet when they were young, never ran out of songs to sing, though she was shyer about sharing her voice.

'I'm not greedy, I'm not easy, I know what's on my mind... it's you and nobody else will do... you and the sky so blue...'

That was it, he couldn't stay down here, not with Livilla singing at him. It was adding insult to injury, and he couldn't kiss her silent or walk out in a huff because she was fucking dead and there wasn't a thing he could do about it.

Women whose bodies he knew more intimately than his own had to stop dying, that was all there was to it.

Somewhere, a child was crying.

Well, fuck. So much for self-pity. Now he had to do something. He couldn't move without pain, but that was of little matter. Pain was hardly a new thing to him.

Thanks for that, Garnet. You thought you were weakening me, but apparently you made me stronger...

THEY HAD CLEARED as much of the rubble as they could without bringing the rest of the building down upon what survivors might be left in there. It was nearly midday, though cold enough to still be nox. The last three bodies they had dragged out of the building were dead.

Velody had gone back into the rubble several times. She could taste nothing but dust. It coated everything. Kelpie was still unconscious, but healing. Lysandor lay some way off, breathing but damaged and slipping in and out of consciousness. Velody had donated far too much of her precious King's blood to the survivors and was feeling light-headed and strange.

'The building should have healed itself,' Celeste said. Her voice was flat. She had stopped panicking and demanding anything. She had accepted that her child was dead. 'The clockwork saints... as long as they are working, the city heals itself from the sky.'

'They did this,' said Velody.

'Priest contaminated them? All of them? How could he do that?'

'It wasn't Priest. He's dead and gone. But the dust from the sky that was inside him — that could be anywhere.'

They were losing the battle. They couldn't even see what they were supposed to be fighting. If they destroyed the saints, what next?

The daylight folk of Bazeppe wandered by at times, and a few gave a second look to the cluster of people around the fallen Emporium, but there was no urgency about them, no sign that they could really see what tragedy had occurred. Bazeppe was no different from Aufleur in that regard.

Kelpie stirred and moaned beside Velody, who squeezed her hand.

They were cold and dusty and exhausted, and there was nowhere to sleep. Nox would come again, and what would come with it?

'We have to get these people out of here,' Velody said aloud, but no one heard her.

~

WHEN LYSANDOR AWOKE, he had to be physically restrained from throwing himself back into the rubble after his daughter. Celeste sobbed as she forced him down, and he grabbed at her, face wild with agony.

It was all so painful and raw, and Velody couldn't look at them. She had lost a family once, a whole city, and it hadn't left a scar. She knew they were all dead, and she loved them still, but it felt ridiculous to miss them after so long not even remembering they existed.

'This is why we don't have families,' croaked a low voice, and Velody saw that Kelpie's eyes were open and watching Lysandor and Celeste mourn.

'That doesn't work,' said Velody. 'We just form new ones. It's what humans do.'

'What made you think any of us were human?' said Kelpie, and then coughed, bringing up dust and blood.

The fallen Emporium exploded from the inside out. A dark, wild creature burst free from its centre, and the remaining skysilver reinforced roof and walls all fell into the foundations, sending up a huge cloud of dust and grime and soot.

The chimaera hovered there for a moment, clad in the ragged remains of Ashiol's clothes. His eyes glowed red. Then he fell hard on the ground, a terrible sound coming out of him as he lay on his back and writhed. Velody could see scars and cracks all along his thick, black flesh and could smell burnt skin. The chimaera shuddered and was still.

She went to him, touched his shoulder. He cried out in a small voice. Slowly, she unwrapped the bundle of ripped cloth that hung across his chest and looked inside. Puppies, curled up as if in sleep. Four of them. Velody hardly dared check to see if they were alive, but then one cracked open a lazy eye. Velody's feet went out from under her.

The puppies tumbled out of the bundle of rags and ran to Lysandor and Celeste, yapping weakly from throats still choked with dust and dirt.

Ashiol keened and shaped himself human. He was broken in far too many places and he shook with the cold. Velody put a blanket over him, though the touch of it made him scream with pain.

'If he can do that,' said Kelpie through her scraped and raw throat, 'anything is possible.'

39

THE NONES OF SATURNALIS

DAYLIGHT

*A*shiol resisted their attempts to heal him. He flat out refused to drink Kelpie's blood, and turned his face away from Velody. All he knew was pain right now. He didn't know how to keep going without it.

Celeste, still clinging to her daughter, was more ruthless than the demmes who loved him. She cut at the pulse line in her throat with a fallen fragment of skysilver and stood over him, blood welling at the wound.

'Don't make me owe you for what you did this nox,' she said roughly. 'I couldn't take that.'

So he drank, and took strength from her. She wasn't a King, but she was Power and Majesty, and even with Bazeppe's stupid democratic system, the blood meant something to his animor. The pain ebbed, and he dozed a little while the rescue efforts continued around him.

Every time he woke, Velody was not far away, and that was fine, it was good.

He needed to think. Velody had broken the illusion for him. The Emporium was gone and the Clockwork Court that seemed so seductive only a day ago lay in ruins. Nothing made sense.

Everything made sense, if you saw the world a different way. If you assumed that no one could be trusted. Velody said that Garnet was conspiring with the creatures beyond the sky. Whom else might they have on their side?

The afternoon was already beginning to fade, and Ashiol was finally capable of sitting up under his own strength. Not enough. He had to do better than this, recover faster. He needed time to think, but there was no time.

He surveyed the scene. There were the dead and injured. Velody and Kelpie consulted with Lysandor and Celeste. No one was watching him; no one but a small child with bright fair hair. She smiled, and it wasn't a nice smile. A moment later, Ashiol realised that she wasn't looking at him. He followed her gaze.

A small cluster of falcons stood at the highest point of the river bank, staring with hungry yellow eyes straight at Ashiol. They turned, flew a little way and then landed again, waiting.

Ashiol shaped himself into cats and followed. The cats allowed this, as there was no more skysilver, and no more roof, and he was heading as far away from the dust and death-stench as possible.

He knew where he was headed, of course he did, but that didn't stop him from keeping the birds clearly in vision as he tracked them across the city. Snow started to fall, a light patterning of cold over Ashiol's fur and the concrete pavements under his feet, but it didn't matter.

By the time he reached the Palazzo, the snow was thick enough that he could see the scratchy falcon's claw prints beneath a particular window. Ashiol could have gone after them directly, but the lantern light streaming out of the Palazzo reminded him of all the other things this place had to offer. Clean skin. Clothes. Boots. A chance to save the city. All good things.

Cat by cat, he climbed the walls and scrambled over the balcony and into the suite he had been given as his own. There, he collapsed into a shaking pile of fur until he was able to shape himself back into a man.

There was no time to bathe, though he caught sight of himself in the looking glass above the water basin and was mildly horrified. His skin and hair were grey with dust and he looked ten years older than he should. His wounds had scabbed over but not healed as well as he was used to.

He washed quickly, and found clothes for himself — a suit in the Bazeppe fashion: grape-coloured velvet with sage-green silk trim. It was hard not to think about Velody removing his last suit, piece by piece.

The soles of every pair of boots he had were too thick. It clouded his judgement not to be able to feel the shape of the ground under his soles. He went barefoot, along the corridor. He should eat while he had the opportunity, but his stomach roiled and rebelled when he considered that option.

Some work was best done on an empty stomach.

He had never been inside Troyes' rooms but he knew they were in the same corridor as his own. For convenience, the young man had said with a wink. Ashiol could smell him on the other side of the door — falcon, man, hurt, blood, fear, panic, dust. So many scents.

Ashiol didn't knock but allowed his animor — angry, hurt, burning animor — to blast the door open.

'What was that for?' Troyes yelled at him, picking himself up off the floor. He was still naked, and covered in bruises. Several long, ragged cuts were half-healed on his legs.

'You left the Emporium in a hurry,' Ashiol said, not bothering to couch his words in diplomacy. He wanted answers, and now that Bazeppe had lost its odd dampening effect on his animor, he was out of patience.

'I have a job to do,' his secretary said sullenly. 'A life to maintain. I couldn't —' he swallowed nervously, his whole body radiating shame — 'I couldn't take it any more. The Court is broken, so many dead. The smell of it was making me sick.'

Ashiol had no way of knowing how far he could trust Troyes. But trust was not needed right now. 'Get dressed. You're right. We have a job to do.'

'What did you have in mind?' Troyes asked warily.

'What else? We have to reveal the Clockwork Court and the skywar to Duc-Elected Henri and save the city.'

Only when he heard the words coming from his mouth did Ashiol realise that this was what he had always had in mind. It was why his paws had led him here.

'You're mad,' Troyes said finally.

Ashiol grinned fiercely. 'That's what they say.'

Duc-Elected Henri and his family were in the crimson parlour watching a show of mummers and gilded marionettes. The air was thick with tobacco smoke and laughter. The Palazzo went on as it always did.

Servants handed around delicate glasses of imperium and hazelnut wine, performing their routines like an awful kind of clockwork, oblivious that there was something terribly wrong with their city.

They wore scarlet, all of them: the Duc-Elected, his family and their guests, velvets and brocades that matched the decor of the damned room. One more elaborate and empty performance. Why did aristocrats of the daylight go to such trouble? It wasn't as if their actions had meaning.

Ashiol's stomach gnawed at him with hunger, but there were only cheese and tapenade and pickled fruits on every platter. How did these people stay alive?

'High and brightness,' he said, his voice harsh and hurting with dust and blood and his own screams of pain. He pressed all that down. No time for weakness. 'I need to speak to you.'

'Seigneur Ducomte!' cried the Duc-Elected in delight, tugging at Ashiol's sleeve. 'We have missed you. There was crab for luncheon, a fine repast, with honeyed carrots. Do you see our new performers? They are such a delight. I should send them to entertain my new daughter-to-be, your cousin the Duchessa. Do they have such marvels in Aufleur?'

Ashiol looked despite himself. There were prancing creatures on the stage, working without strings. Their clanking, uneven gait was familiar. Clockwork beasts. He couldn't restrain a shiver at the sight of them.

'Please, high and brightness, it is most urgent.'

'Have a glass of imperium, my lad, and tell me all about it,' the Duc-Elected said effusively.

The smell of the imperium hit Ashiol hard. It was all he could do not to bury his head in the carafe and never surface again. He jerked his hand back from the proffered glass.

'It is a matter of grave importance, high and brightness. The safety of this city relies upon it.' Surely the man could see how serious he was about this.

The Duc-Elected's face changed slightly as he took in Ashiol's desperation. 'Indeed?' he said, giving away little.

Ashiol kept his voice low, not wanting it to carry to the other guests. 'If you do not listen to me now, high and brightness, Bazeppe could be destroyed. We may only have hours in which to act.'

'Excuse me, my friends,' the Duc-Elected said loudly. 'I

will return to you for the second act.'

He led Ashiol to a quiet antechamber. Troyes joined them, looking nervous and afraid. 'Wait here a moment,' the Duc-Elected insisted.

'He won't listen to us,' said Troyes as soon as they were alone. 'He is daylight. We can change in front of them, buildings can fall around them, and they won't see what we really are. You're wasting time.'

'We can't afford this any more,' Ashiol replied forcefully. 'We can't fight this war with a handful of soldiers. Those of the daylight must be made to see. Velody was right. It's not just Bazeppe; there's something wrong with all of us, with the ridiculous rules we live by. None of it makes sense as soon as you try to explain it to an outsider who isn't twelve years old.'

He paced the floor, back and forth. His cats were yowling to get out of his skin. It would be dark soon, and if the sky fell again this nox, there was nowhere to hide, nowhere that was safe. So little time.

'She's your Power and Majesty,' Troyes said softly. 'Isn't she? Your Velody.'

'Yes.' Of course she was. How could she be anything else?

'She's the most important person — not just to you. To all of you. The Creature Court of Aufleur.'

'Yes, stop talking,' Ashiol said, pacing another lap of the room. 'We're wasting time.'

The doors opened, finally, and the Duc-Elected returned, alone. Ignoring Ashiol's impatience, he went to the sideboard and poured three small measures of imperium from the carafe there. Was there one of those on every flat surface in this damned place? There was a time it would have been the first thing Ashiol noticed when he entered a room. He was under no illusion that he had been cured, but he was far too busy to destroy himself right now.

'Now, my lad,' said Duc-Elected Henri in a pleasant voice. 'Tell me what you are about.'

'My tale is long and I cannot tell you all,' said Ashiol, taking the glass but resolutely not drinking from it. 'You must take me on faith. Seigneur Troyes here will support me in this, and my cousin the Duchessa Isangell will confirm my verity once you are safely in Aufleur.'

Safe being perhaps not the most accurate of words.

The Duc-Elected raised his eyebrows. 'I can see you are disturbed, seigneur, but you surely cannot wish me to decamp to your cousin's city at a moment's notice?'

'Not just you,' said Ashiol. 'Everyone. Everyone in Bazeppe will die if they do not leave now, before nox falls.'

'I see,' said the Duc-Elected, and took a swallow from his own glass. 'And you expect me to perform such an elaborate procedure on your word, my friend?'

'You must. Ask me any question you like, only trust me in this. I am trying to save your people, for the city cannot be saved. The clockwork saints have ensured that.'

The aroma of imperium hit the back of his throat and Ashiol glanced down at the glass. He shouldn't drink. If he started now, he would never climb out of the bottle. And yet, and yet. It was a small measure, and it might clear his head enough to get his point across. He swallowed it easily.

'What are we facing, Seigneur Ducomte?' There was still a level of scepticism in the Duc-Elected's voice.

Ashiol was getting desperate. What could he say or do prove it to him? 'All I can do is show you, and you will have to listen.'

He had never done this deliberately in front of one of the daylight before. Keeping his eyes firmly on the Duc-Elected, he shaped himself into Lord form, glowing brighter than the lamps that hung on the walls.

The Duc-Elected's expression did not change. He smiled

politely, as if waiting for something impressive.

Ashiol went chimaera. His clothes tore, his teeth lengthened and his skin expanded into sinew, muscle, black fur, wide wings. 'This is the least of the monsters you will face,' he said, though the words came out only as growls. His tongue tasted thick, coated with more of that fucking dust.

'Indeed,' said the Duc-Elected, and he was still waiting, damn him. Couldn't he even pretend surprise?

Ashiol stepped forward, unfurling his wings, and fell flat on the floor. He couldn't feel his wings, nor his claws. Everything was numb and strange and lost.

'What was in that fucking drink?' he muttered.

He looked up, trying to see through suddenly blurred vision. There were no wings, no claws, just his own hands scrabbling against the polished parquet flooring. He saw the clatter of footsteps — a man running away. Troyes had escaped, at least. But escaped what?

Ashiol tried to speak, but his tongue was too thick. He fought unconsciousness. More footsteps, more people. Someone coming to his rescue? He heard voices above him, echoing as if spoken inside a brass vase.

'It seems the rumours of the Ducomte's complaint were true, my sons. We were right to prepare for this possibility.'

'What shall we do with him? Send him back to Aufleur?'

'My dear boy, that would hardly be civilised. My dottore shall attend on him until he is in a far more respectable state. We do not want to endanger your upcoming marriage by embarrassing your future wife.'

'She's the one who left us a madman as her ambassador.'

'Not intentionally, I am certain. Families are always the last to be aware of our little foibles...'

Ashiol opened his mouth to scream at them, but he managed nothing more than a grunt before the floor swam up to swallow him whole.

40

THE NONES OF SATURNALIS

DAYLIGHT

*V*elody dozed for a while, long enough to be thrown into the middle of a disorienting dream. Garnet lay draped over a gold throne, his eyes shining brightly. He looked as young as he had that nox when he stole a kiss and her animor in a single breath.

'Tick tock, tick tock,' he teased. 'Time to wake up, little mouse.'

She jolted awake and looked around. The Clockwork Court had no shelter. They were huddled near the river, wrapped in blankets. They looked miserable and defeated. Celeste and Lysandor, down by the bank, were planning the strategy for the coming nox.

'If only they had sentinels, they would have nests,' Kelpie hissed to Velody.

'If only they had a Seer, they might know for certain that they are doomed,' Velody said back. 'It's no use wondering about if only. All they have are the saints, and the dust.' Nests wouldn't protect them if the whole city was swallowed. 'Where's Ashiol?'

Kelpie shrugged. 'Gone.'

Velody swore. Trust him to slope off on his own without saying a word. 'If ever a cat deserved to be leashed...'

Celeste was coming towards them, her face grave. 'Where is Ashiol?' she demanded.

'Gathering his strength,' said Velody, gazing right back at her, daring the other woman to challenge her word.

'As long as he is here for the battle.'

'Of course he will be,' said Velody, though she knew nothing of the sort.

It was a reasonable promise: if Ashiol hadn't got himself killed, chained up or drunk, he wouldn't miss a battle. Sadly, none of those possibilities were unrealistic. She glanced at Kelpie, who looked worried. Oh, yes. One way or another, Ashiol was in trouble.

Velody stood up. 'Your pardon, Power and Majesty. We need to do something. We will return by noxfall.'

Celeste's smile was bitter. 'We never expected you to stay for our fight. You have a city of your own to think about.'

'Your expectations are meaningless to me,' Velody said flatly.

She took Kelpie's hand and they headed away through the city. 'Where do you think he could have gone? He looked too damaged to walk.'

'It's Ashiol — he could be up to anything.' Kelpie looked at her. 'Are you really going to fight at their side? What if you die here? Aufleur needs you.'

'Tierce could probably have done with me, too,' Velody pointed out. 'We do what we can, where we can. This is our battle now. Only we have to get Ashiol back first.'

'Right, then,' said Kelpie, stretching her battered body. 'Train station or Palazzo?'

Velody gave her a hard look. 'You think he might run away?'

Kelpie grinned fiercely. 'Of course not. He's not that smart.'

≈

ASHIOL WAS COLD, shivering all over, his whole body dripping with sweat. He didn't know what the fuck the Duc-Elected had dosed him with, but it was nothing familiar. He was going to die here, like this, helpless.

Every time he fell out of consciousness, he heard Garnet laughing at him.

He couldn't change shape. He rolled, tried to get out of the bed, but the blankets weighed him down and he fell with a crack to the floor, humiliated at his failure.

Some time later, cool hands lifted him back onto the bed. Cold, rigid hands.

Ashiol opened his eyes and stared into the face of a clock-work saint.

≈

'SAINTS,' Kelpie whispered. 'All around the perimeter of the Palazzo.'

They were hiding at the edge of the oak grove, surveying the scene.

'Are they there to keep us out or something else in?' Velody asked. She could not forget the sight of the mechanical men blasting the Emporium to pieces.

'Does it matter? We can't get in, and we don't even know if he's in there.'

'Of course he's in there,' said a voice.

Both women spun in alarm to see a young man standing

before them. Falcon, Velody realised, her animor sparking in response to his. He wore a bright blue and ivory suit, but the dust and skysilver burn from the Emporium collapse still clung to his skin.

'I know you,' said Kelpie. 'You're one of those secretaries.'

'He's Clockwork Court, too,' Velody warned.

Kelpie looked at her as if she had tried to teach her grandmam to darn socks. 'Obviously. Question is, whose side is he on?'

'Yours,' the young man said with a pout. At their sceptical faces, he added. 'Ashiol's. He tried to convince the Duc-Elected to evacuate the city.'

Velody sighed. 'Of course he did. He keeps forgetting that he's not ten feet tall. What happened?'

'He tried to show them how animor works, but they didn't see it properly. They're assuming that he's crazy.'

The light was beginning to fade from the sky.

'We can't get to him in time,' Kelpie said in frustration. 'Not with all those saints standing between him and us.'

'Yes,' said Velody patiently. 'If only one of us had the power to become something small enough to escape their notice.'

Kelpie glared. 'I liked you better when you weren't sarcastic all the time.'

'No, you didn't.' Velody reached out and patted the arm of the secretary, who looked distressed and ill. 'What's your name?'

'Troyes,' he managed.

'We should fetch a few more friends for this, don't you think, Troyes? In case stealth fails us.'

∽

ASHIOL WAS LOST in the darkness now. There were more

drugs, something green and sticky that left a coating on his mouth. Dust clung to it, so he could taste Priest all the way down his throat.

Not Priest. The sky. The sky was not Priest. Priest was dead.

Ashiol was so far gone that his vision was almost clear again. He saw the Duc-Elected cross the floor, coughing, and saw the dust that emerged from his throat onto a hand-kerchief. He saw Velody under him, crying out, her skin so hot he couldn't bear to touch her. He saw Livilla, head thrown back in a laugh, only it wasn't Livilla at all, it was Tasha...

He saw Celeste, blood all over her white dress and wings, shrieking angry owl hoots at Garnet. *A child.* Not one of them had a child they hadn't stolen from someone else or rescued from the streets. If Celeste managed it, it had to mean something. Had to be for a reason.

The next drug they gave him made his skin so hot that he screamed. There were clockwork saints everywhere, holding him down, standing guard at the side of the Duc-Elected and his sons.

Dust. There was dust everywhere.

'Forgive me for what I have done,' said Priest, sounding older and sadder than in the entire time Ashiol had known him. 'I am not myself.'

Ashiol opened his eyes, squinting through damp eyelashes, and a mouse ran over his pillow.

He smiled.

VELODY WAITED, her tiny heartbeat chiming the seconds, until the old man in the brocade suit and his clockwork saints left the room. Then she called in the rest of her, one mouse at a time, and formed her own body. Naked, she leaned over the sweating, shaking figure of Ashiol.

'Wake up,' she crooned. 'Come on.'

He smelled of potions and salt. He opened his eyes easily enough, but only to grin stupidly at her, his face feverish.

It wasn't endearing.

'Nearly nox,' she said. 'Snap out of it. We couldn't get Kelpie in; she's waiting at the trees. You can have her blood, as much of it as you like, but not yet. I need you on your feet.'

'I love you,' he said dreamily, to the ceiling and not in any way to Velody. 'You can't make me stop. You're mine now.'

Velody sighed. 'Fine,' she said impatiently, and shaped herself into chimaera. The power buzzed through her muscles and broadened her back, and she was able to scoop him up from his bed as if he were a doll. He was heavy, but she was strong.

Somewhere, a clock was chiming. Everywhere, clocks were chiming, one after the other. The Palazzo shuddered with the sound of clocks heralding the hour.

Velody went to the balcony doors and pulled back the curtain. Three clockwork saints stood nearby, unmoving. She could hear every whirr and scrape of their inner workings.

'You are too late, my dear,' said a voice.

Velody turned, and saw an older gentleman in a bright red velvet suit — the Duc-Elected — standing in the doorway.

'We do not need protection from the likes of you,' he said politely. 'As you can see, we have everything under control.'

Velody shifted into Lord form, her naked skin glowing white in the dim room, Ashiol's body still cradled in her powerful arms. 'Your saints betrayed the Court.'

'They did as they were expected to do.'

'They're not defending the city,' she said angrily. 'They're working for those... things that lie beyond the sky. Our enemy.'

'Your enemy, perhaps,' said the Duc-Elected. He coughed discreetly into his handkerchief. 'But what on earth made you think that we are supposed to defend the city from them?'

Velody stared at him. 'You're behind this? You sold out your own city to them. Your own people!'

'We will be safe beyond the sky. It is an honour that they want us there.'

'Believe me, I've been there,' she grated. 'It's nothing special.'

There was an eerie light in the Duc-Elected's eyes. 'That is not for you to say.'

Velody made a quick step towards the balcony, but the clockwork saints clanked into her path, preventing her escape. She went chimaera and flew at the Duc- Elected. He shoved back against her, unreasonably strong, and she stumbled, almost dropping Ashiol. She growled under her breath.

The glass doors shattered suddenly, shards falling everywhere. White owls and grey falcons filled the room with harsh cries.

The clockwork saints fell to pieces as a skysilver sword sliced through them as if they were made of cotton. Kelpie sat astride a lynx, swords bared, looking terribly pleased with herself. 'Time to go!'

41

THE NONES OF SATURNALIS

DUSK

*V*elody threw herself towards the balcony in chimaera form, dragging Ashiol into the sky. It was so close to nox, but she couldn't think about that now.

They made it outside the city bounds, and Velody lay Ashiol down. She returned to her own shape, and brushed his cheek with her hand. He barely seemed aware that she was there.

'Those bastards,' said Lysandor, changing from lynx to Lord form once Kelpie was on her own feet. 'What did they give him?'

'I don't know,' said Velody, checking Ashiol's eyes and peering down his throat. 'The dust devils did this in Aufleur, or they tried to. They got into Priest to pull the Creature Court apart from the inside, and they got under the skin of the Duchessa, used her to lower the city's defences.'

'Tierce, too,' said Lysandor. 'Must have been.'

Velody slid her hands under Ashiol's shirt, touching his

bare skin. 'Come back to us,' she said, and pushed at him with her animor. She pictured her power brushing against his, and then pressing more firmly. She visualised the potions inside him, alien and poisonous. She flexed her animor hard.

Ashiol screamed and choked as liquid filled his mouth. Velody pulled him onto his side, with Lysandor's help, and Ashiol vomited onto the paving stones: sticky, dark green gunk.

'He should feel much better for that,' Kelpie said.

Colour was beginning to streak across the fading sky. 'It's starting,' Lysandor said gravely. He clapped Troyes on the shoulder. 'Up for another battle, aye? Who needs sleep?'

Troyes laughed faintly.

Velody looked around. 'Where is Celeste?'

'I'm here.' Celeste walked out of the city on foot, holding the hand of her daughter. The child looked untroubled. 'I have to ask a favour of you.'

'You can't leave her with strangers,' Lysandor protested.

'Ashiol isn't a stranger.'

'Ashiol can hardly walk upright; he's in no position to help anyone.'

'What are you talking about?' Velody interrupted.

'We have to fight for our city,' said Celeste. 'If we fail, I need to know Lucia is safe.'

Kelpie swore under her breath.

'I was planning on fighting at your side,' said Velody. 'We all were.' She looked down at Ashiol, who was now groaning and half-conscious. 'We're not going to leave you to battle this alone.'

'If Velody fights at our side,' Lysandor told Celeste, hope lighting his eyes, 'you could stay out of it.'

'Don't be a fool,' she said sharply. 'Bazeppe needs all of us. All the power we can muster.'

'Lucia needs a mother,' he countered.

'And a father.'

They stared at each other.

Ashiol muttered something and spat more green onto the cobbles.

'This is why we don't have families,' Kelpie translated.

'We've been lucky so far,' said Celeste. 'But I am the Power and Majesty here. I have a duty.'

'Oh, for saints' sake,' Kelpie said crossly. 'I'll look after the pup. But one of you had better come back. I'm not the mothering kind.'

Celeste squeezed her daughter's hand. 'Will you stay with the nice demoiselle while Mama fights the sky?'

'She doesn't look like a nice demoiselle,' said Lucia clearly. She eyed Kelpie. 'Can I play with your swords?'

Kelpie shrugged. 'Sure.'

~

THE SKY PEELED BACK in layers of light, each more fierce than the last. 'And here they come,' Velody said beneath her breath.

The dust devils poured out, one after another. They ignored the Clockwork Court, who hovered battle-ready at cloud height, and streaked straight towards the remains of the Emporium.

'Ha,' said Celeste with some satisfaction. 'Try making your bodies solid with that.' They had stripped every piece of skysilver from the wreckage and put it on the last train to Aufleur. It was far away already; the dust devils were too late.

Velody was just pleased her idea had worked. 'Incoming,' she warned, and then the devils were upon them, swarming from underneath, their eyes glowing fiercely.

There was clanking and whirring in the streets below and

the remaining clockwork saints processed down from the Palazzo to join the battle.

'Hope you've got a really good war cry,' said Celeste.

'I've been working on it,' said Velody, and then the battle started and there was no more time for bravado.

The dust got everywhere, in their mouths, against their skin, biting hard. Every time a wave of the devils was blasted from the sky by the Clockwork Court, there were more to take their place.

Lysandor was killed when a dust devil sank inside him, its false fingers bursting him from the inside out. It wore his skin for a moment, laughing with his mouth, and then tore him to ribbons so that there was no mistaking it.

Celeste did not react, and Velody thought she had not seen it; but the Owl Lord fought with greater vigour, her animor slashing out of her in fiery white bursts, and oh yes, Velody realised: she knew.

~

ASHIOL DREAMED OF GARNET, who was poisoning him. One drop of skysilver in every measure of imperium. They drank, and glared at each other, and each mouthful was pain.

'Hate you,' said Ashiol.

'No, you never will,' said Garnet with glee.

Footsteps sounded outside the room. The handle turned.

'Here you both are,' announced Lysandor. 'Livilla's in a foul mood and, as the only one not sleeping with her, I want one of you bastards to deal with it.'

'Livilla's dead,' Ashiol blurted.

Lysandor looked unimpressed. 'We're all dead. I hardly think that counts as a valid excuse.'

Ashiol let out a startled laugh. 'I missed you, Lysh. Someone around here has to be sane.'

~

IT WAS NOT YET full dark when the last of the courtesi died. There were three Lords left, and then two.

Troyes Lord Falcon lost half his leg in a cloudburst that came close to sucking him entirely into the sky. He fought his way free and Velody went to help him, but it was too late, the blood pouring out too fast. He changed to bird form, but the wound was still there, and he fell, crying out only once as he dropped from the sky.

The dust devils kept coming, faster and faster, shining brighter, and the city buildings were smashed below them, one by one.

The Palazzo was ground to pieces. Velody could not find it in her to be sorry, though a small inner part of her was horrified at the deaths. The servants. The people of the city. So many; too many nameless faces to care about.

Finally it was just the two of them, Velody and Celeste, fighting back to back as the dust devils closed in around them.

'We should have just let the fucking city fall,' said Celeste through a rubbed-dry throat. 'We shouldn't have tried. There was a train. We could have got on it.'

'What else were we going to do?' Velody demanded.

Saving the city was everything. She had been doing this for only half a year and she knew it in her blood and her bones. There was nothing else but this: fighting and struggling against the sky. Postponing the inevitable, perhaps, but that was life for you.

'I'm sorry you're going to die,' said Celeste, still unwavering.

'Be sorry for your daughter,' Velody snapped.

The sky was so bright she could hardly see, and even in her chimaera form her muscles ached with exhaustion. *Help*, she thought desperately, hoping for some kind of miracle, hoping for Ashiol to climb out of his fugue and come to her aid, hoping for sentinels and Lords and Court to stand at her side.

There was blood dripping into her eyes, and she could barely move one of her wings after the last firebolt that had scorched across the top layer of skin. She would give anything right now for familiar faces, for Warlord and Livilla and Priest and Poet.

Seriously? a familiar voice said inside her head. *After everything, that's what you ask for?*

Garnet. Bloody Garnet, so far away. How desperate was she that her call had reached him?

Tierce was on her mind. That must be it.

It's the least you owe me, she sent to him, expecting nothing.

True enough. But now you will owe me, I think.

And then blissful animor was pouring into her from an unseen place, filling her veins with power so bright that it put the sky to shame.

Oh, yes. That.

Velody spun around and seized hold of Celeste as the world flared fiercely around them. The sky itself flickered and disappeared.

They hit the railway platform rolling, their skin charred from battle, both gasping for breath.

'How did we —' Celeste began to say, then choked out a breath as her daughter hit her hard, wrapping her arms around her waist and burying a tiny tear-streaked face in her stomach.

Ashiol sat up, leaning against the wall of the station, his face grey.

'You're alive, then,' said Velody, not knowing what else to say.

'You, too,' he noted without inflection.

The city of Bazeppe creaked and groaned behind them.

'We should go back,' said Celeste, her face buried in Lucia's coat.

'Too late,' said Velody. 'It's gone.'

The city screamed. As they watched, the paved streets tore loose from the ground and hovered, the bronze-coloured buildings seeming to float in the air. The railway platform buckled under them, but held fast. The sky blazed like salamander fire, bright enough to sear the eyes. And then it was calm, and Bazeppe was gone.

Silence fell over the survivors on the platform.

'I always thought,' Ashiol said slowly, his tongue getting in the way of making coherent words, 'that if we had gone to Tierce's aid, if we had listened to Heliora's warning and Garnet had allowed us to leave, we might have saved them. I don't think that's true.'

'No,' said Velody. It was so dark out there with the city gone. No lamps were lit, except the one above them. 'If they want to take us, they just... take.'

'Enough to make you think we might have been wasting our time all these years,' Ashiol said. He smiled wearily, an old man of a smile. 'We're going to need to travel on foot. By tomorrow, no one will remember why trains ever ran this far south.'

'Can you walk?' Velody asked him.

He looked offended. 'That's hardly relevant.'

Celeste and Lucia were crying softly together, wrapped in each other's pain.

'What are we going to do about Aufleur?' Kelpie asked the empty air.

Neither Ashiol nor Velody had an answer for her, and Celeste was too busy clutching her daughter to say a word.

PART XIII
SENTINELS AT WAR

THREE DAYS BEFORE THE NONES
OF SATURNALIS

DAYLIGHT

*I*t was thirteen years ago, and the world had just changed irrevocably.

Ashiol lay on the cold marble tiles of the bathroom, awash in sensation. He was bruised, bitten, sticky, and his mind was such a jumble that he couldn't concentrate on anything, not the smell of Garnet's skin, nor the musky taste of come that still lingered on his tongue. There was a mosaic pattern on the ceiling: a long-winged lizard chasing its own tail. He had never noticed it before.

Garnet made a small sound beside him and Ashiol rolled over, conscious suddenly of the puddles of oil spreading across the tiles, dripping into the now-cold bath. A glass bottle had broken in their first sudden lunge at each other, and it was a miracle that in all their clumsy fumblings neither of them had managed to cut himself.

This. Finally. They had come close on other occasions, there had been kisses and touches and the petting games that

Tasha especially encouraged in them, but this was nothing less than momentous, and he knew that when they looked back, it was this that they would name their first time.

They would have to be careful to hide it from Tasha: that her cubs had chosen a pretty bathroom in the Duc's Palazzo for the occasion of their first fuck, rather than one of the beds in her own den. Perhaps they would have to act out a similar scenario in future weeks, so she thought she was witnessing it. It wouldn't be difficult to pretend it was their first time. Ashiol was sure they couldn't be good at it yet.

'Did I hurt you?' he muttered, certain that all of Garnet's cries hadn't been of pleasure, but he had been wrapped up in the moment and hadn't been careful enough.

'I'll live,' said Garnet in a low voice, and then winced when Ashiol lay his palm across the curve of his arse. 'Ah, hands off.'

'I did hurt you.'

'Maybe I like it that way.'

He always talked like that, like nothing mattered, like he was as old and worldly as Tasha or Saturn.

'Shut up,' Ashiol said into the nape of his neck, kissing and then licking with a flick of his tongue. 'I'll let you do me next time.'

'Ha, I bet.'

'I will.' Ashiol nuzzled in against him, careful not to get too close. 'You liked it when I held you down,' he added thoughtfully.

'Pervert.' Garnet laughed, then arched back against him. 'I liked all of it.'

'Aye.' Nothing was going to be the same again, not now. 'So,' said Ashiol, too pleasantly numb to move, though the cold was starting to leach through his skin. 'Do we bother cleaning up? Or do we let the maids — you know? Figure it out.'

No servant would say a word to the Duc and Duchessa. He wasn't sure whether it made him squirm with embarrassment or if it was even hotter, the idea of people knowing what he had been up to, even if they might not guess with whom.

'We should just scamper out the window and away forever,' said Garnet. 'How's that for the final "fuck you" to your fancy family?'

Ashiol laughed. 'I'd have to come back sooner or later.'

'No, really.' Garnet turned and gazed at him, his eyes intensely bright. 'What's keeping you here? We have Tasha now, and the others. We're the frigging Creature Court. It's time to cut the ties. Leave the daylight behind.'

Ashiol wasn't sure how serious his friend was. 'The daylight has its uses. Why give up everything we have here when we can have both?'

Garnet's eyes did that icy thing that showed he was angry. 'Because I don't want to be your fucking manservant any more,' he said, as if Ashiol was stupid.

Which, aye, he was. Quite obviously.

'That was never real,' Ashiol said, treading carefully now he knew he was in dangerous territory. 'It was just an excuse to keep you with me.'

'Real enough when I have to take dinner in the servants' hall,' Garnet said, half-spitting the words.

'I didn't know it bothered you.'

He should have known. Everything bothered Garnet; he nursed every splinter until it was a bloody great stake through the heart.

'It doesn't bother me,' Garnet said, defensive now and probably lying. He shrugged a shoulder and then smiled one of those secret smiles of his, flashing from anger to sweetness far too fast. 'Most days, anyway. But there's nothing for me here except you, and I have you there as well. Don't I?'

'Of course you do,' said Ashiol, and it felt more of a pledge than any oath he had made to Tasha. 'I'm yours.'

This time Garnet's smile was better. Warmer.

'I'll go soon,' he said. 'To the Creature Court, completely. You don't have to. But if you want to keep a foot in the daylight, you're going to need to hire a new valet.'

'I can live with that,' said Ashiol.

Part of him wanted to order Garnet not to leave him, to stay with him for both the daylight *and* the nox. He knew better. He hadn't been able to get away with ordering Garnet to do anything, not since they were children.

Garnet kissed him suddenly, a rough crush of his mouth to Ashiol's, and the scent of him almost had them falling to the floor again. Not just sex and skin and oil, but the flare of animor, of gattopardo and cat recognising each other. Ashiol felt hot and urgent all over again, and when he reached out a hand he felt an answering hardness in Garnet's cock.

'Bed this time,' Garnet said, his old bossiness returning.

'I thought you were sore.'

Garnet grinned wickedly. 'It's your turn, remember? Let's mess up those pretty linen sheets of yours. Make some more work for the maids.'

Later, dizzy and hurting and so deeply in love that he couldn't think straight, Ashiol thought to remind Garnet that they would have to put a show on for Tasha.

'You think she doesn't know?' Garnet muttered back, groggy and half-asleep. 'You yelled loud enough they probably heard you in the Haymarket.'

The smell of death filled the room suddenly, swamping Ashiol's senses. He struggled to breathe, and saw a third figure lurching towards them in the lantern light.

Livilla's skin was rotting off her in places and the smell was unbearable. She was quite definitely dead, and she leaned over the boy lovers, crooning, 'I told you I wanted to watch.'

~

ASHIOL WOKE UP. He breathed hard for a moment or two, readjusting to his surroundings. He was half-lying on a window seat in his mother's library, crushing her favourite cushions. The air was scented with tea.

He had bathed twice, gargling mint and water until he could no longer taste whatever cack the Duc-Elected had poisoned him with, or the grit of the road, or the soul of a dead city. His mother offered him brandy but the scent of it sickened him. That probably wouldn't last. He was not built for sobriety.

The house was decorated for Saturnalia, all greenery and silver angels and red paper hearts. He had to count the days to be sure it wasn't actually here yet.

The door opened and the Dowager Baronnille Augusta Xandelian walked in. Ashiol's mother was such a neat, respectable matrona. Ashiol never seen her untidy, not even when she was gardening or surrounded by children. Her hair had far more grey in it than when he saw her last, only half a year ago.

She seemed happy enough here, widowed and still mattering to all of her children as they reached adulthood one by one.

'Mistress Celeste and her daughter are settled in a room upstairs,' Augusta said gravely.

'Look after them, will you?' he asked, lowering his feet to the floor.

He felt shaky, more from the two days of walking it had taken to get here than anything else, though it wasn't unlikely he was still suffering the after-effects of those damned potions.

'You're not staying, then?' said Augusta.

She was working hard not to let her disapproval show, but he could feel it radiating out of her. Perhaps that was deliberate on her part. She had always been an annoyingly subtle sort of woman.

'We're needed in the city,' he said.

'You and those demoiselles.'

It was also clear what Augusta thought of Velody and Kelpie, who looked like the ragged war veterans they were and had no adorable moppet to distract her with.

'Isangell still needs me.' A convenient excuse as well as being exactly the truth.

'You should never have left us, dearling,' Augusta said crisply.

'Perhaps.'

Ashiol went to the mantel, which held no less than three of his dead stepfather's clocks. Tick, tick, tick. He reached out abruptly and stopped one of them, wrenching at the hands. The others continued to beat time.

'What are you doing?' Cross at him, Augusta stepped forward to slap his hand away.

'Diamagne did love his clocks,' said Ashiol, and he had always known there should be a legitimate reason to dislike his mother's second husband, hadn't he? 'Where was it he got them mended when ungrateful stepsons broke them?'

Augusta huffed, and opened her mouth, because she was not the sort of lady who let a question go unanswered when she knew the answer perfectly well. Then she closed her mouth, because she did not, it seemed, know the answer at all. 'I don't remember.'

'You've never forgotten a thing in your life,' Ashiol said dismissively. 'Least of all something to do with Diamagne.'

'It's on the tip of my tongue.'

'No, it isn't.' He sighed. 'It doesn't matter. I was just testing a theory.'

Bazeppe was gone. Bazeppe had never existed. Bazeppe was forgotten by everyone of the daylight.

'Will you stay for dinner at least?' asked his mother.

'Is there meat?'

'There's always meat, dearling. One benefit of living in the country.'

'We would be glad to stay for dinner.'

His mother waited, and raised her eyebrows.

'Maybe a day or two,' he conceded. 'I'll see what the others think.'

'As you say.' She was amused that Ashiol might listen to anyone but himself.

When she left him, Ashiol threw himself down on the sofa like he was a child again, his feet piled high on cushions. Livilla was dead, and inside his mind. That wasn't a good thing. He could feel himself slipping into dark thoughts, the kind that helped no one. He could not afford to lose his hold on reality, not now.

Priest was dead, too. Poet had fallen in with Garnet. Lysandor was found and lost again. Celeste was... not his to command. There were hardly any pieces left of the Creature Court that Ashiol recognised from his youth.

How much easier would it be just to curl up as a cat and stay here for the season? He could let his mother dress Velody like a doll; let one of his brothers fall in love with Kelpie. Sit in the grass and snooze in the sunshine. There was always meat on the estate, and wine. They could wait until Ashiol's family no longer remembered what the word 'Aufleur' meant. Let the cities fucking fall.

'There you are,' said a voice, and of course it was Velody. She looked tired, but Ashiol's mother or her maids had given her access to a fresh dress and something approximating a bath.

'Come here,' he said, and stretched out a hand. She came close enough for him to notice how good she smelled.

'Oh, your mother would like that,' she said dryly. 'Canoodling on the couch with a lowly dressmaker.'

'Canoodling, is that even a word?' Ashiol tugged her closer and Velody fell on top of him. He liked that smile of hers. He hadn't seen nearly enough of it.

She breathed out like a sigh as he touched her, and relaxed for a moment, her head resting on his chest, the weight of her body firm on him.

'We're going back, aren't we?' she said.

'Of course we are.'

'I need to tell you something.' He tensed. 'Nothing bad, I think.' She raised her head and he looked into her grey eyes. 'Someone helped me, when I needed to get Celeste out of the city. Shared their power with me. It's the only reason we survived.'

Ashiol frowned. 'That's not a normal skill.'

'It was Garnet. He heard my plea from across the country. He shared.'

'Garnet doesn't like to share.' Ashiol cupped her breast in his hand. Not for any particular reason. It helped him to think. 'Is this the part where you tell me there might still be hope of redeeming him?'

'I don't know,' said Velody. 'I just thought you should know. He's the reason Celeste and I got out of Bazeppe alive.'

Ashiol blew out a breath. 'Something to think about. Does this dress come off?'

She laughed and wriggled out of his grasp. 'Not in your mother's library, it doesn't!'

For a moment, Ashiol was overwhelmed by calmness. A strange sensation. Pleasure, happiness. For one moment, before the impossibility of what they had to do swept back over him, he felt good.

It lasted just long enough to chase Velody out of the library and up the stairs to his rooms, where he proceeded to fuck her breathless before they even reached the bed.

43

ONE DAY AFTER THE IDES OF SATURNALIS

DAYLIGHT

*I*t was nearly noon. The sack was heavy, and Delphine was proud of herself for lugging it all the way underground without asking anyone for help. Not that the other options were all that tempting. Macready would ask too many questions, and that would mean they were actually having a conversation. If they were going to have a conversation after all this time, Delphine didn't want it to consist of him telling her how wrong-headed she was.

Then there was Crane, but since their tumble in the Haymarket, he showed a distressing tendency to want to carry things for her and be extra polite. While Delphine was usually the sort of person to take advantage of that sort of thing, in this instance it made her feel something not too far off guilt.

So, risking her own fingernails it was. She found the secret tunnel near the river and climbed down into the sunshine and desert of the Killing Ground. She wasn't used to being there on her own, and for a moment she felt entirely unwelcome.

The ghosts took an interest in her, drifting stickily around her arms and legs. They were drab creatures, and she never looked closely enough at them to see details such as faces and clothes. She had done that once and realised she was looking at a much younger Macready, even down to the hand with all digits intact. It creeped her out so much that she avoided looking at them in any detail after that.

'Sentinel,' she reminded them crossly, as if they might have forgotten. 'I belong here, so shut up.'

She lugged the sack across the sand. It wasn't only the weight that made it difficult to shift. She could feel the contents of it prickling at her, calling to the blades that she wore again, concealed under a swirling cloak.

She hadn't worn her brown sentinel's cloak for some time. No particular reason, except that it felt heavy with obligation. Besides, brown wasn't her colour. She pinched a length of blue wool from Velody's stash and sewed it into a cloak herself instead, hemming it on the metal sewing machine that she gave Velody years ago when they were apprentices. It was nice to know she still had the skills to sew something larger than a handful of ribbons. Once upon a time, Delphine had been determined to be a dressmaker, before she realised Velody was better at it.

Delphine really hated being second best at anything, and it was well past time she stopped being resentful about being the newest sentinel, the one who knew least about anything, the one they tried to protect. This was her time to shine.

She reached the door of the Smith's forge and knocked on it. There was silence for a long time, though smoke belched through the crack under the door.

Several more knocks elicited no response. Finally she tried to wrench the door open on her own, but pain shocked through her arm with a flash of light.

'Ow!' she screamed indignantly.

No response.

She could so easily walk away at this point, but she had come all this way carrying the stupid sack, and besides, she had questions that required answers. Many questions, many answers.

Delphine sat down with her back against the door, opened the sack and started pulling out the gleaming pieces of skysilver. She had spent hours collecting it, digging the stuff out of gutters and broken slate before the dawn healed the city. Some of it was melted into slag, and other pieces were still pointy and jagged, like lightning bolts frozen into existence.

When the door finally opened behind her, dampening the fabric of her blue cloak with steam, Delphine was attempting to build a little house out of the broken chunks of skysilver. She was rather proud of it. It had three floors, a roof and a chimney.

'Coming in?' said the Smith.

Delphine looked up and up, tilting her head back. All she could see was his massive leather apron. 'I brought you a present.'

He grunted at her, turned around and went back into the heat of his forge.

Delphine gathered up the pieces quickly, her fingers humming as she put them back into the sack, and went inside before he could change his mind.

'I want to ask you some questions,' she told him. 'Velody says you remember all the way back to the beginning of the Court.'

'Many ask,' said the Smith, which didn't exactly suggest he was going to answer any questions, but nor did it refute the possibility.

Delphine hefted the sack up onto a dirty table and, after a moment's hesitation, scrambled up there as well, swinging her legs. 'You told her that the first Power and Majesty was a woman.'

'I say things,' the Smith said, after a long silence.

He was working on a sword, bringing the hot metal out of the coals and turning it as he clanged down his hammer. There were few pauses in which Delphine could make herself heard, and often there wasn't time for him to reply, so she had to wait until the next time the metal was reheating.

'Do the rest of them know how much you know about the old days?' she tried, barely getting the whole question out before he started striking the metal again, filling the air with noise.

After the metal was glowing in the brazier again, she thought he wasn't going to answer as he continued the silence.

'Few have patience enough to listen to history,' he said finally, eight words all at once.

Then nothing for at least an hour, no matter how many questions she hurled at him.

Sometime later, the Smith rested the finished sword in a barrel of water and came over to sort through the skysilver she had brought, his expert fingers flicking away the bits of gravel or tile or rust stuck to it.

'Where does it come from, the skysilver?' Delphine asked.

It wasn't a question she had meant to ask, but it suddenly occurred to her.

The Smith looked at her and smiled. 'Ah,' he said.

'What, did I say something clever?'

Silence.

'Has no one asked that before?'

'They have asked.'

'So what else haven't they asked? What question has no one ever asked before? What do you know about everything?'

He shook his head at her, and sorted in silence.

Patience did not come naturally to Delphine. Impulse was the sphere she was most comfortable with. But if the rest of the Creature Court, with their short attention spans, had been too impatient to listen to anything useful the Smith had to say about their past... Someone had to listen to him. Someone had to figure out what the seven hells was going on, before Velody got all self- sacrificial again.

Home wasn't home any more. Velody was gone, and Rhian was crazy, and Macready had moved out. Saints only knew where he was living now — one of those musty little nests or something...

Where did Delphine have to go anyway? Why not stay and be useful? At the very least, she could think up new questions.

It felt like she had been there for hours. She wasn't hungry or thirsty, despite the steamy heat coming from the forge. The only way to measure time was the beat of the Smith's hammer, the number of times he turned a sword before he quenched it. Delphine dropped slowly into a trancelike state of beats and strikes. She remembered the clock in her hallway at home in Tierce chiming the hour. When she was little, she used to lean against its side and listen to the scratchy workings inside.

Thoughts of home and her forgotten childhood came to her from time to time, but she usually forced them out of her head, unwilling to let herself grieve for what she had lost.

Now, with the heat so thick around her and the sound of the Smith striking a new piece of metal, she let herself wallow in that one single image of home, the home that had been eaten by the sky.

'Aufleur doesn't have clocks,' she said dreamily. 'Only those wretched dripping things. Why is that?'

'The Daylight Duc thought clockwork was cursed,' said the Smith.

So much information all at once was enough to startle Delphine out of her vision. 'Which Duc?'

'The first one.'

'Huh. He was hardly supposed to be mad at all,' mused Delphine. And then, because she was tired and hot and these things made her flippant, she added, 'Was the clockwork cursed?'

The Smith turned to look at her. 'Of course.'

'There aren't any new sentinels,' Delphine said, after a while. 'Who are these swords even for?'

'The future,' said the Smith.

'You're assuming we're all going to get our blades eaten by dust devils on a regular basis? Or are you assuming we're going to drag a whole lot more sentinels into this wretched life?'

He continued to work, ignoring her.

'There's a lot of skysilver here. How many swords will it make?'

'Enough.'

She reached out, brushed her fingertips over the metal, felt it fizzle under her skin. The Smith took firm hold of her wrist and moved it to one side.

'You make each new sentinel their own particular sword,' Delphine said in a low whisper. 'A new sword and dagger every time. So why are you making swords now?'

'It is what I do,' said the Smith, and there were centuries in his eyes.

'What happens to the spare ones?'

He jerked with his head.

Delphine went to a door she hadn't seen before and opened it. A sea of swords hung before her, each perfect. One row after another. Steel, skysilver, steel, skysilver.

'You could make a lot of sentinels with swords like these,' she said.

'I imagine so,' said the Smith.

'You never mentioned these to anyone before?'

'No one ever asked.'

Delphine had come here hoping to learn something, anything, about the Creature Court's past that might give them an edge in the battle against Garnet. This was far more than she had hoped for. Not the past at all, but the future.

'I'm going to be right back,' she told the Smith, and darted out into the Killing Ground.

A thought struck her almost as soon as the sunshine did and she ran back into the forge before he could close the door behind her.

'Since I brought you all that skysilver, do you think you could make something for me? Something important, but a bit different... I don't know. Can you make things other than swords?'

The Smith looked expressionlessly at her. 'I can make anything.'

Delphine smiled fiercely. 'Excellent. Wonderful. I'll draw you a picture.'

Best sentinel ever. Oh, yes.

~

THE SECOND TIME she left the forge, Delphine's cheeks were ruddy and hot, her hair was frizzled and she was bursting with energy. She had a plan, and it was a most excellent plan, and it was going to make Macready sick that he hadn't thought of it first.

'Well, look at you,' said a voice across the desert floor of the Killing Ground.

Delphine whipped her head around and saw Garnet. His animor hit her as an aftershock and she staggered a little under his sheer presence. Power and Majesty and all that, oh yes. Not just an empty title.

'You shouldn't be here,' she gasped. 'Not unless —'

'I am accompanied by a sentinel?' He smiled nastily at her. 'Hello, sentinel. Though you're not, are you? You left that behind when you denied me. You walked away from your duties, just like the rest of them.'

'The Smith recognises what I am,' Delphine flared. 'Velody recognises me. I have my blades. Who are you to tell me I am not a sentinel?'

'I am your Power and Majesty,' Garnet roared, his voice filling the desert space from end to end.

'I don't care what you call yourself,' Delphine spat at him. 'You're not mine.'

Garnet flew at her and she should have gutted him, it would solve so many problems, it wasn't as if she hadn't practised on Ashiol enough times, but he moved so fast and then she was on her back. She had a knife deep in his stomach, but he was laughing at her, giggling like a maniac. She had pulled the wrong knife. Left hand instead of right, oh saints, so stupid.

It was probably a good thing Garnet was going to kill her, as it would save Macready to doing it when he found out how idiotic she had been.

'That tickles,' Garnet hissed in her ear.

Delphine screamed in his face and brought up her other hand, the one entirely lacking in knives, to claw at his eyes. He lifted her and threw her down on the sand hard, so that her whole body juddered under him. He was going to break her into a million pieces and there was nothing she could do to stop him.

'I'm going to enjoy this,' he promised, and then it was his turn to scream as blood fountained over them both.

Delphine choked on it, spat the blood out, and was able to scramble free because Garnet was writhing on the sand, screaming.

She saw Crane standing there, all bloodstained and rumpled. He fell to his knees, dropping his skysilver sword in order to cut his own wrist with his steel knife blade.

'No!' she demanded, furious at him. 'Let the bastard die. He'd kill us all if we gave him half a chance.'

She had given Garnet more than half today.

'That's not who I am,' Crane said, gritting his teeth as Garnet grabbed the sentinel's wrist and suckled hard. 'I'm a sentinel. So are you.'

Garnet's body was still shuddering in shock from the way the sword had sliced him open; his whole side was soaked in dark red.

'He doesn't deserve us,' Delphine said, vibrating with anger as she recovered her blades. She wanted to wipe Garnet's blood off the front of her dress, but there was no way to do it here. Damn Crane and his heroics. 'Anyone he kills after today is your fault,' she huffed.

Crane looked up at her, his eyes very calm. 'The only kills I take responsibility for are my own.' He took his brown cloak off and laid it over Garnet. Delphine wanted to smack him.

'At least come away with me before he gets his strength

back and guts you, like he was going to do to me *half a minute ago.*'

'You could say thanks for saving you,' suggested Crane.

'I would,' said Delphine. 'But I think you enjoy playing the hero rather too much. I don't want to encourage you.'

44

ONE DAY AFTER THE IDES OF SATURNALIS

DAYLIGHT

*T*he Haymarket was deserted, apart from Rhian. She tore through Garnet's rooms, searching for what must be there, what she knew he must be hiding from them all. She found clothes and shoes and all manner of irrelevant ephemera, and hurled them all on the floor, not caring if he knew she had been here.

He had been lying to her for so long, pretending that he and his precious animor could help her control the voices in her head, that he would use his status as Power and Majesty to take the damned futures away from her, to let her stop being the Seer.

Now Poet was missing, and Garnet was more erratic, and he had stopped even pretending that he was going to help her.

She would wait no longer.

Finally, beneath his bed, she found what she was looking for. A book, handwritten, full of some forgotten Lord's scholarship, his notes and theories about the Creature Court, about their history.

Fragments of the truth. She read every word, swallowing them deep inside herself. Oh yes, Garnet had been lying. He would never have been able to help her. She could do it herself.

'What are you doing here?' he snapped, slamming the door open. His shirt was torn and wet with his own blood. He pulsed with anger.

Rhian did not move.

He dragged the book away from her, furious. 'This is not for you.'

'Yes,' she said calmly, standing up to face him. 'You like to keep all your secrets to yourself, don't you, Garnet?'

She could feel his animor blazing around them, filling the room, but it was nothing compared to the heat under her skin. She had been holding it in for so long, and if she had to, she would release it upon him. It would be such a relief, to let go of it all at last.

'You are my Seer,' he said in a commanding voice. 'Tell me where everyone is. Tell me what has happened to Poet. Tell me the truth!'

The angrier he got, the calmer Rhian felt. 'I can't see the present. Only the futures.'

'So read my damned futures!' Garnet snarled, and slapped her hard across the face.

Rhian had not expected that. Her head flew back against the wall, and it hurt. For a second, she lost control, and flames rippled up and down her skin.

Garnet reacted, stepping back and out of range. 'What is wrong with you, demme?'

'You want your future?' Rhian said, reaching out a hand to steady herself against his bed. Where she touched the wooden frame, it burst into branches and buds. Water

dripped from the ceiling, as if they were outside and a rain-
storm was starting. She felt the flames burning hotter along
her arms, though the raindrops put them out with a steady
hissing sound. 'You will die by fire,' she told him. 'Everyone
you love will leave you and the fire will take you.'

He stared at her, and she wondered if it was true or just
the cruellest thing she had thought of in that moment. She
could no longer tell what was true and what was false. She
walked away, water pooling at her feet as she left his rooms.

Too far. It had all gone too far. Rhian knew now how to
rid herself of the futures, but it was far too late to save her
from what would come next.

～

MACREADY SLEPT, deep in his nest, protected from anything
the city had to throw at him. His dreams were not remotely
restful, alight with screams and flames and rose petals.

When he opened his eyes, someone was banging on the
wall. Delphine, he assumed, until he opened it up and discovered Rhian waiting for him on the other side. He didn't ask
how she had known where his nest was. She was the Seer,
after all. Heliora could have guided her feet — Hel had
visited here often enough. Or perhaps Rhian had seen a
vision of herself standing in the street outside.

(the thought that Delphine and Rhian might be on
speaking terms was sadly out of the realms of possibility)

'What is it, Rhian love?' Macready asked carefully.

She looked unwell, too thin for her frame, and her skin was
dry. There were cracks on her lips that she kept running her
tongue over. Her eyes were too dark for the redhead she was.

'Garnet,' she said. 'He mustn't find me.'

Quick as he could, Macready ushered her inside and

sealed the wall from the alley outside. 'He can't come in here unless I invite him, my lovely.'

'I thought he could help me. He did at first. But Poet has gone missing, and I think he was the only one keeping Garnet calm.'

She raised a trembling hand to her mouth and Macready saw that she had a faint bruise across the side of her chin. Anger shot through him.

'Garnet did that to you?'

'I threatened him with fire,' Rhian said in a soft, breathy voice. She wouldn't look at Macready; had barely made eye contact with anyone in days. The futures were taking her and there was naught he could do to stop it. 'He's afraid of fire. He won't listen to me now. I thought I could learn control from him, but he has nothing to teach me.'

'He's long past teaching anyone,' said Macready. His mind was racing. Fire. They could use that somehow, surely. It wasn't a bad thing to know what Garnet feared.

'I set some men on fire once,' Rhian said dreamily. 'Perhaps he's afraid of me.'

'Oh, lass. We're all afraid of you.'

Macready had a little stove, and set it going to make tea for her. Tea and sanity went hand in hand when it came to Rhian. Rituals were important.

He heard the squeak of the bed behind him as Rhian sat down with a sigh. 'It's not just fire,' she said.

Macready turned to her and sucked in a breath.

Rhian was lying back on his narrow cot, her eyes closed. She was wet. Water dripped from her skin as if she had just stepped out of a bath. Where the hells was it coming from? The blankets were soaked, and it poured on to the floor in rivulets.

She opened her eyes suddenly and gasped as if drowning.

Macready grabbed her and pulled her up from the bed. She leaned against him, the water soaking into his shirt.

'What do the voices say?' he asked. 'Hel, and the other Seers?'

'They've gone quiet. I think they know that I'm not really one of them. I don't know what I am but I know it's going to get worse.'

She clung to him, and it was so rare to touch her that he couldn't think straight for a moment.

'Have you ever had contact with something that came from the sky?' he asked carefully, a moment later. He was starting to suspect that what was happening to her was nothing to do with being the Seer. 'Or... have you touched something that Velody made lately?'

Rhian laughed, high and mocking and hardly herself at all. 'You think this is the work of the dust devils? The things beyond the sky? I wish that were true. It would be so much easier.' Then she shuddered again and buried her face into his wet shirt. 'Help me,' she whispered.

'Always, lass,' he said, and held her tight. *Oh, Rhian.*

~

RHIAN AND MACREADY made it to Via Silviana without incident, but even as they turned the corner into the familiar street, she began to cough and lean against him. He steadied her with one hand and saw dirt fall through her fingers. As he watched with horror, she coughed up an entire clod of earth, replete with grass stalks and roots.

He hustled her forward until they reached the threshold, and used her latchkey to get them both inside.

'It's happening faster now,' Rhian said when she could speak again. She crossed the workroom and headed for the kitchen, poured herself a cup of barley water to wash out her mouth. 'The closer we get to Saturnalia.'

'Aye,' said Macready. 'Festivals in the street and a city to save. Business as usual.'

She spat some wet dirt into the cup. 'It's not just the city. Tierce is gone. Bazeppe is gone. If Aufleur is swallowed as well, there will be a wound in the world too deep for us to recover from.'

'So now we're fighting to save the fecking world?' Macready said tiredly. 'Can't say it surprises me.'

'Did someone say saving the world?' said a breathless voice as the kitchen door flew open. Delphine stood there, bloodstained and glowing, with Crane beside her.

Crane had a guilty look all over his face, as he usually did when he saw Mac these days. Macready was going to have to say something to the lad, but not today. Not yet.

Delphine was luminous. 'I happen to have a really good idea how to do that,' she added. 'If you're interested. But first, I have to design a dress.'

THEY LINGERED at the Diamagne estate. One day became three, and then six. Velody was anxious that they had stayed away from Aufleur too long. Anything could be happening. Anyone could be dead or dying.

When she raised the matter with Ashiol, he simply said, 'It won't start until Saturnalia,' and when she tried to find out more than that, he distracted her with his hands and mouth. He really was very good with his mouth.

Velody found Kelpie sitting on a herb-scented lawn watching little Lucia play games with an older demme — Ashiol's ten-year-old sister, Phage, the youngest of his family, though the eldest of his brothers was recently married and had a baby on the way.

Ash had a family. Somehow he made more sense in the city, with the Duchessa as his cousin and no one else attached to him. Velody could not see any part of this estate that felt as if he belonged to it, and yet he had brothers and a sister and a mother and the servants all called him Master Ash. This had been his home for much of his life. The place where he was safe, as opposed to the Palazzo at Aufleur or any territory in the Arches.

Kelpie glanced up as Velody approached and sat beside her on the grass. 'Imagining what it might be like to be lady of the manor?' Kelpie asked.

Velody raised her eyebrows. 'Are you?'

Kelpie laughed. 'I'm a city demme,' she said. 'Still, I rather like it here. It's quiet.'

'Too quiet,' Velody said fervently. 'Can you believe Ashiol lived here for years? He must have gone out of his mind.'

'Perhaps he did.'

That was a fair point. Velody breathed out, watching the children play. She could feel Ashiol's presence inside the house. His animor was like the lamp of a lighthouse, drawing her in. When they were in the same room together it was almost impossible to keep from touching each other. She was certain his mother had noticed.

'Do you think he's afraid of Garnet?' she asked.

'Yes,' Kelpie said quickly. 'No. I don't know.' She gave Velody an alarmed look. 'You're not hoping to mend things between Ash and Garnet?'

'Why not? If I can mend them, I can mend anything.'

'You're cracked.'

'You must have thought there was something to salvage of Garnet, or you wouldn't have chosen him last time.'

Kelpie's face tightened. 'I don't believe in this sacred

marriage thing,' she said finally. 'It's daft. Even those of the Court who are lovers have never trusted each other enough to make something like that happen.'

'And yet it did happen,' Velody said quietly. 'Maybe the Creature Court was different then.'

'Maybe,' Kelpie said dubiously. 'Or maybe they were really stupid.'

Every time Velody opened herself up to Ashiol, she thought: *this time, he could steal my animor.* She wasn't sure if what they had was trust. If one bled the other dry, it meant taking on the entirety of the Creature Court as well. Did they want to share responsibility more than they wanted power?

It wasn't the sacred marriage, this thing they had together now. But it was something worth preserving. And perhaps it was a promise that somewhere, beyond everything, there might be a future.

Garnet, though. They always had to factor in Garnet. 'We're going home tomorrow,' Velody told Kelpie.

'I know,' said Kelpie, eyes on the children. 'I'm almost sure I'm going to come with you.'

~

'How does it work?' Velody asked Ashiol that nox, in his bed.

Buried to the hilt inside her, he grumbled about demmes who liked to talk at such moments.

'I mean it. The sacred marriage can't just be making love, or you and Garnet would have been married years ago.'

'Now that's a scary thought.' He bumped gently against her, making her moan. Heat pulsed between them, ordinary heat of the flesh as they both held back their animor. His slow, steady thrusts sped up into an urgent, breathless rhythm. 'I don't know how it works. Garnet's the one who

401

came up with the idea. Why don't you send one of those thoughts of yours off to Aufleur and see if he can - provide – us – with – any – tips —'

'Oh,' she gasped, and then there was just heat and pleasure and she couldn't find the words, not for some time, as Ashiol worked so deeply inside her there was no way of keeping her thoughts remotely collected.

'I think we need to stop talking about Garnet when we do that,' she breathed against the pulse in his neck, when she finally had breath enough to speak.

Ashiol kissed her, his teeth grazing her lip. 'I will if you will. Was that a proposal, by the way?'

'What?' said Velody, distracted by his kisses. 'No, it was a thought. I'm still working on it.'

'Very well.' He kissed lower, and lower, and then he was between her breasts. 'Let me know when it's a proposal.'

Velody had a very good reply to that, but his teeth closed gently around her nipple and she lost her grip on her animor completely. It collided with his in explosive bursts barely contained by skin and flesh and bone.

Maybe later.

THE TRAIN PULLED into the station at the south gate a little before noon on the day before the Saturnalia. Velody, Ashiol and Kelpie stepped onto the platform surrounded by clouds of steam.

'Aufleur's still here, then,' said Kelpie.

'I suppose that's something,' said Ashiol.

Velody stared into the steam, looking for answers. She received nothing but grit in her eye.

'What now?' Kelpie asked.

Ashiol stood there looking as if the weight of the world

had once more settled across his shoulders. 'Now we end this thing. We save the city and we stop the skywar.'

'Is that all?' Velody said. 'How do you plan to do that?'

Ashiol shrugged. 'It comes down to me and Garnet. That's what it's always been about. Especially now. Lysandor's dead, and Livilla. Priest. We're the only ones left from the last generation. Time to rewrite the next chapter of history.'

A lone figure stepped out of the steam, making Velody jump.

'You always did forget about me, kitten,' said Poet.

Ashiol stared at him. 'What do you want?'

Velody could feel Ashiol's anger swell up inside him and stepped forward to place a calming hand on his arm. It was a mistake, perhaps. She could see Poet look from her to Ashiol with a knowing smirk.

'Do you have a message from Garnet?' she asked.

'Mouseling,' said Poet, terribly pleased with himself. 'you've been away too long. I don't speak for Garnet. I speak for the fucking resistance.'

THE VITTORINA ROYALE was a ruin now, a blight on the street. The holes in the ceiling had let in the rain, and the velvet seats and curtain were already mouldering away. The floorboards creaked worryingly underfoot.

Poet walked through the mess as if he saw none of it, leading them down a back staircase into the dressing rooms, which were, remarkably, untouched.

'Through here, my sweets,' he said with a flourish.

Ashiol did not trust him yet. Might never trust him again. He had never been entirely comfortable about Poet, from the day that Garnet had brought the little rat home with him. He stepped through the door first. If there was a trap, let it fall upon him and not Velody or Kelpie.

Inside, he blinked rapidly. Too many people were pressed into the small room. The new courtesa, Topaz, was curled up in a corner with the rest of those wretched children Livilla had towed around with her since she stole them from Poet.

(Livilla was dead, remember that.)

Mars had the bed, seated against the headboard with an indolent look on his face. His courtesi, all five of them, clustered about his feet.

Poet's courtesi were here, too: the weasel, Zero, and the hound, Shade.

Lennoc sat on the far side of the dressing room beneath a ragged poster advertising 'The Pearls Beyond Price'.

'What have we here?' Ashiol asked.

Velody stepped in behind him, and he could feel Kelpie's presence close to his back.

'Fucker killed Livilla,' said Mars, flashing his teeth. 'I know the rest of you don't give seven damns about that, but I do.'

'I care,' Topaz flared. 'We all do.' Meaning the lambs, presumably, though none of them spoke a word. Mouthy, this one, for a courtesa. 'She was our Lord and we loved her.'

Lennoc gave a long, easy shrug. 'I didn't like Livilla. I don't like any of you. But Garnet has gone too far. He's crazier than you ever were,' he added with a nod to Ashiol.

'Impressive,' said Ashiol, otherwise at a loss. 'And you, Poet?'

Poet snaked around the women to stand directly in front of Ashiol. 'I've lost faith,' he said with a crooked smile.

'Simple as that?'

'Does it have to be complicated?'

'Why should I trust you?'

'You shouldn't, obviously. But then, you never did.'

Poet swallowed, losing his brashness for a moment. 'Garnet killed Livilla for a reason. He's going after Topaz and the lambs next. He thinks it's the only way to save the city. What do you think?'

Ashiol sighed. 'I think it's time we took Garnet down.'

'Leaving you as Power and Majesty?' Mars drawled. 'Or will it be her ladyship again?' He flicked a glance in Velody's direction.

'We don't need to decide that now,' said Velody, finding her voice.

'The hells we don't,' said Lennoc. 'No more civil wars, no more revolutions. If we're going to risk our lives getting rid of Garnet, we need to know what we're in for. Are you two going to turn on each other and fight to the death the second there's a position open at the top?'

'In the old days of the Creature Court,' said Velody, stepping up to stand beside Ashiol, 'there were two leaders. A Power and a Majesty.'

There was a long silence as they all looked at each other, and then Poet began to laugh hysterically.

'How sweet,' he said. 'Mama and Papa will look after us together. I can't see any reason at *all* that could go wrong.'

45

ONE DAY AFTER THE IDES OF SATURNALIS

DAYLIGHT

'*W*hat do you think?' Velody asked Kelpie. They walked to Via Silviana together while Ashiol headed for the Palazzo.

'I don't trust Poet,' Kelpie said instantly. 'I don't believe he'd choose you and Ashiol over Garnet. It doesn't make sense.'

'Were they ever lovers?' Velody asked.

Kelpie rolled her eyes at her. 'It's the Creature Court.'

Well, yes, there was that.

Velody was so anxious to check on Delphine and Rhian, she hurried around to the house by the back way and threw open the back door. The kitchen wasn't there. Only a blank brick wall.

She pushed her hands against the solidity of it, not believing what she felt. 'What the hells...?'

'I'm impressed,' said Kelpie, and she actually sounded it. 'Maybe that ditzy flapper of yours is a real sentinel, after all.'

Velody frowned. 'I don't understand.'

'Isn't it obvious?' Kelpie leaned in, resting her palms on the solid brickwork. It was neat and tidy, the bricks arranged like rows of ribbons between layers of thick granite mortar. 'Someone's turned your house into a sentinel's nest. About bloody time. We should have thought of it months ago.'

Velody stared at her, then hammered on the brick wall. It made no sound, not even a muffled thump.

'Amateurish work,' Kelpie observed. 'That's a dead giveaway.'

'As opposed to a brick wall behind a door?'

Kelpie nodded. 'Always a good idea to get rid of the door.'

'Delphine!' Velody yelled.

The bricks vanished under her hands and a blur of blonde hair and green dress exploded out of the house and hugged her. 'Velody! You're back.'

'And you're... turning the house into a nest?'

Delphine beamed at her. 'I am. Isn't it great? Finally we can keep the bastards out — hi, Kelpie — if they're not invited. Of course it does mean we can never have clients across the threshold again, but who are we kidding? Every-thing's different now.'

The kitchen looked as normal, though the walls were greyer. Once Velody and Kelpie were inside, Delphine closed the wall and there was a shimmer as it sealed them away from the world.

'Majesty,' said Macready with a nod. He sat at the kitchen table with Crane standing behind him.

'Not that,' said Velody. 'Not yet, anyway.'

'You brought our man Ashiol back?'

'Oh yes.'

'We were worried,' Crane said evenly. 'We read the news-paper. Bazeppe hasn't been mentioned in days. We started asking people...' His voice broke off and he looked away, avoiding her gaze.

'Are we next?' Delphine asked in a low voice. 'I'd hate to get swallowed by the sky just when I'm figuring out how this sentinel thing works.'

'I think it depends on whether we stop Garnet,' said Velody.

'Garnet's after saving the city himself, is he not?' asked Macready.

'I don't know,' said Velody. 'I don't like his methods. I don't think he can be trusted to know what's best for the city. The rest of the Court are on our side, as long as we win.'

'That's good,' Delphine grinned. 'Garnet has no idea what he's up against.'

There was a powerful tang of skysilver in the air. Velody stepped through to the workroom and saw the skysilver cage sitting there in the middle of the floor.

'Where did that come from?'

'Poet handed it over as proof he's on our side,' said Delphine. 'I don't believe a word of it, but he seemed happy to be rid of the thing.' She shrugged. 'It gives me the creeps, but if anything should be in the hands of the sentinels, it's that.'

There was something else different about the room. The work surfaces were clear and tidy, except where Delphine's ribboning supplies were spread out near the sewing machine. There was no sign that any floristry had been done here in recent times.

'Where's Rhian?' Velody asked. She saw it on Macready's face first, that something was wrong. 'Tell me.'

'She's upstairs,' said Delphine. 'But I wouldn't —'

Velody ran.

~

WATER SEEPED out from under Rhian's bedroom door.
Velody tugged the door open and stepped into darkness. It
shouldn't be this dim in here, it was daylight, but there was
something thick and porous blocking the window and only a
few cracks of light broke through.

'Rhian?'

There was a low moaning sound that chilled her to
the bone.

The air was thick with many smells — scorched wood,
dampness, and moss. Velody bumped into something that
felt like a tree branch stretched across the room. She ran out
and fetched a lantern from the hook in the hallway and took
it in with her. Branches crisscrossed the room. Heavy webs
hung from them. The floor was wet, and Rhian's old rag rug
squelched underfoot.

'Rhian, where are you? I can't see...'

Velody faltered. There, in the centre of it all, Rhian lay on
her back on the bed. The twisting branches and vines were
growing out of her body. As Velody stepped closer, she saw a
broken pattern across Rhian's face, like cracks in a cliffside.

'What happened to you?'

Rhian spoke slowly, her mouth moving to form the
words, her throat pushing out creaky, hesitant sounds. 'I
happened. It came from inside me. I don't hear the futures
any more...'

And then she was crying, moaning louder, and there was
a terrible sound coming from everywhere, a creaking and
grinding that filled Velody's ears. The branches turned into
smooth arches of stone. Rhian's body shook and broke apart,
and then the greyness came over her and she was stone, too,
the rigid form of a statue.

Velody pressed her hands to her mouth, shaking so hard
she thought she would fly apart.

'It's better this way,' said a low voice from the doorway. 'I think she doesn't feel pain when she's stone. It's awful when she's fire; and when the water comes, she just weeps all the time.'

Velody turned. 'Delphine, what happened?'

'This is what she was hiding from,' Delphine said hoarsely. 'All those months, we thought she was afraid of going outside. But it was this. This future is what she was afraid of.'

There was nothing Velody could say or think to make this all right. 'She's not dead?'

'No. The cycles are getting shorter, though. As if whatever is going to happen... it'll be soon.'

'Tomorrow is the first day of Saturnalia,' said Velody. 'It's happening already.'

She turned back to look at the twisted statue that had been Rhian, that would be her again if Delphine was to be believed. 'Is this from the sky? More of their poison, more of them trying to get under our skin? Or was it here all along? Is it part of their attack, or part of our defence?'

'I'm starting to wonder if there's much difference between the two,' said Delphine. She looked crumpled, as if days or weeks of denial were finally coming to an end. 'I was so mean to her,' she burst out.

Velody went to her, and they both held back in a moment of hesitation before they hugged.

'You're always mean,' Velody said softly. 'She probably didn't even notice.'

Delphine laughed and sobbed into her shoulder. 'Shut up, I was vile. I told her I was sorry, but I don't think she heard me.'

'She heard,' Velody whispered. 'She knows.'

It didn't matter if it was true. They were losing Rhian. The city might as well fall now.

~

AT THE PALAZZO, Ashiol dodged that fop Armand and made his way unhindered to Isangell's rooms.

'You really should hire more intelligent servants,' he began as he entered, then stopped.

His cousin stood in the middle of her sitting room, trying on her wedding gown. It had a wide, starchy skirt with hoops such as those worn by demoiselles of the previous generation. Bunches of white satin were gathered with green silk vines and curling ribbons. The corset had Floralia roses studded on it in pearls and pale pink beading. There was a train. And a cape. And a bonnet, saints help him, a bonnet. It was the ugliest thing Ashiol had ever seen in his life.

'You didn't commission that from Velody,' he said, when he had recovered enough from the shock to speak.

Isangell glared at him. 'I wasn't aware she had time for commissions these days. Besides, this is an *heirloom*.'

'Are you sure you're supposed to wear it? It's not a spare tower someone broke off the Cathedral of Ires?'

'It was my mother's.'

'Oh, by all means emulate Aunt Eglantine's life choices — they worked out so well for her. If you must have an antiquated frock, why don't you send to my mother? I'm sure she has one or two wedding dresses in mothballs that won't make your groom think you're wearing the cake.'

Isangell threw something at him. Ashiol had no idea what it was, but it was white and satiny and went clunk when it hit the wall behind his head. A bridal sack, perhaps? It wouldn't shock him if Aunt Eglantine had installed missiles in her wedding dress.

'Hang on,' he said, straightening up. 'Who do you think you're marrying?'

'Comte Niall of Bazeppe, of course,' she said impatiently.

'You're my ambassador, Ashiol. You've been dealing with the paperwork. Come to that, what on earth are you doing here? You were supposed to stand in my stead at their Saturnalia dinner. I won't have you neglecting the few official duties that I request of you.'

Ashiol stared at her. 'Isangell, Bazeppe is gone.'

Gone, broken, rendered to dust, and she shouldn't remember a single brick of it. His mother and siblings didn't, nor any of the servants.

'Gone where? Make sense if you can, Ash.'

How could he explain it? He'd never had to before, not to anyone of the daylight.

'Bazeppe fell. Like Tierce fell.'

Isangell steadied herself with a hand. 'You mean, smashing into one of my districts?'

'It was swallowed by the sky.'

'Nonsense! It's a *whole city*, Ashiol.'

'A whole city,' he agreed. 'And it's gone. No one of the daylight remembers it even existed.'

Her eyes grew flinty. 'What are you saying?'

'I'm saying that Bazeppe —'

'You must be mistaken.'

'I saw it fall, I know what happened. It's not exactly something you forget, gosling.'

'Forgive me, Ash, but you're not the world's most reliable witness.'

He sat down hard on her floral sofa. 'If you remember Bazeppe and Niall, and... name the Duc!'

'Duc-Elected,' she corrected him promptly. 'Henri. You're being ridiculous.'

'It means you're not daylight any more,' Ashiol said, trying to take it in. 'You're something else.'

Isangell's eyebrows rose sharply. She had never looked more like her mother. 'No. I am not one of your wretched animals. I have accepted the Creature Court's existence, and your ability to spark lightning from your hands and turn into a herd of cats, which explains an awful lot about your personality, I must say, but I am not a part of all that.'

'But you remember Bazeppe.'

'Stop saying that!' Isangell turned with some difficulty and flounced towards her sideboard to pick up a fountain pen. 'I am writing a note to Niall right now. It will be on the train to Bazeppe today, and when he writes back it will prove to you that you are speaking nonsense.'

'There is no train to Bazeppe, Isangell. It doesn't exist any more.'

'So you say.'

Having written her note, she rang for her factotum. 'Armand, please include this letter for Bazeppe in today's post.'

The factotum blinked and smiled politely, taking it all in his stride. 'Bazeppe, high and brightness, as you say.'

'Aren't you going to ask her which country?' Ashiol drawled, putting his feet up on the sofa.

'Don't be a fool. Armand knows which country,' Isangell snapped.

Armand's smile grew wider and more polite. 'Indeed, high and brightness.'

Oh, the little oik was bluffing.

'Go on, then,' Ashiol said. 'Tell us.'

'Ashiol,' Isangell chided 'you're being —'

'An arse, yes, but that doesn't change the fact that he doesn't have the faintest idea what we're talking about.'

'Of course I know,' Armand said, losing an edge of his politeness. 'Bazeppe is one of the cities of Nova Stella.' He smiled, pleased with his clever guess.

Isangell swallowed. 'Oh, no.'

'I told you.' Ashiol let the amusement drain from his

voice. 'Now dismiss your little friend here. We have much to discuss.'

'We have nothing to discuss,' said Isangell, but she still waved Armand out of the room. 'I'm busy, Ashiol. There's a Saturnalia ball this nox, and you're not even halfway up my list of duties. Go away.'

'Your betrothed is dead, gosling, so far dead that no one you know will ever remember he and his city existed. And while I don't intend to be flippant about his passing, that really is the least of our problems. The bigger concern is that you remember him, and that means you're one of us now. You belong to the Creature Court.'

She gave him an imperious look. 'Go away, or I will call the lictors to get rid of you. It's time you learned, Ash. Not everything is about your precious Creature Court.'

ONE DAY AFTER THE IDES OF SATURNALIS

NOX

The sky was quiet that nox. The sentinels made their bed in the workroom of the newest nest in Aufleur. Where else would they sleep?

Macready couldn't get much out of Kelpie about what had happened in Bazeppe, and after a while he gave up trying. What was the point, anyway? Bazeppe was gone, and Aufleur would be next.

He sat up as the others slept, the light from the fire in the grate reflecting on their faces. Kelpie and Crane. Both looked so young in their sleep, the creases smoothed out like ribbon silk.

Macready felt so old he could barely move without creaking. He hadn't been able to save Rhian from whatever the feck was eating her from the inside out. He couldn't protect Velody, or Ashiol. He was wearing thin.

After what felt like hours of sitting still in contemplation, he heard a creak that had nothing to do with him. Then another, on the staircase. He moved silently towards the stairs, hands ready to draw his swords if he needed to.

Delphine, caught in the act, gasped once as he touched her sleeve. 'Frig it, Macready,' she hissed. 'Who taught you to move that quietly?'

'All those bad demmes in my past. Where are you off to, my lovely?'

'None of your business any more. Nothing I do is of any interest to you.'

'When you're sneaking out at the beginning of what could be a war and our Kings needing us? Oh, love, you can't tell me it's not my business.'

She pouted like the old Delphine, playing the spoilt child, but there was something off about her. No stolen perfume, no roses to cloud his senses. She stank of something else.

'Have you been rolling in skysilver?' he accused her.

'You don't know everything, Mac,' she huffed.

'I don't know anything, lass. Educate me.'

Delphine snatched her arm away. 'The sky could explode at any moment. You're not going to leave Velody and the others now. Don't even pretend you think whatever I'm up to is more important than them. Stay here and do your job, Macready. Leave me alone.'

She flounced through the kitchen, and he felt the soft shimmer as she released the entrance to the nest.

'Let her go,' said a low voice.

Macready turned and saw Crane standing there, dressed, his arms crossed in a vaguely threatening manner. Playing the man now, was he?

'You know what she's up to?'

'I trust her. You might want to try it.'

Macready bristled at the lad's tone. 'Know a lot about our Delphine these days, do you?'

Crane stepped forward, and as he came away from the

fire his face fell into shadows. Macready couldn't see anything of what he was about. 'You wanted her to be a sentinel. Did you think that meant she would stop being herself?'

'Careful what you say, lad.'

'Oh, for frig's sake,' broke in Kelpie. She was awake, too, and on her feet. 'If you two are going to scuffle over the blonde can you do it outside?'

'We're not going to fight,' said Macready, eyeing Crane.

'No, we're not,' agreed Crane.

'Good,' said Kelpie, pulling on her leather coat. 'Because I'm going to find out what Delphine is up to, and if you stay on your best behaviour, I'll let you come with me.'

DELPHINE HEADED along Via Cinqueline and up the back slope of the overgrown Avleurine hill, all but bouncing with righteous ire as well as anticipation. She was damned if she was going to let Macready spoil this for her.

Her swords felt heavy on her back as she hurried along. She was almost used to them again, ready for action. She was a sentinel, and after this nox no one would question that ever again.

The club was called the Glass Cat. The owners had taken over the ruined remains of the old Palazzo on the hill (abandoned by the Ducal family generations ago, because of drainage or something), adding domed glass windows between the broken stone and steel frames. They had also put in glass tiles and frescoes to replace stolen mosaics. It was all very shiny.

Jazz music filled the complex, spilling down the hillside. Delphine slipped in close so she could watch the scene through one of the heart-shaped skylights.

The dance floor, once an open courtyard belonging to the Daylight Duc's family, was filled with beautiful people. They danced and clung and gossiped and laughed and drank themselves silly.

Delphine had been one of them, once. She had never questioned why a ribboner might be welcomed among the debauched aristocratic children of the city, or even wondered why her accent was precise like theirs, not as common as Velody's or Rhian's sounded to her ear. Now, of course, with the swords of the Creature Court warming her back, she remembered her childhood in Tierce as a spoilt little rich demme, already rebelling against her parents. Being sent to learn a trade was a punishment, a way to get her out from under their feet during her 'difficult' years.

She knew now why she had fitted in so easily with her gin-swilling crowd, with Teddy and Villiers and the like. She was an aristocrat, even if she hadn't remembered her past. They knew it by her voice and manner; had allowed her into their circle because she was 'one of them'.

As she watched, Delphine recognised other faces. Half the sons of the Great Families were here this nox. She really should make her move before they sank too many ansouisettes.

She slid down the side of the Palazzo and removed her cloak with shaking fingers. Her swords and knives were clearly visible in their harness over a knee-length grey shift that whispered against her skin and an over-dress made from knitted links of skysilver.

It was time.

~

'WHAT THE FECK IS SHE DOING?' Macready breathed, leaning over the skylight.

'Gone crazy,' Kelpie observed. 'Sooner or later it happens to every demme you frig, Mac.'

'Aye, I'm sure that's it,' he said sarcastically. 'Lad, do you know anything about... Where's Crane?'

Kelpie leaned further over the skylight. 'Oh, hells. I didn't see this coming.'

Delphine walked through the crowd. She knew this song. It was a medley of old war anthems, sped up to the modern pace and always sung with great irony. Everyone knew the war was over, leaving nothing but battle stories and ancient songs as relics of the time. Everyone was wrong.

Her dress gleamed with the delicious hum of skysilver. It was cut perfectly: short enough to give her ease of movement, but long enough to drape prettily over her curves. Velody had never made a frock like this. Who was the mistress dressmaker now?

'Dee-dee,' said one seigneur, catching her arm. 'Where have you been, angel?'

She shook him off and walked to the stage where the band played their ironic war songs with lazy grins. 'I need to make an announcement,' she said, and threw a handful of shilleins to the bandleader.

'Announce away, baby doll,' he said with an exaggerated bow.

Delphine climbed up on the stage and faced a crowd who were already protesting the sudden halt of the music. 'I need you,' she said, and didn't that start up a cacophony of catcalls and heckling among the wastrels and wankers. 'All of you. You've had it too easy for too long, and now there's a battle to fight, and if you won't stand up for your city, who will?'

'What powders are you on, Dee-dee?' called one voice, and everyone laughed. "Can I have some?"

Delphine looked towards the voice and recognised Teddy,

with Villiers at his elbow. Maud and Peggy stood with Lisette over by the bar, pointing at her, whispering to each other.

She drew her sword. The steel one, for the satisfying noise it made. Then the other, because of the contrast, the soft hum of the skysilver. This sword liked to be drawn.

'You wanted a war,' she said. 'All of you have been carousing and laughing and living on the milk-fat of a city that has none to spare. You sing songs and write bad poetry about never getting to prove your mettle on a battlefield. It's time to stand up for this city. It can't be just a handful of us fighting to protect it any more — that's not going to work. We need sentinels. The city needs its champions.' She took a deep breath. 'We're going to need a lot of champions.'

'And we're the perfect toy soldiers, are we?' yelled out a young drunkard that Delphine was pretty sure was Atticus Aufrey, one of the sons of the Great Families whose suit the Duchessa had turned down.

'Someone has to be,' she said simply. 'I choose you. You have the most to repay to this city.'

The great doors opened, doors that had once been the entrance for Ducs and Comtes. A huge figure stood there, a large sack on his back.

'Frig me, it's Father Neptune,' snarked one smart-arse.

Crane, also with a sack on his back, stepped out from beside his larger companion. 'It's better than that,' he said, sounding pleased with himself. 'This is our friend the Smith. He does have presents for you, though.'

The Smith lifted his sack high and tipped out an impossible number of skysilver swords. They fell onto the glass dance floor, clattering and skidding, forming an enormous heap. They hummed to Delphine, making her skin warm by their presence.

'What do you expect us to do with those, sweet pea?' asked Villiers with a twist of his mouth.

'I expect you to pick them up and learn how to be heroes,' said Delphine.

'Is that all?'

'Well, if you could manage it in the next day or so, that would be good. The sooner the better, really.' She smiled brightly. 'Luckily I know an excellent place for us to practise.'

~

MACREADY STARED DOWN AT DELPHINE. She stood there in the lanternlight, gorgeous and glowing, so fecking confident that she was doing the right thing, though he knew she had no bloody clue.

'It's ridiculous,' hissed Kelpie. 'She can't turn a rabble like that into sentinels. I don't care how many fucking swords she's got hold of. It doesn't work that way. We were called to this life. You don't build sentinels in a factory.'

'Maybe not,' Mac said slowly. 'But we've a duty to help her, do we not?'

'You're kidding me,' Kelpie said flatly.

Macready leaned over and gave her arm a squeeze. 'We're doing things differently this time around.'

'They say that, they always say that, but it ends up the same. We throw ourselves at their feet and they don't even see us. We get stepped on. They save the world.'

Macready sighed, shaking his head. 'Kelpie, my love, it's time we did something about that cynicism of yours.'

'Last time I was blindly loyal, I got poisoned,' she snapped.

He held his hand out to her. 'One more time. For my sake?'

Kelpie glared at him. 'I really hate you sometimes.'

When they entered the glass-lined room, Macready almost staggered as the taste of skysilver hit him in the face.

Delphine dazzled with it. The music was no longer playing. The toffs and wastrels stood in their shiny clothes, staring at her as she spoke of heroism and bravery.

'What the feck have you done, lass?' he hissed as he got closer.

Delphine turned to him and smiled. Her frock shone with tiny silver scales, chain links so bright that they hummed. How was she doing this? Skysilver should have no effect on those of the daylight, but there was so much of it, and the crowd was falling under its influence.

'Velody didn't make that dress for you,' said Kelpie.

'No,' said Delphine, breaking off her speech. 'I did — well, I helped. The Smith did most of the work. I always wanted to be a dressmaker, you know. I was rather good at it. Not the best, but you don't always have to be the best. Sometimes you just have to let yourself be enough.'

'What's wrong with them?' Kelpie said, surveying the room. 'Are they hypnotised?'

'They're choosing to be heroes,' Delphine said staunchly. 'To be sentinels. Once they have made their choice, they are ours to command.'

Macready could see their faces now. They gazed adoringly at Delphine, but there was nothing alive in their expressions. He shook his head. 'There was no choice here, lass. You can't make sentinels like this, by taking their will away from them.'

'Why not?' she flung at him. 'Is this really any different to what you did to me?'

That stung hard, but he carried on. 'Enough is enough.'

'No, it's never enough. I know it's wrong, and I know it doesn't fit your romantic ideals, but we need warriors. We need to beat the damned sky once and for all — this is our last chance. The sentinels weren't supposed to be a support act. We were great once. We can be great again.'

She believed it so hard she was nearly crying, and it shocked Macready to the core that she had come so far that she would even think of doing something like this.

Like Velody, Delphine didn't know the history, didn't know the rules. Neither of them had any idea of what was impossible. Maybe that was what would make the difference in the end.

'These are not sentinels,' Kelpie insisted. 'This rabble is no use to any of us. You're going to get them killed, or get us killed protecting them.'

Crane, who had been standing silently near Delphine, spoke up. 'Velody needs us. The Court needs us. If we don't stand with them, we might as well give up.'

'Aye, we should stand with them,' Macready said fiercely. 'Not drag some false army along in our wake.'

But he couldn't take his eyes off Delphine, couldn't rid himself of that most dangerous thought of all. *It might work.*

'The Smith has swords enough for all of them,' said Delphine.

'It takes more than swords to make a sentinel!' Kelpie insisted, looking to Macready for support.

He opened his mouth and closed it again. What Delphine was doing was wrong, he knew that. But it was the kind of wrong that could save the city.

Delphine stepped down from her makeshift dais and the eyes of a hundred fops and flappers followed her. 'I know that,' she said in a soft voice. 'You taught me that, Macready. Kelpie. All of you. Now it's time for me to teach you something.'

She drew her skysilver sword and led the way out of the glass pavilion. Her army of dead-eyed courtiers in candy-striped suits and feathered frocks followed her.

'Are you coming?' Crane asked in the silence that followed.

Macready shook his head. 'Do what you have to. We'll work on keeping Velody and Ashiol safe.'

Crane nodded, and went after Delphine and her followers. Kelpie and Macready stood still, watching them leave.

'So that's it, then,' Macready said lightly. 'Delphine will save the world while the rest of us sit back and have a cup of tea.'

Kelpie closed her eyes briefly, looking pained. 'I saw a city die only a few days ago,' she said. 'I'm not sure there's much left of our world to save.'

PART XIV
SEED OF DESTRUCTION

47

FIRST DAY OF SATURNALIA

TWO DAYS AFTER THE IDES OF SATURNALIS

DAYLIGHT

*R*hian was everywhere. The pain in her body — plant, stone, fire, water — was so great that she folded inside herself and flew free. She could see the whole city from here. Stone and water, path and grass, mortar and cement.

There was no pain, this way.

She saw beneath the city: the broken buildings, the bodies in the dirt of the Angel Gardens, the bright sunshine in the Killing Ground, the army Delphine was building. Oh, Delphine. If Rhian was capable of laughter, of sheer joy, that would do it.

She saw the Palazzo and the rooftops and the Forums. She was unable to contain a wave of heat from her body, and it hit the Lake of Follies, making the water churn and boil.

It was starting. She was going to destroy the city and there was no one to stop her.

The scent of mint and lemon brought her back to her

body, to the pain and stiffness and stone and dirt and the ruined remains of her room. She could barely see; her eyes were swollen and crusted with blood.

'I brought you a cup of tea,' Macready said softly, and that did make her laugh, though it was a broken and wretched sound.

'Glad you're here,' she whispered through lips that barely seemed to work.

'Oh, lass.' He came nearer and she felt the brush of his rough hand against part of her — she did not know what. A hand, a tendril, a hip. 'What can I do?'

'You can kill me.' He was silent. All she could hear was his heartbeat. 'Macready, you must.'

'Not that, love.'

'Something has awoken in me. I'm tied to the city, and I will destroy it if you don't stop me.'

'How is that possible?'

'I don't know.'

She was tired, so tired, and the stone would be coming soon. She might never have another chance to convince him.

'Something has been inside me since that day — the Lupercalia, the lake...' But no, those words meant nothing to him. 'I thought it was being the Seer, but that was wrong, it wasn't supposed to be me. Heliora made a mistake. I am the seed of destruction, and I will be the end of all of you.'

He leaned his forehead against hers. 'You have to hang on, Rhian. You're stronger than this.'

She opened her mouth to say, 'You never knew me, Macready,' but her mouth filled with roses, silky perfumed petals, vicious thorns, and by the time she had spat them all to the floor, the stone had hold of her body. 'Please,' was all she managed. Kelpie. She needed Kelpie, but the words would not form in her throat.

Macready kissed her briefly, his mouth pressed to hers,

and then it was cold, so cold, and she couldn't see him any more.

~

VELODY AWOKE in the early afternoon of the first day of the Saturnalia festival. It was strange to not being able to see anything out of her windows. Delphine had made the right call in turning the house into a nest, but it meant that every brick and floorboard felt a little bit wrong. There was no sign that Delphine's bed had been slept in.

She looked in on Rhian, and found her moaning quietly but apparently sleeping. Water dripped from her skin to form puddles on the floor. Macready sat beside her, asleep against the wall.

Downstairs, Kelpie was asleep in a chair.

Velody made tea for herself, and stared at the shapes the steam from the kettle made against the ceiling. She shivered. This might be a nest, but there was nothing that made the house feel safe.

Garnet was nearby. She could feel his presence closing around her. She could stay in here, but what was the point of being safe if she had no chance to change anything?

She stepped outside. The city opened up to her, as if recognising her. The air smelled more real than inside the nest. And yes, there was Garnet; she could taste him on the chill winter breeze.

A body hit the ground, bursting in front of her. Velody jumped back, and then pressed her hands to her mouth, bidding herself not to wail or faint or be sick. It was a child, oh saints, it was a child, and she knew nothing about him, who he was, what animal he had been.

She should have protected him from this. From Garnet.

She stepped into the air and flew up to the rooftop where

he was waiting for her. It was freezing, with the smell of snow in the air, though none had yet fallen. The wind was icy. Garnet wore a dark red woollen coat, his cheeks ruddy in the wind and his hair a bright beacon against the grey sky.

'Why would you do this?' Velody screamed at him. 'What's wrong with you? How can you possibly think this is the way to be Power and Majesty?'

'And what do you know about it?' Garnet said calmly. 'What ordeals have you ever passed, Mistress of Mice? How many times have your ideals been tested?'

'It's not hard, Garnet,' she said furiously. 'Don't kill *children*. Surely that's one of the easier rules in life to follow?'

'So precious, so innocent,' he said, shaking his head. 'Don't you get it, Velody? Sacrifice means giving up something important. Something that it hurts to give up. This city of ours runs on that rule.'

'No,' she insisted. 'There's another way. There's a better way. You stopped looking for it.'

'You are not Power and Majesty!' he yelled at her. 'You never were. If you were Power and Majesty, you would have heard the voices.'

Velody sucked in a cold gulp of air. 'What voices?'

Garnet gave her a suspicious look, as if she should already know. 'The voices that swallowed Tierce. The voices that made me choose.'

~

TOPAZ WAS SHAKEN awake by Bree, who was none too gentle about it. '*He* wants you,' she said, and it was clear from her tone that she hadn't come around to the new way of things.

'What have you got against Poet?' asked Topaz, deliberately not calling him Lord anything. It didn't sit right on her tongue to do that with anyone but Livilla, not now.

He'd lost his right to be Himself, too; the Vittorina Royale was a lifetime ago.

'He's one of them,' Bree said bitterly. 'But he's not ours, is he? He hasn't offered us a Lord's protection.'

'We don't need protection,' said Topaz, pulling on her clothes, the nice ones that Livilla had given her. 'We have the fire. We all have the fire.'

'I was happy being a bird,' Bree blurted. 'I hate being a salamander. It's all hot and scratchy.'

'It's power,' Topaz said sternly. 'If we have it, they can't hurt us. Remember that.'

Bree rolled her eyes.

Topaz found Poet in Livilla's room, fully dressed, hair combed, primped up for company. He looked too thin, and his wrists still bore the marks of the skysilver chains they had wrapped around him when they first captured him. She felt bad about that, but only a bit.

His two courtesi were there: the darkhound man and the weasel boy. Topaz nodded to them both, then turned to Poet.

'You're not going to go running to *him* the second you leave this place, are you?' she asked bluntly. The one flaw in their plan was Poet going dizzy for Garnet all over again.

Poet hesitated, took his specs off to polish them, buying himself some time. 'I won't kill him. I won't let him be killed. I plan to save him from everyone, including himself.'

'How are you going to do that, then?'

'The skysilver cage is at Velody's house. If we can get him there, we can take him out of the battle. It should be enough. The sky is using him, I know that. I think it's my fault.' His voice broke slightly. 'That bloody watch. It gets inside your head. It only had hold of me for a short time, but Garnet... I think he was lost long ago.'

'It would be simpler to kill him,' said Topaz.

Poet laughed and tilted his head to one side. 'You think

so, do you? Think it's easy to kill? We're supposed to be doing things differently now. Isn't that the point of all this? We're breaking the rules and behaving like civilised seigneurs and demoiselles for once in our lives.'

Bree was right. There was no trusting Poet. He might be willing to protect them now, but he could easily turn around, take his dratted head off and hand it to Garnet on a plate. Topaz hadn't missed the wary looks that his courtesi gave him, either.

'Well?' Poet said politely. 'I believe you are going to share something with us before we march into battle with you?'

Topaz nodded. A small voice inside her (sounding a lot like Bree) complained that it was too much of a risk, but a promise was a promise.

She went to Zero first, put her hand over his heart and felt the weasel shapes squiggling and wriggling inside him. She showed him her shape, the shape of the salamander, putting the images right inside his head.

'It's hot,' he said, sounding surprised. Then he blinked and shaped into a sudden pile of fire lizards, scrambling all over each other and burning brightly.

'Excellent,' said Poet, his eyes bright. 'Shade next, my dearling. Then me. Isn't Garnet going to get a surprise?'

～

ASHIOL FOUND Velody and Garnet on the roof of her house in Via Silviana.

'There you are,' Garnet greeted him with glee. 'I seem to have misplaced the entire Creature Court, Ash-my-love. They no longer come when I call. You wouldn't know anything about that, would you?'

'They're safe,' was all Ashiol would tell him. He nodded

distantly to Velody, not wanting to give too much away of how close the two of them had become.

'How can that be true?' Garnet challenged. 'They don't have their Power and Majesty to protect them. I'd say that makes them the opposite of safe.'

'I've seen your idea of safe,' Velody said, sounding distressed. 'How many more of them will die in the name of your madness, Garnet?'

'Now, that's not nice,' said Garnet. 'I'm pretty sure I'm not the mad one here. Wouldn't want our darling Ashiol to feel neglected.' He looked from one to the other of them and laughed out loud. 'Oh, that's rich. You're frigging like rabbits and you still haven't made the sacred marriage. So much for gaining any advantage over me.'

'Who did you suck this so-called wisdom out of?' Ashiol demanded. 'Are you making this up as you go along?'

'I read books,' Garnet said sweetly. 'I keep my ear to the ground.'

'And, oh yes, he hears voices,' Velody said sharply.

Ashiol narrowed his eyes at his old friend. 'Since when?'

'Oh, Ashiol,' said Garnet. 'Isn't it sad? You never knew me at all.'

Ashiol felt the presence of Kelpie and Macready, and wanted to shout to them to keep away.

'Sentinels!' Garnet laughed as the two of them clambered up onto the roof. 'Let me guess. You, Macready, have come to inform your Kings that something is dreadfully wrong with our Seer. And Kelpie thinks you should both know that your rogue sentinel Delphine is building an army against me. You see, I know everything. There's no point in playing, my friends. I know all your secrets and you know none of mine.'

'I know your secrets, Garnet,' said a voice, and Poet joined them on the roof.

'Ah,' said Garnet, sounding sad. 'But you wouldn't tell,

would you, sweet boy? Your loyalty has always been to me.'

'That's the funny thing about loyalty,' said Poet, a fragile figure even in his fine clothes. 'The more you share it, the more you have. That boy on the ground down there was called Wils to his friends. He couldn't dance worth a centime, but he was the best tumbler I've ever seen under ten years old and he had a voice like a Sweetheart Saint. His brother, his only family in the world, was crushed under a sandstone block in the destruction of the Vittorina Royale. My theatre.' His feet slipped a little on the roof tiles. 'Did you never wonder what it would take, Garnet, for the loyalty I have for you to run out?'

'Not for that,' scoffed Garnet. 'A street lamb. You made them for me in the first place. Bred them for sacrifice. They all ditched you for Livilla.'

Poet glanced briefly at Ashiol and Velody. 'He's getting all of his knowledge out of a book, one of a set that Lord Saturn collected. A history of the Creature Court. He stole it from me.'

'Stole,' Garnet said dismissively. 'You would have given me the world and stars.'

'Yes, I fucking would,' Poet snarled. 'He has a pocket watch, too. I gave it to him... I didn't know —'

'Clockwork,' said Ashiol slowly.

'It's been talking to him through it. The sky. Promising him things. Demanding greater and greater acts of sacrifice. Though what's greater than sacrificing a whole city, Garnet?' Poet flung out.

'You know nothing about me,' Garnet spat.

'I know the choice you made! Then and now.'

'Everything I've ever done has been for Aufleur,' declared Garnet. 'I have protected you all from the sky.'

'The sky took you a long time ago,' said Poet. 'You just won't lie down.'

A cruel smile played over Garnet's face. 'You brought me back, ratling. It's your fault I'm here.'

'I know,' Poet sighed. 'And I'm sorry for it. Maybe if you'd stayed dead, I could have let you go.'

He shaped himself in a fast blur, but not into the usual white rats. Instead, he was salamanders, blazing with fire.

Garnet cried out in alarm, stepping back and back until he teetered on the guttering of the roof.

More salamanders poured up and over the roof from below, hundreds of them, far more than one lamb or two or three could make.

Garnet went chimaera and flew off across the sky, and the horde of salamanders followed him, blazing with flame.

Ashiol breathed out for one long moment. Velody looked at him with sympathy. He didn't know if he wanted her to touch him, or if he would hit her if she tried.

'We have to take him down,' he said grimly, and she nodded.

Yes, that was obvious. It had been obvious for a long time. Whatever it was that Garnet thought he was doing, the sky had a hold on him. The only thing Ashiol had to comfort him was that this was not Garnet — the corruption had started in him long ago. He was no longer the boy that Ashiol had loved.

Perhaps it hadn't even been him when he tortured Ashiol and tried to destroy him, so many years ago. Perhaps. It was a single warm light in a sea of frost.

'Time to talk to the Seer,' Ashiol said.

'Aye, about that,' Macready put in, but Ashiol didn't wait to see what he had to say.

INSIDE THE NEST that had once been a house and a shop and a

place of ribbon scraps and warm soup, Velody led the way to Rhian's room. She pushed on the door and it opened into darkness. 'Rhian?'

Was it too late?

'I'm here,' said a calm voice, and Rhian walked out of the room. She looked normal — skin healed, hair trimmed short. She smelled faintly of earth and stone, but otherwise she was as she should be. 'I'm ready,' she said.

Velody stared, hardly able to believe it.

'We need to see into the futures,' said Ashiol as if nothing was out of the ordinary. Of course, he didn't know, hadn't seen the wreckage of Rhian that filled this room less than an hour ago. Macready saw it, though. Like Velody, he stared at this normal Rhian as if she had stepped out of the seven hells unscathed.

'I'm sorry,' said Rhian with a smile. 'It took me longer than I thought. But the Seer is gone now.' She wiped a tear from the corner of her eye and pressed it into Kelpie's hand. 'Give that to her, when the time is right,' she said.

Kelpie dug her hand deep into a pocket of her breeches before Velody could see what it contained.

'What do you mean the Seer is gone?' Ashiol demanded.

'Heliora made a mistake,' Rhian said simply. 'It wasn't supposed to be me. I'm something else. We should go soon.'

'Go where?' Velody asked.

'To the Forum.' Rhian led the way downstairs, and found an old woollen coat in the cupboard, which she shrugged into. 'Garnet and the salamanders are waking something they shouldn't. Then there's Delphine's army, and the sky will attack as soon as nox falls. Really, we shouldn't delay.'

'How do you know all that if you're not the Seer?' Velody blurted out, unused to this Rhian who acted so much like the demme she had known years ago, her sensible friend.

'I told you,' said Rhian. 'I'm something else.'

48

FIRST DAY OF SATURNALIA

TWO DAYS AFTER THE IDES OF SATURNALIS

DUSK

*D*elphine and Crane had been on their feet all last nox and most of this day, building an army. The skysilver did the work that it was supposed to do, turning daylight folk into sentinels through repeated exposure. It would not have had permanent effect if she had brought them anywhere else, but this was the Killing Ground. Skysilver was different here, more powerful. Delphine marched up and down the sands of the Killing Ground, observing the troops. Possibly she'd gone a little nuts, but she wasn't going to admit that to anyone.

The bright skysilver frock was warm on her skin, warm like the artificial sun that beat down on them as they worked. Crane led the fops and flappers in a drill and they copied him perfectly.

There was a light in their eyes that did not belong to any world Delphine recognised, and it made her uncomfortable if she thought too deeply about what she had done. Best not to think about it. She had a city to save. Whatever happened this nox, whatever fate they all met, they would not suffer from a lack of sentinels.

The Smith had not returned to his work. He leaned against the wall of his forge watching the army of new sentinels. Could he see the flickers of ghosts that filled the sands, the ghosts of fallen warriors?

'Are you joining us?' she asked him, striding up to him and staring into his large face. 'Will you fight with us?'

'I do not fight,' he grunted. 'I build.'

Well, it was worth a try.

THIS CLOSE TO MIDWINTER, darkness came early. The traditional ball held at the Palazzo on the first day of Saturnalia began in the middle of the afternoon and it felt already as if it had been going on forever. The great hall was a mess of masks, men dressed as demoiselles and ladies dressed as serving maids. Isangell had drunk too much, quite by accident, and had the taste of violet punch on her tongue as she danced, passed from hand to hand under the boisterous music.

She remembered, as a child, sitting under one of the tables with a bowl of sugared almonds, watching the dancing and the costumes and the merriment. She wished she was there now. Everything had made sense when she was eight years old.

Saturnalia had always been her most beloved festival. There was something delicious about the topsy-turviness of it all, of celebrating the wrong and the upside down and the strange.

Her favourite Saturnalia game was to dress herself as a servant in clean, tidy linens and serve breakfast rolls to her mama, or dress her grandmama's hair. She insisted on eating brown bread and plain cheese instead of her usual favourite pastries or candied fruits. Saints, she must have been an insufferable child, playing at peasantry, surrounded by hard-working servants who had to pretend amusement for her delight.

This year, she embraced the more adult aspects of the festival. There was something extraordinarily freeing about wearing breeches, even breeches made of embroidered gold satin, and a shirt of the finest cobweb silk. Isangell was sure she did not look remotely like a boy, but realism was hardly the point of Saturnalia.

On impulse, moments before she made her entrance, she demanded that her maids bob her hair and, oh, the look on her mother's face had been worth it.

Bazeppe was gone, and that meant Isangell's last attempt at rebellion was over as well. It was time to choose one of the sweaty-handed, glazed-eyed boys of the Great Families of Aufleur.

Many of them had not turned up to the ball. Isangell assumed that her recent attempts to find a husband from Bazeppe had insulted them enough to stay away. Except, of course, that none of them remembered Bazeppe... Saints, it made her head hurt.

Some of the Families may have snubbed her, but there were still plenty of eligible men here. Why not choose one now? Not one of them would make a Duc she wanted to unleash on the city; not one of them was anything close to the princel Isangell had imagined for herself as a child. The more time she spent allowing them to court her, the more irritating they became. Why not let the dance do its work for her? She could reach out blindly into a sea of costumed noblemen and marry the one who took her hand.

The music rose and fell and Isangell spun deeper into the circle of gaudy courtiers, letting the madness of the dance swallow her whole.

Cool fingers slid into hers and drew her out again. She followed, allowing herself to be brought clear of the chaos and even out of the room. Only in the corridor outside did she realise who had rescued her. It was one of Ashiol's precious 'sentinels' who served as lictor to him and his wretched creatures. This demme played a seigneur far better than Isangell in her costume breeches — her clothes were dark and worn, and she wore swords on her back.

'High and brightness,' she said politely, her hand still firmly holding Isangell's.

'Kelpie,' said the Duchessa, remembering the demme's name after a moment's thought. 'Is it Ashiol?'

'Isn't it always,' said Kelpie with a cynicism that Isangell could well identify with.

They hurried along the corridor and into Isangell's rooms. There, she looked around for her cousin, but there was no sign of him.

Kelpie busied herself by drawing her daggers and making firm incisions on the door. Isangell opened her mouth to complain about the scratches in the paintwork, but held back the words. The demme was so intent on what she was doing, she barely seemed aware that she was not alone.

As a child, Isangell learnt much more by sitting quietly in a corner while the adults went about their business than she had when she made a fuss. So she sat, drawing her knees up on the couch (so strange not to have to fuss about skirts — she wondered if her mother would throw a fit if she regularly chose to wear breeches around the Palazzo), and watched Kelpie work.

The sentinel finished with the door and began to circle the room, her knives marking the wall at regular intervals. She made no distinction between wall and furnishings — her blades bit into plaster and tapestry curtain and a portrait of Isangell's grandmama. It was rather fascinating to watch. Isangell shivered once, and it seemed as if the window darkened a little in that moment.

Finally Kelpie tore her eyes from her work and acknowledged Isangell's existence again. 'I need to seal it,' she said, kneeling beside her on the couch.

Isangell did not get a chance to ask what and why before Kelpie put her hands on either side of her face and kissed her. It was warm and sudden, and Isangell felt jolted awake, as if she had been in a daze all this time.

'Oh,' she said faintly, when they came apart.

'It works better with kissing,' Kelpie said with an apologetic shrug. 'Not sure why. It's probably a Creature Court thing. Anything to get laid, that lot.'

She was up again, bouncing on her booted feet, fingers smoothing over the door that... was not there any more.

'What have you done with my door?' Isangell asked.

'I'm keeping you safe.'

'Trapped,' Isangell said sharply.

Kelpie blew out an impatient breath. 'Safe,' she repeated. 'You can leave any time you like. But you're important right now, and not because of the Duchessa thing. Ashiol needs you safe and guarded while the shit goes down, and frankly I'd rather be at his side than in here with you. Don't give me a hard time about it, aye?'

'Is the city in danger?' Isangell asked. 'Is Ashiol in danger?'

'Do you really have to ask?'

'What about everyone else? The Palazzo is full of people. Would they be safer in here than out there?'

'This is a nest, not a ballroom,' said Kelpie flatly. 'We're not bringing anyone else in.'

'I am the Duchessa. I can't hide away in some *nest* while everyone else suffers.'

Isangell hurried over to the blank wall where her door had been. She felt for the crack, the doorknob, for any way out.

'When I said you could leave anytime you like,' said Kelpie, closing her hand over one of Isangell's. 'I lied.'

~

IN THE FORUM, Velody watched the sky turn grey and then dark with the coming nox. She watched as the everyday people of the city, going about their business, began not noticing things — like the several wild animals that strutted back and forth on the grey cobbles, waiting for the battle. She could taste it on the air. War was coming.

The salamanders won their battle. They had Garnet pinned above the great altar, bound to the statue of Iustitia with skysilver chains. Delphine was there, too, with the Smith, obviously the source of the chains. They all looked ridiculously pleased with themselves even as Garnet howled and roared at them.

'We have to stop them,' Velody said in a low voice.

Ashiol was at her side, but she past the point of his presence being a comfort to her.

'Stop who?' he asked. 'Delphine, Poet, the salamanders? I thought you wanted everyone working together. Isn't that what you were trying for all along?'

It was true, absolutely, but there was something wrong about all this.

'We're wasting too much energy going in different directions,' she said in frustration. 'We have to be a strong, united front to beat the sky.'

'This is about as united as you'll ever get us,' Ashiol said. 'With Garnet bound and out from under our feet.'

Velody shook her head, but said nothing else. Beating Garnet was not the point. It couldn't be. They had a war to win.

Ashiol shaped himself into chimaera and flew forth, scattering salamanders this way and that. 'Stand down,' he roared at them. 'Garnet will not die from your bites and scratches. He will fight me.'

Garnet turned chimaera with a fierce roar, shaking his chains.

One of the salamanders shifted into rats and hurled themselves at Ashiol, shaping finally into Poet. 'Fight?' he repeated. 'We've only just captured him. Do you expect us to let him go so you can playact some bullshit ritual of a duel?'

'Traitors,' Garnet growled at them both.

'Shut up and consider the fact that everyone who loves you most wants you locked up or dead,' Poet snapped.

'Those are my chains,' Delphine said, crossing her arms as she stepped forward to stand at Poet's side. 'And I'm not taking them off. This isn't about pawing the ground, Ashiol. Behave yourself or I'll smack you on the nose.'

Ash returned to Lord form, recoiling from her. 'What are you wearing?'

Velody had been so caught up in the fate of Garnet to notice, but yes: Delphine was wearing a tailored tunic of chainmail that gleamed with skysilver. She stank of it, the animor of the metal hitting the back of Velody's throat harshly enough to make her gag.

'Delphine,' she said. 'What have you done?'

There were rumblings from the sky. Delphine glanced up,

then darted a smile at Velody. 'I've been getting prepared, of course. Want to see?'

She put two fingers in her mouth and whistled fiercely, and suddenly the stench of skysilver was everywhere, surrounding them, and Velody could hardly breathe.

An army marched into the Forum. Dozens and dozens of men and women, dressed as if for a fancy party, armed with skysilver swords and daggers. A very specific feeling rolled off them all. Sentinels. Somehow, Delphine had created dozens of sentinels all at once.

Ashiol started to laugh, gleeful and utterly genuine.

Warlord and Lennoc flew overhead, shining in Lord form and surrounded by their courtesi. Everyone was ready for the battle.

They were, in fact, united against their enemy. All of them except Velody.

'It's all right,' Rhian said calmly. She reached out and gave Velody's hand a reassuring pat. 'It will make sense soon.'

Light blazed from the sky, fierce and hot, drawn into a single powerful thread that shot over their heads and burst through the roof of the Basilica, blasting into the ground. Velody leaped into the air, flew over the heads of Delphine and her army, and skidded roughly on the paving stones of the avenue just beyond them.

The light from the sky was channelling ferociously into the Lake of Follies. The water boiled and frothed under the heat and gave off huge waves of steam.

Shapes formed in the steam. Great winged shapes, and there was no way to know what they were, except that they were not friends. Shape after shape clambered out of the lake and lurched in the direction of Delphine's army.

Saints and angels.

For one shocked and quiet moment, Velody had a strong memory all over again of her brother telling her about seeing angels in the steam. Devils made of dust. Saints made of clockwork. *What on earth made me think that the angels might be on our side?*

More light poured from the sky and the last water of the Lake of Follies gave up the ghost into one huge cloud of steam. It formed several distinct shapes and, yes, angels. There was no other word for them. Except, possibly, death.

49

FIRST DAY OF SATURNALIA

TWO DAYS AFTER THE IDES OF SATURNALIS

NOX

*A*shiol had never seen the point of Delphine before. An army of sentinels, brought into being because no one had told her it was impossible. There was no time to stop and admire her now. The sentinels were under attack from the steam angels, and there were fracture lines cracking across the sky, glowing in fierce shades of orange, red and gold.

'Let me go,' Garnet yelled from where he was still chained to the statue of Iustitia, surrounded by salamanders. A glowing skybolt crashed into the tiled portico behind him, and the groove it made in the ground bubbled with molten skysilver. 'For the love of Aufleur. Let me fight.'

'How are we supposed to know which side you would fight on?' Poet snapped back.

Another skybolt arced over their heads and Ashiol threw animor at it, forcing it to explode before it got too close.

'You expect us to have mercy on you, Garnet?' he said. 'You picked the wrong people to ask.'

The steam angels swarmed towards them. The salamanders skittered forward and burst into bright flame, which kept the angels away for a little while at least. But they circled around, darting this way and that, actively looking for a break in the salamander fire.

'Seems it's you they want,' Ashiol said to Garnet.

'All the more reason to let me go,' Garnet replied.

It turned out as Ashiol had known it would, with him standing at the foot of the statue of Iustitia, protecting Garnet from the angels. They smelled like animor and rain, and there were other scents in there too, of familiar skin that made his head muzzy.

One of the angels cried out as he slashed at her — her, of course it was a woman — with his chimaera claws. For a moment her steam blurred thin and he saw a familiar face within. No, not that. No hallucinations of lovers past, not today.

Ashiol lost focus for just long enough to enable the second angel to climb onto the statue of Iustitia, her wings of steam wrapping around Garnet's body. Now he was the one crying out, struggling to breathe. Ashiol went to him, but the first angel held him back, surrounding him in heat and cloud. His body sagged, losing strength.

'That's the way, cub,' a voice whispered in his ear. 'Stand down.'

The angel that had Garnet grew more solid as her hands closed around the skysilver chains that bound him to the statue. She seemed to breathe, and the chains rotted from his wrists, breaking into tiny pieces that the angel took inside herself. She formed colours now.

A long golden dress. Skin more pink than white. Razor-sharp fingernails. Short blonde hair.

'Tasha,' Garnet gasped, and the angel kissed him, tipping his head back and all but swallowing him whole. 'Hello, my cub,' she said, and then changed in an instant to chimaera form, dark and fanged and clawed, before shaping herself into Tasha again, or something very like Tasha. 'Look what I can do.'

'You're a King,' Garnet said drowsily. 'You finally made it. Welcome to the party.'

Ashiol wanted to fight, to shout, to insist that it wasn't Tasha, she was dead and gone, it was a trick. But his own senses were dimming, and the air was full of the scent of lioness. Tasha. Not Tasha. He could not form words.

'We're both Kings,' Tasha said alluringly, her mostly solid hands stroking Garnet lovingly. 'You don't need Ashiol or Velody now. You have me. We can make the sacred marriage and repair what was broken long ago. We can bring the skywar back into the daylight.'

Ashiol opened his mouth to protest, because Garnet was going to doom them all. The steam angel turned to look at him and he felt a wave of agonising heat burn through his veins. As he writhed on the ground, struggling through the pain, he heard Garnet agree, and looked up just in time to see Garnet and Tasha wrapped around each other in a kiss.

Stupid, so stupid. How could Garnet fall for the trick he himself had used on Ashiol five years ago?

It wasn't just a kiss. It was the fucking sacred marriage. Garnet's animor streamed out of him, light pouring from his mouth into the body of the angel, who was far beyond a semblance of Tasha now.

She glowed white and gold, light pouring from between every sculpted feather of her wings. She pulled back from the kiss, leaving Garnet empty on the statue, and screamed with triumph.

~

THE SKY WAS FALLING in pieces — stone and sinew, bricks and pillars. Velody took shelter in the broken remains of the Basilica. She caught Crane's sleeve as he hurried past her.

'Where did all those sentinels come from?' she demanded.

He glanced at her, a brief check for injury, then looked out at the whirling storm in the Forum. 'Delphine's idea. She figured out it's the skysilver that makes sentinels — and the Smith had a whole lot of spare swords. She's brainwashed a bunch of her old dancing partners into becoming an army.'

'And you let her do something that crazy?'

Crane almost laughed. 'Ever tried to stop Delphine doing something crazy?'

Velody couldn't argue with that. 'If the creatures from the sky get hold of that much skysilver, we're doomed,' she said desperately.

'At least this way we can fight.' Crane looked out again. 'There she is.'

Delphine was a blur of light and silver in the darkness, surrounded by her new soldiers and a host of flashing blades. They fought creatures made of cloud and steam.

Velody felt rather than heard Ashiol scream elsewhere in the Forum.

'Crane...' She wanted to wish him luck, or tell him to be careful, or say something that wasn't entirely meaningless right now, with the world coming down around them.

'Go on,' he said, wielding his sword again, ready to run out into the thick of it. 'Call a sentinel if you need us. We've plenty to spare!'

The temple burst into stone and dust as they both ran out of its shelter into the thick of battle.

~

THE PALAZZO SHOOK. Isangell looked with alarm at Kelpie. 'What is happening out there?'

'I don't know,' Kelpie said, then gave her a sharp look. 'You can feel that?'

'Of course I can feel it,' said Isangell. She went to the window, but there was nothing there but blurred shadow against the glass. 'I need to see out. What is happening to my city?'

'We're under attack, but that's nothing new,' said Kelpie. 'You didn't hear or feel anything the nox Heliora was killed,' she added.

Isangell pressed her hands against the glass, willing herself to see beyond this cocoon Kelpie had built for them. 'Ashiol says I am becoming one of you. I remember Bazeppe. As if I don't have enough to worry about.'

'I think I'm supposed to give you this,' said Kelpie, coming close. She unfolded her hand. A small, perfectly round diamond lay in the crease of her palm. 'Ashiol didn't send me. I wouldn't miss out on the battle for *him*.'

Isangell reached out with one finger and touched the jewel. Kelpie's hand was warm, but the diamond was very cold. 'What is it?'

'A tear. A seed. I don't know. Something. When Heliora died, she wasn't supposed to pass her gift on to Rhian. She got confused. Someone else was supposed to be our Seer — and, by the way, can I mention how much I hate that I know this without having been told? My orders fell into my head the second Rhian handed me that stone for you.' Kelpie lifted one shoulder miserably. 'Hate all that mystic shit. If it doesn't involve swords, I don't know what to do with it. There were only a few people present when Heliora died: Delphine, Crane and *you*. I don't think our Crane's cut out to be a Seer. He can't even work out how to fancy a demme who might like him back. And don't get me started on Delphine.'

'I don't want to be a Seer,' protested Isangell.

A tear. A seed. She lifted the diamond slowly, not knowing why, and held it to her lips. It tasted like metal and sadness.

Pain seared through her suddenly, pain and words and light. Isangell fell like a stone, gasping as if the wind had been knocked out of her. Kelpie was there, steadying her with her strong hands.

It's about time, said a sharp female voice directly into Isangell's head. *So you're the one who's going to fix my mistake, are you? I suppose we could do worse.*

Isangell pressed her fingers to her temples. 'Who are you?'

You mean it's not obvious? I'm Heliora, the Seer of the Creature Court. Prepare yourself for a bumpy ride, high and brightness. I'm not the only one in here.

50

FIRST DAY OF SATURNALIA

TWO DAYS AFTER THE IDES OF SATURNALIS

NOX

*a*shiol screamed as an angel dragged him to the ground, its mouth burning his neck. He could see Garnet twisting in agony as his animor flooded the air around him, flattening the Tasha angel that held him down. Lightning struck, plunging straight into Garnet's body and pinning him to the statue of Iustitia.

The angel holding Ashiol reared up and burst into motes of light as it was blasted by animor. Velody threw herself down beside Ashiol, her hair tangled madly around her face, her clothes all torn and charred.

'What are they doing to him?' she demanded.

'Stealing his animor.' Ashiol's voice sounded grim even to himself. He would not wish that on anyone, even Garnet. He had not realised he was so forgiving. 'Putting something else inside him. I don't know what.'

But he knew.

Garnet yelled and bucked and laughed, and it wasn't

his own laugh. As the chains fell away and he pulled free of them, bright colours shone out of his eye sockets.

'Conquest!' he shrieked in a voice nothing like his own.

'The sky,' Ashiol said, sickened by the thought of it. 'They put the sky inside him.'

Garnet howled, flinging his limbs around with abandon. Lightning and thunder crackled around him, coming from him, not from above. He blasted the statue of Iustitia into fragments.

'So,' said Velody softly. 'Do we fight, or do we run?'

She took his breath away. How could she be so calm? She was a frigging dressmaker and she put Ashiol to shame with what a coldhearted soldier she could be.

'Fight,' he said, though he meant 'run'. He wanted to run with every fibre of his being, every drop of animor in his body. But where could they run to?

Velody nodded, and he saw her preparing herself to do it, to attack whatever Garnet had become, no matter the cost. Ashiol had never loved or hated her more than in that moment.

HALF THE FORUM was on fire and Macready couldn't see a damned thing. Smoke and steam filled his eyes, and a smear of blood he couldn't get rid of no matter how many times he wiped his face clear.

The devils kept coming, and the angels were worse.

Macready was using Ilsa's sword. His had vanished into the lake back when Garnet killed Livilla, and this one felt wrong in his hand, but what did that matter, anyway? His real sword was eaten by devils months ago.

There had never been a battle like this. The Lords and

Court hadn't even managed to get into the sky. It was dirty and vicious and fought entirely on the ground.

You wanted this, feckwit that you are.

He saw the Smith, massive figure that he was, beating back angels with a hammer and gleaming broadaxe, surrounded by Delphine's fops and flappers. A fireball burst out from behind the black clouds and obliterated them all. The air was full of acrid, choking smoke and it felt as if the city itself was screaming.

Macready slashed his way through three devils. He was on his hands and knees near the arch at the mouth of the Forum, wheezing for breath and readying himself for the next assault, when he saw the body. There were bodies aplenty in this battle — dozens of Delphine's false sentinels had been sliced down in the first few minutes, choking on dust or steam. But this one was different.

This one was Crane.

The lad lay still, his torn brown cloak covering half of his body. His blood pooled on the grey paving stones and that pretty face of his looked nothing but surprised. No one was home.

A dust devil swooped down, smiling with grainy yellow teeth as it reached for Crane's fallen skysilver sword. Macready roared at the saints-forsaken monster, hurling himself towards it. He scooped up Crane's sword as he ran, so that he had a long skysilver blade in each hand, and fecking hells, this was more like it.

He wasn't thinking straight, his head full of blood and war and his dead lad, and instead of just cutting the bastard to pieces, he ran it down, chasing it out of the Forum and down the wide Duchessa's Avenue, away from the screams of battle and flashes of flame.

The devil was ahead of him, mocking him, right up to the moment that he chased it into the wet mud of the drained

Lake of Follies, still decorated with strings of Saturnalia lanterns, bright red and green and gold. The devil screamed as it touched the mud and exploded into a spray of fine wet droplets.

Macready choked back a sob, and then another. One more devil down. Only one. So many left to go.

Too exhausted to properly lift both swords, he turned to go back to the battle. A sound stopped him. A ripple ran across the floor of the lake, and then another. The mud shuddered and began to swirl, slowly, and then with intent, forming a whirlpool.

Macready stepped back, gripping the hilts of both swords. 'Whatever the feck you devils have to throw at us now, bring it on!' he yelled at the lake.

The mud swirled and spun and shrank into itself until it was a column of darkness twisting in the centre of an empty lake bed. As Macready watched, the column spun hard into the slender figure of a demoiselle holding a sword. She stood there for a moment, then walked across the lake bed towards him. She wore a short red flapper frock, which danced with lights that matched the Saturnalia lanterns.

As she came closer, he recognised that the sword she held was his own, the one that had fallen into the waters on the Neptunalia. He didn't recognise the demme at first. She had brown, tangled hair and a fresh-scrubbed face, and both of those things were wrong.

'You have your hands full,' she said, when she was only a few feet from him. 'I'll hang on to this one, if you don't mind. Things to stab. You know how it is.'

'Livilla,' he breathed. What the hells kind of world was it that let this demme survive when so many had died? 'No,' he added. 'The wench is dead. They quenched her. No coming back from that.'

She gave him a distant smile, as if he was completely

unimportant. 'They quenched me, all right. But do you know the really funny thing about the Creature Court?'

She leaned into him and he could taste the animor pounding through her veins. She didn't smell like Livilla — no perfumed smoke, no wolf — but she was real, not a creature of dust or steam. She was pure animor.

'What?' Macready said, struggling not to show his fear. If this was Livilla, whatever she had come back as was far more powerful than a Lord.

'The rules mean nothing,' she said, and kissed him on the forehead so he could feel how solid she was. Then she turned and walked up the avenue, holding his old sword by its cloth-wrapped hilt.

Her dress shimmered like water, and he wasn't entirely sure that her skin didn't do the same thing. She looked more real than Livilla ever had — no cosmetick or shiny dyed hair, no beads or baubles. But shadows followed her, fluttering like a wide pair of wings.

'You're one of them,' he accused again, shouting after her. 'A steam angel.'

'You have no fucking idea what I am,' she called behind her. 'Try to keep up, sentinel.'

The fight had gone out of Macready. He followed this new Livilla back through the arch and into the Forum. Though his swords were at the ready, no one attacked him as he trailed her into the thick of the action.

They found Garnet. He was laughing, spurting colours and light out of his mouth and hands, dazzled with his own power. A steam angel wrapped her arms around him, basking in triumph. Tasha. Feck it all, she looked exactly like Tasha.

'Oh, I don't think so,' breathed Livilla, rising up behind the steam-angel version of her former Lord. Her shadow wings spread wide, and it wasn't an angel she resembled, but the vengeful spirit of Justice, as she drew back Macready's sword and slashed the angel-Tasha into pieces.

Garnet saw her, and for a brief moment recognised who she was. He smiled, as if this was another victory. 'You came back in time to watch Aufleur burn.'

'You think I'm going to sit back and let the city fall after all the work it took to get back here?' Livilla said in disbelief. 'Oh, *lover*. You never did pay enough attention to my wants and needs.'

She slashed again with Macready's sword and this time she caught Garnet in the chest. He fell, light streaming out from the wound, still laughing. 'It doesn't count as a sacrifice if it's someone you hate, Livilla.'

'This isn't a sacrifice,' she screamed at him. 'It's a mercy. Now lie down and die!'

∾

Ashiol stared at the scene unfolding before the backdrop of lights and explosions the smell of death and shattered stone. He knew it was Livilla, although he hadn't seen her without bright cosmetick on her face since she was fourteen. She radiated power beyond anything he recognised. He had no doubt that it was her.

She was older than the demme he had known. Without her usual mask, she looked less like a caricature of a musette femme fatale, and more like a real person.

'Livilla!' he yelled. 'We can't fight each other, or the sky will win!' It didn't sound like something he would say. They were Velody's words. But Garnet lay bleeding on the ground, damn it, and Ashiol would do anything to make her take it back.

Livilla turned on him, power and confidence bright in her eyes. 'Haven't you been paying attention, Ashiol? Garnet *is* the sky. They took him long ago. If you want to save Aufleur, if that is what really matters to you after all these years, then I have just one piece of advice.' She was glowing, the lights on her gown shining brighter and the darkness of her wings spreading out behind her body. 'Run.'

She burst apart into water, a storm of rain and ice that swept the Forum from one end to the other.

Ashiol felt Velody's hand slip into his. 'Run!' she shouted at him. Together they went chimaera and took to the sky, fighting a path through the devils and angels, leading the others out of the Forum.

~

TOPAZ FELL out of her salamander shape; the cold and ice of the storm was too much for it. She still had fire deep inside her body, and she used it to light a path through the darkness.

The other salamanders had scattered. She could sense them. Some had followed the Kings, and others were hiding or wounded. She couldn't feel Poet anywhere. Had he left them again?

She came to the empty plinth that had held the statue of Iustitia and climbed it slowly, slipping a few times, until she was on her feet, the rain drumming around her. The sky was still falling. The devils and angels were still attacking the city. The rain felt like an assault against her skin.

'You were supposed to run with the others,' said a soft voice

Topaz looked up, and felt a comforting warmth wrap around her, like wings protecting her from the storm. 'Don't want to leave you again,' she muttered.

'Sweet child. You always had more faith than I deserved.'

It was Livilla. Of course it was. She felt different, like the fire inside her had been replaced by something else: cool water and the crackle of an electric storm. But it was still Livilla.

'You're my Lord,' said Topaz. 'Isn't that how it's supposed to be?'

They had quite a view from up here. The rain was falling upwards, and when it struck the devils and angels, they screamed in pain.

'I don't think I'm a Lord any more, dearling,' said Livilla.

It was getting lighter. That wasn't Topaz's imagination. She could see the outline of Livilla now, and her real face beneath the mop of wet, tangled hair. She looked younger than Topaz had thought. More like an older sister than a mother figure.

'Are you a King?' Topaz asked.

'Not that. I don't know what I am. But I'm myself.' Livilla smiled a beautiful, sunny smile. 'I'm not pretending to be less than I am. And I'm not afraid.'

Topaz shivered, the salamander inside her not liking the icy bite of the rain.

'Dawn is coming,' she said. 'So everything's going to be all right. Isn't it?'

'Dawn is coming,' Livilla agreed. She leaned down and kissed Topaz's cheek. 'Let's see if we can make it there in one piece.'

51

FIRST DAY OF SATURNALIA

TWO DAYS AFTER THE IDES OF
SATURNALIS

NOX

*I*sangell sat on the edge of her floral sofa, fingertips pressed to her temples. 'I can see it,' she breathed. 'The battle. All of it. I can't unsee it.'

You might want to get used to that, Heliora advised her.

Kelpie had left her swords crossed on the floor. She sat on the window sill looking miserable, though there was no way she could see out through the blurred seal that covered the glass. 'Hate this,' she muttered. 'I should be there. I should be fighting.'

'What's the point of me being the Seer if I'm separated from the rest of them?' Isangell asked, and they looked at each other.

'I don't know,' Kelpie said finally.

'So open this nest of yours and let me out.'

Isangell didn't know what to believe. But she could see soldiers with bright swords falling and dying, she could see her Forum awash with demons and angels, and there had to

be something better to do than sit here and wait for it to
be over.

Kelpie shifted a little and then shook her head. 'I can't. I
don't know if it was Rhian or that bitch you have in your
head, but I can't move. I don't have a choice.' She was furious,
her hands clenched into fists. 'I never have a fucking choice.
As if I might turn tail and run the second they test me. I've
always been loyal!' She was yelling at the ceiling now.

Isangell stood. She could move. She still had a choice. The
voices in her head tried to interrupt her, but she pushed
them swiftly aside. She had been ignoring meaningless
chatter from inferiors all of her life.

'We will make our own path,' she told Kelpie firmly. 'We
will get out of here together.'

Isangell opened her mouth to say more, but was overwhelmed by the images of the battle, the taste of dust and the
light in the sky, and something almost but not quite like that
feeling in the air before snow fell.

She saw a boy in a brown cloak fall against the arch of the
Forum, and she knew him. She could not hide her reaction
from Kelpie, who sat up straight and stared at her. 'What did
you see?'

'Crane,' Isangell said softly.

He meant nothing to her, except that he was one of those
who would have killed her that nox because the wrong
person was named Seer. But he meant something to Kelpie,
she knew that much.

'Dead,' Kelpie said, to be certain of it. When Isangell
nodded, the sentinel turned away and rubbed her sleeve
roughly against her face. 'Damn it. I promised this fucking
Court would never make me cry again.'

Isangell wanted to touch her, to say some words of
comfort, but what was there to say? Nothing she knew
anything about had any meaning in this new world.

The Palazzo shook from a direct blow, and she felt it break apart. 'Saints, no!'

Be brave, Heliora told her, and then the voices in her head fell silent, though the images did not. Isangell felt every blow, every bolt of fire and ice that struck the building. She heard the screams of the revellers at the Saturnalia ball, saw them running and burning and dying. She heard the servants wail in fear as the walls crumbled.

She saw every death.

Isangell beat her fists on the door until pain shot through her arms, and then she was sobbing, crying out. She felt Kelpie draw her away from the door and they hung on to each other as the Palazzo fell to pieces.

Her grandfather's atrium. Her grandmama's walled garden. The kitchens. The parlours. Room by room, it was destroyed, and the smell of death rose up through the cracks in the remaining walls.

'This is what you saved me from,' she whispered into Kelpie's neck.

'I'm sorry,' Kelpie whispered, and there was nothing flip-pant about it. The demme was honestly sorry that she had saved Isangell like this, that they would know for the rest of their lives that they had survived while hundreds died.

It felt like hours, and then it was over.

Isangell raised her head and looked at Kelpie. 'Now? Can you let me out now?'

'I think so,' said Kelpie.

She stood on shaky legs and placed her palms against the door that was not a door. It shimmered and came apart.

The first body they found was Armand, stretched across the hallway, crushed by a fallen beam. Isangell hardened her heart and stepped over him. There would be worse than this.

Half the Palazzo was too badly destroyed to even walk through. There was rubble everywhere, broken walls, charred furniture. Dead bodies, too many to count or to mourn. The nox sky gleamed through the gaps where ceilings used to be. Colours still flooded across the sky in bursts and patterns. The battle was not over, though no more blows fell on the Balisquine district.

The main corridor was blocked, and they had to crawl and clamber their way through all manner of awkward spaces, slipping on blood-stained tiles and broken glass.

Of all places, Isangell found her mother in the librarion. She and Kelpie were wading through fallen leather-bound volumes and smashed shelves when she saw a familiar skirt sticking out from behind a chair at an awkward angle. When she looked closer, she saw a foot.

'Who is it?' Kelpie asked when she saw her reaction.

'Mama.' Isangell could not say anything else, because the tears were coming thick and fast, and how could she face this alone?

'The sky won't take Ashiol,' Kelpie blurted, as if it was the closest thing she could find to comfort. 'Seriously, it's tried, so often he should be dead ten times over, but he has nine lives for each cat, and that's a lot of cats.'

Isangell could not feel anything but her own heart, beating too loudly. Two steps and she would see her mother's dead body. Was she ready for that?

'Let's go find him,' she said abruptly, turning around and climbing over the mountain of books in the other direction. Thank the saints she was still wearing her Saturnalia costume. The gold trews and shirt might be foolish, but they were eminently more practical than what she usually wore.

'I've never seen so many books,' Kelpie said with a nervous laugh.

'My grandpapa collected them,' said Isangell. 'He loved to read about the history of the skywar and the early Ducs. The origins of festivals. That sort of thing.'

Kelpie's hand slipped and she stared at Isangell. 'People... daylight folk wrote histories of the skywar? Of the festivals?'

'Of course,' said Isangell. She thought she could hear laughter inside her head and firmly pushed Heliora deeper down. 'Why?'

For the first time in hours, Kelpie did not look exhausted or miserable. Hope blazed out of her open face. 'I think I know why we were supposed to survive here,' she said. 'We still have some use after all.'

Isangell stood and watched while Kelpie rummaged through the piles of books, checking the titles and discarding those of no interest. She looked like a woman possessed.

Is this true? she asked the invader in her head. *Is that what we're here for? Can books make a difference?*

There was a silence. *Possibly*, Heliora said finally.

Isangell frowned. *Don't you know? I thought you knew everything! Isn't that what being a Seer is all about?*

I, said Heliora, and then stopped. *I don't know. I'm only a piece of the Seer, and there isn't much of me left. It's getting dark.*

Dark, no, not that. It was getting light. Isangell ran to the window and drew back the heavy velvet curtains, managing to keep her eyes turned away from the fallen body of her mother.

'It's dawn. That means it's all over, doesn't it?'

'Until nox comes again,' muttered Kelpie, still pawing through the books. 'Gives us time to breathe. Regroup. Read.'

Isangell could not take her eyes off the city below. As the sky lightened, she could see straight down the hillside. There were fires in the Forum, and she could see damaged buildings from the River Verticordia all the way across to the Lucretine.

'We can breathe,' she said softly.

Bolts of blazing light streaked through the early morning

sky and blasted the Church Bridge into pieces. Isangell gasped.

Kelpie dropped the books and came to join her at the window, her shoulder pressing firmly against Isangell's. 'Oh, hells,' she said in a low voice. 'Not that.'

They stood there for some time, watching the sky hurl bolt after bolt at the city as it faded from black to pale grey and then a soft winter blue.

Day had dawned, and the battle continued.

52

SECOND DAY OF SATURNALIA

THREE DAYS AFTER THE IDES OF
SATURNALIS

DAWN

*V*ia Silviana was too far away. They weren't going to make it. The streets were too long, and the devils and angels were getting stronger. Velody's muscles ached as she fought her way down Duchessa's Avenue, heading south. She had been in chimaera form too long and the battle rage had died down into something dull and hard.

She had lost track of everyone. Macready and Delphine were together, using their swords to keep the devils at bay, and she could feel Ashiol's presence nearby. Poet and Livilla (if that really was Livilla) and the salamanders could be anywhere by now. Velody hadn't seen Crane for some time. Rhian. She couldn't think about Rhian or the panic would overwhelm her.

Warlord flew with them for a while, but then the storm took him and his courtesi, dragging them back into the maelstrom of rain and light and battle. Velody did not see them again. Shade remained, looking around sometimes as if

466

hoping Poet would join them soon. The boy, Zero, hovered at his side, and Lennoc stayed near enough to keep an eye on them both, though not so close as to make Shade angry at him.

We protect those we love first, Velody thought guiltily, well aware of how many people she hadn't saved today.

They had to survive until morning. Aufleur was holding fast. They had another day's grace, surely. The city was not yet tearing itself up by the roots as Bazeppe had done (though when Bazeppe went it was fast, so breathtakingly fast).

Home drew her in like a lantern in the darkness. Dawn came, finally, and Velody felt as if she could eat that light with a spoon. Light. Morning. Home. Safety.

The skybolt burst the street in front of them into pieces of stone and rubble. Velody was knocked back into a wall, shaping back into her own form from the shock of the blast, and blinked blood out of her eyes. The sentinels had leaped clear just in time.

A rolling wave of animor swamped her before she even saw clearly who had been hit. Lennoc's power surged through her blood and, as Velody was gasping from the aftershock of quenching him, Zero's animor swiftly followed.

Blinking away tears, she saw that Shade was on the ground, alive still. He resisted as she tried to draw him to his feet.

'It's morning,' he muttered. 'It's supposed to be over.'

Oh, saints, he was right. The sky was lightening and there were still deadly bolts raining down on the city. Velody choked back a sob.

'Keep moving,' she told him. 'Just... keep moving.' He gave her a desperate look and she grabbed him around the wrist, pulling him away from the bodies of Lennoc and Zero.

Dawn was here and the battle continued. How could she pretend they had hope now?

Someone was screaming her name.

Velody stumbled through the dust and rubble to find the familiar curve of they alley behind her house. Delphine stood by the gate, yelling.

Ashiol swooped down from above, shaping from chimaera to Lord form as he dropped out of the sky. 'Get inside,' he ordered roughly. 'The nest should protect us, for a while at least.'

Her home was a nest now. Velody nodded dumbly and turned into the gate, still dragging Shade behind her.

Macready was the first person she saw. 'Where's everyone else?' she asked him.

'This is it,' Ashiol said grimly.

The kitchen felt wrong as Velody stepped into it. Rhian was not here. Several of the lambs huddled in the corner, some still falling in and out of salamander shape. An older demme, the one who had been Priest's courtesa once upon a time (Bree, her name was Bree) had put herself in charge of putting out small fires as they occurred.

Bree looked up hopefully. 'Is Topaz here?'

Velody shook her head quickly, and forced Shade to sit down.

Clara, Warlord's greymoon courtesa, made as if to stand, but Macready pushed her back down next to Shade. 'Once you're in here, you stay,' he barked, and then strode out the kitchen door into the storm himself, passing Ashiol on the way.

Velody could not sit. 'This isn't right,' she said. 'We can't just hide away and let the city fall around us.'

'The dawn didn't stop the battle,' Ashiol said harshly. 'The sky's a deathtrap. I just saw Mars burn up trying to make it to the south wall with some of his courtesi. There's no escape.' He sounded unemotional, like he was reporting something he had read in a newspaper.

Clara made a small noise, pressing her hands to her mouth. Shade glanced at her but did not react.

'Rhian is out there,' Velody said wretchedly. 'Kelpie. Isangell.'

'I'm sure they would be delighted if we got ourselves killed in sympathy,' Ashiol snapped.

Velody wanted to touch him, but if she did, one or both of them might fall to pieces.

'Underground,' she said finally. 'Can we shelter underground?'

Some of the others might have made it to the Arches. There was hope, surely. Where there was life...

'I don't know,' said Ashiol, and he looked so bleak.

Don't touch him, don't touch him.

'Where are the sentinels?' Velody asked.

Shade opened his mouth and blood poured out of it, onto the kitchen table.

MACREADY CAUGHT Delphine as she headed for the alley, stepping over the rubble in that fecking skysilver frock that stood out like a beacon.

'Where do you think you're going, lass?'

'Back out there, of course,' she said fiercely.

'We need you here — the Kings, and any other survivors who make it this far. Can't seal your nest properly without *you*.'

Delphine set her chin. 'My army, Mac. I brought them into this. I made them fight; made the Smith come out from the safety of his forge. You think I'm going to leave them now so I can hide out in a safe little nest? Not going to happen.'

'They're all fecking gone, love,' Macready insisted, forcing himself to feel nothing. Time for that when dawn came, the real dawn, not this false sunshine that ebbed across the sky, pretending the all clear. 'The Smith burned and died. I saw it happen, and half your toy soldiers with him. The rest of them can look after themselves, or they can't. Our duty is here, with the Kings.'

Delphine wasn't giving up. 'But my army —'

'Cannon fodder,' he said brutally. 'They were never going to be anything else.'

'I won't leave them to die.' She smacked him hard against the cheek and he took the blow, appreciating the brief sensation for what it was. The noise of the storm and the battle (hard to separate the two, they were part of the same thing, a whirling cloud of death and danger) grew louder.

'They're already dead,' Macready shouted at her.

The wind howled around them, tasting of snow and light and blood.

'We were going to save the city,' Delphine screamed. 'What's the point of being a sentinel if we can't save everybody?'

A deep crack ran along the alley, as if this was the line where the city was being torn in two.

'Jump,' Macready yelled, and all but threw Delphine across the crack, towards the nest and safety.

Too fecking far away.

～

VELODY LET Shade drink from her wrist, willing him to heal even as she scolded him for not telling her he had been wounded in the blast. Her animor was slow and difficult to work, and it took far too long to bring him back.

'He doesn't care,' Clara said flatly. 'Why should he live? Our Lords are dead. There's nothing left.'

Shade moaned and turned on his side, spitting out some of his own blood mingled with Velody's. 'Poet's not dead,' he said in a rasp. 'I know it. He wouldn't go so easily.'

'I believe you,' Velody said, thinking of Garnet. Regardless of whether he was on their side or that of the sky, it was impossible to imagine he had succumbed to his wound. This was a man who could not stay dead, even when swallowed by the sky.

A loud cracking sound reverberated through the house and the floor rumbled. It felt for a moment as if a hillside had come down on top of them, the ceiling pouring dust into the kitchen even as the nest held tight.

Ashiol went to the door, scrabbling for the catch to open it, but when the wall unblurred to let him through, there was nothing but more stone and brick on the far side.

'Street's come down,' he said. 'This entrance is blocked.'

Velody went to his side and they worked to dig through the barrier with their animor. She found her power as slow and clumsy as it had been when trying to heal Shade. 'What's wrong with us?'

'The nest stifles our powers,' said Ashiol. 'We don't need animor while we're safe, remember? If a more experienced sentinel had made this one it wouldn't be so bad, but Delphine's still a beginner.' He pulled back, stretching his fingers painfully. 'Don't suppose you have a pickaxe in the house?'

ISANGELL HAD NEVER GREETED a dawn with such despair. She

drew in a shaking breath as she stared down at her ruined city spread out beneath the Balisquine.

It's good, said the Seer's voice in her head.

How could this possibly be good? Isangell thought back.

I never saw this future. A battle that burns through the morning. None of us have ever seen this. It's new.

And that's a good thing?

I don't know, said Heliora. *But it's new, and that means there's hope. All is not lost.*

Isangell shook her head in irritation. *You'll forgive me if I find that difficult to believe. If new is so very important, why are you still here? You died!*

That's a very good question, Heliora said after a short while. *You're not like the others.*

That's because she isn't one of us. Another voice broke into the cacophony in Isangell's head. *I'm sorry about that. But you should know by now what a liar I am.*

Rhian, said Heliora. *Are you... are you dead?*

Not yet. I couldn't make it all the way to the Palazzo. Had to send Kelpie in my place.

If you're not dead, what are you doing in here?

Please stop treating me like I'm not a part of this, Isangell broke in. *It's my head you're using like a parlour to pay calls in!*

Can we take all the apologies and explanations as read? begged Rhian. *We're running out of time. Does Kelpie have the book?*

Isangell lifted her head. 'Kelpie?'

The sentinel sat with her back against a broken bookcase, an elderly volume teetering on her knees. 'Did you know that you have a whole shelf of books about the festivals of Aufleur and the history of the skywar?' she said in disbelief. 'How did Ashiol not know this?'

'They're books,' Isangell said simply. She didn't think

Ashiol had ever opened a book in his life. 'What do we do now?'

Hold tight, Rhian said inside her head. *The cavalry is coming.*

The library shook and buckled as if the Palazzo was breaking apart all over again. The wall burst open in a shower of heat and sparks, and two figures stood there: an oddly familiar woman in a red frock like swirling water, and a very young demme with flames flickering along her bare brown arms and legs.

Isangell blinked. 'Did we take tea once?'

'Not *you*,' Kelpie said viciously, clutching one of the books to her stomach as if she feared it might be snatched away from her. 'Can't you even die like ordinary people?'

Livilla gave a wolfish smile. 'Is that any way to speak about your rescue party, dearling?'

SECOND DAY OF SATURNALIA

THREE DAYS AFTER THE IDES OF SATURNALIS

NOT DAYLIGHT

*D*elphine was underneath half of Via Silviana, and the other half of the street was apparently lodged in her throat. She tried to move and cough, and realised with a sudden scrabbling fear that she could do neither.

Surely her chest wouldn't feel so heavy or so sore if she was dead?

'Up you come,' said a voice that sounded reliable. Delphine gasped in a deep whoosh of air as the weight was relieved and she could breathe again. Everything hurt. Was that a good thing?

She was clutching someone who turned out to be Kelpie. 'Street fell on me,' she managed to say when the world was the right side up again.

'Good to know,' said Kelpie.

Delphine looked beyond her and saw Livilla — a new dust-smeared and heroic Livilla whom she was pretty sure she didn't like any more than the last one. Livilla held something, an armful of stones and sticks and tree roots. When Delphine realised what it was, her legs almost gave out from under her.

'Rhian.'

'She's not dead,' insisted another demme, a slender blonde in breeches whom Delphine struggled to place before realising that if her hair and clothes were tidier she would look a lot like the Duchessa d'Aufleur.

'Then what is she?' Delphine demanded.

'Inside my head for now,' the Duchessa said. 'She says it's not over yet.'

'Oh, I like that "yet", full of hope,' Delphine snapped back. She took a step and found it possible. Nothing was familiar. 'What happened to the street?'

'Some explosions south of the Lucretine brought on a landslide,' said Kelpie. 'We were lucky to find you. We must be close to the nest, are the others safe?'

Delphine gazed around, searching for a fencepost or something that separated her own house from the rest of this chaos. She saw a body flung flat on the ground some way from them, one leg twisted grotesquely out of sight. Her body reacted, knowing it was Macready even before her mind identified him. 'Oh, *no.*'

She leaped across the wide crevasse in the street and ran to him, breaking her nails on the stones that pinned him to the ground. She held her breath, remembering that boy in the Vittorina Royale and how quickly he had died once they pulled the stones clear. She might not love Macready any more, but that didn't mean he was allowed to be dead.

It began to rain, huge dollops of water that splashed on his dusty body. Delphine tried to check his pulse, but realised halfway through the process that she didn't know how to do it. He was warm; was that good?

'Let me,' Kelpie said roughly, kneeling on the other side of him, running her hands over him with an air of confidence. 'Alive,' she said finally.

Delphine started breathing again.

'No offence, sweetlings, but we're going to need to get undercover,' called Livilla. 'The rain is starting to burn.'

Delphine could feel the heat of the water as it splashed onto the back of her head and arms, but the sting she felt was nothing to what it would do to the Lords and Court.

'Get to the nest,' she yelled, letting Kelpie scoop up Macready.

Delphine looked around wildly, and then realised that she was a sentinel, stupid. She didn't need to use her eyes to find the nest she had wrought out of that funny little shop she had lived in for so many years. The nest was hers — the house was hers — and she let the skysilver she wore draw her towards it.

'There,' she cried, pointing at a heap of rubble and broken remains of the next-door bakery.

Topaz threw herself at the heap and tore it apart, throwing charred pieces of stone and brick aside until the kitchen was revealed, the warm light of Delphine's kitchen.

They ran inside, all of them, Delphine ensuring that she was last. As the rain gave way into a thick, pounding down-pour, she sealed the nest behind them.

~

SEALED OFF LIKE THIS, away from the storm and the war and the crumbling city, it was almost possible to pretend nothing bad had happened. Ashiol leaned against a wall and watched them all gather into Velody's kitchen, dusty and wounded and damaged. Not a group of people he would ever want to see in the same room. He made no move to greet Isangell or

Kelpie. How broken was he that he felt nothing at knowing they were still alive?

The city called him. Aufleur itched under his skin and hummed in his ears. You didn't hide when the sky fell, not even in daylight. Not if you were Creature Court.

Ashiol watched Velody as she tended Macready as best she could within these power-dampened walls. Saw her avert her face from the twisted statue of a thing that remained of Rhian. Velody took the time to give a word or a hand-squeeze to everyone, even Livilla.

He had to get out of here. This was no time to nest.

Of all people, it was Livilla who met his gaze and nodded in agreement. She looked so different shorn of her false black hair and coloured eyelashes, thick cosmetick and elegant props. Her smile was warmer, and there was humour in her eyes.

Livilla left Velody's side and came to him, shaking back that oddly natural brown hair. 'Driving you crazy, isn't it, my cat? You never liked to be contained for long.'

'There could be other survivors out there,' he said, trying not to remember the sight of Mars burning up before his eyes.

'Yes,' Livilla said. 'It's an excellent excuse. Shall we tell them that, or just slip away?' He must have given away his surprise in his face, because she laughed at him. 'I've been at this almost as long as you, dearling. I won't die in a cage.'

Velody was distracted with the wounded. She might not notice they had gone, for a while. It wasn't her that they would have to convince, in any case. Delphine stood with her back to the door, arms crossed and a defensive look on her face.

'No,' she said as Ashiol and Livilla sidled up to her. 'I'm not opening it again. Everyone I love is in here and I won't endanger them so you can pretend to die heroically.'

Ashiol had never liked her. 'You'll be rid of us, at least,' he suggested.

Delphine gave him a dirty look. 'Don't think I'm not tempted. This is a new world order, Ashiol Xandelian, and I don't give a flying frig how many titles you people make up for yourselves, or who is claiming to be Power and Majesty. I answer to Velody. Take it up with her.'

Ashiol opened his mouth to continue arguing, but a familiar cry from outside the door snapped him to attention. 'There's someone out there,' he said.

ISANGELL SAT on the floor of the kitchen beside the twisted form that the others insisted was Rhian. 'The others' included not only Kelpie and Delphine but the voices in Isangell's head.

Ashiol was here and he was alive and she was damned if she was going to admit to him that he had the right of it — that she was part of this sorry mess of a Creature Court now. She belonged here.

Is that what is going to happen to me? she asked the voices, staring down at Rhian. The former Seer was partly formed from marble and partly from granite, with plant roots twisted wetly around her limbs. Her face was barely recognisable as human.

Not at all, said the voice she had come to know as Rhian's.

But if I'm the new Seer...

You're not.

Isangell blinked. *But the voices, and the visions...*

I lied to you. I'm sorry about that. It's true that Heliora made the error, that the Court was calling you and not me to be the Seer. But once it came to me, there was no changing it. I am the last Seer of the Creature Court. But I am something else, as well, and the futures were getting in the way of that. I needed to get rid of being Seer for a while.

So you passed it on. Will I be stuck with it forever?

When the time is right, you can give it back. I'll tell you when. You'll be free of it, Isangell. I promise.

The other voices sounded fainter in the background of Isangell's mind.

Don't trust her, Heliora warned suddenly. *What she's doing, it's not right...* But then her voice was overwhelmed by others, voices and visions, and try as hard as she could, Isangell could not hear Heliora again.

∼

VELODY COULD NOT HEAL MACREADY. He remained unconscious, and though she had stopped the bleeding everywhere she could, his left leg was still a mess.

The nest numbed more than her animor. The sounds of the storm were dampened in here. The mice were mostly quiet inside her. But if she concentrated, pushing her senses beyond the thick, blanketed walls of the nest, she could hear the screams of the city.

Quite clearly, a single voice cut through her like a knife. *Time to pay back what you owe, little mouse.*

Velody looked up and around.

Ashiol was shouting at Delphine, threatening her. 'Open the door! Can't you hear them? They're right outside.'

Delphine shook her head resolutely. 'We can't risk everyone.'

Ashiol turned to Velody as if seeing her for the first time in hours. 'You can hear it, can't you? Poet is outside. Make this bitch let him in.'

Livilla gave a hollow laugh. 'After all this time you expect us to believe you would risk everyone to save *Poet?*'

'Garnet is with him,' Velody said steadily, staring Ashiol down. 'The sky infected him, you know that. For all we know, it's taken Poet, too.'

'Is that who you are now?' Ashiol accused. 'Saint Velody, who saved Poet from my claws, who saved Garnet after he was swallowed by the sky. Now you'll let them burn?'

'Would you risk everyone in this room to save them?' Velody shot back, hating that she was on this side of the argument. She owed Garnet for saving her neck back in Bazeppe, before the city fell. She owed him for Tierce, for bringing her home, even if it was to die here with her friends.

Ashiol did not reply, but his face said everything. Velody spoke quietly to Delphine. 'Let them in.'

'Let the enemy into the one place in the fucking city we've managed to keep secure?' Delphine said in amazement. 'I betrayed my own army to bring you all here, to keep you safe. But saints forbid we abandon the man who left you both in a pool of your own blood!'

Velody looked at Delphine. 'Letting them die is not who we are,' she insisted. 'It took me long enough to drill that into the Creature Court. I can't become the monster now, in the last moments.'

Delphine released the catch.

A blast of rain and ice-cold wind burst through the doorway and two half-dead figures stumbled forward, crashing on the floor. Poet had burns down half his face and body, and he was hanging onto the limp, bloodstained figure of Garnet as if he had forgotten how to let go. Garnet's body glowed with light, and waves of cold poured off his skin.

Delphine closed the door up again. 'Of course, that means we're shut in here with him,' she said pointedly.

'You still have the cage,' Poet gasped. 'Don't you?'

Ashiol was almost gentle as he prised Poet's fingers away

from Garnet. 'You would have made it faster if you'd left him there,' he said.

Poet laughed hollowly. 'The thought honestly never occurred to me.'

'That was your first mistake.'

54

SECOND DAY OF SATURNALIA

THREE DAYS AFTER THE IDES OF SATURNALIS

NOT DAYLIGHT

*W*ith Kelpie's help, Velody dragged the ice-cold body of Garnet into the workroom, where they locked him in the skysilver cage.

'Is there anything left of him in there?' Kelpie grunted as they finally slammed the door closed.

'Sadly, yes,' said Velody, staring through the bars. 'It would be much easier if there wasn't.'

'Don't you dare even hesitate,' Kelpie added fiercely. 'If it takes sacrificing him to save the others, to save Ashiol or the Duchessa or even that bratty blonde flapper of yours, you do it.'

'Yes,' said Velody. 'I will.'

Garnet's eyes blazed with all the light of the sky. 'Ah, Kelpie. You were always my favourite.'

'I'm shocked you remember my name,' Kelpie spat.

The others came into the room, a few at a time, gathering

around the cage. Garnet only had eyes for Ashiol. 'It's come to this, my cat. So sad.'

'Don't pretend you're him,' said Ashiol furiously. 'I know what you are. The sky. The enemy.'

Garnet laughed. 'And if I am?'

'You've been doing this for centuries,' Velody said softly. 'Attacking us. Wearing down our defences. Why? What was it all for?'

Livilla snorted. 'Don't tell me you plan to negotiate with them.'

'What else is there to do?' said Poet, who was barely on his feet. He shivered despite the blanket someone had wrapped around his shoulders. 'Don't you see? We've never been able to beat them, not really. Now we have a chance to talk to them. Maybe that's the only way to stop the war.'

'War,' Garnet repeated, still sounding amused. 'Is that what you call it?'

'What is it to you?' Ashiol growled. 'A game? Some idle amusement?'

Garnet leaned towards the bars, close enough to kiss. 'Not play. Justice.' His eyes glowed like skysilver. 'You are the thieves. We hunger for what you stole.'

'This war has been going on longer than any of us have been alive,' said Ashiol.

'Your kind. You stole the light from us and we want it back.'

'Animor,' Velody realised. 'It came from you.' Yes, she had known that part of it, deep in her bones. If the skysilver was a side effect of the cracks in the sky, then the animor must be as well. 'We don't have a history. We don't know what happened, but it was so long ago.'

'But we do have a history,' Kelpie said. She shrugged and looked embarrassed when everyone stared at her. She waved a blue-bound volume at them. 'At least, the Daylight Ducs had a history. The librarion in the Palazzo is full of books about the skywar: when it started, how they fought it, old rituals of the daylight. The early Ducs each had a team of lictors called the Sentinel Court to defend his body from the sky!'

'Put that book away, sentinel,' Poet said impatiently. 'If there was anything important in that librarion, Lord Saturn would never have left it for daylight folk.'

'I would have thought it the perfect hiding place,' Isangell observed.

'Saturn and his books,' Ashiol snorted. 'What good did they do him?'

'I'm missing something again,' said Velody. 'Who was Saturn?'

'Poet's first kill,' said Ashiol.

Poet gave him a venomous look. 'Saturn was one of us, the Lord of Hawks. He worked as a bookseller, supplying all the librarions, and along the way he gathered every scrap of history he could find — every reference, every story about the Creature Court and the skywar. He had a theory that Aufleur and Tierce and Bazeppe were built upon weak points in the world, and that the weight of the cities broke something between us and the sky. Perhaps that's how animor came into our world.'

'You broke the sky, you stole our light,' snarled Garnet, pacing the cage. 'Thought you could hide your crime.'

'It wasn't us,' Velody said in frustration. 'Centuries have passed. You've shattered two of the cities, and all but destroyed this one. Haven't you punished our world enough?'

He gave her a vicious look, which, had she not known about the possession, Velody would have described as 'all Garnet'. 'Not nearly. Everything you have, everything you are, belongs to us.'

'Tell us,' Velody pleaded. 'We want to understand.'

Garnet stretched. 'You want to die knowing exactly why you are all monsters? I am happy to oblige.' His voice took on a singsong quality, like he was staging a grand performance. 'Once there was a world of light and spirit and goodness. All were loved and serene and content, except for three wicked creatures. They broke a hole in the sky, searching for other worlds, and for their punishment were doomed always to stay in the world they had discovered. Never to return home. But they were so angry and resentful that they took the light of our world with them into this place, this unclean den of nox and daylight, of humans and steel and steam and clock-work.' His lip curled with disgust. 'With the power they had stolen, they built cities. Three beautiful, impossible cities. Abominations.'

Velody shook her head. The story didn't fit, even if you discounted the obvious hatred for whomever those creatures had been. 'That's not true. It can't be.'

She looked across at Ashiol who stood there with his mouth in a set line. Isangell had crept forward and was holding his hand. He didn't seem to mind.

'Hush,' Garnet commanded. 'I'm not finished. The crea-tures peopled the cities with daylight folk, playing with them like dolls. Mayors and priests and proctors and mad Ducs. Great Families,' he added, with a sudden grin at Isangell that made her flinch. 'They gave them memories of a longer history, gave the world memories that these cities had always been there, that they meant something. When our people learned what the exiles had done, we came to take back the light and power. To take back what was ours.'

'So you really have always wanted to destroy us,' Ashiol said calmly.

'We wanted to destroy every stone of the false cities that were built with our light,' said Garnet, sounding almost reasonable. 'But instead of falling on our mercy and returning what they stole, the exiles built themselves armies to defend their cities against the rightful vengeance of their people. They took creatures of this world and perverted them into Kings and Lords and courtesi. They took the silver that fell through the cracks in the sky and forged swords and knives for mortals to hold. They gave visions of the future to chosen ones and made them guide you. They built the Shadow Court, the Clockwork Court, the Creature Court, and you continue to act out their filthy work like the weapons you are.'

~

TOPAZ HUNG back as the adults talked to the cage. She did not care whether Garnet was from the sky or himself — she didn't want to hear him talk. She slipped back into the kitchen instead.

One of the sentinels, the one with a missing finger, lay there under blankets, looking like a dog's breakfast. Then there was the other body.

It looked like a woman, but was shaped from stone and root and dirt. It was wet to the touch, as Topaz found when she couldn't resist brushing a fingertip against it.

Its eyes snapped open.

Topaz jerked back in horror, but the statue's eyelids fluttered again and fell shut.

A large ginger tom cat wound his way through the table legs and curled up near the statue, purring.

~

ASHIOL COULDN'T STAND THIS, couldn't stand talking through

Garnet like he was some kind of window into the sky. It
made him sick to his stomach.

Velody was talking patiently about negotiation, about
making some kind of deal, and every word out of her mouth
was another stab to the chest. Negotiation be fucked. He
wanted to fight something.

He moved away from the cage, to find Isangell following
him. She looked battered and exhausted and more like their
grandmama than he had ever realised.

'I'm glad you're all right,' he said in a low voice.

Isangell gave him an exasperated look and said nothing.

Poet circled the cage, trying to talk to the creature inside
Garnet's skin. 'You've told this story before, haven't you?
Through that damned watch. Did Garnet know all this?'

'Oh yes,' said Garnet, smiling widely. 'We spoke to him,
many times, as we did with Saturn before him. He didn't take
it very well.'

'If your argument is with the exiles,' Delphine broke in,
'then take it up with them, not us. If these creatures are so
damned powerful, let them solve this mess. Where are they?'

Garnet met her gaze and seemed to bask in the muted
glow of her skysilver dress. 'The last one fell in battle this
nox. You called him the Smith. It is of little account. You all
have what we want returned.'

'So we'll return it,' Velody insisted. 'We'll negotiate a
treaty. Are you their leader? Can you speak for them?'

'Leader,' their enemy said scornfully. 'We are all as one.'

'Then you can help us end the war,' said Velody. 'The Smith
and the others like him are gone, so you've had your vengeance.'

The creature smiled with all of Garnet's teeth. 'Once this
city is dust as the other two are dust, the war will end. The
light will be back where it belongs, on our side of the sky.'

Isangell let go of Ashiol's hand and stepped forward. 'We

can't let you destroy another city full of people,' she said, speaking firmly. 'There must be some agreement we can make to save everyone who is left.'

'You people love to make sacrifices,' said the sky-Garnet. 'By all means, sacrifice to us. Burn your honey cakes, wave your ribbons, build your statues. It is meat and drink to our world. But we will still eat you alive. We will not rest until every stone they placed, every weapon they forged, is destroyed.'

Ashiol was exasperated. Would these demmes do nothing but talk?

'You can't negotiate with them,' he insisted. 'Don't you get it? We're the weapons. The only way it will be happy is if we're all destroyed.'

'Ashiol's right for once,' said Kelpie. He tried not to resent that 'for once'. 'The battle or storm or whatever is still going on while we make small talk with this... random piece of cloud. It's distracting us from the main event.' She stepped closer to the bars, hatred all over her face. 'Kill it and be done.'

Ashiol knew all of Garnet's moves, and he saw this one happening before he could stop it. Garnet's hand darted out to grasp the skysilver knife on Kelpie's left hip, and as she shifted back on one foot to keep it out of his reach, he grabbed the other knife, the steel one, and plunged it directly into his own chest. It slid in like butter — steel could not draw the blood of one of the Creature Court — and Garnet's face cleared. His eyes were suddenly far more hungry and alert.

'Right then,' he said. 'That's better. We can talk.'

'What are you up to?' Velody demanded.

Garnet met Ashiol's gaze and raised his eyebrows inquiringly.

Ashiol sighed. 'This is the real Garnet,' he said.

Poet nodded in confirmation.

Kelpie's face didn't change. 'Not an improvement,' she sneered.

'This won't work for long,' Garnet said quickly. 'There's something about steel — it mixes up their signals. Back when they were speaking to me through the watch, putting a steel blade to my skin would shut them up for nearly an hour sometimes. It was the only way to get a decent sleep.'

'Why should we believe you?' Velody asked.

Garnet gave her his best 'bored now' expression. It twisted in Ashiol's stomach like the knife was sticking into him instead of his oldest friend. 'If you can't contribute anything useful, little mouse, keep your mouth shut. The fucking army on the other side of the sky has been grooming me for years for this moment. This day. As long as they're inside me, they don't need to break paths through the sky any more. They can come through me.'

'So if we kill you,' said Kelpie helpfully, 'it's all over.'

'A sweet thought, sentinel,' Garnet sneered. 'But whatever they are is well and truly tangled up in my body. They took my animor and put something *else* inside me. Something valuable. We need power, dearlings, raw animal power, enough to beat them back and seal the sky over for good. There's only one way to get that kind of power.'

'The sacred marriage,' Velody said breathlessly.

Garnet snapped his fingers at her. 'See, I knew you had to be smarter than the rest of them. It's the only explanation for why they like you more than me.'

'That's what happened last time,' said Kelpie, waving her damned book. 'The old mad Duc married a flock of ducks or whatever, and the skywar went away. Only it didn't. We know it didn't. It shifted into the nox and the Creature Court were left alone, the only ones who could see the danger.'

Poet snatched the book from her and threw it against a

wall. 'Don't you get it? The book doesn't matter. Our history is false. Our whole fucking city is false. Nothing matters.'

'That's hardly a useful contribution,' Delphine snapped, picking up the book and handing it back to Kelpie. 'Why not let them make the sacred marriage? Better to try something than to die whining.'

'They didn't do it right,' Garnet said. 'Not the mad Duc. No one since the very first Powers and Majesties.' His eyes flicked in Ashiol's direction.

Ashiol swallowed.

'How is it done?' Velody asked, all businesslike. 'Is it documented in any of these books? Do the Seers know?'

'The Seer is a pile of stone and firewood in the kitchen,' Ashiol snarled.

'No,' Isangell said. 'I'm sorry I didn't tell you before. But the Seer is in my head right now.'

Ashiol stared at her. After everything else that had happened today, that shouldn't be the thing that broke his brain. 'Hel?'

'Heliora and Rhian both,' Isangell admitted. 'The Seers know all about the sacred marriage. They say they're not the only ones. Better to ask the King who tried and failed.' She frowned, not understanding what she was saying.

Velody understood, though. In that moment, at least. Ashiol could see the surprise and disappointment cross her face.

'You knew all along about the sacred marriage,' she guessed, staring at him. 'When Garnet stole your powers, all those years ago...'

'That was what he was trying to do,' Ashiol admitted. 'He found the books Poet was hoarding. We stole one — Saturn had pieced together how the sacred marriage worked, what it was supposed to do. Garnet offered —' His voice broke on that. He could not continue.

Garnet was gripping the bars tightly, his knuckles almost white. 'I offered to *share*,' he said. 'I was losing you. I had lost everything else, and I offered to share. We would be Power and Majesty together. But you still couldn't trust me.'

He had the balls to sound upset about it. Ashiol wanted to punch him.

A shock wave from outside shook the nest.

'I tried,' Ashiol said between his teeth.

'You held back, lover. You wouldn't give me everything. That's what the sacred marriage is, Velody-my-sweet. You pour everything of yourself into the other vessel. Exchange animor fully. But even with everything I was offering, he held back.' Garnet smiled horribly. 'So I took it from him instead.'

'You didn't give me the chance,' Ashiol said. 'It was only a moment.'

'That was enough.'

'A split second of hesitation!' Ashiol roared at him. 'After everything you've done to me, *that* was the unforgivable act?'

Garnet gazed at him, mouth twisted. 'Yes,' he said simply.

'I can't do this any more,' Velody said suddenly. She looked from Garnet to Ashiol, throwing up her hands in frustration. 'The sacred marriage can't be about you and me, Ashiol. I'm not the one you have to work things out with.'

Garnet began to laugh.

'You can't be serious,' Ashiol said.

'I mean it,' Velody snapped. 'It's up to you and Garnet. I'll be defending the city while you talk in circles and try to tear each other to pieces.' She turned and headed for the kitchen.

Ashiol ran after her. She had obviously gone insane. 'You can't be suggesting that Garnet and I make the sacred marriage. The sky will infect me, too.'

'Will it?' Velody's eyes were luminous in the low light of the kitchen. 'The sky couldn't have taken him over unless he

491

let it. Maybe he thought he was strong enough to handle it; maybe he really did think it was necessary to keep them believing he was on their side. But it was his choice. You have a choice, too. You've spent your whole life trying to let other people decide for you. I won't do that, not now. Sort it out, Ashiol.'

'Stop saying that!'

'I need to fight the sky,' Velody said furiously. 'The city is coming down around our ears and we are running out of time. I can't perform the sacred marriage with you because you're never going to trust with me everything you have. You won't even give me a *piece* of you.'

Ashiol kissed her then, caught her face in his hands and kissed her as hard as he could. Velody kissed him back, and they leaned into each other. Ashiol felt her animor pulsing against her skin and against his, but they were both holding back, preserving what they had.

'It's you and me,' he said in a low voice.

Velody shook her head. 'How could it possibly be about you and me? If the sacred marriage is about uniting the Creature Court, then it's all of us. Every single one of us.'

Ashiol drew away, and went back into the workroom where Garnet stood in the cage. 'You were wrong,' he said quietly. 'My hesitation wasn't because I didn't trust you, or because I was trying to hoard my power. I didn't *want* to be Majesty to your Power. I didn't want to share your rule. I was happy to be ruled by you, always. You never believed me.'

Garnet stared at him as if seeing him for the first time, and then held his hand out through the bars. 'Save the fucking city,' he said hoarsely. 'It's all we're good for.'

Ashiol clasped his hand and felt animor flooding his fingers. It wasn't Garnet's, nothing like it, but it was stronger than anything he had ever felt before. It came faster and faster, like rushing water and a fierce alien light. He was dizzy with it, power heating every inch of his skin. Garnet's gattopardo stretched inside him, along with Ashiol's own black cats. There was a nameless creature there, pulsing with the voice of their enemy, but the cats and the gattopardo surrounded it, not letting it take control of his body.

Ashiol stumbled away from the cage and towards the kitchen.

Poet caught him as he leaned against the staircase, and placed a slow kiss on his forehead. 'Let's not do this by halves, kitten,' he said, and Ashiol felt a new surge of animor press inside him. He was almost bursting with power now, his head full of white rats as well as the other creatures.

Left without power, Poet looked surprised and then oddly relaxed. 'It's over for me, then,' he said. 'Good luck.'

The enemy animor that Ashiol had taken from Garnet was a smaller piece of him now, a shock of cold inside his thudding, heated body. He stood in the kitchen doorway, breathing. The enemy voice thudded inside his head, but he kept it at bay. Ignoring what he did not want to hear was one of his greatest skills.

He looked down and saw the lamb, Topaz. She held the old ginger tom that Ashiol had left here with Velody so long ago. One of the many cats that were always drawn to him when he was in Court shape. Old Tom filled her skinny arms, all bulge and fur.

Yes, that.

Ashiol reached out and placed his hands on the cat, giving the enemy inside his animor a sudden push out of his body and into that of Old Tom. The cat yowled and glowed fiercely with all the colours of skybattle before Topaz released it and it went running across the floor.

Kelpie brought her swords around in two sweeping arcs, cutting the cat in half before it reached the door. The steel blade made no mark, but the skysilver blade cut true. The cat's body burst into blue flame and burned there for a moment.

'I really hate you for making me do that,' said Kelpie.

'Add it to the list,' said Ashiol.

He reached a hand out solemnly to Topaz, who nodded and took his loosely in hers. Suddenly his head was full of fire and rage and the cool skin of salamanders.

One by one, the children came forward, either to him or to Velody, and gave them their animor.

Livilla caught Velody in a gleeful kiss, handing over her power as easily as breathing. 'Since the world is ending,' she said with a twisted smile.

Shade went to Velody, as did Clara. Bree hesitated before coming to Ashiol as Topaz had done. There was no one left to share what they had. There were so few of them left.

Ashiol looked at Velody across the kitchen. 'A city to save, you say?'

She almost laughed, but caught herself. She was glowing with power, brighter than he had ever seen her.

'This is better,' she said finally. 'A marriage really should be about the whole family.'

He took two strides across the kitchen and grabbed her again. She wrapped her arms around his neck and they sank their animor into each other, giving everything.

For once in his life, Ashiol did not hold back.

55

SECOND DAY OF SATURNALIA

THREE DAYS AFTER THE IDES OF SATURNALIS

NOT DAYLIGHT

*V*elody felt hot and cold all at once. She gave everything to Ashiol and received the animor he channelled back into her skin. She had never felt so alive and alert. The world was brighter than it had ever been before.

'Now you have to return it,' said a soft voice.

Velody broke off the kiss, but she could not take her eyes off Ashiol. He was glowing, all dark and shiny, smiling so stupidly at her that it was hard to pay attention to anything else. Eventually she realised it was the Duchessa who had spoken.

'We did that,' said Ashiol, and even his voice was beautiful, like power and sex and ciocolata all poured into one. He had never sounded that good before.

'Not to each other,' Isangell said patiently. 'You have to give it to Rhian.'

Velody turned then, still in Ashiol's arms, and let herself look. She had avoided the twisted statue that lay prone in the corner of her kitchen, not wanting to believe that was all that remained of her friend. But it was Rhian, when you looked at it. Her face was unmistakeable, even if she was half stone and half wood, with rose vines wrapped around her thorny ankles.

'Why Rhian?' Velody asked.

'Because she was never supposed to be the Seer,' said Isangell. 'Or a sentinel, or King, Lord, Court. She is something else. She is the seed of destruction.'

'How can we know this is the right thing to do?' Ashiol asked.

Isangell gave a small smile, her eyes distant. 'You have to trust your Seers. This is what they were here for, all this time. Give her everything, and Rhian will save the city.'

Velody hesitated too long. She felt Ashiol's fingers curl into her own as he held her hand.

'We have to trust,' he said, and made the first move.

As Velody watched, Ashiol poured everything he had into Rhian. Light burst out of her, haloing her twisted body as he filled her with the animor of the Creature Court. His body sagged as he let go of all that power, letting it bleed out of him.

Isangell held out her hand, too, and something silver shone out of her fingers, streaming into Rhian's body. Isangell crumpled into a faint and Kelpie leaped forward to catch her.

Rhian stood up. She was still stone and plant and water and sun, roses and wood and light and dust, but she was human, too, and whole. More whole than she had been in a very long time. Velody stared at her, feeling Rhian's power. The animor was there — from Ashiol, Poet, Garnet, so many of them. The flame of the salamanders.

When Rhian held a hand out to her, though, Velody hesitated. 'We can do it together,' she said.

Rhian shook her head. 'I am the last weapon. Forged by the Smith of Tierce before she fell into the sky. Placed here to be the final redemption. It is up to me to heal the shattered sky once and for all, and to give back what was stolen. To make amends and end the war. It's time to lay down your burden, Velody. This is my task.'

No. Velody couldn't do it. It was all right for Ashiol, who had never wanted the responsibility of being Power and Majesty. But she had taken on that duty, and she could not relinquish it now.

'You can't sacrifice yourself to the damned sky,' she said, unable to stop her voice from shaking. 'That never works. I tried, remember? I won't let you.'

'You're so used to protecting everyone,' said Rhian, her voice so very confident. 'You can't fight this battle for me.'

'Yes, I can,' Velody yelled at her. 'It's the only way.'

They were all looking at her like she was the crazy one, hoarding power. Like it made sense she should give it all up and trust Rhian to save the city. Rhian had barely left this house in two years.

'It's a trick,' Velody said. 'Garnet, the sky, all of it. How do we know it's not a trick? We'll lose you and get nothing back. They want us to give up all the animor and be left defenceless!'

She felt Ashiol's hand rest against her shoulders. It was a shock to get no spark from him, no sense of his power. He had given it all up. How could she be the last one standing?

'We've been fighting for years,' he said. 'Centuries, maybe. What if not fighting is the only way to end the war?'

'Don't you dare be on her side,' Velody choked.

Rhian was what she had been fighting for. She would not lose her like this.

'You heard it from Garnet's mouth,' Ashiol said softly into her ear. 'The animor was never ours to keep.'

'You don't have to trust Garnet, or the sky, or any of them,' Rhian said. 'You have to trust me. Do you?'

Velody took a deep breath because Rhian had once been the most reliable person that she knew. A friend whose strong hands built their kitchen table, whose even temper had kept things calm between Velody and Delphine.

With something like a sob, Velody let go of her animor. It fought, not wanting to leave, and she had a vision of hundreds of blindingly bright mouse bodies streaming from her and into Rhian.

Then it was over and Velody was empty.

'Open the door, please,' said Rhian in a voice that radiated power.

Delphine had tears running down her face as she released the catch on the door. Suddenly the kitchen was full of sounds again, of crashes and breaking stone and icy rain hitting the broken, rubble-strewn remains of their courtyard. 'Give them hells,' said Delphine.

Rhian stepped out into the yard, glowing brightly, new vines springing up where she walked, pushing their way through the stones.

Velody stood still, unable to move until Ashiol tugged her by the hand and led her outside, where the battle still raged. The rain felt like ordinary water on her skin. Daylight. She was daylight. They were all entirely human; all of them except Rhian.

Her friend smiled at her, looking for a moment just like that demme who wanted to be a florister when she grew up.

'Take me home to Tierce,' Rhian said. 'When it's over.'

As the scrappy remains of the Creature Court emerged from the kitchen one by one, blinking in the sunshine, Rhian rose into the air. She glowed brighter and brighter, and then flew straight up into the sky like an arrow. For one long moment, everything was achingly, painfully white from one edge of Velody's vision to the other.

The rain stopped.

~

RHIAN HAD NOT FELT SO MUCH LIKE herself in years. Strength flooded her body; the kind of strength that hauled heavy loads of stems and branches, that built their kitchen table and mended the broken furniture they had refurbished when making their house a home.

The whole city spread out beneath her, wide and scarred and aching. Buildings lay in rubble, hills had become mudslides, there were fires and floods in every street.

Rhian felt the dust devils become aware of her, and then the steam angels, and all the other faceless, voiceless creatures of the sky. She blazed like a beacon, like a thousand skysilver blades flashing all at once. They smelled her, tasted her. They wanted her dead.

See me, she cried across the city to them. *You think you can take us? Think we're easy meat? That we will crumple like Tierce, like Bazeppe? You think we are not defended?*

She could feel Velody inside her, and Ashiol, and Garnet, and Poet, and Livilla. So many other faces and voices and songs. After holding the Seers inside her for so long, it seemed almost easy to take the whole Creature Court, those who had died and those who lived.

They rampaged inside her, a tumbling mess of cats and mice and wolves and gattopardi, of rats and salamanders and hounds, of panthers and bats and feraxes and birds and lions.

She was Warlord, she was Lennoc, she was Priest, she was Dhynar, she was Lief, she was Saturn, she was Ortheus, she was Tasha, she was sentinel and Seer.

Rhian stopped, finally, so high that her human body could

barely breathe, surrounded by a thousand different fractures in the sky. They swarmed to her, devils and angels and skybolts and gleamspray. She smiled politely at them as they closed in around her.

'My name is Rhian,' she said aloud. 'On behalf of the city of Aufleur, I am here to negotiate a truce.'

Her body burst apart into salamander flames and she took every fucking one of them with her.

This time, the sky would mend clean.

56

SECOND DAY OF SATURNALIA

THREE DAYS AFTER THE IDES OF SATURNALIS

NOT DAYLIGHT

*T*opaz did not go outside with the other lambs. She crept back into the room with the cage.

Garnet sat leaning back against the bars that he could now touch because he was human, like the rest of them, and skysilver would not burn. One hand was painfully curled around a spot just above his belly, and she realised too late what it was.

Poet knew. She saw his hands shake as he unlocked the door of the cage and fell down on his knees beside Garnet. 'What can I do?'

'Not a lot,' Garnet said, sounding almost lazy. 'Come closer.'

Poet crawled to his side, and Garnet messed up his hair. 'Not long now.'

'You couldn't have taken the fucking knife out before you gave him the animor?'

Garnet shook his head slowly. 'Sky would have taken back control. It's okay. Doesn't hurt or anything.'

'Liar.'

It was a painfully private moment, but Topaz couldn't look away from them. They both looked so small and hurt. She reminded herself of how much Garnet had hurt others and felt less bad about watching.

'If you pull the knife out of me,' Garnet said after a moment, 'it'd be faster.'

'Is that what you want?' Poet's face crumpled at the thought of it.

'No, ratling. You know me. Always took one curtain call too many.'

Poet started to cry quietly, and when he turned to kiss Garnet briefly on the mouth, his face was wet with tears.

'Better than last time,' Garnet decided. He coughed, and his body shuddered with it.

Topaz left them alone. She ducked back into the kitchen and found Kelpie there, sitting next to the unconscious Macready with an unreadable expression on her face.

'Is Garnet dead yet?' Kelpie asked quietly.

'Getting there,' said Topaz.

Kelpie nodded, patted Macready's limp hand once, and then went to join the others outside.

A few minutes later, Poet joined Topaz in the kitchen.

His face was dry and he was as poised and together as always. 'Still here, are you, little fireball?' He held a hand out to her. 'Shall we go see what kind of mess those reprobates have made of the sky?'

She squeezed his hand and they went out to the yard together. The sky was blue. Not scary battle blue, just... blue. It was a clear sort of day for the middle of winter. No clouds, and a deep chill on the air.

'Is that it, then?' Poet remarked, too loudly. 'I was

expecting fireworks. An ovation at the very least, possibly a parade. If I'd been given enough notice, I could have composed a song for the occasion.'

'Maybe the war didn't stop,' the blonde sentinel said. 'Maybe none of us can see it any more. It's just Rhian out there on her own for eternity, fighting the sky, and we're blind to it.'

'Lovely thought,' someone said sarcastically. Topaz wasn't sure who.

'It's the Saturnalia,' said the one they called the Duchessa. She sat on a broken piece of wall, leaning against Kelpie.

'Are you suggesting we exchange gifts?' Ashiol said acidly. He was still holding Velody's hand.

The Duchessa gave him a dirty look. 'It's the second day of Saturnalia. There are rituals to perform. Songs in the Forum. Lights on the lake. If we keep the rituals, then perhaps...' She gave a helpless shrug.

'Perhaps the city will heal,' said Kelpie.

'It's worth a try,' said Velody, looking around at the wreckage of the street.

'We can sing,' Topaz volunteered. When everyone looked at her, she ducked her head, annoyed at them all. 'Well, we can,' she muttered.

The other lambs nodded, though they were all as reluctant as ever to speak.

'Of course you can,' said Poet, his hand cool in hers. He managed a half-smile down at her. 'Everyone can sing. That's what the Saturnalia is for. Singing, and roasted nuts, and hot bean syrup. I can taste it already.'

Some time later, the sky started raining rose petals.

FIFTH DAY OF SATURNALIA

SIX DAYS AFTER THE IDES OF SATURNALIA

DAYLIGHT

*T*hree days after the world ended, the city healed.

Isangell had performed every arcane Saturnalia rite the city had ever observed, and many they never had. She and Kelpie combed the librarion for ancient texts and used everything that they found to celebrate the festival.

They *all* thought she was crazy, Isangell was well aware of that. Not only the ragged survivors of the Creature Court, but every living person she found in Aufleur was given a ritual to perform.

'It doesn't work like that any more,' Ashiol told her, impatient with her attempts at festivity, at staging a Saturnalia pageant around the few undamaged streets of the city. 'There's no animor left. We're on our own.'

'Would you rather do nothing?' Isangell demanded.

Velody helped, and Poet, and the children. Even Livilla seemed to enjoy a chance to do something, no matter if it was hopeless.

As dawn lit up Isangell's bedroom on the morning of the fifth day of Saturnalia, she awoke to hear the voice of her mother berating Kelpie for having the ill manners to sleep on Isangell's couch.

Isangell blinked awake and stared at the smooth ceiling over her bed, which had been so badly cracked the nox before.

'It worked,' she said softly to herself. Ashiol was wrong.

Isangell barrelled out of her room, hugged Mama, and then heartlessly abandoned Kelpie to run out into the Palazzo itself.

For days it had been a crumbling tomb filled with the scent of death and decay. There was an awful silence about it, as if the whole place was waiting for its mistress to declare it was time to fall to dust.

Now Isangell spotted one familiar servant, and then another. As she rounded the corner of the corridor, she ran full pelt into a huddle of ministers and priests, who looked very alarmed when she kissed each of them on the cheek.

The Palazzo had not emerged unscathed. One of the kitchens was smashed beyond repair, as was the Old Duc's atrium. The ballroom still looked as if it had collided with several temples, and dozens of bodies lay in a cleared area of it, prepared and ready for burial.

Isangell ran up staircase after staircase until she came to the picture window that offered the best view of the city. A long scar ripped through Aufleur. Both the Forum and the Lucretine had taken some damage, but nothing like the destruction that had been there only yesterday. It was not perfect, but the city had given her this one last gift.

Ashiol found her some time later. 'A petition for thanksgiving ceremonies for making it through the return of the skywar,' he said, handing over a silver- sealed scroll. 'I've never been so glad to be accosted by priests in my life.'

Isangell accepted the scroll and hugged it to her. 'I had given up hoping.'

'No, you hadn't,' he said warmly, holding her eyes with his. 'That's why you're so good at this. Grandmama wouldn't have given up, either.'

Isangell laughed and hugged him. 'I was right.'

'Yes, you were.'

'This city is never, ever skipping another festival. Not one. We might even start new ones.' She felt him shift uncomfortably, and knew he wanted to tell her not to bother, that the time of festivals and animor and the Creature Court was over. 'Ashiol?'

He pulled back out of the hug. 'I didn't say anything. You're the Duchessa.'

'Yes,' she said, grinning stupidly. 'I really am.'

When she finally returned to her rooms, Isangell found that her mother had set up camp there, fortified by a large tea tray, a harried-looking Armand and a stack of blank invitations. Kelpie hovered by the window with a desperate expression on her face.

'Do you really think it's appropriate to hire a female lictor?' Mama grumbled, having made sense of Kelpie the only way she could.

'Very appropriate,' Isangell said, shooting a grin at Kelpie. 'I have the perfect dressmaker to sort out her livery.'

Kelpie stuck her tongue out where Mama could not see.

'I'm glad you're here, Armand,' Isangell said, sitting down primly and pouring herself a cup of tea. 'I'd like you to take a letter to my Aunt Augusta, the Dowager Baronnille of Diamagne.'

Armand nodded, preparing himself to make notes. 'Of course, high and brightness.'

Isangell smiled. 'I'd like to suggest that she visit the city with her children — apart from the current Baronne, of course — so that I may select an heir from one of my cousins.'

Mama almost dropped her teacup. 'Isangell, what on earth?'

Isangell had been hoping that she would have a chance to make this speech. She had practised it late every nox, her own ritual to add to the Saturnalia revels.

'It's rather simple, Mama,' she said, folding her hands in her lap. 'I won't marry without love, and love is complicated. It may take time. Perhaps I won't even marry at all.'

She risked a brief glance at Kelpie, who was trying not to laugh out loud.

Mama's hands shook, and she carefully put her cup down. 'Not Ashiol?'

'I think we all know he's not cut out for leadership,' Isangell said gently. 'I need an heir who is actually willing and able to do the job. What do you think, Mama? Is it not an acceptable plan?'

Her mother gave a good impression of someone who had been chewing a lemon. 'A tolerable plan,' she conceded finally.

'You hear that?' Isangell teased Kelpie later, when her mama and the servants were gone. 'A tolerable plan. I finally won an argument with her!'

'Congratulations,' said Kelpie, leaning forward to kiss her softly on the side of the neck in that way that made Isangell shiver with happiness every single time. 'When are you going to tell her the rest of it?'

'Oh,' Isangell breathed, 'I think we'll ease her into it. Very, very slowly.'

58

FIFTH DAY OF SATURNALIA

SIX DAYS AFTER THE IDES OF SATURNALIA

DAYLIGHT

*a*lso on the fifth day of the Saturnalia, Topaz and Poet went to survey the damage at the Vittorina Royale. The theatre was still a wreck, sticking out like a sore thumb along the street that otherwise was gleaming new, like someone had built it out of spun sugar.

'Cities shouldn't be this clean,' Topaz muttered suspiciously. Even the pavement was bright white, sort of blinding.

Poet was staring at the Vittorina like he hadn't seen it in years. 'It will take some fixing,' he said finally.

Topaz rolled her eyes at him. 'Tell me something I don't know. You have coin, don't you?'

'A centime or two,' he admitted.

'And you know more theatricals you could invite to fill out a revue in the new year? In other cities, perhaps?'

That was apparently a more painful question.

'I might,' said Poet in a cracked voice. "I don't know if they'd come, but... I can extend an invitation."

'Well then, shut up and let's start working.'

Topaz liked being rude to Poet. It it was the only time he looked like a real person instead of a plaster statue with a broken heart.

Inside, the theatre smelled all musty and damp.

'It can't be done,' Poet sighed, shoulders sagging as he saw how bad it was. 'There's no fucking ceiling. It's too far gone. I'd be better off razing it to the ground and selling it off to housing developers.'

Topaz wanted to kick him. Every time he got like this, her hope of a home for herself and the lambs went up in smoke. She opened her mouth to chew him out, and was interrupted by a voice singing from behind the mouldy curtains.

Livilla promenaded her way out of the wings, wearing a slinky scarlet gown that was all sparkles and spangles. She carried a top hat in one hand and a cane in the other, and had jammed her head into a bright scarlet wig, all curls and shimmy.

'How do you like me as a redhead, dearlings?'

'What are you doing, Liv?' said Poet. He sounded tired.

Livilla posed for him. If she was here to screw around, Topaz would kick her, too. Bloody grown-ups, never stopped thinking about themselves.

'Topaz and I had a chat,' Livilla said. 'We were thinking that you're entirely unsuited to the position of stagemaster. All that shouting and organising things is dreadful for your throat, you know.'

Topaz wanted to scream. That wasn't what they had agreed. Poet looked more pissed off than tired now, and it wasn't an improvement.

'What do you suggest?' he snapped. 'Nice little apothecary

business? Take my vows as a Damascine Virgin? Or shall I find a wealthy seigneur to buy pretty things for me?'

Livilla tapped her foot, and put the sparkly top hat on her head. 'Silly boy. I'm applying for the position. You're going to be the stellar. Topaz can lead the chorus and sell tickets. Write a damned letter to bring Kip and Ruby-red *home*, with as many of their talented friends as they like. I want to be a stagemaster. Tell me I wouldn't be frigging spectacular at it.'

Poet blinked, and tilted his head to one side as he thought about it. 'We'll have to rename the theatre if we rebuild it,' he said finally. 'Bad luck to keep the same one.'

Livilla's teeth gleamed like she was a wolf on the prowl. 'I thought Pearl Beyond Price had a nice ring to it,' she said. 'I always liked that old poster. Reminds me of a little town called Oyster. It's important to remember where you come from, if you want to get anywhere interesting.'

Poet stared at her, and nodded.

That was all right, then.

'I'll get the lambs,' Topaz said, sagging with relief.

They had a big job ahead, but at the end of it there would be something real, she hoped. Something they had built themselves, instead of falling into. That was a future you could believe in.

59

EIGHTH DAY OF SATURNALIA

SIX DAYS BEFORE THE KALENDS OF VENTURIS

DAYLIGHT

On the eighth and final day of Saturnalia, Delphine caught a train north. She had Velody with her, and Macready, whose leg still gave him pain from the street that had collapsed on him, even though the street itself was back where it had once been. Delphine had no idea how that worked, but she wasn't going to argue the point, not when his face went all grey every time his foot stumbled against an uneven paving stone.

Velody carried a small wooden box on her lap. Inside was everything that remained of Rhian.

They found her on the roof some days ago, long after the rose petals fell from the sky. At least, they thought it was her. It was a long tangle of roots and branches wrapped around a stone arm that crumbled when they touched it. They had gathered what they could and cremated the remains. A small, hard lump was found among the ashes. It might be bone, or diamond, or the biggest bloody rosehip imaginable.

Delphine hadn't slept well since the battle. She dreamed of her army of sentinels screaming at her, of the wind and the rain and the burn of skysilver against her palms.

She had seen Teddy and Maud since the city had healed itself, though neither of them recognised her when she passed them in the street. She went to Villiers' apartment on the Octavian, only to find it closed up, a funeral notice on the door.

The city was full of funeral notices. So many of the dead had returned, yet the daylight folk were well aware of this one most recent skybattle that came down upon them after so long. People were wary and afraid. They had no way of knowing that it was over; that Rhian had sacrificed herself to bring an end to the war after so many years of silent, invisible deaths.

Delphine hated everyone right now.

~

THE TRAIN WAS HEADED for Atulia, but they hopped off long before that, at a station that no one else thought was worth bothering with. Fair enough, really, as it was in the middle of nowhere.

Macready was struggling to hide how hard it was to walk, but he refused to stay back in the city. He had missed the end of the war that filled his whole life for so long. No fecking way he was going to miss the chance to say goodbye to Rhian.

If you looked the right way, you could see there had been a city here. The river diverted for no sensible reason, and the old lines of canals lay the right sort of marks on the landscape. It was all grass now, greyish green grass as far as the eye could see. The sky was grey, too, with the promise of snow. Macready could feel an icy bite in the air.

Velody asked too many times if he needed to rest, and he bit her head off about it. She was reproachfully silent after that. Delphine pretended not to care by simply not looking at him, refusing to see the smashed-up leg and the way he leaned on the cane. He liked that better.

Kelpie had done that, he remembered, back when he lost his finger. She refused to acknowledge it happened, and that suited Macready down to the ground.

Velody buried Rhian's remains in the hard wintry earth, and they sat around in the cold air for a while, talking about her. Macready listened, mostly, as Velody and Delphine mixed up their fractured memories in one big soup.

He could really go a bowl of Rhian's soup right about now.

It was getting late, and they had to make it back to the train station before dark. They turned away, leaving her there, though everything in Macready's soul screamed out that they couldn't do that, leave her alone in the shadow of a city that didn't exist any more. It was all kinds of wrong.

His leg gave from under him and he heard an almighty CRACK that seemed to divide the world in halves. He fell into blackness, swearing at himself for being so fecking stupid, for risking his chance to heal out of some misplaced sentimentality about a demme who never looked twice at him, not really.

'Macready,' a voice said from a long way away. 'Wake up!'

Velody. It was Velody, and he was lying in a field, and if he didn't wake up, those two would have to carry him all the way back to the station.

He opened his eyes and stared at the sky. Still alive, then.

'Look,' said Velody.

Macready rolled over, cursing himself and the aches in his limbs. He saw Delphine capering around like a mad thing, and then he saw the tree.

It was growing thick and strong, and, unless the demmes had moved him, it was right where they had buried Rhian's remains.

'That's no ordinary tree,' Macready croaked.

Velody nodded, the wind blowing her dark hair all over the place. 'I know.'

'If she was a seed of destruction, now she's something else,' Delphine screeched into the wind. "A seed *grows*."

The tree was still growing. It wasn't a trick of the light. As Macready watched, its branches snaked into the sky, and they weren't all made from what you might define as "tree". There was stone there, yellow stone, and tangled vines of roses, and a spray of white camellia flowers right here in the middle of winter.

The ground rippled and roots bulged up at the base of the tree as if it had been there for fifty years.

Delphine stopped dancing around and ran back to Velody and Macready as the earth swelled and brought forth stone: whole pillars and arches, a high mezzanine, and then another.

Slowly they moved back, and then again, as the city of Tierce rebuilt itself before their eyes. Macready had been here once or twice in his youth and he knew it wasn't the same city. The canals were in different places, the buildings not so high, and there had never been so many roses tangled around the gateways, let alone at this time of year.

There were no people. They were long gone, swallowed by the sky. There were no souls to be returned here, no miracle family reunions. Macready saw that hope rise and die in Delphine's face as the three of them explored this new place, the city that had grown back.

'The bakery's not here,' said Velody, sounding almost relieved. 'It's different. It's all different.'

'What's the point?' Delphine demanded. 'Who gives a flying frig about the city coming back if there are no people?'

'A new beginning,' said Macready, staring out across the locks and the canals that were pumping with fresh water. A new city, barely getting started. A man could make something of himself in a place like this.

He closed his eyes and inhaled the scent of roses.

~

RHIAN BREATHED, and the city breathed with her. This was her body now. The canals were her veins, and every building an organ. Part of the whole. She could see out of her walls and doors and windows, but it wasn't really seeing, nor feeling. She simply was.

Her strength had followed her here. Her walls were tough and long lasting. She dug deep and stretched tall.

She was beautiful.

She watched — or listened — or felt — as Macready and Velody and Delphine discussed her like she was dead and gone, like they would never hear her voice again. Like she was something that had been lost.

Roses grew everywhere, and she inhaled their scent. It would do. It was enough.

Eventually, they left her, heading back towards the train station that had no name. She was going to have to do something about that. A city needed a name, and there was something of ill-luck about clinging to 'Tierce' or indeed to 'Rhian'.

Macready looked back more than once as he left, and she knew that he would return. Perhaps they could choose a name for the new city together.

60

EIGHTH DAY OF SATURNALIA

SIX DAYS BEFORE THE KALENDS OF VENTURIS

NOX

On the eighth and final nox of Saturnalia, only a handful of days before the turn of the year, Ashiol and Velody met on a rooftop. It was a hard habit to break.

'You expected her to come back, didn't you?' he said, about Rhian.

Velody nodded reluctantly. 'Stupid. But we've lost too much, and I wanted...' She shrugged. 'I wanted her to come home.'

'Understandable,' he said.

They were silent for a while.

'My mother's coming to visit Isangell,' Ashiol told her. 'When she returns, I'm going with her. Back to Diamagne.'

Velody had expected it, or something like it, but it still hurt. 'I didn't think Diamagne was home for you. Are you sure this isn't you running away again?'

She would not beg him to stay. She would not.

He gave a little hand gesture, somewhere between

'frigged if I know' and 'of course not'. 'Maybe it is,' he said. 'But I've been hiding from my family a long time. I owe them something. If I'm going to start again, it should be there. Aufleur doesn't make sense to me without the Creature Court in it.'

There was another long silence, which Velody refused to fill.

Ashiol said, finally, 'You could come with me.'

There it was, the offer, and it was a huge relief for Velody to realise how much she did not want it.

'Aufleur without the Creature Court makes all kinds of sense to me,' she said. 'I have a life here, one that's not hard to rebuild, and I want that life. This is my home.'

Ashiol didn't look particularly upset. Part of Velody wanted to crawl into his lap and demand to be kissed, and part of her wanted to push him off the roof.

'You'll go back to making dresses,' he said, obviously trying hard not to make it sound like he thought it was a stupid idea.

Velody felt inappropriate laughter bubble up inside her, and pushed it down. Ashiol had never really understood her.

'Beautiful dresses,' she said. '*Spectacular* dresses. Dresses that make the world a better place. It is possible, you know. To be spectacular without animor running through your veins.'

'I hope that's true,' he said, and smiled. Her stomach squeezed hard, damn it, as it always did when he remembered to be charming. She was never going to be entirely immune to Ashiol Xandelian, the Ducomte of Aufleur.

It could have ended there, with them going their separate ways, not too many regrets, but then he reached a hand out to hers. Velody found herself bracing for the inevitable spark of his animor against hers, no longer there. His hand was warm and, oh yes, she grew warmer at his touch, but there was something missing. Perhaps, if they stayed together, the absence of animor would always be there, a visible scar that meant neither of them could move on with anything.

'We could go somewhere else,' he said, his fingers grazing along the back of her hand. 'Find a city where we make sense.'

They could, oh, they could.

Velody smiled and drew her hand away. 'Ashiol,' she said, meaning every word she was about to say, 'I don't think there's a city in the world where we make sense.'

He accepted that, for now, and they sat in comfortable silence, gazing out over the city of Aufleur, damaged but still beautiful under a nox sky that had nothing but stars in it.

THE END

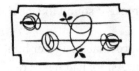

CABARET OF MONSTERS

A PREQUEL NOVELLA TO THE CREATURE COURT TRILOGY

- ISBN: 978-0-6483291-0-7 (ebook)
- ISBN: 978-0-6483291-1-4 (print)

Saturnalia in Aufleur is a time of topsy-turvy revels, of the world turned upside down and transformed before your eyes. The city's theatres produce an annual display of reversals, surprises and transformations. In Aufleur, flappers can transform into wolves. Even the rats are not what they seem.

Evie Inglirra is on a mission to infiltrate the theatrical world of Aufleur and discover what lies beneath their glamorous cabaret costumes and backstage scandals. What secrets will she uncover?

CALENDAR NOTES

The Ammorian calendar, or Fasti, has three named days —
the Kalends (first day of the month), the Nones (nine days
before the Ides) and the Ides (full moon — which falls more
or less in the middle of the month). Generally people refer to
days in relation to these, e.g. "four days after the Ides," or
"two days before the Kalends."

The day after each Kalends, Nones and Ides is considered
nefas/unlucky.

Market-nines or nundinae are the closest thing they have
to the idea of weeks — these refer to the markets held in the
city every 9 days regardless of other festivals.

MONTHS OF THE YEAR:

- Venturis (winter)
- Lupercal (winter)
- Martial (spring)
- Aphrodal (spring)
- Floralis (spring)
- Lucina (summer)

- Felicitas (summer)
- Cerialis (summer)
- Ludi (autumn)
- Bestialis (autumn)
- Fortuna (autumn)
- Saturnalis (winter)

GLOSSARY

- **Alexandrine Basilica** — once the largest church in the known world, constructed by the fourth Duc d'Aufleur, mad old Ilexandros. His successor, Duc Giulio Gauget, declared the Basilica to be an unholy abomination and stripped its rich furnishings to ornament his own Palazzo. The hollowed-out and falling-down Basilica is now used as a marketplace, and a merchant's lot here is worth a small fortune.
- **Ammoria** — a principality once consisting of three duchies: Silano (capital city: Bazeppe), Lattorio (capital city: Aufleur) and Reyenna (capital city: Tierce). When the city of Tierce vanished, Reyenna became one of the baronies of Lattorio.
- **Animor** — the energy/power contained within the bodies of all full members of the Creature Court. Seers and sentinels do not hold animor, though they are touched/contaminated by it, which gives them a status between the nox and daylight worlds.

- **Ansouisette** — a fashionable cocktail of aniseed and lemon liqueur.
- **Arches, the** — ruined city that exists below Aufleur, where the city's inhabitants once lived after being forced underground during the old skywar. Now inhabited by the Creature Court. Also known as 'the undercity'.
- **Artorio Xandelian** — former Ducomte d'Aufleur, son of Duc Ynescho Xandelian and Duchessa Givette Camellie. Artorio refused to marry in his youth, but at age thirty-three was prevailed upon by his father to marry nineteen-year-old Eglantine in order to produce an heir. A year later Isangell was born. Artorio died of the Silent Sleep when his daughter was thirteen.
- **Ashiol Xandelian** — Ducomte d'Aufleur, son of Augusta and Bruges, stepson of Diamagne. Cousin to Isangell, Duchessa d'Aufleur. Member of the Creature Court; rank: King; creature: black cat.
- **Atulia** — region to the north of Ammoria.
- **Aufrey** — one of the twelve Great Families of Aufleur.
- **Aufleur** — capital city of the duchy of Lattorio in the principality of Ammoria. Ruled by Isangell, the daylight Duchessa.
- **Augusta Xandelian** — second child of Duc Ynescho Xandelian and Duchessa Givette Camellie. Married Bruges Lanouvre and had one son, Ashiol. A year after Bruges's death, Augusta married the Baronne di Diamagne and retired to his estate. She and Diamagne had four sons: Bryn, Keil, Jemmen and Zade, and a daughter, Phage (Pip). Now widowed again, her official title is the

Dowager Baronnille though she is technically entitled to use the title Ducomtessa.

- **Avleurine** — one of the hill districts of Aufleur; location of the Temple of the Market Saints.
- **Bree** — member of the Creature Court; rank: courtesa to Livilla, formerly to Priest; creature: sparrow.
- **Bridescake** — ornate wedding cake traditionally covered in spring flowers.
- **Bruges Lanouvre** — late husband of Augusta Xandelian; father of Ashiol (died when Ashiol was seven years old).
- **Burnplague** — a spreading sky pattern of blisters that spit motes of light and acid.
- **Camellie** — one of the twelve Great Families of Aufleur.
- **Camoise** — country to the far east of Ammoria. One of many cultures that trades extensively with Aufleur. Providers of the exotic and expensive 'real tea', the best of which is Camoiserian leaf.
- **Carmentines** — bright scarlet flowers with long stems.
- **Cathedral of Ires** — place of worship dedicated to the Crone Ires, who is venerated by the Irean Priestesses. Place where wills are lodged for safekeeping.
- **Celeste** — former Lord of the Creature Court who left with Lysandor during the tyrannical reign of Garnet as Power and Majesty. Member of the Clockwork Court in Bazeppe and mother to Lucia. Creature: owl.
- **Centi opera** — portable stalls featuring puppet shows. Sometimes a young female performer, an ingénue, performs among the puppets.

- **Centrini** — affluent mercantile district in the centre of Aufleur.
- **Cheapside** — part of the market district of Tierce, where Velody's family own a bakery.
- **Chimaera** — a monstrous dark shadowy shape with claws, teeth and scales; an amalgam of every devil and forbidden creature imaginable. Only Creature Kings are able to take chimaera form; used in battle.
- **Christophe** — formerly known as Kip, this performer from the Mermaid Revue rose to first harlequinus (male lead dancer) at the Vittorina Royale before leaving the city of Aufleur with friends. For his story, see the novella *Cabaret of Monsters*.
- **Church Bridge** — traditional starting point for festival parades; finishing point is the Forum. One of two city bridges across the River Verticordia, the other being the Marius Bridge.
- **Ciocolate** — a very expensive delicacy brought over from Nova Stella. Served as a fondant or as a hot, spicy drink called ciocolata.
- **Circus Verdigris:** a central arena in the city with a grass surface, used for public games.
- **City Fathers** — the members of the City Council, who meet in the Curia: this group is made up of the Duc's Ministers, a Proctor for each of the city districts, and the three senior priests who between them form the ruling body of the city, under the hand of the Duc or Duchessa. The three senior priests are the Matrona Irea of the Irean Priestesses (the only woman allowed to be a city father), Brother Typhisus of the Silver Brethren, and the Master of Saints.

- **Clara** — member of the Creature Court; rank: courtesa to Warlord; creature: greymoon cat.
- **Coinage** — the coins of Aufleur are divided into gold ducs, silver ducs, copper shilleins and copper centi.
- **Columbine** — a female dancer who performs in musette and theatre revues.
- **Coronets** — delicious lemon-glazed breakfast pastries, shaped like crowns and unique to Aufleur.
- **Courtesi (courteso: male; courtesa: female)** — the lowest rank of the Creature Court; must ally themselves with a particular Lord for protection. Too vulnerable to exist alone.
- **Crane** — youngest of the sentinels. Weapons: blue-hilted daggers and swords.
- **Creature Court** — the courtesi, Lords and Kings who hold animor within their bodies, belong to the nox and have the ability to fight the sky. Ruled by the Power and Majesty, the highest ranked of their Kings. Peripheral members of the Court include the sentinels and the seer, but they often consider themselves separate from the Court.
- **Crossroads** — any part of the city where two streets meet is considered sacred to the protective spirits or household gods of Aufleur. Casual sacrifices (for example chickens or honey cakes) are often made here for greater effect.
- **Curia** — slope-roofed building in the Forum that houses meetings of the City Council.
- **Cyniver** — brother of Rhian and lover of Velody; lost when Tierce was swallowed by the sky.
- **Damascine Virgins** — an order of priestesses in service to Damascus the war-angel. They sacrifice to him on the eleventh day of Martial.

- **Dame** — appropriate form of address for a respectable matron, diminutive of 'madame'.
- **Damson** — member of the Creature Court; rank: courtesa to Priest; creature: gull.
- **Delphine** — friend to Velody and Rhian; ribboner and garland-maker. A sentinel of the Creature Court. Sword and knife hilts: rose pink leather.
- **Demoiselle** — unmarried (young) woman; 'demme' for short.
- **Duc/Duchessa d'Aufleur** — ruler of the city of Aufleur.
- **Dhynar** — member of the Creature Court; rank: Lord; creature: ferax.
- **Diamagne** — farming and wine region south of Aufleur; part of Lattorio. Also the name of the Baronne di Diamagne (now deceased), who married Augusta Xandelian (Ashiol's mother) as her second husband.
- **Donagan** — reputed to be the finest tailor in Aufleur, a master craftsman.
- **Dottores** — medical practitioners, mostly male. The only women allowed to practise in Aufleur as dottores are those registered as midwives, although many of them dispense other forms of medical advice on the side.
- **Edore** — region to the north of Ammoria and Atulia.
- **Evander X** — a popular writer of newspaper adventure serials, pen-name for Evanderline Inglirra.
- **Farrier** — member of the Creature Court; rank: courteso to Warlord, formerly to Dhynar; creature: slashcat.

- **Fionella** — member of the Creature Court; rank: courtesa to Priest.
- **Floralia** — six-day festival commemorating the glory of spring and the fertility of the coming summer. It begins in the month of Aphrodal and ends in the month of Floralis. Honours maidens, sweethearts, brides, household gods, passion and abundance, each on a different day. The first day (maidens) is celebrated with a public parade by the Spring Queen (the highest-ranking female in the city) and her Spring Consort, both dressed in pink and white.
- **Flame-and-gin** — common bar drink.
- **Florister** — artisan who works with plants and flowers; often works in conjunction with a ribboner or garland-maker to produce festival garlands.
- **Fornacalia** — festival from the sixth to the seventeenth of Lupercal in honour of the harvest saints, and the baking of the corn. Citizens wear ceremonial baking aprons for the rituals. Overlaps with the Parentalia, Quirinalia and Lupercalia.
- **Forum** — the public centre of Aufleur, a large area lined with temples and public buildings such as the Alexandrine Basilica and the Curia. The city market is held here every nine days, events such as the apprentice fairs are held here, and this is the traditional climax of most public parades and pageants. The Duchessa's Avenue connects the Forum to the Lake of Follies. Other cities, such as Tierce, also have a Forum, though the Forum of Aufleur is unusually large.
- **Gardens of Trajus Alysaundre** — gardens covering one side of the Lucretine hill in the

centre of Aufleur; built over the top of the
decadent public baths established in honour of the
third Duc d'Aufleur, Trajus Alysaundre. The
gardens face on to the Lake of Follies and
the Forum.

- **Garnet** — member of the Creature Court; rank:
  Power and Majesty; creature: gattopardo
  (mountain cat). He is the son of the cook and the
  groundskeeper on the Diamagne estate, and was
  Ashiol's boyhood friend.
- **Giacosa** — bustling merchant district at the
  southern end of Aufleur.
- **Giulio Gauget** — fifth Duc d'Aufleur. Known for
  excessive modesty and piety in contrast to his
  predecessor, Ilexandros Alysaundre.
- **Givette Camellie** — the Old Duchessa, wife of
  Duc Ynescho, mother of Artorio and Augusta,
  grandmother of Isangell, Ashiol, Bryn, Keil,
  Jemmen, Zade and Phage. Became Regenta when
  her late husband was mentally incapacitated; pre-
  deceased him after a long illness.
- **Gleamspray** — a rare and lethal element of the
  skybattles which is known for killing daylight folk;
  victims appear to succumb to the 'Silent Sleep'.
- **Grago** — member of the Creature Court; rank:
  courteso to Warlord, formerly to Dhynar; creature:
  stripecat.
- **Great Families** — the twelve Great Families of
  Aufleur: Xandelian (ducal), Leorgette, Lanouvre,
  Gauget, Paucini, Aufrey, Alysaundre, Vittorio,
  Giuliano, Camellie, Delgardie, Octaviano.
- **Halberk** — member of the Creature Court;
  courteso to Poet; creature: bear.
- **Harlequinus** — a sad dancing clown, main male

role in the harlequinade, a regular feature of musette revues.

- **Haymarket** — located in the Arches. Formerly a packing and storage facility; now a large space where the Power and Majesty resides. A canal runs water from the River Verticordia right through the Haymarket and down through the Arches, emerging at the Lock in the side of the Lucretine hill, which is the main entrance to the Arches.
- **Heliora** — member of the Creature Court; rank: Seer. Joined Court as a sentinel; became Seer during Ortheus's reign as Power and Majesty.
- **Ilexandros Alysaundre** — fourth Duc d'Aufleur; also known as 'mad old Ilexandros'. Built the Alexandrine Basilica, largest church in the known world, in the Forum of Aufleur.
- **Imperium** — a distilled alcoholic beverage made from fermented grain mash.
- **Inglirrus** — a small country across the strait from Orcadia.
- **Irean Priestesses** — powerful priestesses who venerate Ires the Crone, otherwise known as Saint Grandmere. The priestesses wear white and are said to have communion with the dead. Wills are lodged with them for safekeeping, and the priestesses are responsible for public readings of said wills. Their chief priestess is the Matrona Irea, one of the three priests included in the City Fathers.
- **Ires** — the Crone, or Saint Grandmere, worshipped in the Cathedral of Ires and venerated by the Irean Priestesses.
- **Isangell** — Duchessa d'Aufleur (full name/title: Duchessa Isangell Xandelian d'Aufleur, First Lady

of the Silver Seal); daughter of Artorio Xandelian and Eglantine; granddaughter of previous Duc d'Aufleur, Ynescho Xandelian, and his Regenta, the Duchessa Givette.

- **Isharo** — an island country to the Far East, a trading partner with Aufleur, particularly for flowers and fabrics.
- **Islandser** — a person from the Green Islands, to the west of Inglirrus, with a distinctive accent.
- **Janvier** — member of the Creature Court; courteso to Livilla; creature: raven.
- **Jardin Falcone** — editor of the Aufleur Gazette, a popular city newspaper.
- **Kelpie** — sentinel. Refers to her swords as her 'Sisters' and her daggers as her 'Nieces': hilts are wrapped in dark leather.
- **Lanouvre** — one of the twelve Great Families of Aufleur.
- **Laudinon** — the capital city of Inglirrus
- **Lemuria** — festival during Floralis to placate the shades of dead ancestors and lost loves.
- **Lennoc** — member of the Creature Court; rank: Lord (formerly courteso to Lief and then Dhynar and briefly Poet); creature: brighthound.
- **Leorgette** — one of the twelve Great Families of Aufleur.
- **Librarion** — Aufleur's city library.
- **Lictors** — honour guard that protects ranks of Duc, Duchessa, Ducomte or Ducomtessa, as well as select City Fathers, priests of high status and the Chief Minister. Lictors travel in multiples of three, carry ceremonial rods of state, are armed with axes and wear black and scarlet.

- **Lief** — deceased member of the Creature Court; rank: Lord; creature: greathound.
- **Livilla** — member of the Creature Court; rank: Lord; creature: wolf.
- **Lucian** — one of the districts of Aufleur, known as the theatre district.
- **Ludi** — as well as being the name of the first autumn month, this word means 'games'.
- **Ludi Aufleuris** — fifteen-day series of games held during the first month of autumn, Ludi. Women traditionally wear scarlet shawls when attending these games and wave the corners of the shawls to favoured gladiators and performers.
- **Ludi Megalensia** — Games of the Great Mother, held in the month of Aphrodal. Unlike other Ludi, there are no fights, animals or mock battles; instead, the games feature theatrical performances.
- **Ludi Sacris** — Sacred Games, held in the month of Felicitas. On the chief day of sacrifice (day four), everyone in the city makes a sacrifice to their chosen saints or gods.
- **Ludi Victoriae** — Victory Games, held in the month of Cerialis, in which favourite historical battles are re-enacted in the Circus Verdigris by gladiators and actors.
- **Lupercalia** — one-day festival in Lupercal during which men carouse in the streets wearing goatskins, goat masks and fake phalluses. Not unheard of for their real phalluses to hang out, for extra authenticity.
- **Lysandor** — member of the Creature Court; rank: King; creature: lynx. Fled with Celeste during Garnet's tyrannical reign as Power and Majesty. Member of the Clockwork Court in Bazeppe.

- **Macready** — sentinel. Original weapons: Alicity (steel sword), Tarea (skysilver sword), Phoebe (steel dagger), Jeunille (skysilver dagger); hilts wrapped in green leather. New weapons: hilts wrapped in grey leather.
- **Madalena** — the stellar of the Mermaid Theatre in the small town of Oyster, and the first stellar of the Mermaid Revue at the Vittorina Royale. Murdered unexpectedly by wild animals in a city street.
- **Margarethe** — one of the lower districts of Aufleur, run- down and poor.
- **Market-nines** — every ninth day (nundinae) is a public market day, regardless of other festival constraints. The phrase 'market-nine' refers to these nine-day groupings. Market-nines fall on different days each year.
- **Mars/Warlord** — member of the Creature Court; rank: Lord; creature: panther (Khatri zaba in Zafiran). Born Maziz dal Sara, he was the son of the Zafiran ambassador.
- **Mask** — an actor who performs with their face covered in musette and theatre revues.
- **Matralia** — festival during month of Lucina, when mothers and maternal relatives everywhere are crowned with silverbreath and ivy.
- **Mercatus** — grand city-wide market festivals held in Cerialis and Ludi, the two months with the most sacred games.
- **Mermaid, the** — the local musette in the seaside town Oyster.
- **Mermaid Revue, the** — a theatrical show featuring the company from the Mermaid Theatre in Oyster, who were brought to Aufleur some years ago by Lord Saturn of the Creature Court.

- **Musette** — a theatrical establishment or performance, usually in the style of a music hall, variety show or pantomime.
- **Nefas** — means 'unlucky', particularly in relation to a day; for example the day immediately after the Kalends, Nones or Ides of each month is nefas, and business transactions are rarely performed on these days.
- **Neptunalia** — a winter festival held on the Kalends of Saturnalis, celebrating the ancient Sea-father with sweetmeats, sacrifice and rituals involving paper boats.
- **Nova Stella** — a land far to the West of Ammoria, discovered and colonised two hundred years previously by explorers from Stelleza. Source for ciocolate and tobacco.
- **Nox** — the opposite of day.
- **Orcadia** — north-western region, known for its gentle climate and bubbled wine.
- **Orcadian Strait** — a body of water between Orcadia and Inglirrus.
- **Orphan Princel** — Poet's theatrical alter ego, stellar and stagemaster of the Mermaid Revue.
- **Ortheus** — former member of the Creature Court; rank: King; Power and Majesty (before Garnet). Creature: serpent.
- **Oyster** — a small seaside town in Ammoria. Birthplace of, among others, Poet, Livilla, Christophe and Ruby-Red.
- **Palazzo** — home of the ruling ducal family, located on the Balisquine hill and surrounded by other opulent residences. A former palazzo, now abandoned, is located on the Avleurine Hill.
- **Parentalia** — nine-day festival from the thirteenth

to the twenty-first of Lupercal, during which all citizens of Aufleur travel to place flowers and sweetmeats on their family tombs and grave markers. White silk garlands are traditionally worn.

- **Paucini** — one of the twelve Great Families of Aufleur.
- **Pearls Beyond Price** — an old stage act featuring Madalena and Poet's mother.
- **Piazza Nautilia** — public square at the conjunction of three major streets in Aufleur: Via Delgardie, Via Leondrine and Via Camellie; location of Triton's Church and the best public baths in Aufleur.
- **Poet** — member of the Creature Court; rank: Lord; creature: white rats. Moonlights as the Orphan Princel, a famous musette performer.
- **Power and Majesty** — leader of the Creature Court; must hold the rank of King.
- **Priest** — member of the Creature Court; rank: Lord; creature: pigeon.
- **Proctors** — public officials elected each year; one for each district in Aufleur. Included among the City Fathers.
- **Quirinalia** — One-day festival on the seventeenth of Lupercal, overlapping with the Fornacalia and Parentalia. Bunches of myrtle are exchanged and worn at the belt to ward off ill-luck for soldiers. Vigiles and lictors are allowed this day off public duties for religious observance.
- **Raoul** — former Seer of the Creature Court, who passed his powers on to Heliora upon his death.
- **Reyenna** — formerly one of the three duchies of Ammoria. After the disappearance of its capital

city, Tierce, Reyenna became known as one of the baronies of Lattorio.

- **Rhian** — friend to Velody and Delphine; florister. Seer of the Creature Court.
- **Sage** — Velody's brother, who was lost along with the rest of her family when Tierce was swallowed by the sky. Originally a dock worker, he was injured in an accident and ended up taking recreational potions for many years before cleaning up his act and getting factory work.
- **Saints** — worshipped by the daylight folk through rituals and festivals. 'Saints and angels' and 'saints and devils' are two common swearing phrases heard throughout the city.
- **Samara** — legendary former member of the Creature Court; female Lord who took in too much animor and blew apart. Cited as evidence that women cannot be Kings.
- **Saturn,** former member of the Creature Court, lover of Tasha. Rank: Lord; creature: hawk.
- **Saturnalia** — an eight-day festival, held from the seventeenth to the twenty-fourth of Saturnalis, in which masters and servants traditionally swap roles, men and women wear each other's clothing, etc. Also sometimes known as the Feast of Fools, it celebrates all things topsy-turvy. Traditional refreshments include hot cider, bean syrup and roasted chestnuts. An important theatre season.
- **Scratchlight** — weapon used by the sky in battle; kills one in fifty mortals it hits — not as effective as the rarer shadowstreak or gleamspray.
- **Seer** — member of the Creature Court, outside the usual hierarchy. The seer has the ability to look

into the future and pull out visions of what is to come.

- **Seigneur** — a polite term of address for men, which gets politer the higher in rank they actually are.
- **Sentinels** — the loyal armed servants of the Kings of the Creature Court. Each bears blades of steel and skysilver to represent the thin line they tread between the nox and the daylight. They are ready to give up their blood to their masters at a moment's notice.
- **Seonard** — member of the Creature Court; rank: courteso to Livilla; creature: wolf.
- **Serenai** — patron saint of gamblers and good fortune. Friendly bets often include promises for the loser to sacrifice to Serenai or other saints and angels on the winner's behalf.
- **Shade** — member of the Creature Court; rank: courteso to Poet (formerly courteso to Lief and then Dhynar); creature: darkhound.
- **Silent Sleep** — a fatal illness that tends to affect the very young and the elderly. A side-effect of skybattle, but to daylight folk a mystery illness that attacks without warning and leaves no contamination trail.
- **Silver Brethren** — a chaste order of male priests, who wear silver chains and shave their heads. They never speak once they have taken orders, only sing and chant during their street processions.
- **Silver Captain** — Nathanial, former leader of the sentinels. Died on the eve of Vestalia, three years before the return of Ashiol.
- **Silverstorm** — shards of skysilver generated by the sky during battle.

- **Skybattle** — when the sky opens and attacks the city, using all manner of deadly phenomena. Only happens at nox, and only the Creature Court and their allies, such as the seer and sentinels, are aware of this. The Creature Court exists to battle the sky and protect the city. Any damage to buildings or other parts of the city is repaired at dawn, and any daylight folk affected by the sky's weapons recover and return to normal. Occasionally there are fatalities if a person has suffered a direct hit, particularly if they are very young or elderly. Such fatalities are referred to by the daylight folk as the Silent Sleep.
- **Skyburn** — the effect of some sky weapons on the sentinels. In its lightest form it is similar to sunburn; more serious symptoms include deeply reddened or bruised skin, fever and weakness.
- **Skyfall** — to be swallowed by the sky. Death by skyfall means a Court member's animor goes with them into the sky and is lost forever, instead of being shared among the survivors of the Creature Court. 'The sky is falling' is an expression often used to indicate that a skybattle is beginning.
- **Skyseed** — a red cloud that is the seed of a deathstorm. Deathstorms bring flaming hail, 'devils' (violent animated dust clouds) and 'angels' (poisonous bursts of steam)'. A skyseed can be destroyed by lancing — similar to lancing a boil, only a million times more disgusting.
- **Skysilver** — a metallic substance that falls from the sky. The Creature Court believes it comes from the stars. All skysilver is the property of Kings and given to the Smith, who forges it into weapons for the sentinels.

- **Slow rain** — a force of destruction from the sky, liquid that can burn a hole right through a member of the Court and give a sentinel skyburn. Usually occurs a couple of times a month, often heralding worse to come.
- **Smith, the** — a figure who is both part of and apart from the Creature Court, only accessible for an hour at noon each day. The Smith crafts the skysilver into weapons for the sentinels, and has been around since before Aufleur was built.
- **Songbird** — a singer who performs in musette and theatre revues.
- **Star tar** — hideous black muck that oozes through the cracks in the sky during the worst skybattles.
- **Stellar** — the most prominent and popular performer in a musette or theatre revue.
- **Stelleza** — an affluent country to the west of Ammoria, known for its adventurers and explorers. Strong trading partner with Aufleur.
- **Surrender** — a party potion that makes the user high and giddy.
- **Sweetheart Saints** — patron saints of romance and sweethearts.
- **Tanaquil** — mistress of birds, one of the ancient saints of Aufleur.
- **Tasha** — former member of the Creature Court; rank: Lord; creature: lion. Recruited Ashiol, Garnet, Lysandor, Poet and Livilla as her courtesi. Died forsworn, and returned as a shade who dragged corruption and disease through the city before she was stopped.
- **Temple of the Market Saints** — located on the Avleurine hill. The Market Saints are the patron saints of all traders and merchants.

- **Tierce** — capital city of Reyenna, and where Velody, Delphine and Rhian come from. When Tierce disappeared, Reyenna became a barony of the duchy of Lattorio.
- **Trajus Alysaundre** — third Duc d'Aufleur; see also 'Gardens of Trajus Alysaundre'.
- **Velody** — friend to Rhian and Delphine; dressmaker. Sister to Amber, Thaya, Iris, Sage (all deceased). Member of the Creature Court; rank: King; Power and Majesty; creature: little brown mouse.
- **Vestalia** — a rural festival on the ninth day of Lucina in which people dress up in milkmaid costumes, aprons and other 'peasant' attire. Other features are green paper lanterns and sacrifices of honey, cake, bread and salt. The day is sacred to bakers and millers.
- **Via Ciceline** — a vibrant shopping strip in the heart of the wealthy Centrini district.
- **Via Silviana** — a narrow street crammed between the affluent Vittorine hill and the shabby, bustling Giacosa commercial district. The shop belonging to Velody, Rhian and Delphine stands at the halfway point between Vittorine and Giacosa, under the Sign of the Rose and Needle.
- **Vittorine** — one of the hill districts of Aufleur; also extends below the foot of the hill into an upmarket shopping district that meets the thriving merchant district of Giacosa.
- **Vittorina Royale** — a theatre in the Vittorine district, under new management. Current and former performers at this theatre include Christophe, Sunshine, Ruby-red, Zephyr, Topaz, Bart, Adriane and Madalena.

- **Warlord** — member of the Creature Court;
  see 'Mars'.
- **Xandelian** — one of the districts of Aufleur. Also
  the name of the current ruling ducal family, whose
  members include Ynescho, Augusta, Artorio,
  Isangell and Ashiol. One of the twelve Great
  Families of Aufleur.
- **Ynescho Xandelian** — the Old Duc, grandfather
  to Isangell, Ashiol, Bryn, Keil, Jemmen, Zade and
  Phage, father of Artorio and Augusta. Ruled with
  an iron fist until his wits gave way; his wife,
  Duchessa Givette, took over as his Regenta.
- **Yvette LeBeau** — former mistress of the Old Duc
  and former columbine; in her retirement she owns
  a house on the corner of the Marius Bridge over
  the River Verticordia and entertains theatricals.
- **Zafir** — an eastern country rich with culture,
  source of the popular 'princessa and djinn' plays
  that are a regularly revived trend in the Aufleur
  theatres and musettes.
- **Zero** — member of the Creature Court; rank:
  courteso to Poet; creature: weasel.

AUTHOR'S EDITION AFTERWORD
(2018)

I already wrote these books once.

Around a decade ago, I sold a fantasy trilogy to Harper-Collins Voyager which was a huge moment in my career. For years, I wrote and edited and hustled to complete the Creature Court, my most ambitious writing project. The book of my heart.

When I started writing Velody's story, I was a PhD student with no children, and a remarkable amount of free time. Seven years later, when I wrote the last word of the final book, I was a mother of two working off very little sleep.

Now, my children are 13 and 9. My doctoral thesis is a distant trauma that hardly ever gives me nightmares. And these books, the books of my heart... they're back.

For those wondering if these Author's Editions are different to the originals that were published in 2010-2012... well, yes they are. Because apparently, I can't publish a book without editing and re-editing, and rewriting, and... well, I like to think I'm a better writer than I was then. A tweak here, a word there... and of course, writing the brand new prequel, Cabaret of Monsters, at the same time as republishing the originals, gave me the opportunity to lay in a few more connective threads than existed before.

If you have and still love the first printed versions of these books, I'm delighted… but the new ones are better. Tell your friends.

Many people contributed so much to help me on this second journey, to bring the Creature Court back to print. Obviously I would have not been able to do this at all without the 400+ Kickstarter backers who pledged to make these new, beautifully dressed editions a reality.

Kathleen Jennings and Cathy Larsen, my wonderful artist and designer, are a big part of the success of this project. Combining fantasy fiction with Art Deco imagery and 1920s styling is still a very rare thing, and a far cry from what most commercial fantasy looks like, so I am grateful to have these two talented women working to make my books look spectacular.

And of course, my mother Jilli Roberts, the artist who drew the original Creature Court maps under very stressful circumstances… I'm so glad to be able to use these again, as they delight me whenever I look at them.

All my love to my supportive family: to my husband Andrew who learned how to produce audiobooks for me, and has always supported my writing career. To Lee and Jemima, who cope valiantly with having a writing mother constantly perched at one end of the dining room, nose in laptop. To my father Tony, still the biggest cheerleader of my books.

All my love to the support teams I have on Slack: the Twelfth Planet and Galactic Suburbia communities contain so many of my favourite people, and I lean on them constantly for support, feedback, cheer and advice.

The same can be said the love and support of our Friday

night crew, a weekly found-family gathering that is a touchstone in my life. Hugs and desserts all around — and a special shout out to Isabel who took one look at my Kickstarter and decided that it needed a hand-stitched flapper doll to lure in the punters.

Then there are those who helped the Creature Court come into existence the first time around: My former agent, Anni Haig-Smith. Stephanie Smith and Anne Reilly from HarperCollins. Nicola O'Shea, the best structural editor I've ever worked with.

The RoRettes: Marianne de Pierres, Rowena Cory Daniells, Margo Lanagan, Maxine McArthur, Trent Jamieson, Richard Harland and Dirk Flinthart, who read *Power and Majesty* at various stages and contributed so much to the structure of that vital first novel.

Kaia, my Swedish writing fairy, first *first* reader and sharp wielder of the red pen. She made these books better.

Finally, all my gratitude to Professor R. L. Dunbabin, who taught at the University of Tasmania between 1901-1939 and left behind a generous bequest towards a travel scholarship for Classics postgraduate students. This enabled me to spend several weeks in Rome in 2001, building on my knowledge of imperial statuary in museums... and, quite by accident, imprinting an imaginary version of the city on to the underside of my feet, which later emerged in a story about shapechangers, skybattles and little brown mice.

I regret nothing.

Tansy Rayner Roberts, 2018